The Archimage's Fourth Daughter

Lyndon Hardy

Volume 4 of Magic by the Numbers

Bartizan Press
Los Angeles

Version 4
Print ISBN: 978-0-9991320-1-2
Library of Congress Control Number: 2017910323

Other books by Lyndon Hardy

Master of the Five Magics, 2nd edition
Secret of the Sixth Magic, 2nd edition
Riddle of the Seven Realms, 2nd edition

Visit Lyndon Hardy's website at: http://www.alodar.com/blog

Cover by Tom Momary http://www.tomomary.com

Map by Ana Maria Velicu http://facebook.com/ancart7

1. Fantasy 2. Magic 3. Adventure 4. New Adult

To my granddaughters, Alison and Zelda

Contents

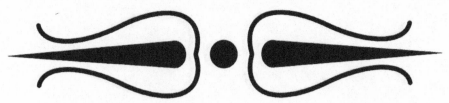

Part One *Stranger in a Strange Land*

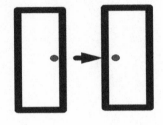

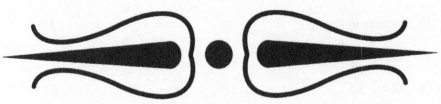

Part Two *So Many Women, So Little Time*

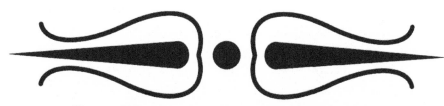

Part Three *An Expanded Reality*

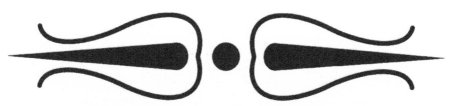

Part Four *Turn of the Ratchetwheel*

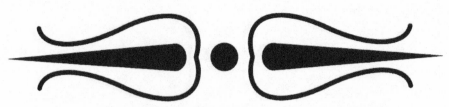

Part Five *Eightfold Path Neverending*

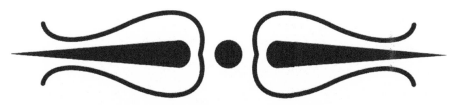

Part Six *Briana's Choice*

The Laws of Magic

Thaumaturgy

The Principle of Sympathy — like produces like

The Principle of Contagion — once together, always together

Alchemy

The Doctrine of Signatures — the attributes without mirror the powers within

Magic

The Maxim of Persistence — perfection is eternal

Sorcery

The Rule of Three — thrice spoken, once fulfilled

Wizardry

The Law of Ubiquity — flame permeates all

The Law of Dichotomy — dominance or submission

Prologue

DINTON HESITATED for a moment and felt the luxurious fur on his arm ripple under his tunic. Without some specific tag to search for, he had no control over whose mind he would latch onto next. They flowed by in a fast moving stream without any rhyme to the order by which they came. Such was the nature of the charm.

But this one, the one he was in contact with now, might serve well enough. No strider on this world's stage to be sure, but he would be ideal for the experiment he had wanted to try.

Primitive and stupid, the natives missed what was essential for true alchemy time and time again. Yes, they dabbled in concocting all manner of ingredients to see what would happen, but no one, not a single one, had ever stumbled on the necessity for having activation formulas as well.

So, with a simple suggestion, one so subtle that his target would not even suspect that it came from elsewhere, would start him down the correct path. A second hint that he create potions that released great passions and the deed was done.

Dinton hesitated a second time. Even if he never returned to this mind, it did make sense to get a tag, just in case. But probing further ran the risk that the target would begin to suspect, and everything he had planted could be lost.

Just for a moment, he told himself, and he began scanning random memories as they emerged. A name would be best of all.

After fruitless monitoring for a dozen heartbeats, the target mentally began to stir. No identification had appeared. Dinton grabbed at a last garble as it floated by. Reluctantly, he pronounced the final words that ended the charm. All contact with another mind was no more. The sorcery was complete.

"No more craft," he said. "Yes, this would be the very last time."

3

Part One

Stranger in a Strange Land

1

The Magic Portal

"IF I don't do something soon, my life is as good as over," Briana thought. She was a sylph of a girl; barely twenty, slender as a reed, and with long flaming red hair like her mother. Pale skin; large, deep green eyes. In the fashion of all proper young ladies, she wore brown leggings, tunic, and cloak.

Briana shook her head. How could she have been so stupid? So stupid as to sign a contract for marriage after only a single day of attention, some smooth, flattering words, and three glasses of wine. And betrothed to Slammert of all people. The worst possible choice — so disgusting, so coarse.

Everyone could talk about nothing else when it was finally disclosed what he had done to his first wife. At the time of her mistake, Briana had not known. At the harvest festival, sitting with his bride up on the dais in the feasting hall, Slammert had ripped her bodice away and fondled her bare breasts while his minions watched and roared with laughter. The next morning, they discovered the unfortunate girl had hanged herself, one of her belts tight around her neck and her body stiff like a slaughtered lamb.

Briana grasped the chairback of the wizard seated in front of her to bring her focus to what was happening now. The massive round table in the center of the council chamber had been removed to make more room for spectators. Alodar, her father and Archimage sat in the very center of the row of chairs, leaning forward, as eager as the rest. On either side like pieces in a board game were arrayed the most senior practitioners throughout all of Murdina: thaumaturges, alchemists, magicians, sorcerers, and wizards. From Procolon, the Southern Kingdoms, and even Arcadia across the Great Ocean. Everyone seated wore their robes of office: scarlet red for the archimage, brown, white, deepest blue, gray, and black for the others. At the far left, she even recognized one of her childhood tutors: Fordine, the Master Thaumaturge.

The finery denoted in which of the distinct crafts each master was proficient, but even without them, one could tell. The eyes of the sorcerers were deep and piercing, able to enchant others with their charms and see far in space and time. Haughty and unyielding as steel, the faces of the wizards seemed almost to dare demons from another realm to challenge them for dominance.

Although they wore pristine and unblemished garb reserved for ceremony, the alchemists' hands were soiled and blotched with stains from the exotic substances they manipulated to produce sweetbalms and potions of love. The magicians had a faraway look, always contemplating the rituals from which came the swords, mirrors, and rings of true magic .

The lowly thaumaturges were the friendly ones, eager artisans hoping for a few coins in exchange for raising heavy beams to the top of a new tower or causing trees to drop their fruit all on the same day. Only Fordine was different. He had been brilliant with counterspells in his youth, but practiced no more — instead was quite wealthy running an academy to train apprentices and journeymen for others.

Five distinct skills, each with its own disciplines. Only one, her father, had mastered them all.

The chamber was as somber as a tomb. Wall frescos had faded centuries ago. Heavy curtains blocked any incoming daylight. On the other side of the room, tall sconces with multiple arms upraised with flickering candles illuminated a small, hastily constructed platform.

No one spoke.

Standing at the chairback on Briana's left was a young lordling still in his teens. He flexed his grip and looked nervously about. Obviously, this was his first time.

"It will be all right," she whispered to him and smiled. "We are only here to emphasize the importance of the masters. All we have to do is stand erect and look serious, no matter what is said."

She returned her attention to her own thoughts. It was because she was so sheltered, she concluded. Confined within the compound for her protection, her only experiences were simple flirtations with a few of the pages her own age. And when the baron from the far west, a man and not a boy — tall, muscular, smoldering eyes, a beguiling smile. He had said he was lonely and asked if he could dine with her. Of course, she had said yes.

Had her three elder sisters done the same? Anything to get out of the dull, polite conversations with men old enough to be a grandfather. Snap up the first one younger with a pulse. Wed him, see some of the world,

8

have children, perhaps even adventure a bit on their own.

As a muffled chime from a clock in an adjacent room marked the hour, the air in front of the chairs started to shimmer, at first barely perceptible, but then with increasing violence; like smooth water encountering rapids, it distorted more and more until the blank wall behind was no longer visible.

A door took shape within the swirl, solidified, and, after a few moments more, swung open. Briana gasped, as did more than one master, even some nearing a hundred years of experience. Wrapped from head to toe as if for burial, a figure stepped forward and with effort raised one arm in a sign of greeting.

He was shaped like a human in every respect: head, neck, torso, arms and legs, hands and feet, but the coverings hid every feature. Not thin sheets of linen, but bulky strips from what looked like brilliant white woolen blankets swirled around the entire body. No eyes or mouth could be seen. In their place were opaque goggles and below them a circle of thin parchment where there would have been a mouth. Bulky gloves covered his hands. So, this was the purpose of the formal council meeting — a parlay with the one who had brought the tome.

"You may call me Randor, Randor of the Faithful." A tinny voice in a strange accent vibrated from the paper beneath the glasses. "Do you understand everything in the volume left for you? Are you confident you can work the controls?"

"Yes, the high council has studied the contents," Alodar answered. "And if your doorway had not appeared so suddenly and unannounced a year ago, they would have no credibility."

Briana watched the visitor intently as did everyone else. The being must be of such grossness that he dared not appear in his natural form, she thought. In the writings that had been left, there were illustrations of what looked like men — beings that could easily pass without notice here on Murdina. But there were no pictures of any other type of creature, no hint of what unwinding the swathing would reveal.

She should not even have been allowed to see the book after it was deposited in the great library for study by the masters, but the page had told her how to bypass the safeguards for a single kiss. She had spent many late evenings reading and rereading what the tome contained.

"I have asked you a direct question," the visitor said. "I expect a direct answer."

"We have questions as well." Alodar's tone hardened. "Why did you leave this book with us that speaks of another world in the cosmos? Is that where you are from?"

"*Two* questions rather than a single answer," Randor said. "Your race is an impertinent one." One of the enveloped hands waved the concern away. "But no matter. It is one of the reasons why you were chosen.

"Our entire race is not exiled on the orb of which I speak. We, the Faithful, remain pure. Only the vanquished of my kind, the ones who call themselves the Heretics Who Proclaim the Truth, have been imprisoned on the hellish world described in the text. The descriptions in the tome concern only the primitive natives, not ourselves. We judged that such information would make your own journeys more efficient. You would not have to spend time relearning what we had gleaned from so many trips ourselves."

"Heretics?" Alodar asked. "Our own journeys?"

"The heretical crimes committed by those now banished is a matter of no concern to you. And yes, we, the Faithful, have made the journey many times, once every hundred or so of your years for some ten times or more. Now, we grow, let us say ... less able to guard against the possibility of the return of contamination."

"Over a millennium!" the magicians with the neatly trimmed goatee exclaimed. "You live that long?"

"No, as individuals, we normally do not. Only the exiles wear rings of eternal youth — and only if they so elect."

"A ring of eternal youth!" The magician grabbed at his beard. "Then the suspicion in our guilds is correct. One can be made! Your magicians have done so. What is the ritual? How is it performed?"

"Some say we should have killed them." Randor ignored the outburst. "But that would be only a passing satisfaction. Instead, as of our last visit, the Heretics remain imprisoned as we planned. Originally eleven hundred were entombed; now only some seven hundred are still alive.

"Death is swift and is but a shadow of the agony of an *eternity* of captivity. Death is too gentle a fate for what they continue to experience. The only way they could escape from their confinement is by the use of one of the crafts. And for that, our sorcerers enchanted them all, forced them to forget everything they knew about any of the arts when they were defeated. By now, the despair of their situation should have caused them to end their existences by their own hands. It is exquisite for us to contemplate. Ones so proud reduced to ending defiance by the exercise of their own crumbling will."

The strange one adjusted his swathing for a moment. "Some have already done so, but not yet all. Some still remain."

"If they have remained in captivity for so long, then why not accept the situation for what it is?" asked the wizard seated in front of Briana. "Not bother to check on how they fare anymore?"

Randor hesitated a second time. "Because," he said at last. "Because there is a possibility, however slight, that the sorcery might wear off. The skill in the arts by the Heretics might eventually return. Return gradually, and then, using magic, they might escape.

"The natives of the orb are quite backward," he continued. "As far as we have detected, they employ none of the arts at all. So, evidence of a large enough use of the crafts by the Heretics before they had regained their full power would be a trigger — a trigger to take more drastic action against them. The chances are small, but all of us that remain are too... too engrossed with other things to continue with the task.

"And so, here is our proposition. Moving among the natives will be no problem for your kind. That is one reason why you have been selected. All we ask you to do is to check periodically for evidence of any incantations, charms, or other spells, and then do what is necessary to snuff out the practices.

"Catch the banished as they emerge. It will be easy enough using the mature proficiency of your own crafts. In exchange, this magic portal is yours to use according to your own desires. In an instant, you will be able to travel across your great ocean for a meeting such as this. Send crops or even men-at-arms to wherever they are needed with but a few steps anywhere within our entire realm."

"But the writings say only a single person can use the portal at one time," Briana burst out. "To transport an army would take days."

All the masters in the room turned to stare at Briana, now very well aware of her presence. "Oops! Sorry, Dad!" She blushed.

Alodar frowned, but chose for the moment to ignore the interruption. He returned his gaze to the bundled visitor.

"If what you say is true, this portal has great power," he said. "Great *disruptive* power for any society using it — perhaps a curse rather than a boon." He looked at the masters seated around him. "Is this truly what we want? Is it any better than a bargain with demonkind?"

"It is most ingenious magic," Randor said. "The door at one end of the portal is in our realm — our own universe — yours and mine . Although the traveler is unaware of it, the central portion of the device travels through the realm of demons while preventing any contact with the vile beings who dwell there. There is no bargaining with them involved at all."

11

"The path then loops back to a destination of one's choosing — possibly even one that we could reach by other means," Randor continued. "By placing the two entrances properly in our realm, we can connect them to what seems like mere paces apart, a shortcut regardless of how long the journey might otherwise be.

The two doors do not even need to be situated on the same orb within our realm," Randor plowed on. "I come from my home to your earth here. We desire you to travel from here to yet a third orb in the sky."

"Yes, I understand it now," an alchemist said. "The opportunity to explore. A chance to visit other worlds, exchange formulas and harvest exotic ingredients that here are rare."

"Trade and exchange," a thaumaturge chimed in. "Murdina could become the commercial center for our entire universe. We all would prosper. This Randor says that their internal politics are no concern of ours. I agree. The chance for great benefit is too great."

"Progress cannot be stopped, Archimage Alodar," Fordine said. "One way or another, each step forward has to be addressed, and undesirable consequences dealt with when they occur. As you and this high council have done many times before."

Alodar was silent for a long while. He lowered his chin onto his chest to think.

What decisions her father had to make all the time, Briana thought. No wonder he has become so tired and overworked — so irrational in some of his decisions. He needed help. Why couldn't he see she was the one who should be his aide?

"It is decided," the Archimage said finally, raising his head. "We accept the offer."

The masters around Alodar began burbling like brooks breaking the surface for the very first time. No voice raised in objection.

Briana's thoughts raced. A possible way out of her predicament! This was an easy task. She remembered the instructions about controlling the portal. They were quite simple. Snoop around a few places to see if there was any craft being performed and report. A two or three-day job at the most. Perhaps this could be the task opening her father's eyes to how useful she could be. Enough of a reason for him to declare her marriage contract void.

"When will you make the first journey?" the visitor asked.

"The traveler has not yet been chosen," Alodar said, a hint of irritation entering his voice. "But he will be soon enough to satisfy your desire."

"Then I return now to my peers. Their purity will refresh. The parchments given to you contain the coordinates of the world that imprisons the exiles."

Without anything further, Randor returned the portal and shut the door. It shimmered again for a moment and then was still.

Alodar stood and faced the masters. "We will meet again in seven days. Bring with you candidates for who is to be the journey-taker. We will discuss and then decide."

A page entered the chamber and gave a note to the Archimage. He read it and scowled.

He looked in the direction of the wizard on the far right. "All are dismissed — all except one, that is. Briana, please remain. Your *fiancé* is here on an unannounced visit."

2

Father and Daughter

BRIANA TOOK a seat next to her father, and the page ushered in Slammert. "May I approach my betrothed to bestow a kiss of greeting, mighty Archimage?" he said.

"No, you may not," Alodar answered through gritted teeth. "Words of your deeds precede you. What is this about?"

"From the tone of your greeting, I infer your daughter has thought it better for me to announce the wonderful news. Here, look at the document I bring. I am sure you will find it in proper order."

Alodar quickly read the contract, looked at Briana, then back to Slammert, and scowled.

"I have not consented to this," he said.

"But consent was given, venerable Archimage. Perhaps with the distractions of state, you have lost track of the time. Your youngest daughter is of age." He smiled at Briana. "She has been for some time."

"I will abrogate the agreement," Alodar thundered. Briana had never seen him like this. Usually, he exhibited complete control.

"But you cannot." Slammert smiled. "You know that very well. The Archimage is not a despot holding sway over all of Murdina. Your decisions are accepted by those who rule because of the respect given to you — accepted *only* because of that respect. You *cannot* arbitrarily reverse something freely agreed to by another. The matter is concluded. It is done. Time for you to move on to your next crisis."

"Decisions are altered all the time," Briana burst out. "New information is not ignored."

"It has taken years of reasoned logic and gentle prodding," Alodar said, "but even the kingdoms to the south have seen the value of what I have espoused — the value of open borders, free trade, the expansion of commerce. Even the Iron Fist is now an inn for tourists.

"Except for the ceremonial palace guards," the Archimage continued, "standing armies have been disbanded throughout the world. There is no longer any need for the expense. Everyone abides by what I decree. For that to work, I must be beyond reproach. I, more than all others, must abide by the law.

"This crawling slug is right, Briana." He sighed. "You have been most foolish, but you have agreed. You are bound."

There was a moment of silence, then Alodar said "Slammert, why exactly are you here?"

The lord glowered at Alodar. "Perhaps to remind everyone why the wedding must go forward as planned." He smiled at Briana. "And to inform you, my beloved, that in your honor, I will be replacing one of the posts of our wedding bed with a new one. The old lumber is almost already notched from top to bottom. Yours will be the first on the new. Then every time we spend the evening together, you can count for yourself how many other notches have been added for those days we are apart."

Slammert's tone hardened. "Make no doubt about it, wench. I always get whatever woman I want. Always!"

Rage contorted Alodar's face. He curled his fists in frustration. "Get out," he managed to command through clenched teeth. "Somehow... somehow, I will find a way to get this undone."

"That we shall see." Slammert bowed. "As you wish, mighty Archimage, I now will leave. I have other kings and lords to visit and extend invitation to the wedding — and remind them also about the agreement you must honor."

AFTER SLAMMERT had left, the silence hung like a dark raincloud over the two who remained.

"Am I not worth something more to you than a mere pawn in the world of politics, Father?" Briana asked.

"Of course you are," Alodar said. "But in that world, you are only a beloved daughter, not a wielder of power."

"You do not command armies either."

"Yes, but it is my knowledge, my experience, my reputation that serves instead."

The decision rushed into Briana's thoughts and solidified. She twirled a loose strand of her hair in her fingers while she decided what to say. "Let me be the one who ascertains the situation with the exiles, Father. And after that, there are other tasks you could give me, too. Then, the royalty and their lieges could understand why you broke the betrothal, why I have value more important than the desires of a border baron, value of importance to all of Murdina."

"What? The exiles? No, that is impossible. No one knows if what this cloaked visitor says is true. A proven champion is needed." Alodar's brow folded in a fatherly frown, and then he managed a weak smile. "Someone who has a very good chance of returning unscathed."

"But wouldn't that be the proof you needed? An example of what my worth to everyone would be? Reason enough to nullify the agreement made with Slammert. Everyone would understand."

Briana continued without thinking which words were tumbling out of her mouth, words she did not even know were there. "I want to go on an adventure, Father, as you did before becoming the Archimage, before checking off all the steps in the same boring ritual: courtship, marriage, children, and then old age. I want my name to be added to those in the sagas, triumphing over adversity, righting great wrongs, saving the world... or at least a little part of it."

She smiled, "Tales like those recorded of the deeds of my famous father. You were scarcely older then than I am now."

Alodar startled at the words. "Aeriel warned me it might come to this — that is, if we had had sons as well as daughters."

"How can you say that?" Briana exploded. "What difference does the gender make? Was not your final victory as much because of what mother did as you?"

Alodar was silent for a while and then answered softly. "No, you are right. Of course, I would not be here today. The *world* would not be as it is now if not for her. And to this day she completes me still."

"And so, I want to be the one who goes through the portal and visits this other orb. The natives look almost the same as ourselves. It could be a woman's task as well as a man's."

Alodar started to answer, but then frowned. "Wait a moment. You said, 'One traveler at a time.' How do you even know that?"

"From the writings given to us by the shrouded one on his first visit last year." Briana shrugged, trying to make light of it. "A library page has been kind enough to gain me access."

"I have studied the tome well," she continued. "There is a dictionary, a tutorial on one of the dominant languages, what the alphabetical symbols look like, and a pronunciation guide."

"Yes, yes, you are an apt student, able to discover secrets from even the most ancient of texts. Few of your age are your equal. But — "

"And most important of all, the natives are primitive." Briana rushed on. "They have no knowledge of the five crafts. Even if they did, the laws would be the same as they are here. I would not be going to another realm. It will be easy to explore a world that is like ours. How hard could that be? I will be back in a few days.

"Unlike other magical items, this portal has controls, settings for where and when to go and such," she continued at a slower pace. "I have studied that also. After all, we have had these parchments for a year."

The Archimage shook his head, "We have only the shrouded stranger's word that the natives do not use the crafts. I do not trust him… at least not yet. Not until whomever makes the journey reports back what he has learned. Trust me. I will somehow find another way to correct the error you have made."

He placed his hands on Briana's shoulders, paused for a moment more, and then said softly, "The answer is no."

"You can't do that!" Briana yelled back. "Even the Archimage has limits to his power. You admitted as much yourself. You cannot order me around like some serf of an Arcadian lord."

"I do not order you to stay because I am the Archimage," Alodar said. "I do so because I am your father."

Briana felt the anger well within her like a brush fire suddenly out of control. She clenched her teeth so as not to say more. The library page had a key to this council chamber, she thought fiercely. It might take more than a single kiss to get it, but that is what she would have to do.

17

3

Preparation for Adventure

BRIANA PLACED the small disk over the keyhole. Its magic gently tingled her fingertips. With a satisfying click, the bolt in the door retracted. She grabbed the handle, thrust her backpack into the opening, and then buried the disk into the potted plant standing beside the doorway. The page would retrieve it later, and the only mystery would be how the council room had somehow been left unlocked.

Briana entered the chamber and let the door swing shut. The heavy drapes had been pulled back earlier, but because it was a moonless night, the blackness was deep. Perhaps the two rows of chairs were gone, and the council table returned as well. She reached into her pack in order to snap a glowstick, but then halted. Now she only had five left, and to waste one here would not be wise. She had to start thinking like an adventurer, not some pampered doxy wondering about dinner the next day.

Feeling along the wall, she felt a sconce and found the indentation nearby containing matches. The flickering glow of a single candle was enough. Yes, the chairs were gone, and the large round table had returned to its usual place. The door into the portal still stood on the other side of the room, beckoning like a seductive siren.

Briana set her equipment on the ground for one last check before proceeding. She would have to hurry. Dawn was not far away, and she needed to be gone before anyone else would come — before anyone would stop her from what she was going to do.

She smiled with satisfaction. Her cloak would be cover if the climate turned out to be cold. The surface of a goatsack of water filled almost to bursting was completely dry; there were no leaks. A dagger for the left side of her belt and a stout baton of ironwood for the right. Two loaves of hard bread and a change in underwear completed her essentials. She would wear her tunic, leggings, and boots for the entire journey. There was no need for anything more.

Briana looked over the provisions a final time. She replaced one loaf of bread with a sack of sweetmeats. After all, she was only to be gone for a few days.

The instructions for the portal, native dictionary, and the language guide left by the visitor joined a coil of string, a slim journal, some quills, and a small bottle of ink. How her father had managed to keep everything in his head on his own saga, she could hardly imagine.

Her father, Briana thought. What would he do if she were caught? He was widely regarded as just and level-headed, but when it came to his own family...

She turned her attention to her small trove of precious objects — toys from her childhood, things long since put away. None was powerful of course — those were too rare, too expensive. But what she did have might come in handy in dealing with the primitives. She had one for each of the five crafts: Thaumaturgy, Alchemy, Magic, Sorcery, and Wizardry.

From a thaumaturge, a short metal cylinder, shorter than the width of a hand, cut into two pieces lengthwise — one piece named the 'king' and the other the 'queen.' It was a teaching tool for youngsters for 'once together, always together' and 'like produces like.' Briana remembered hiding one-half under something like a handkerchief and then manipulated its twin so the first would soar and scare her older sisters

Next, her collection of glowsticks from an alchemist. She had bought a batch of two dozen when she was twelve, and she had wasted most of them over the years until she realized that those remaining should be saved until there was a real need rather than an imagined one. Snap one apart and there would be a soft glowing light lasting for many minutes.

She grasped the dark crystal of columbite, its color an unusual deep brown-black. It was a source of niobium, the magician had explained at the bazaar. Used in rituals producing strange forces that never faded. Useless unless the iron was stripped away first, but it was all a child needed in order to pretend.

The sorcerer's telescope came next. Yes, a telescope, but somehow rendered the size of her hand, sights for both of her eyes rather than only one. The light bent back and forth inside, the sorcerer had said, so that the telescope need not be long and cumbersome. The best part was that the chant one had to say in order to make the device work was short and simple. Despite what everyone knew — how difficult it was to recite correctly three times through, and the headache that would occur when there was a miscasting — each time she had used the strange telescope, she had not faltered. Each time she saw clearly images from many paces away — a charm of far-seeing, as potent as any in the sagas.

Finally, five mitematches bound in string, their tips coated in alchemical preparation that caused the shafts of ironwood to burst into flame when rubbed against a coarse surface. The imps from the demon realm on the other side of the fire were almost the smallest of all. Although they had surprising strength, they were as tiny as baby moths and their wills feeble and easy to dominate. Briana remembered how her sister had swatted helplessly as one whined around her head as it had been commanded.

Briana brushed the direction of her thoughts away. Yes, these were juvenile things, most likely cheap diversions to keep children occupied while parents bargained for items of true craft at the bazaar. That did not matter. The important thing would be the reaction of the natives to them if the situation arose.

She reassembled her pack, attached the bedroll, and shouldered its straps. The sky outside was growing lighter. Soon, someone would come to the chamber. There was still the workings of the portal to be mastered. She started to drop a note saying she was going, but then thought better of it and slid the parchment into her pack. She toyed with a loose strand of hair for a second and then slowly walked over to the waiting door. Its handle tingled to the touch — yes, true magic.

4

Planetfall

THE DOOR closed silently behind her as Briana entered the portal. A soft light illuminated a narrow white corridor perhaps ten paces long and ending in another door like the one now behind her. The wall on her left was featureless as a perfectly calm sea. On the right, near each door was an array of controls arranged in rows. Each row looked the same — a selection button, some illuminated text, and a long sequence of counting wheels. Halfway between the two entrances, an array of small, ornate drawer pulls, no two alike, budded forth from the wall. There were no loose artifacts to be seen: no papers, quills, charts, or discarded swathing. There was none of the elaborate scrollwork and decorations like those in vogue with the magicians of her own world. The whole effect was one of sterile efficiency.

Briana retrieved from her backpack the instructions left by the shrouded stranger. Inside were translations into her own tongue what the writing and symbols meant. The top-most inscription in the panel at her side said 'location' and immediately below, two more, 'Murdina' and 'Nowhere.' All the counting wheels showed zeros.

She hesitated a moment. This portal is magic, she thought. Nothing can go wrong. Nothing can fail. Get on with it. With a last bit of reluctance, she pressed the button next to 'Nowhere.' Almost instantly, a sharp click of a bolt sliding into place came from the door. The entire structure began to shimmer. A wave of nausea washed over her, sending her to her knees. Her eyes watered, and she could not keep them in focus.

After a short while, the vibrations stopped. The nausea went away. A warning disk of angry red shown in the middle of the door. She rose and tried the handle, but it did not budge. Evidently, the portal had moved the gateway from Murdina, from the council room to Nowhere, and it was not safe to see what lay outside.

Next, she dialed the right most counting wheels adjacent to 'Murdina' to one hundred and then again pressed the selection. As she expected, the vibrations did not start immediately. Instead, the numbers in the wheels began to decrease — ninety-nine, ninety-eight…

When the count returned to zero, she braced herself, and the shimmering began again. Better prepared, the upset stomach did not feel quite so bad, and when the vibrations finished, the latch clicked a second time. Now, the handle turned easily. She opened the door and glanced out into the dimly lit council chamber. A pleasing comfort like that from sliding into familiar slippers washed over her. She was back to where she had started.

With gathering confidence, Briana shut the door and selected 'Nowhere' from the list of locations a second time. After the vibrations had ceased again, she smiled. Things were working as she had expected. Each listed location was a place the door could be positioned to open upon. And the corresponding countdown determined when the translation would start to take place.

She decided to leave the door through which she had entered parked at Nowhere. It would do no good to use the portal and then have some minion of her father immediately follow.

And the second door. It must open to the shrouded stranger's world. How else could he have gotten home? A peek there before she returned would be an added bonus to report about to her father. When she did, he would maintain a gruff exterior of course, but inside, he would be proud. Thinking about it gave her a warm glow.

She moved to the other end of the portal. The only choices on the wall there were 'Nowhere' and 'The Vanquished' — nothing that would indicate Randor's home. He must have wanted to keep his location secret, but, if so, how did he manage to get there after he had visited Murdina?

Briana pushed the thought away. Something to figure out later. There was no time for that now. She shouldered her pack, selected 'The Vanquished,' waited for the vibration and nausea to go away and opened the door.

It was dark, not as dark as a moonless sky, but dim enough that she could make out nothing. She snapped one of her glow sticks and cautiously looked outside. The air was tainted with a strange odor she could not identify, something stale and heavy like that of a room unopened in years, but evidently not toxic. She felt no ill effects from what she had inhaled.

Reassured, she studied what she saw more carefully. In the near distance in front of her were what looked like the bars of a cage! She whirled about. The bars gently curved off into the gloom on both sides, hinting at a giant circle of confinement.

Randor had said the natives did not practice any of the crafts. So she had naturally assumed they were primitive as well — living in simple huts, perhaps with plowed fields and tethered animals nearby. But metal bars...

Maybe when Randor's people last visited here, there was no cage. It would make sense to put the portal in an uninhabited location. But the circular barrier now changed things. The first thing she would have to do was... escape.

Holding the glow stick in front of her, Briana stepped out of the portal, paced to the line of vertical bars, and started walking the perimeter of the confining wall. After a few dozen steps, she gasped aloud at what she saw — a narrow opening through which she easily could walk!

She started to step through the opening and then stopped. The reality of what she was getting into started to rumble in her head. Her confidence began to falter. Things were not going to be simple; already there was a complication. The enclosing cage was here for a reason. Come the dawn, perhaps natives would arrive to inspect its contents. Even if she were not here, they would see the portal door. She would not be able to leave it unguarded and wander about.

For a few moments, she thought about what to do. The *setter*, she finally remembered from the instructions. Yes, that was what was needed! She returned into the portal, found the correct drawer in the wall now on the left, and extracted a small, slender device that she could hold easily.

She ran her free hand over the bottom of the container but felt only smooth metal. There should have been a tracker in addition to a setter, she remembered from the instructions. But there was none. On the controller she held, the selection choices near the two doors were reproduced along with their nearby selection buttons and counters. She exited the portal, and back outside, carefully read the instructions for the setter's use. She studied them a second time to be sure. Even the smallest mistake here could maroon her forever.

When Briana was satisfied that she understood thoroughly, she began pressing tiny button-like objects protruding from the setter. She set the counter for the 'Nowhere' location near the door she had exited to one hundred, then set the counter for 'The Vanquished' to an additional hundred more.

Next, she started the countdown for the 'Nowhere' location to begin — to move the portal door to Nowhere when the count reached zero. Before it completed, however, she started 'The Vanquished' countdown as well. The counters for both choices began spinning down.

Just as Briana was beginning to fear something had gone wrong, the portal vanished. Briana twisted her loose curl into a tight spiral. Waiting for another fifty was agonizing, but finally, the magic transport again reappeared. It had gone to Nowhere and then returned.

The instructions said a day on this, the exile's planet, was forty-three thousand three hundred and twenty heartbeats. Using that number for the length of time before retrieving the portal from Nowhere meant she could hide it for an entire day. And she could set things so that she was present when it appeared and none of the natives was about.

Briana quickly browsed through more of the instructions. How to add and delete location choices was complicated. More complex still were explanations of how the portal worked. It was not a simple matter to have a door stay in one place. A planet spun on its axis and also hurtled through the cosmos. While on the outside, it might look that a door was standing still, it was in fact continually in motion.

Briana made the necessary portal control setting and felt her confidence return, although not quite as high as it had been at first. But no matter. Now for the adventure to begin.

She scrambled through the opening. On the other side, she looked up at a wooden placard attached to the wall written in the script of the natives. With the help of the language guide, she spoke aloud what she read.

"Wattles Mansion and Garden. City of Los Angeles."

5

A Typical Street

BRIANA WAITED until dawn started to break rather than explore any further in the dark. She was near a gently sloping path paved with large flat and smooth stones. Next to it and a bit lower was a wider surface, dark, and laced with black repairs that looked like giant wandering worms.

Lined up on both sides of the dark surface were rows of what must be carriages for the wealthy. Through glass windows, one could see plush interiors, elegant enough even for a queen. The surrounding shells were smooth steel and painted in bright colors, although some appeared much fresher than did others. For all of them, there was neither purchase for a driver on top nor any means of connecting horses or oxen in the front. And so many! It could not be possible there were so much affluence in one place.

Briana looked downslope, southward if this orb rotated the same way on its axis as did Murdina, in the direction of strange whishing noises that sounded as if a hundred scullery maids were sweeping in unison. In the distance, one of the coaches sped by from left to right, faster than any team of horses could possibly pull. Shortly thereafter came another from the other direction, and then two more from the left.

On top of posts near where they raced were circular lamps gleaming an angry dragon-breath red. After a few moments, they blinked out, and green ones below them began to shine. A screech filled the air, and two more carriages came to a stop on the cross path below. A short time later, a third light beamed yellow and then the red one shown again. When they did, the wagons roared away.

Magic coaches, not one but several. And controlled by imp lamps. Magic and wizardry in blatant display. The exiles *had* escaped their prison! Not here more than moments, and already she was done. This first adventure was going to be easy!

.

For confirmation, Briana reached out and touched one of the carriages directly in front of her, but no tingle of magic caressed her fingertips. She shook her head. No, they were not magic after all, and besides, there were too many of them. Better not to conclude in haste. She needed to find out more before she returned home, and she had a day before she could anyway.

Briana started walking southward next to the broader path that she concluded should more properly be called a street or road — for carriages rather than travelers on foot. She touched each vehicle along the way to be sure, but none held any trace of magic.

When she reached the intersection, she noticed there were lamps above the larger avenue cycling on and off also. Although no coaches traveled north or south, the lamps shining there synchronized with those for the east and west. Looking at the signage on shorter poles near the glowing orbs, she mouthed out what must be the name of the larger street.

"Hollywood," she said, and then the much harder to pronounce, "Blvd."

The yellow lamp came on and then the red. One of the carriages pulled to the side near where she stood. A door into the interior swung open. A gaunt man who had not shaved in what must have been several days and wearing shabby clothes like those of a beggar leaned across from where he sat and pushed the opening wider.

"I will give you twenty bucks for a quicky," he said. "How about it?"

A man, Briana thought. Not shrouded like the visitor to the council chamber. Dressed properly, he could pass without notice back on Murdina. And he was speaking in the native tongue. A man. Not an exile.

She felt a moment's hesitation, even though she had told herself when preparing for the adventure that at some point she would have to speak to the natives. This barter probably was a good a test as any for a first try.

"I... do not have a quicky," she said as she struggled for the meaning of the words. "But I am wondering — "

"Bitch!" The man slammed the door. A loud growl escaped from the front of the carriage as the lamps changed, and it bolted away.

The possibilities expanded. The growl could be that of a demon hiding in the front compartment of the carriage. Maybe the native had been enchanted by the exiles' sorcery. Maybe the thought about imps in the lamps was still valid.

AS THE sun began its climb into the sky, the road traffic increased in both directions. Briana remained at the street corner, trying to understand what she was seeing. Although still early morning, the number of carriages was far greater than what would be seen in Ambrosia, the capital of Procolon, at midday. She looked both ways down the street. There was no royal palace in either direction that would explain why there was so much rushing about with no apparent purpose.

Her stomach began to growl. The initial excitement of adventure waned, and her energy began to sag. After all, she had been up the entire night.

It was all so kinetic, the scene so... so enormous, she thought. Yes, that was the word for it, enormous. She began to feel small, insignificant as a gnat on the back of a djinn. Like a small pebble in a boot that could not be moved out of the way, the thought began to ferment and trouble.

To shake off the feeling, she decided to walk east, hoping a different venue might be more understandable, more representative of the native culture, something she would be able to comprehend.

AFTER BRIANA had travelled for some while along Hollywood Blvd., she began encountering natives coming from side streets and passing her by — more and more, the farther east she went. She felt some apprehension as the first had drawn near, but he did not pay her any heed, nor did any other as they approached.

None of the men were threatening; they displayed neither sword nor dagger. Their clothing was much more colorful and varied than back at home, and thinner rather than practical, the sort of thing young lordlings would strut in order to show off their wealth in the safety of a noble's court.

The women were the amazing ones. She studied them more intently as they passed. They walked in twos and threes and sometimes alone, all unescorted. And some showed the swell of their breasts for anyone to see. Ladies of the court also did this, Briana knew, but only after the blush of youth had faded as it had for the queen. The younger women on Murdina had no such need.

And their legs! They were bare, some brazenly to above their knees. More astonishing was that they were clean-shaven, as smooth as the face of a man! Those lords who maintained such appearances paid skilled barbers to keep their skins fresh, but certainly, no woman would permit such intimacy by a stranger. That was impossible to understand.

As Briana continued, the structures on either side of the street became taller, some of three stories or more. Not all were simple boxes, but instead looked as if built by drunken masons with tilted and uneven walls. Subdued browns were replaced by a rainbow of colors, sunburst yellows, scarlet-reds, and deep-ocean blues. Large panels of imp lamps danced in intricate repeating patterns, drawing attention to themselves almost as if they were the result of a sorcerer's charm. Signs were bounded by what looked like alchemists' glowsticks, but longer and brighter, able to shine fiercely in the daylight. The lamps pulsed on and off in deliriums conveying a mania even more manic than that of the rushing carriages.

Storefronts? Briana puzzled. But far grander than any she had ever seen before. And for none could she recognize what wares were sold. There were signs enough but most with words she did not recognize from her dictionary. And those that she did made little sense. 'Hard rock'? Of course, they were hard. Why would anyone have to pay for one?

The path on which she walked became grander — wider, darker, and containing an embedded series of white stars blazing the path even though such an aid was not needed. Like a line of marching warriors, tall trees with long naked trunks and plumed with branches at the top sprung out of the smooth stone.

She continued to marvel why no one spoke to her. With her thick tunic, leggings, and pack, she was the one who stood out from the others. But still no one gave her any notice, edging around her, or even jostling her, without a word.

After traversing two more cross streets up ahead, she glimpsed the reason why. There were others dressed the same as she! Some even wore cloaks or capes. Some had masks. Other women in wore sequined costumes, so short as not to be believed.

They rapidly twirled metal cylinders with white bulbs on the both ends and occasionally tossed them high into the air. Around them clustered others, garbed like the ones who had already hurried past her.

One structure was impressively higher than the two to either side — an entryway built like a helmet worn by a general in a victory parade. It stood at the rear of a large courtyard bare of greenery and underfoot completely covered with a random array of indentations looking like the prints of hands or boots.

Larger carriages came into view, some with seats on the top as well as inside. They pulled to the edge of the street and disgorged their content into the courtyard. The natives that had been discharged ran from one set of indentations to another, obviously delighted, and yelling to others what they had found. It reminded Briana of the rituals of magicians, but here it was too disorganized to have any such a meaning.

As Briana pondered, two young women suddenly surrounded her on both sides. "Selfie!" yelled one and extended a small mirror-like object on the end of a stick.

"What movie?" asked the other. "I don't recognize your costume. Is it not out yet? Are you one of the stars or only an extra?"

"You are supposed to smile," the first thrust the mirror in Briana's face. "Like us. See. Instead, you look like a blank faced idiot."

"She's in character, Hester," the other said. "Don't you get it? She is playing the *role* of an idiot."

The second woman thrust a small book into Briana's hand along with what looked like some sort of writing quill.

"Well, autograph it," she said. "Your name, your real name. Who knows? Some day you may be famous, and this will be worth a fortune."

Briana thought for a moment how her name would be composed in the native's lettering system and slowly began to make the marks across the page.

"Look at that," Hester said. "Look what she scribbled. Worse than a kindergartener".

"That precisely is my point. Like I said. She is in character. Go ahead and give her the tip."

"This is not worth even a buck," Hester said. She thought for a moment. "Okay, if you are playing the idiot, you would probably like a nice silver coin, right?"

She reached into a purse, extracted one, thrust it in Briana's palm.

Briana bristled. Idiot indeed! This was not the way to treat a daughter of Alodar the Archimage. She should…

The coin *was* silver! Maybe…

She examined the disk more closely. Her anger had subsided for a moment, but then it returned. Counterfeit! Counterfeit and a bad example at that. It was silver all right, silver *overlaid* over a copper core. She could see that the baser metal had worn through around the entire circumference.

Briana turned to confront the two women, but they were already moving on through the crowd, looking for additional targets to accost.

It took a while for the heat to dissolve away, but Briana found she could not return to a complete calm. The noise and flashing lights on the storefronts were becoming too much to process all at once.

She needed something to focus on, but the visual bombardment continued its relentless onslaught. Closing her eyes did not help. If she did, the unfamiliar sounds intruded even more. She decided to continue in the direction of a tall tower farther to the east. There, in the distance, the furor of activity seemed to be much less.

But as she did, her discomfort grew. She needed to relieve herself, but no convenient bush or tree was in sight. Her shoulders slumped under the now heavy weight of her pack.

When she reached the tower, Briana looked at the sign across the street. 'Ripley's Believe It or Not', it said. What could that possibly mean? Believe it? Believe *what*? And if not, then what happened? Her thoughts reeled. Even here, where relatively it was quieter, everything was still too kinetic, too vast, too frenzied, and complex.

The experience was so unlike those recorded in the sagas. When heroes went to an unchronicled land, they coped almost immediately. That would not be possible here. Her original plan of taking a few days to sample the culture was not going to work. It could take a lifetime to figure it all out.

This adventure could be a big mistake. When the portal reappeared tomorrow morning, perhaps she should go home. For a moment, the thought surprised her, but then it rooted, and she had to consider what to do.

Go home? But what would happen then? Be carted off to a grubby fortress in the west? No, she could not do that. She *would* not do that. Not yet. Not even if *many* days had to pass. Whatever it took. No return until she had something of value to report.

Her stomach rumbled again. Her tongue was thick in her mouth. She had brought enough sustenance for a few days, but not for how long this was going to take. In addition to puzzling about the existence of the crafts, she would have to take care of the basics too — food, water and a place to sleep. How was that to come about? Could she even eat the food, drink the water? There was nothing familiar here, nothing she

30

understood — nothing she *could* understand in any reasonable time.

With a sudden jab of fear, Briana realized the predicament in which she had placed herself. The last of her energy ebbed away. She did not want to return, but neither could she stay. She leaned against the wall of the tall building. No one noticed or offered to help as she sagged to the ground. In all of her life, no situation ever had been this bad. There was nothing worse than this.

And as she did, she felt a twinge that rapidly grew into a cramp. She was wrong. It *could* be even worse. Her time of the month was starting — starting a week early. She had brought nothing for it. And something had to be done now, sooner rather than later. Otherwise, her leggings would have a stain for everyone to see, one that would set and could not be removed.

But by now, she could do nothing. Briana folded her arms over her knees, lowered her head onto them, and quietly began to weep. If the exiles could see her now, she thought, they certainly would be laughing.

6

Exiled forever

ANGUS, THE exile, reached behind his head and smoothed down his long, flowing hair. It would reach his waist soon and he would have to have it sheared. A daily ritual of shaving kept his face bare. Black eyes like machined spheres of hematite marked him as cunning to the other Heretics; one to be dealt with only when necessary and then with caution. Only the tips of his fangs showed when his mouth was closed. Nor did his tunic cover his arms as it did most of the others. Rather, he bared them proudly, the thick fur as sufficient as sleeves. When he stood to full height rather than slumped, he was as tall as the natives roaming freely above.

He ran his fingers over the polished wood grain of the orange-brown table, but its beauty gave him little satisfaction. Neither did the expanse of the rocky alcove about him, though it was larger than all but two others. More than three times his height, its smooth walls rippled like waves on a placid sea, a wrinkled bubble of air far beneath the ocean's surface.

Small flakes of gold shimmered in a narrow vein snaking above Angus' head. Flickering candles standing in indentations chiseled into the walls gave only enough light so that the objects on the tabletop could be seen, but the rest of the alcove was in shadow. The wax was too precious to waste on reminding one of the crushing reality of confinement.

Untold hours had been spent by the Heretics chipping away at the alcove floor to create the flat space on which the table stood and a pathway to a small oval opening leading to more caverns and twisty passageways beyond. Caverns and passageways — the entire world of the vanquished, the exiles, the Heretics Who Proclaim the Truth.

Angus looked at the small clock on the tabletop, its pendulum swinging back and forth in frantic haste, far faster than the glacial slowness the humans used to mark their time.

The humans. The puny, primitive humans. If they knew of his true status and that of the others of his kind, they would be laughing. He was a powerful alchemist. His brothers were potent practitioners of the crafts as well. Unfettered, subjugations of the surface dwellers would be easy. Yet despite this power, they were hopelessly confined in underground caverns. And so fearful that any use of the magics would alert the so-called Faithful, the oppressors who put them here, his brothers insisted no craft be practiced at all.

The Faithful. Faithful to what? What an ill-fitting label. Sheep that move from one fad to the next with only the slightest prodding. The merest hint that something new was going to be more popular than what had come before. The idiots did not think, did not consider, did not engage with exercises of the mind.

But then, it was no better here. Dinton, his eldest brother, how could he be so stubborn, so unseeing, so afraid? Whenever he had possession of the baton, the depression of the flock members always increased. There was always the risk one or more would remove their rings and surrender — unable to accept who knows how much longer — more centuries encased in rock before they might possibly be free.

Dinton and Thaling would be here shortly, so Angus shoved the thoughts away. As always, Dinton would arrive first; Thaling would be the last to appear — the diplomat, his middle brother with the glib words to douse the rising anger boiling between Dinton and himself. Never venturing opinions of his own so they too could be attacked. His two, so unalike, brothers. He wondered how much longer he could keep his secret from them.

Without preamble, Dinton entered the alcove, breaking through Angus' reverie. He was shorter but broader like an over ripe gourd. His hair also cascaded to his waist behind, but rather than the uniform dull brown of Angus, the roots showed silver. Even in the dimness, his eyes squinted nearly shut, as if he were afraid to let anything from the outside accost his senses. His fangs did not protrude. A long rod of polished wood hung from his waist on one side and a short dagger from the other. He carried a colored cardboard box in his hand.

"You have gone above again, haven't you?" Dinton said without preamble. He slapped the staff at his side. "Even when I explicitly forbade it while the baton is mine."

Angus glanced up at Dinton, but did not rise. His brother's time as agreed upon absolute leader was almost over. Let him feel a little more aggravation before it was finished.

"We have been over this many times before," Angus said. "A grandfather over a hundred native years ago, and then his grandson when his elder was soon to pass. They are the only two of which I have interacted. There is no way any other of these primitives would find out about the trades I have made."

"It is not the natives I worry about," Dinton thundered as if were orating to everyone in the caverns at once. "It is the oppressive ones, the Faithful, the ones who overwhelmed us and cast us out. If they discover there is traffic with those who call themselves humans, or that the charm placed upon us has worn off, or if any new exercise of craft is detected, their next punishment will be even worse than this. We all would be given to the tigerwasps. *All* of us. Continual pain with no release."

Angus prided himself on how he carried himself in the caverns — back straight as a sheer cliff, untroubled by any threat unless directly challenged to a duel one-to-one. But every time he thought of the wasps, he could not help but wince.

His eyes closed nearly shut and his cheeks stretched high on his face. "We should have destroyed the colony of the loathsome pests long ago," he shuddered. "The Faithful left those huge beasts with us so we would come to use them on ourselves — even when there was the most petty bickering."

Dinton nodded slowly. He cleared his throat before speaking as he often did. "What the feeling would be, I, too, find it hard to think about. Boring into one's stomach and then consuming the organs from the inside — slowly and carefully, leaving only enough of each to continue functioning until the very last."

"But it is the ultimate deterrent," Dinton continued before Angus could reply. "No one dares to commit a capital crime. The punishment would be too great. For the thousand years we have been here, the tigerwasps have been employed only twice."

"Count the rings in your alcove," Angus ignored Dinton's words. His brother had a tendency to run on and on. "How many do they number now? Haven't more than three hundred already taken their own lives, from their loss in either a half-heartedly fought duel or an overwhelming sadness they can no longer put away? What good does it do to wait any longer? Soon there will be none of us left, and then it will not matter."

"We must have patience," Dinton answered. Now his eyes were totally shut. "The primitives are accelerating the destruction of their world. In a few hundred more orbits about their star, they all will be gone and this entire planet will be ours."

"This entire hell-hole, you mean," Angus snapped back. "Of what use is it to us, if we must remain below the surface even after the humans are gone?"

Angus waved his arm around his alcove. "And while we wait, what do we have to bring us joy? A meandering collection of lava tubes and gas bubbles. Small cracks in the surface to let in sunlight for our crops, a trickle of water from the rains above. No sky overhead, no wind. Once every nook had been explored two or three times over, only numbness is left."

"Back on the home world," Dinton put a tone of considered reasoning into his voice, "our so-called heresies were a matter of debate — the beliefs of one flock against those of another. But here, the risk of discovery is unforgiveable. Your dabbling, the skirting on the edge of safety must stop." The sound of the orator resumed. "I have commanded it. Stop or else."

"Or else, what?"

"Or else the wasps."

"Yet, you enjoy an even bigger table than this one in your alcove," Angus said. "Without what I have done, how could these little tastes of beauty even have been possible? The monotony would indeed be complete."

"Mere shadows," Dinton scoffed. "Native trinkets with no depth of meaning."

"Trinkets!" Angus shouted. "The objects I have obtained at great peril, mere trinkets?" With a snarl, he withdrew the dagger from his waist. "I'll show you a trinket. But first, you will have to remove it from your gut!"

"You are the youngest, Angus," Dinton growled. The box he was carrying dropped to the floor and flew open. Cards and tokens scattered about. Ignoring the mess, he drew his knife in reply, his eyes now wide open and glaring. "You are the youngest, Angus, if only for a few moments more."

"Stop!" a third voice interrupted the argument. "What is it this time?" Thaling rushed in and placed restraining hands on his brothers' arms. "We have made the agreement that we will not succumb to our baser emotions when we meet. We are to decide who will possess the baton for the next turn of the wheel of time. Nothing more. Why is that so hard to remember?"

Thaling was the shortest of the three, hunched over like a rat trying to walk on only its hind legs. Long fangs protruding from his lips interfered with his speech, but his brothers had grown used to his slurs. As adults, they no longer jeered when he tried to mouth human words.

For a few heartbeats, Angus and Dinton stared at each other. Like two feuding children, they played at who would resheath his weapon first. Finally, Angus sighed in exasperation and plunged his into its scabbard. Dinton waited a moment longer, smiled, and put his away as well.

"If only father had publically chosen one of us before he gave into the monotony and took his own life," Thaling said. He straightened up as best he could. "We would have no need for the periodic bickering and waste of time."

"Yes, certainly," Angus said. "Our daily schedules are so *very* busy, that we can hardly find a few moments for this stupid ceremony."

"We have agreed," Thaling said, his slur more noticeable when he became excited. "It is the only thing that has kept us from destroying *all* of ourselves in a struggle to determine who was to rule."

"I am the eldest," Dinton said. "By rights, it should have been me."

"We made an agreement," Thaling pleaded. "Why do we have to go through with this each and every time?"

"If Dinton would only stop harping about being the oldest — " Angus began.

"I choose my words carefully each time I speak," Dinton cut in. "You are the one who pollutes the air with your hot-headed outbursts."

"Enough," Thaling shouted. "To the business at hand."

"You are not yet the holder of the baton," Dinton turned his attention to Thaling and withdrew his dagger again. "You cannot give me commands. I demand the respect that is my due."

"I do not cower to words that are merely loud," Angus said as he brandished his stiletto as well.

Thaling took a step backward and bared his own knife. "So this is the way of cowards? Rather than duel properly, instead, gang up two against one?" He showed his teeth, and a drool of foam began to drip from the side of his mouth.

The three brothers stood facing one another in a tight circle, first threatening the one on the left and then the right. After a few dozen heartbeats, a gentle chime from the small clock on Angus' table broke through the tension. Like the uncoiling of intertwined springs, all three men relaxed.

"Yes, it is time to choose," Thaling said, lowering his blade and resuming his usual slump.

"If it is my turn again," Dinton said, "my edicts remain the same. No contact with the natives. Reduce the frivolous use of water. Store it instead against when there will be drought. And above all, patience. Wait for what eventually is going to happen — for when the humans will be gone."

"Action now," Angus said. "If it becomes my turn, then there will be tasks that I will command what you and your flocks are to do." He turned and looked at Thaling. "And you, brother. Every time, you are always silent. "Have you even thought about what would be your commands if the baton were to pass to you?"

"No thoughts, my brothers." Thaling's slump grew even deeper. "Not until such time as they are needed. Let us continue as we have done before."

Dinton grunted. He stooped and began retrieving the box and its scattered contents. Thaling and Angus bent to help. Soon a flat board, the tokens, and the cards were in their proper places.

"Before we begin, the oath," Dinton said. Angus and Thaling nodded.

In unison, they orated, "I agree that the winner of the game gets the baton for the next cycle. For so long as he holds it, his word is absolute, and I shall obey."

"And regardless of who holds the baton, I shall practice no craft. But if I transgress, the tigerwasps shall do what they will with me." Dinton then continued alone.

"And regardless of who holds the baton, I shall practice no craft. But if I transgress, the tigerwasps shall do what they will with me," Thaling repeated.

"And regardless of who holds the baton, I shall practice no craft. But if I transgress, the tigerwasps shall do what they will with me." Angus spoke as the last.

Angus held his thoughts to himself. He pushed away the images of the wasp depositing an egg in his stomach bulges. There was high risk in what he was doing. He could not deny it. But then, neither could he continue with things as they were.

The three turned their attention to Angus' tabletop. Dice rolled and the tokens moved. No one spoke until Thaling said, "I suggest it was done by Miss Scarlet with the revolver in the lounge."

7

A Second Encounter

SOMEONE WAS shaking Briana's shoulder. Her eyes sprang open. She was still where she had sagged to the ground, but it was night. She must have fallen asleep.

"The police patrol will be here shortly, missy," a voice told her softly. "They will take ya in rather than telling ya only to move off the boulevard."

"Take me to where?" Briana croaked. Her voice was parched from not having drunk anything all day. She looked up to the figure stooping over her. It took a moment to decipher what she saw. Long mouse-gray straggly hair, knotted and unkempt and a beard like a bird's nest on a face deeply creased and smudged with dirt. A man then and not a woman. The clothes were in tatters — dirty browns and grays. Toes gnarled like stubby roots from an uprooted weed sprouted from bare feet. The stench of the unbathed filled Briana's lungs.

Definitely not a lord like the others she had seen, she thought. Were the serfs only allowed out at night?

"They call me Slow Eddie," the man said. "But I know what I'm talking about. If ya got an ID, they'll drop ya off somewhere else in the city. If ya don't, well, ya could end up on the next bus south, back to where ya came from."

"I don't think so." Briana shook her head and tried to clear her thoughts. "I come from... too far away."

She looked up and down the street. It was almost deserted. The swish of the speeding carriages was absent. Except for the pools of light cascading from strong imp lights, the darkness was heavy.

"An illegal, eh?" Eddie smiled, showing only three teeth in a cavernous mouth. "I figured as much. Do ya have a place to stay?"

Briana frowned and did not answer. What was this old man hinting at?

"No, no, I don't mean anything like that," Eddie said quickly. "Ya look like too nice of a missy for ... well for someone like me. I only mean ya have to get off the street before the cops come crusin' by."

Briana's stomach growled, loud enough for Eddie to hear. "Betcha haven't eaten since ya arrived, too. Well, ya picked a good day to show up. Tomorrow, over a few blocks and then south a few more there is a Sunday handout. Have to get there early though. They run out before everybody in line gets something."

He scratched his head. "Look, meet me at this place tomorrow at noon, and I will walk ya there. Get a meal in ya, and things will stop looking so bad," He wrinkled his nose. "And sometimes they have a shower truck there, too... though it has been a while since the last one showed up."

Briana blushed, remembering her predicament. How long had she slept anyway? She had to take care of herself and return to where the portal was due to reappear before anyone else could see it.

And... Eddie sounded kindly enough. Different from everyone else so far who had disregarded and jostled her as they passed...

Return or stay? The question boomed back into her mind. She needed time to think things through. For now, she decided to leave all options open in case.

"Yes, tomorrow, I will be here at noon," she said. "But do not wait for me long if I do not come."

Eddie smiled again weakly and then sighed. "Don't worry about it, missy. The years have made me slow, but not so slow I can't understand what words mean a brushoff when I hear them."

He turned and began to walk away. "But I will be here at noon nonetheless. I only wanted to have a friend to talk to."

"No, wait, I did not mean what you think. The language is new to me."

Eddie did not respond but continued a slow shuffle up the street to the east.

Briana watched for a moment, toying with her hair and then stopped. She had things to do.

BRIANA WALKED back the way she had come in the morning. Like a warm, comforting blanket, the quiet and darkness were soothing. Only occasionally would one of the carriages rush by. And after a few of those passed, they did not seem to matter much either.

When she was almost back to where she had first entered the boulevard, she turned south onto a cross street populated with smaller dwellings on either side. Most of them were dark, but for a few lights pierced through large glass windows onto the street like the eyes of huge dragons looking for prey. She ducked behind a large hedge of one of the unlit houses, stripped out of her leggings and undergarment, and relieved herself.

The walk had done her good. She had figured out what to do next. She removed the dagger from her waist and her cloak from her backpack. For a moment, she hesitated. Her father had given the garment to her on her eighteenth birthday, and she had to admit she felt quite special when she wore it to a bazaar and everyone knew she was the daughter of the Archimage.

And now, without it, what would she then be really — a heroine on an adventure but now in disguise or only a mere girl who should return home and accept what fate awaited her?

Briana shook the images out of her head. "It has only been one day," she whispered to herself. "Far too soon to tell." Holding the cloth tight in one hand, she slashed the cape into pieces, creating two aprons, one to drape her in front, and one for the rear. The appearance would look bizarre, but then she was from a different world so what difference did it make.

Briana cut four more banners of cloth from the remainder of the cloak and folded them up into hand-sized pads. She climbed back into her leggings, placed one where it should be and put the remaining three in her pack. What was left of her cloak and the soiled undergarment she disposed of in one of the curious looking boxes with small red flags standing in the front of some of the houses. Shortly thereafter, she was back in Wattles Garden, drinking from her goatskin, munching a hunk of her bread and waiting for the return of the portal. Perhaps tomorrow would be a better day.

8

Magic castles

AT DAWN, a woman pushing a child in a contraption of metal tubes, cloth, and small wheels entered the garden. At the same time, the portal door reappeared. Briana fumbled for the setter out of her pack and sent the magical device away for another day.

She looked with apprehension back at the woman, but the caretaker appeared not to have noticed what had transpired. Instead, she was busy bending over and speaking what must be baby talk to the child.

The setting of the countdown in the portal had been too long, Briana realized. She needed to make the interval shorter, so there was a greater margin before anyone else came to the garden. This was the wrong place for the portal to be anyway. It needed to appear in a much more secluded spot, not exposed in such an open space as this.

The full stomach and hours of quiet had settled her thoughts. Regardless of how bizarre these surroundings were, they did not appear to be threatening or dangerous. Leaving after a single day was not something a true adventurer would do. She would have to stay longer — long enough to convince herself if there was any craft being used by the exiles in this world or not. When the portal returned tomorrow, she would set the countdown interval shorter.

The first step had to be to determine whether or not the natives were using craft themselves. There were so many marvelous things she had seen that could not easily be explained. If they were practitioners, then whatever the exiles might be doing would be completely masked.

Briana twisted a loose curl while she pondered. Her task was going to last more than another day or two — maybe as many as ten. When she finished, her wedding would be almost a fortnight closer, but that could not be helped. And to stay so long, she needed silver coins rather than counterfeit ones. Enough to buy the food and drink, to pay for a place to stay. A room at an inn with a lock on the door, somewhere that would be safe for the portal to materialize and disappear at any time of the day.

For silver, she had to work. Menial jobs certainly. There was no hope of doing anything sophisticated, but with so many people along this one street, surely there would be tasks she could perform. It would only be a matter of looking for them rather than gawking at what she did not understand.

Yes, merely gazing around was going to be too inefficient for everything she needed to comprehend. She needed to find a palace of magicians where there was a library, or at least what passed for one.

With renewed purpose, Briana returned to the boulevard and started to retrace her path of the previous day. When she reached the place where she had been given the coin, she watched intently as bizarrely clad others performed the same ritual she had done before. But no silver changed hands — instead only small rectangles of green-colored paper.

She moved on eastward, farther than she had gone before. This time, the rush of carriages, the frenzy of the signage, the crush of people did not bother her as much. She had seen it all before — strange and incomprehensible — but already familiar, nevertheless.

Crossing a street with a surge of others, Briana smiled inwardly at her newly deduced knowledge of what the colored lights, arrows, and flashing hands of restraint meant. She looked at a shopfront that appeared quite approachable on her left. In a large window of glass, she read a sign she realized she understood. 'Help wanted,' it said.

Briana peered into the window. There were many inside, eating at tables and others on high stools perched at a long counter. Among them flitted women dressed in blouses, leggings, and wearing aprons like herself, passing out plates they carried skillfully on their arms.

Serving wenches! She could do that! Bread and rolls covering meat and cheeses top and bottom. Leafy salads far larger than any she had ever seen before. And where there was food there should be lodging as well. With a smile of anticipation, Briana pushed open the door and entered.

"Take a seat anywhere," the waitress nearest called out.

"Help wanted?" Briana asked.

The waitress looked Briana up and down for a moment and then shrugged. She reached under the counter and pulled out a piece of parchment and what Briana now knew worked the same way as a quill that somehow contained its own ink.

"Here. Fill this out. We will get back in touch if you're needed."

Briana nodded. She walked to the counter, sat down on a stool and began studying the paper she was handed.

"First name," she mumbled to herself. "Well, that is easy enough." As she had done the day before, she carefully filled in the blank with her name.

"Last name." She paused for a moment. 'Fourth daughter of Alodar, the Master of the Five Magics, Archimage of all of Murdina' would not fit and probably would require a lot of explanation. Best to leave that empty.

"Street." That one was easy. She looked through the window toward the nearby intersection, saw what she wanted, and entered 'Hollywood Blvd."

"City." Briana pulled the notepad out of her backpack on which she had copied the very first sign she had seen when she exited the park. 'City of Los Angeles' it had said.

But the rest of the blanks offered no clue — State, Zip, Phone, and SSN. Perhaps what she had done would be enough. After all, it was only for the duties of a serving wench. How hard could that be? Briana held the form up and waved for attention.

"You left out your social," the woman said as she scanned the form. "We got to have that for the withholding."

Briana's face froze in puzzlement. It was like her first encounter about the 'quicky.' "I do not have a social," she said.

"No social, no job."

Briana opened her mouth to protest, to ask more so she could understand, but the woman had immediately turned away to resume her duties.

It was not that she was again overwhelmed by the number of differences, Briana thought. She felt that with a little patience, she could handle such a thing now. But each difference might well have its own peculiar pathblock that needed a key. With a sigh, she nodded and exited the shop. Some of her morning optimism began to erode. She looked up at the sun. It was still several hours until zenith. May as well explore some more on her own and then meet Slow Eddie at noon. Perhaps he could help.

BRIANA SAT crossed legged next to Slow Eddie on the stone walkway on the side street. She took a swig of water from her goatskin to wash away the taste. The food she had sampled was far too salty, but she had managed to swallow nevertheless. Now to wait for a while to see if her stomach could accept what it was being given, and more importantly, if there were no ill effects.

"Are you all the serfs of a single lord?" she asked.

"Serfs? You mean like slaves?" Eddie asked. "No, we are free. Of course, we are free..." Eddie waved at the others sitting or squatting down the walkway like the heaps of trash waiting to be picked up by the garbage wagon. Most wore clothes in tatters, gray with age and grimy dirt. A few huddled near their collection of haphazard discards stuffed into metal cages mounted on tiny black wheels

Eddie sighed. "Free, but homeless."

Briana surveyed the huddled forms. She had been fortunate to be among the half receiving a meal. The others that had obtained none had already vanished.

"Then, how do you...?" Briana reached for a word she did not yet know.

"Survive?" Eddie finished her thought. "There are more handouts like this one, but ya have to know where they are. And there are the bins at the backs of the groceries."

He shrugged. "Water is more of a problem than the food, but occasionally, the DWP installs temporary drinking fountains in Skid Row. It takes almost all of your time moving around from place to place."

This was not what Briana wanted to hear. Occupied with staying alive would leave very little chance to find out if the exiles were using craft, if they had escaped from their imprisonment... Exchanging labor for silver would be a much better way to go.

"What is a social?" she asked. "I tried to be a serving wench, but I did not have one."

"And ya ain't gonna get one either," Eddie shook his head. "Ya need a birth certificate or some documentation proving you have an authorization to work in the US."

He looked at Briana keenly. "When ya say serving wench, what exactly is it you mean, missy? There are always jobs like that around. Ones dealing in cash only, especially for women."

"Take an order and bring the food," Briana answered. "What else could it mean?"

"Ah, a waitress," Eddie smiled. "Good for ya, missy."

He screwed up his face in thought for a few moments. "Well, this is hardly better, but it might be something. A bit east of here, there is a place where ya work as a waitress, but only for your meals and tips. How you get your tips is your own business. It draws in the customers, and the owners do not have payroll taxes. Everybody wins."

"Tips?"

"The extra money a customer gives to the waitress beyond the cost of a meal."

"How much is the tip?"

"Well, I don't know. A couple of bucks I guess, two dollars or three."

Briana tried to put things in perspective with her limited knowledge so far. "So if I serve ten meals, I get enough dollars to buy... one 'quicky'?"

"No, no, women sell quickies. They don't buy them! But missy, I thought ya didn't want to do that, right?

"How many dollars for a single night at an inn?" Briana ignored the confusion. "How much of a day could I work?"

"You wouldn't get enough," Eddie shook his head. "Rent around here is too expensive. Why do ya think there are so many of us out here on the street?"

"How much of a day could I work?" Briana persisted.

"Around eight hours in a shift, I guess," Eddie said. "The standard thing. Ya know. One third of a day for sleeping, one third for working, and one third for whatever else ya desire to do." He looked down the street at the others finishing their meals and moving off. "Yeah, whatever else ya desire to do."

No lodging for her labor then, Briana thought quickly. And her stomach was still feeling good. At least her food problem would be solved. She could still sleep in the Wattles Garden in the hours of darkness until she figured out something better to do about the portal and where to stay.

"Where is this place?" she asked.

Eddie grimaced. "Maybe I shouldn't have mentioned it," he said. "The mildest ones going there are bottom pinchers. Then there are the gropers and others worse than that."

Briana ignored the warning. Eddie was proving to be quite useful. Perhaps he even could provide additional help. She felt a growing empowerment. "I think I can handle myself," she said, "but there is more I want to know."

"Sure, missy. What is it?" Eddie smiled. He acted as if the attention of a fair young thing was the highlight of his day.

"There are magicians where I come from. Any around here?"

Eddie scratched at his cheek, as if trying to root out a flea about to bite. "Well, there is the Magic Castle up on Franklin. Is that what ya mean?"

"Yes, a magic castle!" Briana exclaimed. "How far away is it? How do I get in?"

"Never been there since... well, that's of no importance now. How do ya get in? Get a sponsor to let ya in to watch the shows."

"Watch the shows?"

"Ya know, the usual stuff. Up close table sleight of hand. Escape from the locked cabinet up on the stage — "

"Oh, that is nothing," Briana interrupted. "Anyone could do those things. I mean *real* magic."

"There is no such thing," Eddie said.

Briana started to rebut, but then thought better of it. "I ask because where there are magicians, there are also ..." She faltered again. "There are also many ..." She pantomimed opening and closing her hands several times as if they were hinged together at the bottom. "Also many words so I can learn faster than walking about."

"A library," Eddie said quietly as a great sadness descended over his face like the final curtain of a tragic play. "Yes, I know where there is a library. In fact many of them. But that was so long ago."

"Where?"

"UCLA," Eddie said. "About seven miles west of here."

"Ella?" Briana asked. "There are libraries where you can see someone named Ella?"

"No, no. Letters of the alphabet. 'U. C. L. A.' — a university, a place of higher learning."

"How far is seven miles in steps?" Briana asked.

"Well, let's see. About two thousand steps in a mile..."

Her excitement began to bubble. A complete plan started to fall into place.

"So fourteen thousand in all," Briana said. "Two hours of very fast walking there and back. Sleeping, working, and then whatever else, you said. I can be there four of your hours every day. Thank you, Eddie. You have been very helpful. Now, tell me, how do I go from here to the inn and this... this 'You see Ella.'"

46

9

The Purchasing Agent

ANGUS SMOOTHED his long flowing hair and eyed Jormind carefully. The other exile was a foot shorter, and his eyes were wide with fear. They stood before the plugstone in the wall of a small, roughly circular antechamber, the ceiling barely higher than Jormind's head. Fashioned by the Faithful with magic chisels when they were entombed, the seal as perfect as that of a ground glass stopper in a flask. No one else was near. Others would come only when it was their turn to tend to the crops.

Have I made the right decision, Angus thought? What if this helper told? He shrugged in the manner of the humans. If Jormind did not work out, he would have to die in a duel or an unfortunate accident — have his ring added to Dinton's depressing collection.

"This is merely a precaution," Angus explained as he inspected his swathing. Using a small mirror of the natives, he checked his back and saw no gaps. He wanted no hint about coarse body hair and fangs for the human they were to meet. Although it was difficult with the thick gloves, he managed to tie the small pouch of gold dust around his waist.

He turned his attention back to Jormind. "For my plan to be completed, someone else must know how to carry on this part of it. Dinton will still want his newspapers and Thaling his candles while I am busy with other tasks."

He should be suspicious of his brother's needs, Angus knew, but there was no time to ponder that. All of his attention had to be devoted to the steps he had deduced to be taken.

When the two exiles were both completely covered and ready, they strained against the plugstone, rolling it to the side. It could be moved by one, but two made the job so much easier. After entering the tunnel, Jormind squatted while Angus arched over him. Placing their hands in four chiseled indentations in the displaced boulder, they rolled it back into place, plunging them into darkness.

Angus fumbled a small candle from a pouch beneath his wrapping, and with some difficulty got it lit. The tunnel sloped steeply upward to another opening. Feeble light illuminated beckoning steps.

"At first, I used to do this only as a test," Angus called over his shoulder as they climbed, "to see how long I could endure before having to return below. When I did, I would sit and wonder, examining all of the fissures and openings and pondering how close they were to the surface."

They reached the upper tunnel entrance and climbed into the largest alcove of them all. Compared to the others, it was enormous, five times the height of a native who lived on the surface above and more than one hundred paces across. Leaves, some large and dark green, others in small clusters, almost canary yellow, covered the indented floor from wall to wall. Here and there, gourds and ripening fruits poked their way through. A stand of bristly succulents commanded one corner. Trickles of water dripped down the walls from cracks overhead and flowed into the garden. A pool in the very center glistened with the excess.

It was their livelihood, their lifeline. Without the bounty of the soil and the water that nurtured it, all of them, every single one, would have starved to death long ago. No one begrudged his duty when his turn for cultivating or harvest came around.

"There." Angus pointed to an opening in the ceiling, barely visible in the candlelight even though it was larger than the rest. "I sat where we are standing now, and I wondered how large it was. Could one fit inside and climb even higher? Where would it lead?"

"Flock Leader, it is so far above us." Jormind's voice quivered.

"I chiseled handholds into the wall. The ascent is easy once you know where to place your grip."

"How could you stand it?"

"I could not for long, only enough to carve one indentation each time I visited. It took many trips, but, then, what else was there to do?"

"That is something I will never try," Jormind said. "No matter how important you say it is."

"If you will not, then our flock will fail to be the one ultimately dominating."

"Is it such a bad thing that Dinton or Thaling would be in charge of our... our commerce with the natives?" Jormind asked.

Angus did not answer. Jormind, he thought. Was there not one who would be better?

IT TOOK much goading, but finally, Jormind agreed to the climb. After many hundred heartbeats, they were in a smaller cavern than the one containing the garden.

"We will not stay long," Angus said. "Do not worry. We will return in time." He used the candle to light one of several torches lying on the smaller grotto's floor. "This way." He pointed with the flame at another opening on a far wall and started walking toward it.

Jormind nodded and followed. Angus thrust the torch through the hole and motioned Jormind to place his head there as well.

"It is a cave!" the shorter exile exclaimed. "Not an alcove but a cave on the surface! I see lights in the distance. Look! There is sky! This is all so beautiful!"

"Yes, the surface," Angus said. "It has been here from the very start of our imprisonment, waiting for discovery. I think the so-called Faithful placed our prison here deliberately so we would find this crypt, be able to see freedom but unable to grasp it."

Jormind followed Angus through the aperture. The two of them scrambled over an uneven floor and eventually stood at the mouth of the cave. The sunlight outside was bright. In the distance, it glistened off a jungle of lush green plants, some soaring high overhead. Above them, tall, stately palms like guardian soldiers stood in disarrayed attention.

Jormind inhaled as he was directed and then looked about with calmer eyes at the unfamiliar surroundings. "But why?" he asked.

"The reason approaches," Angus said as he pointed out of the cave's entrance. "He calls himself Oscar Garbell, two names rather than one in the manner of the humans."

As both of the exiles watched, an old man limped closer. A white and untamed mange like that of the oldest of lions cascaded from the back of an otherwise bald head. He wore a long, colorful shirt that draped over loose fitting knee pants, completely casual in the world of men. One hand quivered as it directed a cane in front to keep an unsteady balance. His other arm cradled a bundle of newspapers and a small brown bag with bulging contents. With each step, it looked as if the entire load would burst like a balloon and the cargo tumble to the ground.

"There is more than one of you!" the man rasped with a voice rusty from disuse. "Do many more of your kind dwell in the bowels as well?"

"That is of no concern of yours, ancient one," Angus said, then turned to address Jormind in their own tongue. "This one first came when he was but a boy some seventy orbits ago. Accompanied his grandfather who had done so another seventy years before that. Now, unfortunately, there is no new heir to perform the task when this one is gone."

"Have you brought what I have asked of you?" The exile's attention returned to the human standing before him.

"Of course, although the burden gets more onerous each time. I am an old man now. Can't you tell?" Rheumy eyes dimmed by cataracts squinted at Angus. "And have you brought payment for it as we have agreed."

"Let me see the flat scrolls first, then we will exchange."

"I have always provided as I said I would," Oscar said to Jormind. "As my grandfather before me did as well."

"Yes, yes," Angus said, "but as always, I insist on inspecting the goods first before the trade is made."

Oscar proffered the sheets of paper, and Angus grasped them and began reading their content.

"What are you doing?" Jormind asked. "What knowledge do you seek?"

Angus grunted in satisfaction. "Yes, these instructions are what I sought, old man. This time you have done well."

"Then the gold dust." The old man held out his hand.

Angus ignored him and pointed to the newspapers. "It took many years of instruction from this one's grandfather to learn the speech, and then many more to read and write. Now even Dinton can understand much of what goes on among the natives, although why what he concerns himself about is so important I do not know."

He opened the bag at his feet and then counted softly as he inspected the contents.

"Only ninety-eight candles." He looked back at Oscar. "It was supposed to be an even hundred. When they are divided into two lots, Thaling will be displeased."

"Close enough for payment," Oscar rasped back. "There have been times there were overages as well."

Angus studied the old man for a moment, then detached the pouch from his waist and fingered it. "Go to wherever you get them and return with two more. I will pay you then."

"My bones are weary. Each trip is harder than the last. If there is no dust to pay for the journey, then perhaps it is best if I decide to no longer make them."

"You are but a primitive native," Angus growled. "I barter with you only at my pleasure. If this is to be your last journey here, then I will make sure that indeed it is so."

He reached for his dagger and then cursed because he could not grasp it under his bundling. Growling, Angus stepped forward almost completely out of the cave.

"No, wait, Flock Leader," Jormind grabbed at Angus from behind. "It will be too dangerous to venture any farther."

Angus stopped and nodded. Oscar ignored the threat. Without saying anything more, he dipped his head slightly once, turned, and started to shuffle off the way he had come.

"He lives alone a small distance from here," Angus said. "No grandson to take his place when he is gone. No one to pass on the tale of how his own grandfather had ventured to the mouth of the cave to discover what moved in the shadows."

Angus watched the ancient one vanish from sight. "It does not matter," he said at last. "When he has wasted all of the dust I have given him before on some liquid that addles human brains, he will come when the moon has orbited twice more to accept a new list of commands. I will need him only for a few additional times, and then he and all the others will be an irritation no more."

10

Steps Along the Way

A LABEL for the Janss steps on a nearby map had pointed Briana in the direction Slow Eddie had indicated. She had prided herself on how fit she was compared to the daughters of lords her own age, but her legs ached after she had completed the long climb to the entrance to the Powell library. Across the square stood another massive structure in cherry-red, flanked by towers on either side, but curiously each having a different number of windows at the top. The library itself was capped by an octagonal cupola that looked outward in every direction.

It had taken five exhausting days before she could come to UCLA for the first time, but at the shabby café, Briana had learned quickly what she had to do. First of all, ignore the surroundings: a floor sticky with dropped food from a week ago, faded and ripped curtains shutting out almost all of the outside light, rickety, mismatched chairs clustered around a mismatch of tables covered with stained paper.

More important were the standard moves. The swift turn as a hand darted menacingly behind, the shove to divert a grope, and all the while smiling and returning the banter the customers wanted to hear. It certainly was something she did not want her father ever to find out about.

The other wenches shielded her from the most challenging customers — at least until she could handle herself, they had said. And she was gaining confidence in the language, and more importantly, an increased sense of being able to take care of herself in this alien world.

Yes, she had made progress, but she had been away from her home on Murdina for a week now and not a single step closer to finding out if the exiles had escaped their bondage. Briana ran her hand through the snarls in her hair. None of the other women at the café knew anything about the shower truck Slow Eddie had mentioned, and the best she could do was sponge herself off with wet towels of paper in the women's room before the start of each shift.

At least her clothes felt fresh, her blouse far smoother than those worn by the richest of Procolon's ladies. Three full changes of clothes she now possessed and petite shoes to use instead of her sturdy but quite heavy boots. She still had no coins or rectangles of paper of her own, however. All of her tips for a night's work she had to surrender to one of the other wenches in exchange for a castoff garment.

But despite whatever else was strange and foreboding about this planet, there was no doubt about desserts. They were delicious, especially ice cream. She savored the delightful shock of how cold it was when the first bite hit her tongue. How smooth it was; firm, but not rock-hard. And more than one flavor! Chocolate. Strawberry. French Vanilla... The best part was that Irma was on a diet. She could have two desserts at dinner rather than only one!

Briana looked back down the slope she had climbed. UCLA could be no less than the palace grounds of the king of the entire world, she thought. Massive multistory buildings rose majestically into the sky. Thousands of young lords and ladies swarmed like ants from dozens of unseen hills, some solemn and alone, others in groups chatting at matters that clearly had nothing to do with the affairs of state. And there were so many! For each, there must be a dozen serfs somewhere laboring to produce the wealth that fueled the idleness and lack of purpose.

To the task at hand, Briana jolted herself out of her reverie. Joining the bustle of entrances and exits, she was surprised to see no guardsman standing at attention on the library steps. In her newly acquired garb, she looked the same as many and passed in unnoticed and unremarked upon. Indeed, even some of the other women toted backpacks like her own. Inside, she climbed a staircase emptying into a vast room floored with huge squares of marble like the surface for a game that could be played as far as to the horizon. A huge chandelier glowing white hung from a high, vaulted ceiling over a cluster of benches and tables, all sparsely occupied. Alcoves radiated in every direction with tall shelves of books filled to bursting on their surrounding walls and containing long tables of more lordlings and ladylings in silent study and contemplation.

Briana could hardly believe what she was seeing. Books and more books! Books in every direction! On Murdina, they were valuable things, almost as priceless as the magic objects they explained how to build. Here, displayed within the grasp of the most inept thief, were treasures almost asking to be taken. And this was only on one floor! There were stairways leading upward to more levels. Were they all filled with riches as well?

The overwhelmed feeling of Hollywood Boulevard on Briana's first day surged back into her gut. Certainly, what she was looking for was here, but the vastness, the overpowering and numbing vastness squeezed her chest like a relentless vice.

"Can I help you?" a voice called out from the alcove to the right. It looked different from the rest. A long, paneled barrier ran from side to side like a high sandbar guarding a beach, cutting it in half.

Briana took a few cautious steps toward a woman standing behind the barrier with a smile on her face.

"I… I want to look in a book about the crafts," Briana said.

"The online catalogue is on the table here. Come, I will show you how to use it."

Briana drew closer and tried to fight through the daze seizing her thoughts. Follow what the woman was doing with her hands.

"Type in the subject or author and their call numbers will appear besides them."

"I call a number, any number? Aloud?"

"The catalog lists where you can find the book up in the stacks. The entrance is over there."

"Anyone can read the book?"

"Of course. If you want to use it elsewhere, you will have to check it out first. Show your student ID card."

Briana's spirits began to recover. Evidently, as long as she perused them here in the library, she could examine any book as much and as long as she wished. She could ascertain if any of what she had been seeing in this strange land had a basis in the crafts or not. And if so, was it the doing of the natives or exiles running free. This was going to be easier than she had feared. She would be back home in plenty of time.

Aping the woman, Briana entered 'magic' in the device in front of her. Nothing happened for a moment, and then the illuminated window became alive with activity. One line after another appeared in rapid succession, scrolling upward and vanishing at the top in order to make room for a new one at the bottom.

She jumped back away from the table as the text kept scrolling. Of course! There were so many books here. There had to be hundreds of them devoted to the craft of magic alone, not only one or two. Apprehension began to bubble again. Briana felt as if she were the disk bobbling up and down on the end of the string on a child's toy.

She could not keep doing this she scolded herself. This world was not like Murdina. Accept the fact. Get over it. And she had witnessed only a few of its marvels; there must be many, many more. When the next deluge of the new and unusual happens, she could not hide within a shell for a day before venturing out again. Savagely, she willed the discomfort away.

The scrolling stopped. She picked one of the book titles at random and wrote down the number by its title on one of the small scraps of parchment placed nearby.

"Where are the stacks?" she asked

THE CHOSEN book was not helpful. Only one word in ten did Briana understand. The second and third volume were no better. She gave up trying any other, exited the library, and hastened back down the long steps leading to it.

When she reached the bottom of the slope, she sat down in the shade of one of the trees lining the staircase. Under another one nearby and up a bit on the left she saw a lordling bending over one of the thin metal boxes she had seen so many of in the library. Next to him, a young ladyling occasionally tossed leaves of grass at the illuminated window and giggled, obviously not interested at all in the books and devices she had brought with her.

Briana managed a smile. See, she told herself, not everything here was different and complex. Evidently, some things were the same throughout the universe.

From where she sat, Briana could see the upright window of the lordling and watch him wiggling his fingers on a flat horizontal plate connected at the bottom. She withdrew the sorcerer glasses from her pack and zoomed in on what was happening. After a good part of an hour, as the natives called the time interval, Briana started to understand the pattern.

The lordling was making notes! Making notes like an initiate magician, recording for his own use some particular content from a scroll somehow crammed into the device before him. Briana watched until she was sure. Yes, although not in a completely repetitive sequence, he performed the same simple steps over and over. She grabbed a quill and some parchment from her backpack and jotted down the motions he was making with his fingers and then described what was happening as a result in the illuminated window.

Briana felt a shock of discovery. There was no need to search through all of the books about the crafts one by one! Somehow, all of the contents in the massive library must be accessible from the strange devices everyone carried. One could ask exactly what they wanted to know. No need to peruse laboriously text after text. And there was even a dictionary — a definition appeared when you simply entered the spelling of a word.

Almost as remarkable was that these devices clearly were not magic. Briana had felt no tingle when she had performed similar manipulations in the library. With the hundreds, perhaps thousands, of these devices being used and carried by all of the nobility here, they could not be anywhere near priceless.

Filled with the satisfaction of what she was learning, Briana turned her attention back to the lordling. His search was not continuous. More and more frequently, it was interrupted by the ladyling at his side. Rather than a few leaves of grass, the lass tossed an entire clump that spattered against the illuminated window. When he looked up with a slight smile acknowledging what she was doing, she suddenly stood upright and began running up the slope. The lordling laughed and bolted after. For what Briana judged were several minutes, the young women feinted and turned, just out of the lordling's grasp, retreating another few steps away from him.

Briana watched the progress of the chase and concluded the ladyling was the swifter of the two. He would never catch her on his own. The lass finally would have to deduce this and slow herself for anything more to happen. That could take quite a few minutes more, and in the meantime…

Briana did not think any further. She put away the sorcerer glasses, shouldered her pack, and raced over to where the two thin boxes lay on the grass. The lordling's stood open and ready for the next manipulation, and the woman's was closed. She grabbed the lass's and bolted onto the walkway leading south at the foot of the steps. Now, finally, after two false starts, she could see a way to make some real progress to achieving her goal.

"Stop! That's *my* laptop!" the ladyling yelled from up the slope. "Carl, she is stealing my computer."

Briana started to run. Coming downhill, the woman might be able to cut her off before she could be safely away. With a burst of speed, Briana accelerated. Thank the random factors she was not wearing her boots, she thought. She chanced a glance behind. The ladyling had reached the pathway behind her and was in pursuit. The lordling, already panting, struggled to keep up.

"Stop!" the woman cried again, but her voice was not as loud as before. Evidently, she too was a little winded from her evasions on the hillslope. Curiously, others on the path did not move to block Briana's progress as she continued running. Instead, they scrambled to get out of the way.

Briana sucked in the air deeply as she cradled the thin box under her arm. She was suddenly thankful of the running she had done back in Procolon to clear her mind after a long session looking at scrolls in the Grand, well, now perhaps not so Grand, Library. She sped past a cross path lined with tables and short billboards and pushed aside eager lordlings trying to thrust a handbill for her to take. Up ahead she could see the path ended at the entrance to one of the other buildings that were scattered about everywhere. Should she go to the left or right or perhaps go inside? Maybe a place in which she could hide.

When she reached the building steps, Briana looked back. There was a greater distance now between her and her pursuers. In fact, the woman had stopped running, continuing now only with a walk. Now, she could get away easily, away to a safe place and start using the device. Her exploit was only beginning, and already there were words waiting to be added to the sagas — how she had deduced the value of the thin boxes and managed to take one away almost under the nose of...

Briana stopped. No, this was not right, she thought suddenly. She was more than a petty thief. Her adventure was important, one she must complete. But not like this, not without the honor that should accomplish the deeds of the true hero. In the Cycloid Guild, her father had used his skills to create deceptions, but never once did he take something that was not rightfully his.

Briana sighed. Slowly, she held out the thin metal box and began walking back toward her pursuer.

"Give me my laptop!" the ladyling commanded as she and the lordling drew near.

"Laptop?" Briana shrugged as she handed it over.

"Laptop. Computer. Whatever," the young woman snapped. She glanced over her shoulder as the lordling caught up. "Giving it back is not enough. We should turn you over to the campus police."

Police! Briana remembered Slow Eddie talking about them. Her pulse began to race again.

"Oh, lighten up, Kathy," the lordling said as he looked at Briana closely for the first time and then smiled. "No harm, no foul." Unlike most of the young men she had seen, he was tall and thin, like a slender reed growing in a marsh of squat ground cover. Eyes of blue were the best feature on a plain oval face.

"She can't run around like this. Someone else's will be snatched."

Carl studied Briana. "If you really want a computer, buy one at the student store," he said. "They aren't that much. Use your student ID to get the discount."

"Buy my own!" Briana exclaimed. "Of course. That is what I should do. What is the price?"

"I don't know. Around five or six hundred, I think. Show your ID and that is all there is to it."

Briana scowled. "A quicky, then a social, now a student ID," she said. "The list gets longer and longer. It looks like everything is open and unguarded here, but there is always a catch, something standing in the way."

"You are not a student, are you?" Carl asked. He seemed intrigued. "They are even cheaper at Better Buy. About four miles south of here on Pico. Bottom of the line models; under three hundred, I think."

"Three hundred dollars?" Briana's eyebrows jumped in surprise.

"Yeah, I think so." The young man smiled again and stuck out his hand. "My name is Carl. Let's the three of us go for a coffee so we can end this up by being friends."

"Oh, Carl, don't you get it?" Kathy said. "Let's turn her in and get back to what we were doing. No student ID and no computer. Sounds very suspicious to me."

"She doesn't need an ID," Carl said. "Whatever she wants a computer for, she can use 'UCLA_WEB.' It's public access."

Briana found herself smiling back at Carl in return. On Procolon, many of the lordlings were smiling and friendly. But that was because she was the daughter of the Archimage. She had long ago stopped reading anything more important into them. And Slammert, she had misread completely. But here — perhaps she might be a bit attractive to the other sex after all. Perhaps...

She squeezed shut the way her thoughts were going. There were more important things to focus on. Under three hundred dollars. Under three hundred. She could earn that in a little more than a fortnight at the café. Less than three weeks more and she would have the means to do the exploring that was necessary.

She glanced at Kathy's growing frown and then smiled back at Carl. "Thank you for the offer. I have other things to do. But perhaps you will tell me the path from here to, what did you call it, the 'BetterBuy.'"

11

Surfing the Net

BRIANA EXITED the bus at the north entrance to the UCLA campus. It was early morning, and she could stay until a half hour before her shift at the café began. One of the other serving wenches, waitresses, she corrected herself, had told her about the buses. Down La Brea to Sunset and then westbound from there.

To be sure, she had accumulated more than enough money to buy the computer. The extra paid for the bus fares. In addition, she had ventured into the shops on the boulevard and been able to buy a few sundries and souvenirs of this world as well. Curious little glass jars of red paint that came in a bewildering variety of shades, cylinders of similar colors that one twisted in and out of hiding from small tubes. A little bird that dipped its head into a glass of water repeatedly, never stopping. Useless trinkets called 'jacks' and perhaps a half-dozen other toys.

She shook her head from side to side, feeling her curls bounce with life. Shampoo, glorious shampoo. If anything would be worth taking back to Murdina, it would be shampoo. Also now, in her backpack, a small clock was ticking. Dozing on and off fitfully as dawn approached and worrying about the portal being discovered was no longer a problem. A gentle chime woke her in plenty of time each morning so it could be sent back to Nowhere for another day.

'Plenty of time', she thought. That certainly was not right. The tension she could not put aside grew stronger each day. Five days until she visited the library, and then sixteen more to buy one of the thin metal boxes. A good fraction of the time before her fate was to be decided was already gone.

When she reached the grassy slope next to the Janss steps, she started her laptop. The clerk who had sold the computer to her had run through a set of basic instructions very quickly, and some of it she already knew from watching Carl, three weeks before. But other concepts were new.

Before she forgot, she had had to write them down hurriedly when she exited the store.

Getting the Wi-Fi connection to UCLA_WEB working had taken her more than a day. Her first efforts put the machine into strange states, and she had to resort to putting more boots on it and starting over. After a few hours of frustration, she realized she had to make a detailed recording of every click or cursor movement so that after each rebooting she could quickly return to where she had made her last mistake.

Then another day was spent using the dictionary to find the equivalent for some words of her own tongue that were not in the guide left by Randor, the stranger from yet another world. By starting with a guess from her limited vocabulary and then examining the definition of each similar word appearing in turn, she could follow the trail until she found what she needed.

Each new definition she dutifully copied into what was called a 'spreading sheet' and after some additional trial and error was able to sort her newly defined words into a semblance of order. Finally, she could use the words she had assembled to start her first real search… a search for what was written about the seven laws of the magical crafts.

'Like produces like' she entered and saw the first of some twenty-eight thousand matches appear. Yes, there was thaumaturgy here!

This time, she was not immediately dismayed by the large number. She clicked on the first chain link at the top of the window: — 'Sympathetic Magic - Wikipedia, the free encyclopedia.'

"Ready for that coffee break?" a voice broke through her concentration. Briana looked up. It was Carl, smiling at her as he had done weeks before. Kathy was nowhere to be seen. There could be no doubt about it. He *was* interested in her, and not because she was the Archimage's daughter.

But then, *why* was the interest there? He knew nothing of her, who she was, where she was from, the reason for her quest. It was only the way she appeared, nothing else. Flattering to be sure, but superficial. She was wiser now. At the bottom of it all, he was no different from Slammert, from the customers at the café.

"No, this is a bad time," Briana said. She was anxious he should leave. Now that she had a tool to use, she wanted to continue without someone looking over her shoulder and asking questions about what she was doing. "Perhaps… perhaps later."

Carl did not immediately reply. Briana returned her attention to the computer. "All right then, some other time," he said at last. "See you around." Like a little boy whose friend could not come outside to play, he slinked off.

Briana waited a few seconds until Carl was safely away and then returned to her search. "Sympathy and Contagion," she mumbled to herself as she read the text at the top of the window. But when she tried to read further, as had happened in the library, she bogged down with the vocabulary.

She opened a new window and copied into it the text being displayed. Then for each word she did not understand, she studied its definition and synonyms until she understood enough to paste over the word in the second window with a simpler substitute or phrase.

The going was slow. It took her until it was time to catch the bus back to the café to translate only a few paragraphs. More troubling, near the very top, the text attributed to someone named James George Frazer was incorrect. According to him, the laws of sympathy and contagion did not work together. And there was no mention of the necessity of coupling a source of energy in order to perform an incantation. Another day completely gone and only a single step taken of what now was looking to be a long journey.

THE NEXT week was more of the same. Many pieces of text described the beliefs of primitive cultures, but in every case, those beliefs were treated as mere fantasies with no basis in truth. Search after search lead to discussions of wizardry, magic, alchemy and the rest, but all of them concerned discarded conjectures or the contents of fictional tales meant for amusement.

On the morning of the ninth day of searching, Briana slammed the laptop shut. She had been staring at a screen and concentrating for so long! Except for one wordsmith who somehow got the statements of all seven of the laws correct, there was no direct evidence that people of this planet knew any of them, *any* of the laws at all.

There had been so many false trails. Like the enchantments of a sadistic sorcerer, each new possibility at first created excitement that was dashed by what was learned after. The sciences of Earth knew about catalysts. But they were more akin to alchemy than thaumaturgy. Transmutation of elements had no alchemy involvement at all. The study of Monster groups discussed nothing about assemblies of djinns and other demons.

The only mention of anything remotely dealing with natural laws was about the work going on at a place called CERN — something about having found proof of the Higgs boson. But as far as Briana could tell, 'elementary particles' had nothing to do with the elementary laws she was looking for.

She was fatigued. Her brain was numb. Had she overlooked something, something fundamental the next query would reveal? Surprisingly, she felt that, at least for the moment, she did not care. Why had the sagas never recorded something like this? The hero always continued undaunted until he reached his goal. But right now, she could not. As important as her quest was for her own future, she needed a break.

She put away her laptop, shouldered her backpack, and started walking away eastward, back toward Hollywood Boulevard. The bus ride would be for another time.

THE SUN was below its zenith when Briana passed Vine Street. She was somewhat surprised that, mingling in the crowd, she now could recognize emblems on bags and shirts identifying some of the lordlings and ladylings as also frequenting UCLA. Perhaps they too needed a break from the burden of study.

Up ahead she recognized someone. It was Slow Eddie talking to a well-dressed lord while holding out his hand palm up in front of himself. The baron's garb stood out, even at a distance. The front creases of the slacks were as sharp as knife blades. The shirt of silk was a vibrant red unbuttoned half way down the chest like the revealing blouse of a doxy. Not one but two bracelets of gold circled a thick wrist. He stood next to a sculptured white stele with the word 'Tesla,' whatever that was, written on it over a large boxy opening that did not seem to serve any purpose.

A sleek, pearl white chariot lined up nearby the stele with a snake-like hose stuck into an opening on the side and near the rear. 'Tesla' also adorned the vehicle. A dozen or more of the homeless milled about nearby, apparently watching to see how successful Eddie was going to be.

"It is both the voltage *and* the current." Eddie's voice strained with frustration. "Here it is direct current not alternating and at 440 volts, four times the 110 at your home. That's why it takes so long to recharge there."

"I still don't understand," the lord said. "You are not helping me at all. Putting the station up here on the street was a big mistake. It should have remained in the basement of the parking structure on Argile. No nuisances like you came there."

Slow Eddie thrust his upraised palm closer to the lord's torso. "What I have told ya is worth at least a little something," he said. "Come on, gimme... give us a break."

The lord scowled, pushed Eddie's hand aside, and turned to disengage the hose from his vehicle. The rest of the homeless grumbled and inched closer to the pair.

The noble climbed in his chariot and started to back out of its stall. But as he did, two of Eddie's companions suddenly circled behind the vehicle and sat on the ground, blocking its exit. The lord stopped short of bumping into them, reversed direction, and tried to maneuver to the left. More of the homeless joined their comrades, surrounding the Tesla on all four sides.

For a while, there was a stalemate. The Tesla could not move. But then, neither would the homeless be getting a handout. Finally, one of the black and white chariots that always seemed to be on the street pulled to a halt. Two men emerged. These must be the ones Slow Eddie had talked about.

A crowd of boulevard walkers formed around Briana. A second group collected on the other side of the charging station. One of the police officers sprinted back to his chariot and began speaking to a small device suspended in easy reach.

It took several minutes, but it seemed like almost immediately, that three more black and white chariots swooped into sight down the boulevard and halted. Like bees with a clear target, additional officers poured from the vehicles. Two grabbed the nearest homeless man under his arms and began to pull him away from the Tesla. Another one shrugged off the policeman who tugged on him, and his assailant responded by striking back with a baton.

Several of the younger lordlings in the crowds suddenly shouted, "Police brutality! Police brutality." They ran forward and sat on the ground, forming a second row of containment of the Tesla outside of the first.

64

The police struggled with the sitting homeless as additional bystanders arrived to support them. More black and white chariots appeared. More protestors surged forward, this time even some of the ladylings joined in. Those behind Briana surged, and she was propelled along with them, scrambling all the while not to trip and be overrun.

When she arrived near the Tesla, two ladylings next to her yelled, "Sit! Sit!"

Briana looked about for a way to retreat, but another row of bodies was forming behind her, cutting off any escape route. In under a minute, the Tesla was surrounded six rows deep. Reluctantly, she knelt down to the ground.

The police among the squatters retreated and waited for more reinforcements. As they did, Slow Eddie started a chant. "Brutality against the homeless! Give us a break!"

The seated around the Tesla echoed in unison, "The homeless! Give us a break! The homeless! Give us a break!" The mood was infectious. Briana did not want to call attention to herself. She began shouting with the rest.

A few minutes later, several large black and white vans arrived. A tinny voice radiated from the top of one, "Clear the area! Disperse! Clear and disperse."

The two chants blended into a garbled cacophony as police began dragging protestors from the outermost row. Some went limp as they were carried into the vans. Others bolted and ran away. They were not pursued.

Briana hesitated. What should she do? There *was* an injustice here. The homeless man had been struck when he did not threaten. She understood why so many of the lordlings and ladylings of the street had sided with him. The retaliation was not consistent with the offence. But she also remembered Slow Eddie's warning about what would happen to her if brought to the police's attention.

She looked about. The rings of protesters were no longer unbroken. Fleeing lordlings left zigzag paths among the others who remained. Not feeling good about herself, Briana rose and fled back toward the calm of the Wattles Garden. It was still two hours before her shift at the café.

As she ran, she thought about what she had witnessed. The homeless. And lordlings and ladylings. Two cultures that surely never mixed — never mixed unless they had, what... common cause? What was it about these denizens of the Earth? Some inner sense of what was right and what was wrong? Something that made them abandon certain security and fight for something greater? And was that any different from what happened on the battlefields of Murdina when challenged to defend what was just and true?

12

No Need for a Philosopher's Stone

ANGUS CLIMBED the steps toward the farming alcove slowly. He strained to make sure the large glass condenser he carried did not touch the rock walls and shatter. It had taken him too long to build one the first time, and he did not want to construct another.

Behind him, Jormind grunted under the weight of the rest of the equipment. "Flock Leader, what's in this bag?" he asked. "It is as heavy as if it were filled with rocks."

"Precisely," Angus said over his shoulder. "Gold ore and, if we need it, cinnabar as well."

"But why are we doing this?" Jormind persisted. "You say you have done it yourself alone many times before. Why do *I* have to come along?"

Angus grimaced. A little less complaining would be welcome. "Soon, I plan to be busy with other things. Your new task is to be the one who barters with Oscar. I am going to show you how to smelt the gold dust you will need."

Jormind said no more. In silence, the two reached the garden alcove they had visited before. Jormind dropped the large sack to the ground with a thud before Angus could stop him.

"Careful, idiot!" he growled. His fangs bared for a moment, but then retreated. "There are fragile objects in the sack along with the rocks."

Jormind shrugged and opened the bag, seemingly oblivious of Angus' wrath. He pulled out a small iron tripod and a porcelain bowl with many holes in the bottom.

"Set the colander in the plant stand," Angus ordered. He shook his head. "It took Oscar three trips until he got a pair that fit together. Such a combination is not common among the primitives."

"Fill the colander with some gold ore," he continued. "Not heaping over the top. Precisely full. Put the glass bowl underneath, directly on the ground. Then watch while I perform the alchemy."

"Alchemy!" Jormind exclaimed. "Flock Leader, that is forbidden."

"Do as you are told," Angus said. "It is only for the first step — getting the gold in the rock to bind into a mercury amalgam. The primitives above go to great lengths to cause this to happen. With giant hammers, they crush the rocky ore into fine grains, using inordinate amounts of energy and effort. Energy and effort that we do not have."

Angus fumbled out a sheet of blank parchment from the folds of his swathing while Jormind followed the instructions. "Now, pay attention. You must remember it all if you are to act in my stead."

He waited until Jormind nodded he was focused. "As I finish placing the formula, quickly pour the mercury over it and into the ore."

Angus retrieved a pen and wrote arcane symbols in a brilliant red. With a flourish, he made the final stroke and smiled as he watched it dry. "The formula is completed," he said. Carefully, he draped the paper over the top of the colander. "On our home world, we used the blood of vanquished enemies to construct the words of power. But it is not required. Any ink will do."

Jormind poured the silvery liquid onto the colander and watched it seep through the parchment and disappear.

Nothing happened for almost a minute, but eventually, drops of gold amalgam and mercury that had not bonded began to drip from the holes in the colander into the glass bowl.

"The rest of the process needs no alchemy," Angus said. "Even the primitives have been performing them for thousands of years." His smile bared his fangs. "Thousands of years of only employing a portion of what mercury can do. They never discovered The Doctrine of Signatures — 'The attributes without mirror the powers within.'"

When no more droplets fell, he picked up the bowl, connected it to the condenser he had brought and performed the rest of the steps needed — heating the amalgam to release the mercury as vapor from the gold, recovering the gas and returning it to liquid form for use again.

"I do not want to be doing this, Flock Leader," Jormind said as the process completed. "Others have told me mercury vapor is poisonous. And if for only one step or not, it does not matter. Alchemy is *forbidden*. We will become meals for the tigerwasps if we do not stop." He sucked in a gulp of air and then blurted. "And I must tell Dinton about this."

"Silence!" Angus shouted. "Dinton wears the baton only most of the time. But I am your Flock Leader for every cycle of every day, no matter what. You must do as I say."

"But, Flock Leader, as your brother has explained many times over, the consequence of discovery by the Faithful is too great. He must know of this."

Angus thought for a moment, then spoke in a quiet voice.

"You are as guilty, Jormind. As guilty as am I."

"No, Flock Leader. I performed no craft. I do not even know how."

"Then you examined the breathing tube before inserting it into your helmet and substituted another before we ascended?"

"No. Why?"

"Because, I placed a special product of alchemy there. It is what gave us so much extra time before we had to return. *You* used the fruits of the craft, Jormind. If you go to Dinton, you too will face his wrath. Is that what you desire?

"But I did not know. Surely, Dinton will understand."

Angus' anger exploded. "I will silence you one way or another," His fangs lowered. He fumbled for his dagger and growled in frustration that it could not be reached. Then he lunged at Jormind and began unwrapping the covering from the other man's head.

"No!" Jormind shouted. "No, I will die!"

"Perhaps so," Angus growled.

"Please, Flock Leader," Jormind gasped. He had slumped to the ground and frantically began trying to bat Angus' arms away, to keep himself swathed and safe.

"I... I misspoke," he cried as Angus continued the uncoiling. "Yes, yes, you are my Flock Leader. I will do as you say. This is our secret to share."

Angus stopped for a moment, deciding if he should continue. As quickly as it had blossomed, the rage inside abated, and he released his grip. It would take too long to seek out another helper. There were the other things that had to be done.

"It was the sulfur that gave me the grand idea," he said at last. "It is a chemical of many useful properties throughout the realm and the key to freeing us from this hateful swathing.

"'I will not perform any craft,'" he continued and then snorted. "Hah! Without it, I would not have found the path to our salvation."

13

Zero

THAT EVENING, at the café, all of the other waitresses were busy as the big hulking man entered. Briana hesitantly walked toward him, and then stopped when she saw his leer.

"Ah, a new one," the man said. A rough stubble like newly planted grass filled his face, barely covering the scar down his left cheek. His smile showed yellowed teeth. Heavy, like a giant mobile potato, he lumbered with each step. Around his neck was a collection of metal chains. Worst of all were the deep-set, cruel eyes.

"Don't be shy," he continued as he reached out to grab for Briana's wrist. "My name is Zero. We haven't met, so sit on my lap for a while. We can talk about what comes up."

Briana pulled her arm out of his reach while at the same time forcing the corners of her mouth to turn upward, as she had been taught.

"Now, Zero," she said as breezily as she could. "You know there are others waiting for me to serve them. Do you have a usual, or is there something else you want?"

She slammed her mouth shut and the beginning of her smile vanished. Those were not the words she should have used.

"Something else I want, most definitely," Zero laughed.

"Come on, Zero." Another waitress came to stand beside Briana. "Give the girl a break. She hasn't figured out yet how to deal with somebody like you."

"Not you, Irma," Zero said. "You have got a little long in the tooth. I like mine fresh and young, like this one here."

"Gimme your order, Zero," Irma said. "Briana is going to be busy with that table over there."

"Foxy?" Zero snorted. "His stable is already too big. He has enough to handle. He should give the rest of us a chance."

"So, you want to suggest that to his face?" Irma asked.

"No, you know I don't," Zero growled. He stood and looked back at Briana, and then again in Foxy's direction. "But as long as this one remains untaken, she's fair game for the rest of us. I will be back in a few days to see if she is still available."

Briana backed away. She began to shake. Zero was going to be more of a challenge to deal with than any of the rest so far. She glanced at the other waitresses standing near the pickup table. Besides Irma, no one showed any sympathy. She understood now why they had been so friendly when she had arrived, letting her buy some tattered clothes, giving her tips about things like buses and shampoo. It was probably the same with each new wench. After some training, the newcomer would have to be the one to handle the worst customers. She looked at Irma, hoping her conclusion was wrong.

"There is no secret to it," Irma explained. "To keep the worse ones at bay, you need a protector, someone with some muscle and the reputation to use it if need be."

Briana looked in the direction of Foxy's table and his rowdy entourage and shuddered. "Protection... in trade for what?"

"You can't be that naïve, girl. What do you think? Your protector provides for you in exchange for services you perform for him. He takes a cut off the top, and everyone wins."

"And Zero?"

"He's the same as many of the rest. Getting started with the crumbs falling from the table from a Foxy. Right now, it looks like if you make the first move, it can be your choice."

"I do not want to make a choice. Just continue working here, collect my tips, and — "

"It doesn't work that way. Either you hitch up with one of them, or you leave and go somewhere else."

Zero or Foxy? Somewhere else? The words ricocheted in Briana's head. If she left, she would be back at the very start, Spending all of her time wandering from handout to handout like Slow Eddie. Not able to learn a single thing more. Somehow, she was going to have to come up with a way of dealing with Zero and the others like him on her own.

14

A Purchase Order

ANGUS GROWLED for a moment to be sure. The air this far away from the alcoves tasted differently, but otherwise, it was sufficient. Oscar's ramshackle dwelling on the surface stood before him. In the near distance were other shacks, and the one closest to the city, the old man had said, had an ISDN line and the Wi-Fi access point servicing them all.

Yesterday, the old man had not shown up at the cave entrance after all. Angus had waited as long as he could, but the recluse never appeared.

The exile alchemist had had to retreat to the prison below, his rage boiling higher with every step. The wait until morning the next day was an agony of frustration, but eventually, the feeling passed. Now he had purpose and could act. Oscar was undoubtedly inside his hut. Where else could he be?

At one time, there had been paint on the door Angus faced, but now what remained was faded into peeling strips of gray. Windowsills on either side of the door were bare wood, cracked and weathered like the jawbones of fossil whales from long ago. The roof of nailed-down tarpaper barely slanted enough to dispose of the torrential rains. There had been no attempt at upkeep. There was no need. In between the times he ran errands for Angus in exchange for gold dust, Oscar passed the hours drinking beer and harder liquor.

Angus did not knock before entering. Such civilities were for the humans, not a Flock Leader of the exiles. He shook his head. Yes, the exiles, the vanquished. The ones who had proclaimed themselves victors gave those names to him and his brethren to shame them, to make them feel small and insignificant. But he, his brothers and all who followed their lead, bore the titles proudly — a constant reminder of what they must do: defeat the so-called Faithful and usher in the new age. An age of their own chosen title, The Heretics Who Proclaim the Truth.

Dinton and Thaling. They meant well enough, but they had

insufficient vision, no boldness, no plan that would save them now, nor in a distant future. It was he who would lead the way.

Angus creaked the door open. Oscar rose from a folding chair next to a card table, startled.

"Why… why are you here?" he managed to say. "I told you I would visit no more."

"And so, instead, I have come to *you*," Angus said. "Enough wealth has been accumulated. I have decided your use to me now has little value."

He looked hastily around the room. A cot with yellowed sheets and a crumpled blanket was next to the far wall. Empty bottles littered the floor amidst a sea of crumpled papers, moldy shoes, and discarded cardboard boxes. The door to the left opened onto a small kitchen in which Angus could see a sink piled with dishes next to an ancient stove.

The card table wobbled uncertainly as Oscar reached out to steady himself. "Careful," the old man said. "The monitor probably will break if it falls." He hesitated and then blurted. "I still get to keep the computer, right? After all, *I* bought it with the dust I earned from you. That you asked I do so had no bearing on who is the rightful owner."

"You will not need it any longer," Angus growled. "I am displeased, and you must pay the price."

Oscar backed away from the table, looking for his cane. He spotted it against the wall, limped to retrieve it, and then pointed it at Angus with a trembling hand as best he could.

"I have taught you much," the old man said. "Computers, the internet, Wi-Fi, money, commerce, the stock market, factories, entertainment, business…"

Angus bared his fangs in irritation. "Yes, yes," he said. "But that took so many years."

"Because of the problems with the words. Because first of all, you had to learn the basic concepts of how we live."

"And now, all of that I do understand… understand enough that your use to me has diminished to that of a gnat needing to be swatted."

"You don't know everything," Oscar said. He glanced quickly at a notebook on the card table next to the keyboard. "There are still the user names, passwords, and such. Subscription bills to pay. Online banking. You cannot type with any speed."

Angus did not answer. Instead, he continued his survey of the room and spotted what he wanted. Near the door leading to a small garden in back were a rake, hoe, and other instruments for taming the lush vegetation outside. He walked past Oscar's cane to the wall and picked one of them up.

"I believe you have taught me the name of this one," he said. "A machete, is it not?"

Oscar dropped his cane and slumped to his knees. He closed his eyes and placed his hands together as if he were praying. "Please," he said. "Let me be."

Oscar started to say more, but Angus did not hesitate, moving surprisingly fast even though he was completely swathed. The blade sliced through the air and then Oscar's neck as if it had never even been present. With a dull thunk like that of a melon rolling off a wagon, the old man's head fell to the ground.

The body crumpled, and Angus pushed it aside. He went into the kitchen for some towels and returned to mop up the blood that had sprayed the computing machinery. When he was done, he tested the air again, and it still did not hurt. He would have more time than he thought.

He recognized the thick notebook that had fallen to the floor. Oscar had brought it with him after all the things to remember became too much. Angus thumbed through the page and stroked where his long hair would be if it were exposed. As he had thought, the instructions, the passwords, everything was there.

The urge to place the order welled up within him, but he pushed it away. Tidying up should come first. He found a shovel, dug a shallow grave outside, and disposed of the head and body.

The electric bill was paid automatically from Oscar's bank account, the old man had told him, and with a little study, he would figure out how to access it and compute how much more time the power would continue to flow to the house. The newspaper delivery was handled in the same way, but now he would have to come periodically to take them back to their prison, so no one would suspect Oscar was no longer there. Dinton would still want them in any case. No matter. Now that the access was directly his, he would not need to smelter the gold and go through the tedious communication process to get things done.

Angus relaxed and allowed himself a moment of reflection. Oscar's grandfather had been a young boy exploring the cave when they had first met. The lad had been more curious than afraid, and by a long process of grunts had worked out the beginnings of communication. Angus had given him a nugget of gold to get him to return, and although it took several years and pointing at picture books, the exile had learned enough to communicate in English at a higher level.

The boy was eager for the gold. In exchange for more nuggets, the tables, clocks, candles and other small sundries were procured. Eventually, the lad grew into a man and then tottered into old age. Before he could come no more, he brought his own grandson, Oscar, to the cave, and the barter continued.

After many years, all of the gold nuggets were gone, at least those that easily could be pried from the alcove walls. Angus smiled. He had dared to use alchemy almost as an act of defiance to his brothers, but in the end, it served his purposes well. And along the way, Angus had learned from the old man much of the native's culture that proved to be so useful. But now, the deed was done. He should have done this long ago.

Angus broke out of his reverie. He opened the notebook and began to read.

THE INSTRUCTIONS were simple enough. Despite his drunkenness, Oscar's mind had been precise. Every step the old man documented clearly. The original list of 128 names and email addresses was still there. Lucky number seventeen still circled. Angus turned on the computer and slowly, a single letter at a time, began typing the email to the broker in New York.

'Purchase the rights to any and all salt domes in the Gulf of Mexico region, abandoned or not. Price is no object. Use the funds in the trading account. Conduct yourself as you have been instructed before.'

15

The Noose

BRIANA LOOKED up from the screen, focused on the red-bricked buildings below the Janss steps, and stretched. She had had no more trouble at the café in the last seven days. Zero had not yet reappeared. Refreshed, she was looking for more clues with her laptop.

The culture of the natives was not based on magic as it was back on Murdina, she had concluded. Of that, she was now convinced. And therefore, if she discovered even a hint of the use of craft, then the exiles *must* be the ones involved.

But there were only some seven hundred of them among who knew how many millions of humans. Any indications of such use would be faint. Her searches had to be focused sharper than the finest needle to find what she was looking for. Despite everything contained on the internet, general queries on 'thaumaturgy,' 'magic,' 'sympathy'... would not succeed.

But, just as for her, Briana reasoned, the human culture also would be intimidating to the exiles. Free of their confinement and then discovered, they would be powerless against the onslaught of Earth's knowledge and vibrant energy — perhaps even stripped of the shrouds that hid their hideousness and put on display at Ripley's Believe It Or Not.

Powerless that is except for what they *could* accomplish by exercising the crafts — skills unknown throughout the Earth by any human. That then was the question: of all the incantations, rituals, and charms that the exiles had knowledge, which were the ones that they would exercise?

Suppose she were a lady newly awakened after centuries of sleep back on her own orb and unaccustomed to the protocols and intricacies of court — what would happen?

She would be instant prey to the charlatans and schemers at court, unless... unless she could *buy* protection from men-at-arms, advice from counselors, and the security of a fortress of her own. Yes, that was it. She would need wealth and a vast one at that — so large that by doling it out, she could buy the time needed to learn how to survive.

Briana started typing rapidly. Gold was the key! The exiles would use the crafts to accumulate and horde gold. And then, when they had enough to insure safety, they would effect their escape.

AFTER SEVERAL hours, Briana stopped looking. She could find no indication of new discoveries of gold, of sudden disappearances from fortresses, or unexpected changes in price. For a few moments, she tried to consider alternatives, but none satisfied the need for portability and easy division into small parts as needed. She slumped, trying to reason what to explore next.

"I see you almost every day here on the slope with your pretty brow wrinkled in thought," a voice broke through Briana's concentration.

It was Carl again. She reached to shut the top of her computer, but then realized that there was nothing showing that would hint on why she was on Earth.

"Hmmm, gold," Carl said. "Are you a geology major? No, that can't be right. You aren't even enrolled.

"From ancient times, gold was the primary basis of wealth upon which everything else depended," he continued without waiting for an answer. "Originally, all the other forms of money, like paper, derived their value from it. They were mere tokens representing what was safely stored away. But with the advent of banking, now almost all wealth is merely entries in balance sheets. There is no one-to-one relationship to precious metals behind it."

"How can that be?" Briana asked. "You mean that I cannot take the little slips of paper I get for my tips and go somewhere to trade them for precious metals and gems?"

"Yep. That's right," Carl said. "The supply of money is far greater than the supply of gold." He shrugged. "Believe me; the whole thing is rather complicated. I am an accounting major and I should know."

"But if there is more paper than gold, most of it must be... be worthless," Briana began.

Carl rolled on. "Most money is intangible. You cannot touch the gold that is behind it. And there are other things like that as well — stock and bond certificates, good will, brand names, copyrights… But no matter, at the bottom line, they are all components of wealth."

Briana's interest perked up. "So wealth can be in different forms than land, jewels, and gold?"

"Absolutely. And they can be traded in markets, merely by modidying the appropriate lists."

Briana gave Carl a big smile and patted the ground beside her. "It would have taken me many days to understand all of that," she said. "Sit awhile and tell me more about intangibles and markets." As he sat, she reached out and gently squeezed his upper arm. "After that, maybe I would be interested in some coffee — and perhaps a piece of pie."

BRIANA CAUGHT Zero's eye as he lumbered into the café several nights later. It was fortunate that she had had the time to prepare. But she was not sure if her plan would work, and if it did not…

Zero caught her glance and smiled. Briana smiled back. She motioned for him to follow and ducked into the passageway toward the restrooms and then to the lot out back. Outside, only a single bulb pushed feeble light into the dimness. The smell from the rotting food made her cough as she looked around in the litter for a relatively smooth place on which to lie.

A moment later, Zero pushed open the door and spotted where Briana now stood. Slowly, as if to heighten the anticipation, he shuffled up to her. She held her ground. There was no turning back now.

Zero noticed her clenched fists and laughed. "What are you going to do, little one? Beat against my chest in protest when things start getting a little rough?"

Briana did not answer. She shuddered as she pushed herself against him and threw her arms around his neck, hoping that he would not react too quickly. She gagged at the foul smell. How many weeks had it been since he last bathed? Closing her eyes, she kissed him as hard as she could.

"Well, this is more like it," Zero pulled her tighter. He ran one of his hands down her back and tugged her even closer. "You want a little bit of foreplay? Okay, I'll give it to you."

Briana opened her left hand. It contained one of the bars of metal she had brought with her from Murdina — the king. A trip to what was called a hardware store had produced the little hook and chain to which it was now attached. While Zero began gyrating against her, she slipped the hook into one of the chain links that circled his neck and started whispering the incantation.

"Okay, that's enough," he grunted after a moment. "Let's get to the main event." He reached up, slapped Briana's arms aside from around his neck, and thrust her onto the ground. Briana's hands flew over her head as she finished the incantation that connected the king and the queen thaumaturgically together — The Principle of Contagion — 'Once together, always together.' Then, as she had learned from her computer searching for how it was done, she began twirling the bar in her right hand as she had seen one of the performers do on the boulevard. What one of the metal bars did the other would follow — The Principle of Sympathy — 'Like produces like.'

The queen twirled in her hand. The king, attached to a link in one of Zero's chains did likewise. And as it did, it began to kink the links, intertwining them together, each revolution of the queen making the chain shorter and shorter.

Zero paid no attention. Pressing his bulk against her, he began pulling at her slacks, trying to wiggle them off her hips. So far, everything was going according to plan. Briana had taken in the waist as tight as she could with a few stitches of thread and had been barely able to squeeze them on. Hopefully, that would give her the time she needed. She concentrated on keeping the queen twirling. To drop the bar now would be a disaster.

"Damn! How do you women manage to wear these things?" Zero cried in frustration. He tensed his arms, put his hands into the waistband of the pants, and with a grunt burst apart the sewing that had taken up the extra room at the waist. Briana felt her trousers begin to slip downward. Zero's unclipped nails gouged flesh on her hips.

For more than a minute, nothing different happened. Zero struggled to lower the barrier to what he was after, and Briana continued the manipulation of the queen with her fingers. Each full revolution became harder than the one immediately before. It took more and more energy to complete a single rotation. The pace slowed, and her hand began to ache. Relentlessly, inch by inch Briana felt her slacks continue to slip downward.

Too fast, too fast: the thoughts raced through her head. It was going to be too late. She squirmed as much as she could from side to side, but that did not help. In seconds, her pants were down to her knees.

Then, as Zero fumbled to unzip his fly, he stopped for a moment, puzzled. He reached up to his neck and felt the tightness of his iron necklace. He tried to slip a finger between it and his throat but could not do so. Briana kept twirling. As she had hoped, the king coupled to one of the links at the back of his neck was twisting the same as the queen in her hand. And as it did, the chain coiled about itself until there was no more freedom. Each additional turn was tightening the noose around his neck.

Zero pulled his other hand from his crotch. He sat up on his knees and pulled at the chain. Even though the effort was getting harder since Briana had not coupled an external source of energy in the incantation — relying instead on what her own body could produce, she continued to tighten.

Zero's attention now was entirely on the noose that was cutting off his air, and Briana wiggled out from underneath the brute, and stood facing him with her hands behind her back. For another minute, he looked at her, eyes bulging wide, and gasped to speak. Briana stared at him without moving, and then finally, Zero passed out and fell on his face to where she had been on her back.

With some reluctance, Briana twirled the queen in the opposite direction so that the chain around Zero's neck relinquished its strangling grip. After a moment, he coughed and struggled to his feet. There was confusion in his eyes, but he managed to lumber forward toward Briana a second time all the same.

Backing up out of Zero's reach, Briana again twirled the noose tight and waited. Again, the giant fell unconscious to the ground.

Now for the tricky part, she thought. There was the risk that Zero was not yet convinced. She stooped beside his unconscious form, removed the king that was hooked to the chain around his neck, and unwound the tangled links. After a few seconds more, Zero began to come to for a second time, and Briana bent down and placed her face directly in front of his.

"You try something like this with me again," she said, yanking the chain about his neck for emphasis, "this is what is going to happen. Only next time, wearing a chain or not, I will not stop choking you until I am sure. Sure that you are not going to bother me anymore ever again."

Briana warily waited for a reaction as Zero rose to sitting. He could decide to try again and she was not sure she could go through the ordeal a second time. But the giant did not say another word. He looked at her in wonder, not fully able to comprehend what had happened, what she was able to do to him. He rose, massaging his neck. Without a word, he lumbered to the rear gate of the lot and vanished into the alley beyond.

She had defeated him! A sense of relief poured through her body, and then after that a growing sense of... a sense of self-worth. Yes, she had *defeated* him. And if she had to, she would do so again. All of the anxiety leading up to the encounter had been wasted. A heroine did not spend energy speculating about what *might happen*. Instead, she focused on the moment, the problem immediately at hand.

It was the same way she should regard the passage of time, Briana suddenly realized. Yes, the days were ticking away until her wedding. But that was not tomorrow. Finding out about the exiles was the only thing to be concerned about now. Focus on the task at hand. She could do no better than that.

As these thoughts formed, she felt a sudden release in tension. The rising tide of discomfort that had haunted her since she had first learned of her betrothal retreated into the background. It was still there but not something that would grow and grow with each passing day.

16

Partners in Crime

ANGUS SHIFTED uncomfortably in the folding chair. Holding the native device near his ear felt strange, like listening to the roar of the ocean with a shell. He looked about the interior of Oscar's shack yet another time. It looked the same. No one had disturbed it since his last visit.

"I am a stockbroker, Mr. Angus," the voice over the phone said. "Not a business manager. I purchased the abandoned salt domes as you directed, but doing so is not part of my usual duties."

"You received a handsome commission, Mister Emmertyn, did you not?" Angus said.

"Yes, yes. But that is not the point. I am unskilled in these transactions, unsure you are getting the best value for your money."

"The price was no object. I told you that. Now, there is another task I have for you."

"Mr. Angus, our relationship has been a long one, many, many years. I did you a favor because of that. A token of friendship, one man to another."

"Friendship, one man to another?" Angus could not stop himself. The laugh billowed up from deep in his chest and exploded through the speaking tube, sounding like the roar of a hungry lion who had smelt fresh prey.

For a moment, there was silence. Then Emmertyn spoke again.

"If I may ask, *why* are you dealing with me directly?" the stockbroker said. "Is Mr. Garbell not available? He and I usually use written communication."

"Mr. Garbell is… is no longer in my employ," Angus said. "From now on, we will be communicating directly. And by phone. It is too slow for me to type out messages one letter at a time." The exile squirmed in his swathing. This was taking much too long,

"I want you to get the mining operations started again," he said. "Hire a management company to run things. Get the flow of sulfur to resume."

"Mr. Angus, with all due respect, I must advise against such an action. The domes have been depleted, all of them. The cost of the electricity to boil the water to flush out the remaining sulfur will be far greater than what you would ever hope to recover by its sale. It is a waste of your money, pure and simple."

"You are my agent, are you not?" Angus said. "One who acts on my behalf?"

"You will have to get someone else," Emmertyn said. "It would be unethical for me to be a party to such an action."

Angus had anticipated it might come to this. He chose his words carefully. "Mr. Emmertyn, you mention ethics. But isn't breaking the law even worse? What do you think your FBI might say if they knew that for over six decades of making trades for me, never a single one was for a loss?"

There was silence on the line. A dozen heartbeats passed.

"Mr. Emmertyn?" Angus asked. "Are you still there?"

"You have never complained about what I have done for you," Emmertyn said at last. "A few thousand dollars have been turned into millions, tens of millions, hundreds.

"I would surmise your skill is also used for your own personal account. And I strongly suspect how you accomplish what you do. I have... associates who are versed in the same craft. I am sure the ones you call the 'feds' would certainly like to learn more about it."

There was another long pause, this one tens of heartbeats more.

Finally. "Please, please, Mr. Angus. What I do is my... my life. I cause very little harm by it."

Angus' tone hardened. "Do as I direct, and our arrangement will proceed as it always had. No one else needs to know. Otherwise..."

A long sigh came over the phone line. "Very well. Start the mining of sulfur from the Gulf again. Find a buyer for it. I will do so."

"No, not a buyer," Angus said. "I do not intend to sell what comes from the domes. Instead, arrange for delivery directly to me. Rent an empty warehouse for the cargo when it arrives. Arrange to have it transferred. Lock back up when they are done. Have the owner mail me the address and a set of keys."

"To where?" Emmertyn asked. Resignation now pressed onto his voice like a great boulder.

"Hilo, on the big island of Hawaii."

"From the Gulf to the Pacific? That's impossible! I have learned a little from arranging the purchase of the domes. Liquid sulfur is hard to transport and store. Over 130 degrees Celsius so it will not solidify; less than 154 so no explosive vapors are created, That requires temperature controlled tanks, special trucks and ships, permits and documentation."

"Emmertyn, listen to me!" Angus felt the battle lust begin to rise in his gut. "Go ahead and let the sulfur cool. I am not interested in making sulfuric acid. Place the powder that results in airtight shipping containers. Mislabel them with something innocuous. Use shippers who will look the other way for a few extra dollars."

"Now, who is talking about illegalities?" Emmertyn asked.

"So we are now, how is it said? 'partners in crime'. Do it Emmertyn, or your next visitors will be from the FBI."

"Oscar had become a friend," Emmertyn said.

"I am not your friend," Angus growled. "Just do it!" He inhaled the surface air through his speaking tube but still did not like the flat taste. "And get the request for a quote out to the company in California. That also is part of my plan.

He slammed down the receiver and prepared to return to the caverns below. Worrying about the tigerwasps was enough distraction. He did not want to waste any energy in concern about lackeys as well.

17

Fetid Air

CARRYING THE stool and the glass jar, Angus walked down the twisty corridor toward the plug — not the one leading to the garden, but another, one most probably no longer cared about. He remembered the excitement of discovery when the source of the foul air had been first discovered. One of the initial tasks for his father's flock was to find a stone large enough to seal off the opening. That in itself was a challenge. Soft enough so it could be sculpted to exactly fit the contour of the passage, yet strong and non-porous so the fluorine smell would be contained.

Thanks to the books and internet search results Oscar had brought him over the years, Angus understood the chemistry. Uranium, the humans called the element. Radioactive. It and its decay daughters, among other things, produced beta rays. They, in turn, stripped electrons from nearby fluorine atoms, and that ended up creating the gas. A fortuitous coexistence. A large cavern with a floor of high-grade yellowcake mixed with cryolite, the sometimes ore of aluminum. Copious uranium and a fluorite mineral. That is where the vile smell came from.

Angus stopped in front of the plug. Without a path to the surface, the pressure of fluorine had built and built. Would there be enough of it now? He was not absolutely sure. That is why he had come. The last measurement he took was high enough he had started the process of procuring the sulfur. Now, this gauging should show an even larger margin to account for any error. He shrugged away the lingering doubt. The only direction now was forward. At least, the alchemy to catalyze the combining he had worked out many orbits ago.

He stood on the stool and stretched his arms over a jutting rock. Like a surgeon removing a tick, with his dagger he pried loose a second tiny plug sealing an additional hole — one he had drilled into the congealed lava. The gas started to hiss out, and he placed a jar over the opening until the pale yellow cloud swirled around the edges of its mouth.

Then Angus screwed on the cap and replaced the little plug, coughing a bit at what he smelt. Now, back to his own alcove and measure the pressure. A mason jar, he mused. One of the inventions of the humans Oscar had scavenged for him. They may be primitive in the working of the crafts, but in some ways, they had compensated for their lack quite well.

18

Initiative

BRIANA REACHED the third level of one of the parking structures at UCLA before she found what she was looking for. No one was about.

Carl, long-winded though he was, had given her a new perspective. From the way he described things, it seemed to her there was an ideal place in which to acquire and hold wealth if one had abilities in the crafts.

She removed a mitematch from her backpack, and looked about a second time. Another car had entered the level and was searching for a place to park. She fiddled some more with the contents of her pack, trying to look inconspicuous until he had left down the nearby stairwell.

Unfortunately, when she had become convinced about where she should search, another blockage appeared in the way. The data accessible in her computer did not include everything there was to know. There were more accumulations of information on Earth protected by walls of fire. Ones she could not access with a simple query. She was going to need help in order to find out more. And the first step to getting that help had brought her here.

Briana dragged the mitematch across the concrete floor of the landing, dominated the will of the first imp whose presence she felt through the flame, and commanded him to place the leaf over the lens of the surveillance camera hung nearby. 'Flame permeates all' and "Dominance or submission.'

She was not going to get access to a database she wanted with the earnings of a waitress in a broken-down café she had reasoned. What she needed was a lordling who had a fortune — sufficient enough that access to the records she wanted would be no more complicated than what she had already learned to do.

And to get that lording to do as she wished, she had needed to improve her command of the native tongue. The language CDs and the second-hand player she had found in the thrift store had helped a lot. By lightly enchanting herself to block out all outside distractions, she had had to listen to each recording only once to absorb its contents and burn the exercises into her memory.

No longer did she surf the internet. Instead, she studied English at least eight hours a day — for how long she could not exactly remember. But now, she felt ready for the next step, finding her target.

Briana coiled a strand of her hair. This was not as bad as stealing, she rationalized. A retelling in the sagas probably would not even mention it. She checked one more time that no one else was present and grabbed out of her pack the hammer she had purchased. With both hands, she plunged it the through the passenger window of the obsidian black Tesla parked in front of her.

An alarm from within the automobile immediately began shouting. Briana crouched out of sight by the car's side and waited a few seconds until she could hear guardsmen climbing the steps nearby. When they were almost to her level, she directed the mite to ascend to the next landing, and then, as the first guard appeared, commanded the imp to shove the stack of empty cans Slow Eddie had found for her down the stairwell. The first guard pointed upward toward the clatter, and he and the one following climbed to investigate.

Then she directed the little imp into a jar and fastened the lid. If she were careful and provided for its needs, the sprite could be useful again.

Briana used the hammer to widen the hole she had made in the window, reached in, and grabbed the first textbook piled in a jumble on the passenger's seat. *Buddhism: A Beginner's Guide to Inner Peace.* She flipped open the cover and saw 'Jonathan Waverton III' and "Comparative Religions 101.' The neatly typed word 'Jonathan' was hard to read; several horizontal ink bars ran through it. Above it in block letters was written 'Jake.' The three capital 'I's also deliberately obscured.

Briana tossed the book back into the car. Everything had gone according to plan. The next step was to see if the internet has entries for a 'Jonathan Waverton.' If it did, then she would find out when and where 'Comparative Religions 101' met. Squaring her shoulders, she started to descend the stairs with a slow, regal air.

She was no longer paralyzed by the wonders of Earth — not totally at ease, but not paralyzed either. She had defeated a brute three times her size. The specter of her impending marriage was manageable.

And she had a definite plan of what to do next. Find Jonathan

Waverton. From what she had seen on campus, he was probably no more sophisticated than a pageboy back on Murdina — someone she could twist around her little finger with a few smiles.

Perhaps she *did* have the makings of a heroine. After all, she was a daughter of the Archimage.

Part Two

So Many Women, So Little Time

The Waverton Family

THE BEEPER on the intercom buzzed. "Jonathan, your father will see you now," the receptionist said.

"It's not Jonathan," Jake said as he strode toward the wide oak door. "It's Jake. How many times do I have to tell you?"

The receptionist smiled briefly and returned to whatever kept her occupied.

Jake pulled open the door adorned with the nameplate 'Jonathan Waverton, Jr.' and entered his father's office.

Even though he had seen it countless times before, the view was still breathtaking. The Golden Gate, the Pacific, San Francisco Bay, and the 'City' itself lay out before him as a feast for the eyes. The rent on the office was probably ten times more than his monthly allowance. It was sparsely furnished — a single desk twice as big as the receptionist's outside with a single guest chair facing it. The surface was completely clean, adorned only with a screen, keyboard, and mouse. There was no credenza, no filing cabinets, and no art on the walls.

Jake was a younger version of his father. The older man was tall and lanky, hair a distinguished gray and close cut with no recession at the temples. Only the beginning of small creases framed his eyes, and the square chin radiated confidence. His suit — impeccably tailored, fitting him without a wrinkle and shimmering in a subtle iridescence when he moved.

"Have a seat, son. As always, I am anxious to hear about your progress," the elder Waverton said.

"Same as usual, Bio-Dad," Jake answered as he slid into the guest chair. "Same as last month and the month before."

"Not flunking anything this time around, right? What is it again you're taking?"

"Comparative Religion 101, Women's Studies, and Gender Lit."

"Why do you waste time on crap like that?"

"Because that's where the women are. Duh."

"You know eventually you will be kicked out for not making sufficient progress toward a degree."

"Yeah, I know that, but eventually can be a long time away. Look, it is no different from what you are doing. What is her name this time, Margo, Margaret, something like that?"

"Don't speak about your mother that way!"

"She is not my mother! Only my stepmother. Only number three in your list of conquests."

"And you have a list, too, I suppose."

"Yeah! Each one a notch on my bedpost. And I'll show it to you, if you show me yours."

The elder Waverton sighed. "Usually it takes a few more minutes before we get to this point."

"Why do we even bother?" Jake asked. "What's so important for us to discuss?"

"What is so important is for you to start doing something useful. At your age, I had already made ten million."

"Yeah, yeah. How could I forget? You remind me of it so often." Like a prune, Jake's face puckered into a frown. "But I'll never be another you, accomplish all you did, et cetera, et cetera."

"You don't have to be another me, son. Just be… something."

"And if I never do?"

"Then the free ride will be over." Jake's father straightened his back and adjusted his tie. "After considered thought, I am reducing your allowance by two thousand dollars a month."

"Two stacks! No way! Why are you doing this?"

"I've tried reasoning with you. I've given you small projects I thought would be interesting and a challenge so you would shape up. None of that has worked. So, starting now, I am reducing your allowance two thousand a month and two thousand more every month thereafter until you start working to get a useful education."

"But my place down at Redondo. It looks right over the ocean. Six stacks by itself. Are you in some sort of financial trouble now?"

"Far from it. I would never let that happen."

Jake moaned. "This is really going to cramp my style."

"You can change that very quickly." The elder Waverton adjusted his tie again. "My big data project with the SEC got renewed. The one looking for inside trader transactions. I can create a spot for you there."

Jake pushed back from the chair and rose. "I'll think about it."

As he turned and walked back to the door, his father called after him. "Since you are already in the city, say hello to your mother while you are here."

THE FRONT door to the condo opened almost immediately, as it always did. Jake smiled at the woman who presented herself to him. Tall, but not too tall. Blonde hair that must take two hours to do up right. A chest that stuck out a mile.

"Hello, Jake," she said. "You are a little ahead of time."

"Hello, *Mother* Margo," Jake replied. "Yeah, the old man and I did not go the full hour this time around. The bastard. He says he is going to reduce my allowance two stacks a month."

"Well," Margo smiled as she ushered him in. "Let's talk. Maybe there is something I can do about that. Do you want something first to calm you down?" She waved her arm with a practiced ease at a credenza groaning with a dozen fancy bottles of cut glass.

Jake shook his head. A hint of a blush began to color his cheeks. "No, not until after. You know that. Before, before — "

"I know, Jake." Margo smiled. "Pleasure first and then business after."

She took him by the hand and led him into her bedroom. They disrobed, and soon were forgetting about anything else.

AFTERWARD, THE two were sitting up in bed, Jake hunched over, and Margo with her back stiff and straight, showing her figure to best effect.

"If you *are* my mother," Jake said, "then that makes me a motherfu —

Margo put her finger to Jake's lips. "You know I don't like hearing that," she said.

"Then both you and I are fu —"

Margo silenced him a second time.

"But that's what we are doing, really," Jake persisted. "Both of us want to get back at the old man for one reason or another."

"Yes, yes, Jonathan probably is trying to relive his life over again through you, and you resent the manipulation." Margo shrugged. "And me, I thought he was through with the philandering. Two wives and their alimonies should have been enough. But once the thrill of the chase had faded, I became like the ones who preceded me. Like before, he is cheating whenever he can get the chance. It's as if he had a bedpost somewhere where he was carving notches."

Jake laughed.

"What's so funny?" Margo asked.

"Never mind," Jake said. "You said we could talk about the problem I now have with cash flow."

"Yes, Jake, I get an allowance, too. I could be increasing what I send you each month."

"That would be Gucci, Margo," Jake said.

"But there is a catch," Margo persisted with a foxlike smile. "Your weekly flights up here. Now they would have to be two times a week instead of only one." She wagged a finger in front of Jake's nose and then extended a second one next to it.

Jake frowned, and he stared into the distance as if he were considering. "Well, I am a *college student*," he said with a smile. "Classes, homework, tests. All kinda stuff taking a lot of time."

"Oh, poor baby," Margo pulled Jake's head down onto her breasts. "Somehow, I think you will manage to survive. Now, let's get back to what we were doing."

Comparative Religions 101

JAKE PULLED the door open to the hall as quietly as he could. The lecture had already started, and the professor had glowered at him when he was late the time before. No sense in calling attention to himself again.

"Hi, my name is Briana. What's yours?"

Jake's eyes widened. A young woman was standing in the landing leading to the seats. A redhead, and slender. Not too much on the top, but enough. Her clothes were faded and frayed. Probably immigrant parents trying to give her an education. She carried what looked like a full backpack over one shoulder. He looked about and frowned. It was as if she were waiting for him.

"You are the one with the Tesla, right?" Briana smiled. "I really would like a ride in a chariot like that."

Jake's frown flipped into a smile. *Kaching!* The bait had worked again. And about time, too. The trips up north kept him satisfied on a physical level, but, like with his old man, what was easy and familiar had begun to grow a little stale.

"Ahem!" the professor coughed.

"Not so loud," Jake whispered. "Let's get a seat, and we can talk when the class is over."

He led Briana to the back row, and made a big production of setting the swing-table in place and opening a notebook. Briana mimicked his motions, but with a jerky hesitancy as if she were doing so for the very first time.

"According to Buddha, the first Noble Truth is that life is frustrating and painful." The professor resumed his lecture. "And the second is that such suffering has a cause. The third states the cause of suffering can..."

Jake's eyelids felt heavy. Staying up until three the night before a class day probably was not a good idea.

JAKE FELT a gentle touch on his shoulder. The babble of students filing out beside him filled his ears.

"I selected the assignment for you from the first pile on the table in front. All twelve choices were face down so it would be random chance," Briana said as she waved a sheet of paper in front of his eyes.

"What assignment?" Jake shook his head. Short naps made his brain feel as if it were a bowl of mush. He probably would have been better off fighting to stay awake.

"The meditation lesson," Briana said. "It has been arranged. This one is at the Kalasandra Buddhist Center. Afterward, you are to write an essay about your... your, yes, that is the word, your *experience*."

Jake stood up and waited for the last of the other students to pass. He appraised Briana a second time. Yeah, she would do for the next notch. "You wanna ride in a Tesla? Then come along. We can get to know each other better on the way over."

JAKE HAD expected something more elaborate, but the building was quite simple. A small covered entrance in the center and two slits for windows on either side. Except for a half-dozen gilded adornments on bare white stucco, it could have passed for a small Spanish missionary church from a couple hundred years ago.

A smiling monk dressed in yellow and red greeted Jake and Briana as they entered. "The meditation room is to the right," he said. "I will be your resident teacher this morning."

Like the monk, the room was adorned with brilliant colors — yellow walls, tables draped in red, and on the floor, a dozen two-tiered cushions of deep ocean blue. Most of the seats were already occupied — legs crossed in front on the larger cushions underneath and smaller ones on top supporting the buttocks. Hands relaxed in laps with fingers curled upward.

Jake and Briana imitated what the others were doing and focused on the teacher who moved quietly to a position in front.

"There are many ways to meditate," the monk began. "All have merit. Today I will instruct you in the Mindfulness of Breathing.

"There are four steps," he continued. "Place, posture, prohibition, and practice. Look about you. You are here in this serene environment. You have achieved place. Straighten your backs and close your eyes and you will achieve posture.

"Now, try to rid your mind of your thoughts. Try to prohibit them from occurring. Focus instead on one single thing — your breathing, in and out. Continue the practice, making it more natural.

"As you do so, your mind will begin to wander. Irritations will arise — a cramp in your leg, an itch needing to be scratched, will you finish this in time in order not to be late for work. These things are natural. But when they occur, continue to concentrate on breathing, nothing else. Do not satisfy the itch; do not worry about how bad the traffic will be. You will discover that with each breath the distracting thoughts become weaker and weaker."

Jake felt himself start to nod off again. He might even tumble into the person sitting next to him unless he was careful. Cautiously he opened his eyes. Everyone else had theirs closed, even Briana and the instructor.

He rose, tiptoed to the doorway, and exited back into the hall. Everything was still and quiet as he expected — everything except what sounded like a raised voice further down the corridor. Whoever was speaking was not in a serene state. Jake decided to move closer so he could make out the words. Anything was better than the boredom of concentrating on his breathing.

"But the resident teacher said the only thing that remained was your final approval," the voice became clearer, and Jake stopped at a curtainway on the left. "I have taken both the beginner class and the intermediate ones as well. I have sold all of my possessions and given the proceeds to charity. The clothes on my back are all that I have left. I want to exchange them for the robe of a monk. I want to achieve enlightenment. I really do."

"Your words betray the state of your mind," an older and softer voice replied from behind the drapery. "*Craving* enlightenment is no different from craving anything else in this world. One has to relieve himself of all earthly desires, even the desire for awakening itself."

Curious, Jake leaned closer, hoping to hear more. He glanced back the length of the hallway to see if anyone was watching him. He saw two heavyset men in dirty T-shirts and low hanging pants striding purposely down the corridor toward him, and he promptly stood.

"I lost my way to the meditation room," he blurted as they drew close. "Perhaps you can tell me which way I should — "

Without speaking, the taller of the two men pushed Jake to the ground, flung back the curtain, and entered the chamber on the other side. The second followed.

"Hey!" Jake scrambled back onto his feet and clambered after them. "You can't push me around like that!"

The room was occupied by the two speakers standing close together. One was big and black. Like a newly sprouting lawn, a curly stubble adorned his cheeks and chin. His head was shaved bald, perhaps in imitation of the other. The second was much older. His age bore down on him like a huge dragon settling into a nest. But despite the interruption, his face, like a pond on a windless day, was serene and untroubled.

"The premium is overdue, your holiness or whatever you call yourself," the first intruder said to the older one. The second grabbed a tapestry displaying umbrellas, fish, vases, conch shells, and other stylized symbols and tumbled it to the ground.

"Stop that!" Jake said. "Hey! Look at me. I'm talking to you."

"This is none of your business, nosy." The first intruder said. "Gonzo, take care of this twerp while I continue talking to the master here." He grabbed the old man's robe by the collar and squeezed it about his neck.

"No!" the big man shouted. "Buddha teaches we shall not cause harm."

Jake turned his attention back to the second thug who was smiling as he walked purposefully toward him. Uh-oh! What was that self-defense class he had taken? He should have paid more attention. Now everything about it was a blur.

"Oof!" the first thug exclaimed. The second hoodlum approaching Jake turned to look. But only for an instant. The big man's upraised foot slammed into the goon's face, sending him flying. As the first ruffian regained his footing, he reached into his waistband for a gun. A second kick sent it reeling out of his hand and clattered across the tiles.

Jake took a stance in imitation of the big man who was doing all of the defending and tried to look as fierce as he could.

"All right," the first thug said. "There is no need to continue the conversation." He rubbed the side of his face, moving his jaws from side to side. "Look at your precious tapestries," he said after a moment. "More of that could happen unless... unless you pay for our protection. Think it over. We will be back in a month. Have a dime ready then, and you will not have to worry."

100

"And as for you two." He looked at Jake and the defender. "You had better not venture in the neighborhood too much unless you have a lot, and I mean a *lot*, of friends with you."

Without waiting for a reply, the two men left the temple.

"You see, Master," the big man said, "There is more I can provide the temple than only serene contemplation. I have studied martial arts, more than one in fact."

"You must go, Maurice." The master shook his head. "Your act shows how shallow still are the words you have learned to mimic. There is still too much of the world within you that has to be expunged. A mind full of quotations, but no understanding of them in your heart."

"But, if I had not — "

"Go, my son, go. Go forth and first find inner peace. Remove your inner confusion. And when you have done that, then you may return and begin to walk the Eightfold Path."

Maurice's shoulders fell. He started to say more, but then turned and exited the chamber. Jake followed him out.

"Buddha says, 'On life's journey, faith is nourishment, virtuous deeds are a shelter,'" Maurice whispered. "But my deeds were deemed unworthy, and now I have no place to go."

Briana emerged from the meditation room as they passed. "There you are," she said. "I was beginning to wonder."

An idea popped into Jake's mind. He turned to face Maurice. "You know about all of this Buddha mumbo-jumbo stuff, right?" he blurted.

"I have studied some, yes. But apparently not enough."

"Perfect. Here's the deal, Maurice. I have a pad right on the ocean. Three bedrooms and I am only using one. The second is for the stuff I have stored for a while. We can put that in the kitchenette… at least for a few days anyway."

"So?"

"So, you have no place to stay. I have an essay on meditation I need written. Move in with me. Room and board provided gratis. And while you are there, you can write my paper. This will be great. I will ace the thing!"

"Three bedrooms?" Briana asked.

"Yeah, why?"

"I want to move in with you, too," Briana said.

Jake smiled. The next notch was going to be easier than he thought.

Repeating Opportunity

THALING AROSE from sleeping on the table in his alcove and listened. Often, Dinton and Angus got into squabbles between the times when they all three met. By the time the echoes reached him, the words usually were unintelligible, but their intent always was clear.

Today there was silence. A full twenty-four hours with no bickering. He straightened his back, and grunted in irritation at his thoughts, at how even he, like everyone of their band, had converted to use the native's measures of time. Then he focused his attention on the far wall of his alcove, closed his eyes to concentrate, and beckoned the nearest rockbubbler imp to attend unto him.

"Practice no craft, indeed!" he muttered. Then, "Lilacbottom, attend unto me," he said with his normal voice.

A small circle appeared in the rock and then grew in size rapidly. Through the opening, Thaling saw the rest of the sphere irising into the alcove and the large glowing sprite hovering in its center.

Like almost all smaller demons, the bony arms crossed in front of a shallow chest and its legs coiled into a knot. The forehead bulged with bumps and mounds. Tufts of coarse hair protruded from tiny ears. The nose lay smashed across a broad and pockmarked face. Except for the whine of rapidly beating wings, it looked like the well-preserved remains of a grotesque child.

"Your wish, Boss," the imp said.

"You are to call me Master, not Boss," Thaling growled. "I have told you this many times. The language of the natives is hideous enough without adding any slang to it."

"Got it. Master, not Boss." The sprite hesitated a few seconds. "And I would prefer you call me 'Heroic Avenger' rather than the nickname the others give me." It hesitated a few seconds more. "And your wish, Boss?" it asked.

"To the lab, Lilacbottom." The exile exhaled in frustration. The little brains evidently could only hold so much at one time. Reinstalling proper respect would be dealt with later. He stepped through the iris and, like a child on a slope of snow, slid to the bottom of the sphere.

The orb centered on the small demon. Except for the opening into the alcove, in every direction at its boundary, Thaling saw solid rock. The empty volume in which he sat had not disappeared, Thaling knew. It still existed, but somehow the sprite temporarily displaced it to be somewhere else.

Lilacbottom retreated from the alcove. The opening shrank in size and finally closed all together. Like a bubble in a dull gray sea, the sphere started moving through the surrounding basalt, opening the passage ahead and closing it behind. Although he had made the journey countless times, Thaling still marveled at how smooth it was. As the surrounding rock oozed by, he felt no motion, and only an occasional large crystal of quartz or feldspar marked the passage,

Some distance from the alcoves and passageways of the exiles, the imp's sphere opened onto a vast cavern. A dozen sprites with the surfaces of their spheres touching one another created a two-dimensional array. In the base of each orb sat a flat, circular table of stone supporting precisely ordered collections of artifacts garnered from the world of sky and wind above. All contained human artifacts, all that is, except for one.

"Let there be light," Thaling said, and the small demons scurried to ignite the dozen or more candles standing on each of the tables. The feeble body glow of the sprites faded in comparison to the vibrant yellow filling the chamber. The expenditure of the precious candles was extravagant, Thaling knew, but Angus always managed somehow to provide more to him than his fair share. Perhaps Dinton did not protest because of the stack of newspapers he received instead. In any event, his eldest brother's protests about not visiting the surface was no more than bluster to nettle his younger siblings.

Thaling climbed up the not-quite-slippery curved slope of the sphere that had brought him and then slid into the bubble adjacent. When he had contacted and dominated the initial rockbubbler some time ago, he had gone almost insane collecting more and building an empire vaster than the entire prison confining all the other exiles. He had even dared to command one imp to rise to the surface, but then quickly reversed direction when he felt the first hint of the outside air.

Now, his domain was only the size necessary, what was needed for the means of revenge. Dinton was delusional. None of their kind would last as long as the eldest brother said it would take. And Angus was so undisciplined, always suggesting wild escape schemes that had no chance of success. Thaling surveyed the extent of his laboratory and smiled. What would his brothers think if they saw all of this? Spools of copper wire and solder, bolts of precisely the correct length and threading, perfectly cut squares and rectangles of aluminum, a vial of etching acid. He had assembled it all.

To keep his focus, Thaling recited the steps of a remembered ritual in his mind. The hint of sulphur in the air was soothing. It calmed his thoughts like a female's caress. His was the true method to achieve victory, not only escape from the captivity in which the ones who called themselves the Faithful had placed them, but return to the home world for vengeance as well.

Sliding from one sphere to another, he arrived at the most important. Though it had been a millennium, the anger was still fresh within him. After the defeat, they had been forced by the Faithful to walk through the portal one by one to the horrible prison now containing them. Dinton, Angus, and all the others had submitted. Thaling and his mate, Alika, had been the only ones remaining to transfer.

He remembered the last he saw of her. She entered the passage, the door shut, and after a short time, it opened again. If she had complied like the rest, the portal should have been empty, but it was not. Alika stood there, hands on hips, fangs bared, and growling. How could one not be attracted to one such as that? The very embodiment of the Heretics Who Proclaim the Truth.

The reaction of the self-proclaimed victors was swift. Good to their threat, she was hacked to pieces before Thaling's eyes. Then with no time to grieve, he was the one forced to collect the pieces of her body for disposal and clean up the ichor. Only when that was done, did he make the very last transfer.

Alika. Fiery Alika. Gone, because of the so-called Faithful. She alone had the will to resist to the last. The desire for avenging her death seared all of his being.

"What is your command, Boss?" the rockbubbler in whose sphere he now sat asked.

Thaling broke out of his memories. Now, after a thousand years, there was opportunity. Now there was work to do.

"Mintbreath, I need five rings," he said. "Of silver, and a size that slips over my wrist but small enough you could wear one about your waist without it falling off. And a dozen birds, the ones the natives call 'pigeons,' alive and robust. Finally, a jar of glue that can bind together metal. My brother, Angus, informs me such a substance exists on this wretched orb."

"Our domain is restricted to be only within rock, Boss," Mintbreath replied. "Raw metal, yes. But not forged rings. You know such things would not be found anywhere we can fly."

"And you know to do what you have done before. Barter with the imps of the air. They can find what I want."

"But, Boss, their price is too steep. They want to perform gross acts upon our bodies — "

"That is no concern of mine," Thaling snapped. His willed his back ramrod straight. "Do as I command. The rings and ink that is pigeon-blood red are needed for the next step in the ritual I will perform."

"Yes, Boss," Mintbreath, answered softly.

His wings started to buzz in a modulated cadence that Thaling could not follow, but it did not matter. Wizardry was not his proficiency. It was magic at which he excelled. He looked at the single device standing upright on the table, a slender cylinder with a translucent bulb on top and a few toggles adorning one side.

Why he had thought to do it, when he entered the portal so long ago, he did not remember. But he started opening each of the drawers along the side one by one — as fast as he could before the Faithful opened the door to verify he had gone.

Most were empty, but in one was the tracker, the device that showed the location of the gateway when it was separated from it. A necessity if an explorer ever got lost when investigating a new orb. The way back to his transport home.

Thaling had grabbed it and spirited it away when he emerged on the Earth. Evidently, none of the victorious ever discovered the loss nor did Dinton or Angus ask about such a device. And for almost the entire exile it had been his secret reminder of Alika — of what might have been.

Over the years, most of the time the tracker was mute, but whenever the victors visited to check they were still confined, it came to life beeping that the portal was present and within range.

He touched the device in front of him and waited a few moments more. Again, it happened as it had recently, not once, but more than two dozen times — a soft light radiated from the translucent bulb and a gentle repeating beep filled the air. Every day at the same time, it had come to life, and except for the first visit, each activation was only for a few moments, and then the tracker was silent again.

A strange behavior, but Thaling was not concerned about *why* the visits were now occurring after so long an absence, only that each day they presented an opportunity. After centuries of waiting, finally, it made sense to act on his idea. The portal was the key. Neither Dinton nor Angus could reason their way to see that, but he certainly did.

Dinner at Eight

JAKE FLUNG open the door to his apartment. The other two were going to be impressed. He knew it. The floor to ceiling window covered the entire west wall, and the glow of mid-morning sun danced on a smooth and windless Pacific. To one side, a few pieces of Danish Modern faced a massive flat screen.

"Behind the couch and chairs are the doors to two of the bedrooms," Jake said. "The farther one is mine, and you, Maurice, can have the one nearest. On one side of the TV is the passage to the kitchen; on the other, Briana, is the door to where you can toss your stuff."

"Everything I have is here in my backpack," Briana said as she set it on the floor. "But I must be at work by six. I am not sure how long the busses will take me to get from here to there."

"Busses?" Jake said. "There is no need for busses. No need for you to work any place at all when you are staying here with me."

He studied Briana a bit more closely. From the way she had come on, she obviously must be hot to trot. But if that was all it was, he already had Margo. Was there something else she brought to the table, something that might make her more interesting than only a one-night stand?

"There is something else," Briana continued, as if she could read his mind. "A task I have to attend to near Hollywood Boulevard."

"Really, what is that?"

Briana did not immediately answer. After a moment, she said, "Now that I think about it. Now that I am making progress. Now with a place to stay. I don't really need to do that every morning. I will make the return interval ten days instead of only one. Ten days should now be enough to finish everything up… I hope."

Briana's words made absolutely no sense, but maybe, just maybe, there was something about her worth finding out about.

"Well, whatever," he said. "For now, let's the three of us clean out

Maurice's room and cram everything into the kitchen. The Electric Girl action figure and the others are on display on top of the dressers, and their boxes are hidden in the closets." He thought for a moment. "You know," he said at last, "Electric Girl with the bustier thingy she wears. One would think that in the movies, with the action and all, they would pop out every once in a while."

Then he gave Briana his most dazzling smile. "After this stuff is put away, our martial arts champion here can scrounge up something from the pantry while the two of us go out for a little fine dining."

"Maurice is not coming, too?" Briana asked.

"I'm cool," Maurice said. "I need to practice my meditation at least two hours a day, or I get rusty. I start to get migraines too. As Buddha says, 'Meditation brings wisdom; lack of meditation leaves ignorance.'"

IT WAS already dark by the time Maurice emerged from his bedroom with a final armload of action figures, a riot of muscle and colors — The Violet Tanager, Miracle Woman, Hawkbabe, and five or six others. Jake and Briana sat in the center of the floor carefully putting each doll back into its original packaging.

"Might be my way to cut my ties completely from the old man when they become scarcer items," Jake said. "In the meantime, when I am not surfing…" He smiled again at Briana. "Not surfing or doing other things, I like looking at them."

"They are all female figures," Maurice said.

"A coincidence." Jake shrugged. Time to start finding out if there was something more behind the pretty face, he thought. Something more that would make it worthwhile. "So, change out of what you have on now into your best dress. I am going to treat you to no less than Spago's."

"This is my best," Briana said. "What I have in my pack is not nearly as good."

Jake hesitated for a moment. "Well, no matter. My father's money is good enough they should not care at all about what I show up with. Grab a wrap and we can be off."

"I don't have a wrap either," Briana said.

THE WAITER brought the 'American Sampler for Two,' and Jake reached for the serving spoon. Briana set her hand gently on his wrist for him to stop. She took the spoon from his grasp and added a portion of the *maïs à la crème* to his plate. Then she did the same for hers.

He grabbed his own fork, ready to begin when Briana placed her hand on his wrist a second time.

"Until we both are ready," she smiled. "It is part of a, what is the word, a ritual going back hundreds of years."

He watched her continue and felt a surprising surge of pleasure. It was enjoyable to be treated this way. It was as if she were a geisha. No, that was not right. She did not look Japanese at all.

"I cannot place your accent," Jake said. "Where are you from? South America? Eastern Europe?"

Briana shook her head. "No, not those places. Far, far away."

"India, then? Bhutan? Nepal?"

"You would not find my home on any of your maps."

This was mysterious. Why was she being so evasive? Trouble with immigration? A criminal in hiding maybe? He reached again for his fork.

"One more step and then we can begin," Briana said. She cupped her hand around his upper arm and gently squeezed.

"What was that for?" he asked.

"Where I am from, it is traditional when a warrior and a princess share a meal. It indicates she is thankful for his protection, and…"

A hint of blush rose to her cheeks. "And the possibility that sometimes, not very often to be sure, but that, sometimes, there are more pleasures to come." Briana lowered her eyes and concentrated on her plate.

She did not hold the fork in a way he had ever seen before, Jake realized. It was as if she were getting ready to shovel heavy snow. He bent closer and looked into her eyes. They were so large and alive, a deep green contrasting perfectly with her cascading red hair, a face pale as alabaster, a face he had seen in no other woman he had ever met. He inhaled deeply and caught a hint of her essence, a scent he could not place. Not perfume with its musky base, but something more natural, a mixture of nutmeg and cinnamon, deliciousness of the natural world.

Shangri-La! The thought rose out of nowhere. He had read *Lost Horizon* when he was in high school. The mythical valley hidden in the Himalayas and the harmonious people who lived there. It was nonsense of course, but, for some reason, it made sense. Briana was from somewhere like that. She was so... so *exotic*. Yes, that was it. She was exotic.

And more pleasures to come, she had said. His pulse quickened. Now, he could hardly wait to get her into the sack. What new delights would she show him? What exciting ways not even dreamed about in the West? The next notch on the bedpost was going to be great!

"MILADY," JAKE said as he pushed open the apartment door a few hours later. It had gone well enough. Teaching Briana on the proper use of each of the pieces of silverware served as an icebreaker. But then, he had done most of the talking. She had said little about herself.

"Now that we are back, we should finish the tour," he said. "Let me show you my room."

They entered together.

"It may seem a little ostentatious for a single guy..." Jake began.

For a moment, Briana focused on the canopied bed and then froze as stiff as a rod of iron. A rich brocaded quilt covered a California king. A tall, intricately carved sentinel stood at each corner holding aloft what looked like a parachute gently descending to the earth. The finished bedpost nearest was marred by the series of notches starting from the mattress level and marching ceilingward.

"Slammert," Briana said softly. "Another Slammert! You are not like a pageboy at all!"

Page boy? He was no pageboy. What was she talking about? Jake shook his head to fling away the thought. Not now, not yet. Time to plunge ahead and see how far he could get on a first date. He reached out and turned her to face him. He put his hand on her back and drew her close. His lips puckered and he lowered his head toward her.

To his surprise, Briana deftly pushed away and twirled out of his grasp.

"Waitress training," she said in a disapproving voice like that of a teacher disciplining a disruptive child.

Well, Okay not a 'slam, bam, thank you, ma'am,' Jake thought. But maybe at least, a little something.

"This is a mistake." Briana took a step back. "I'm… sorry, but you… your type is not what I am seeking."

"Didn't you enjoy the dinner?"

"Yes, the dinner was wonderful, especially the dessert. It was delicious. Where I come from, we do not have anything like, what did you call it, Baked Alaska?" She looked suddenly flustered. "Thank you. Thank you very much, but I have to go."

Jake puzzled. Some women blew hot and cold, he knew. But there was something else going on with this one.

"You've avoided this all evening," he said. "Where *do* you come from?"

"You want more than a mere kiss, don't you? And you expect it now."

"Well, at least a kiss wouldn't hurt. Do you know how much that meal set me back?"

Briana did not immediately answer. "You're talking about the going rate for a single kiss?" she finally said. Her befuddlement changed into indignant anger. "Is it about the same as the charge for a quicky?"

"You mean for the drive-by sluts on the Boulevard? I have no idea. I don't need to know. I have never spent a cent on a woman that way, and I never intend to."

"So what do you call what you spent on me tonight? Wasn't it money in exchange for favors? Is there any real difference? What does that make me if I agree?"

"No, no, that's not it at all," Jake protested. "It was so we could get to know each other better."

What was happening here? Exotic, yes, but this …

"I see the notches on your bedpost, Jake. I do come from faraway, but I know what they represent."

"Look, it is not what you think. I have experience, lots of it, true. But each and every notch was because my partners…"

"Your partners, what?"

"Because my partners just, just *wanted* to. Gifts freely given with no strings attached. Not obligations that had to be paid."

"Gifts, freely given?"

"Yeah, absolutely. Look, our first meeting at the class was not an accident, right? You sought me out. You want something more than a ride in a car. What is it?"

Briana again was silent. Her brow wrinkled in thought. "I *do* want you to do something for me," she said at last. "Probably more than a single thing before it all is over. But the price... the price is more than I am willing to pay."

Jake felt the impulse to show her the door. There always were more sardines in the can. But there was also a challenge here. Some notches turned out to be deeper and more satisfying than others — *Shangri-La!* Maybe a slower approach would work, one that let fair play and guilt play a part.

"Suppose there were no price?" he began carefully. "Suppose the things you asked of me, I just did for you — true gifts because I give them unconditionally, not expecting anything in return. How many dinners do you want? Perhaps a few shows thrown in as well?"

"It's not about your money, Jake." Briana shook her head. "Although in the end, there probably will be some involved. It is about the accesses you have because of your wealth."

"Accesses? Okay, accesses. Whatever. But to be fair, you have to play the game too. Keep an open mind about me. As we get to know each other better, if it seems appropriate to you, give me gifts, too."

"How is that any diff — "

"I will keep my hands to myself. No obligation on your part at all. Only do what your heart tells you to."

Briana pondered for over a minute, her face a mask hiding what looked like serious calculation. Finally, she said, "Okay, to start, you can drive me to Hollywood Boulevard in the afternoon tomorrow. For now, good night. I'll see you in the morning."

"Sure," Jake said. "I'll behave like a saint, like a monk, like Maurice — waiting for you to make the first move."

The Circles of Life

THALING STOOD ready in the bubble containing the tracker. He glanced at one of the little clocks Angus had obtained from the surface. Soon it would chime, indicating that the rest of the ritual could begin. He could only hope the incessant tittering of the sprites would not spoil the next step in the augmentation. It was problematic enough that he could not use the grit of the finest rubies for the ink but had to settle for the bird's ichor instead.

"We do not like this, Boss," Littlebutt said at his side. "Listen to all of the rest. The six of us are quite embarrassed."

"I have explained to you why you had to shrink your spheres to nothingness," Thaling said. "Otherwise, the half-dozen of you could not assemble so close together. Now pay attention to keeping the silver rings from slipping off your waists. Refill your quills with ink often from the belt vials I have fashioned for you. Any small deviation from what is required will nullify the magic, and we will have to start from the beginning again."

"But, Boss," Littlebutt protested. "We are naked. The rest of the sprites can see."

"You look absolutely no different than you do when you are surrounded by your sphere. The orbs are transparent. What difference can there be?"

The tittering surrounding the six increased. Thaling felt a sudden swelling of pressure against the grip he held on the sprites. One or two were easy to dominate, but not so many at once. He glanced again at the clock and scowled. He would have to take the time now to reaffirm who was the master. Get that done first before the ritual step began.

"Silence!" Thaling commanded. He straightened his posture and thrust out his chest. "The rest of you in the other bubbles, stop your chattering."

He closed his eyes, tasted the refreshing air, and focused on the sprite

113

in the nearest sphere. The Law of Dichotomy — 'Dominance or submission' — one of the two laws of wizardry that was quite clear. At some deep level, he did not really like interacting with others that way. But that was how the craft worked. Yes, now the resistance was greater than it had been when he first had dominated the demons' wills.

He sent his thoughts forward as the image of a vice, its two jaws surrounding the rockbubbler on either side. Hesitating for a moment, he mentally began tightening the device's handle against the resistance of the sprite's puny arms. For a moment, the lever refused to turn, but then gradually, the opposition began to weaken. Not too much, he reminded himself. He did not really want to cause deep harm to their psyches, only enough so they would follow instructions the first time they were given without an ocean of complaints.

As Thaling reasserted himself, he felt pressure from another source. A second sprite was starting to struggle for dominance since he had focused his thoughts on the first. I am no accomplished wizard, he growled to himself for the dozenth time. A magician skilled in ritual, yes, but not also experienced dueling with the minds from another realm. He could handle the basics but had no training in dominating more than one demon simultaneously. The ritual would be far easier to perform with others of his own kind handling the steps. But the risk of one of his brothers finding out what he was doing was too great. He would have to deal with these irksome sprites instead.

Thaling visualized an array of vices in his mind, one for each of the rockbubblers, and mentally began turning the handle for the one who now challenged him. But as soon as he did, two more pushed back with their own wills, mounting defiance. Like an entertainer trying to keep a score of plates simultaneously spinning on sticks, he flitted his attention to where it was needed most.

A sense of panic began to well up within him. Alone the sprites were puny, but acting together, acting as one…

Acting as one! Yes, that was what he had to do. In his mind, Thaling arranged all of the vices in a row and welded a horizontal metal bar to the handles standing in line. Then when he moved the rod in a small circle, every one of the jaws simultaneously would contract. At first, the bar did not budge, but then he thought of his mate, and anger added energy to his exertion. Slowly, the vices all tightened about the sprites. In a few moments, the image faded as the small demons bowed their heads.

"Silence, I said," Thaling growled.

"As you wish, Bo… Master," the demons said and then became quiet.

"To your positions then," Thaling commanded the six 'naked' rockbubblers wearing the silver rings. "There on the diagram, to each point of the compass as I have indicated the paths. Step exactly to the cadence as I call it out. Trail your quills on the parchment as you proceed."

As Thaling counted, the ink left by the six sprites curved out from the common starting place. When they reached a certain distance, they reversed direction and returned to the center following a slightly different path. Soon, the pattern looked like symmetrical leaves radiating from the center of a flowering plant. Next, the leaf tips were surrounded by an encompassing circle, and using where the leaves touched the circumference as starting points, the design was repeated six more times. The exile made them write a third set of motifs surrounding the second, and finally, two concentric circles circumscribed the entire design.

Thaling waited a few moments for the ink to dry. "You may retreat to the periphery and reestablish your spheres," he said. "Continue your silence until I have finished my own part."

He placed the tracker at the very center of the pattern and then adhered the little clock into a flat place on the backside with the mineral glue. After waiting a few moments more, he dusted a basalt sand over the ink, drying it completely. The ritual was complete.

Thaling stepped back to admire what he had done. "The circles of life," he said aloud to no one. "The design is perfect, useful as a basis for so many rituals, and it will last forever."

"I don't get it, Boss," Littlebutt said.

"It is all according to the fundamental law of magic, Thaling said. "The Maxim of Persistence — 'Perfection is Eternal.'"

Not So Safe

TWO WEEKS went by quickly. A few more dinners, a show or two, even a movie sitting in an empty loge, and Briana did not surrender even a single smooch. One day near the end of the period, she had requested another ride to Hollywood. But other than that, nothing.

This woman was a loser, Jake thought. He was wasting his time. His first impulse had been correct. He should give her the heave-ho. But then, yes, she *was* a challenge. Eventually, she would come around, wouldn't she? And exotic as ever. He had to have her, find out what it would be like.

Except for the two scoops of ice cream every night, her dent in the pantry was far less than what it took to keep Maurice from getting irritable. The rest of the time, Briana occupied herself with her computer and watching classic movies on TV. She was learning about cultural things faster that way, she had said. But every time he tried a move, she rebuffed him. "You promised," she would always say. Fourteen days, and nothing.

The essay did garner an A, and somehow Maurice moving out never did come up. The monk-wannabe handled the cooking when they ate in, and Briana did the dishes afterward. The two of them shared the laundry chores as well. More time for surfing and occasional study when he felt like it.

Jake approached Briana from behind while she was intent on the TV. He gently placed his hand on her shoulder and leaned over, hoping to see something down the front of her low-cut top. Without losing concentration, Briana lifted his hand away.

"Okay, Okay!" Jake growled. "I have not tried anything for two frigging weeks. I am as much of a saint as that Buddhist hiding in his room all day. I give up. Be explicit. What *deed* do I have to perform to get anywhere with you?"

Briana clicked off the TV, turned her head, and smiled. "It took you a while finally to crack," she said. "But this will be a gift, freely given, right? Nothing in payment expected."

Jake studied Briana intently. Her smile looked genuine enough. Maybe with only a little more time... "Yeah, a gift," he growled.

"The stock market." Briana stood and faced him. "I want to be able to query transaction records."

Jake frowned. This was unexpected. "What in hell for?" he asked.

"I have my reasons."

Was this an act? Making stuff up. Playing him? But if so, then why? Or was there a true mystery here? Something adding to her allure.

"Access to market transaction records?" he said. "Be reasonable. How am I supposed to get my hands on stuff like that?"

"Aren't you Jonathan Waverton, the third?"

"Yeah, so?"

"And isn't your father, Jonathan Waverton, Jr?"

"So wha... Oh, yeah, my old man. SEC big data. He can get to that."

"So, ask him."

"It doesn't work that way with him."

Briana came up to Jake and gently squeezed his arm.

Shangri-La! and everything that might mean danced tantalizingly back into his mind. He sighed. If this was the hoop he had to jump through, then so be it. "Asking him directly probably will not cut it... But I do know someone who can help."

"HE LEFT an hour ago for a trip," the receptionist outside of Jake's father's office said as he and his stepmother, Margo, sailed by. "You shouldn't be going in there."

"Shhh! A birthday surprise." Margo held up a decorated package tied with a large bow and kept walking.

The receptionist opened her mouth to say more, but by the time she had come up with something, Jake and Margo were in the office and had shut the door.

"It's like I remember," Margo said. "A large desk and one chair on either side."

"Most of the filing cabinets are behind the oak panels," Jake said. "We will have to search behind each one until we find the safe." He began pushing on the panels one by one until they popped open. About a quarter way around the room, he found what he was looking for.

"Good! The same one he showed me when I was in high school," Jake said. "Cheap bastard. Bragged about not spending several grand on a Class One Diebold. A few hundred for this toy from an office supply store. I figured he would never upgrade to the newer one. He has had this for years."

Rather than a tall, narrow filing cabinet, the panel hid a small almost cubical safe that was bolted to the floor. On its face was a numerical keypad and a lever; there was no dial like the older models of a generation ago.

Jake reached into his pocket and withdrew a long hockey sock. In its toe was a short, round cylinder.

"What did you say the magnet was made of?" Margo asked. "Neodin... neodin..."

"Neodymium," Jake said. "It is a rare-earth element. The world's strongest magnets are made from it. Something I learned last year in the 'Science for Liberal Arts Majors' class."

"Why is it in the long sock?"

"It is so powerful that if I stuck it to the safe itself, I would never be able to remove it again. Now watch this."

Jake grasped the magnet through the sock padding and placed it on the safe in the upper left-hand corner. He clutched the lever with his other hand and tried to twist it.

Nothing happened.

"What are you doing?" Margo asked.

"There is a solenoid inside the safe that retracts the locking mechanism from the door when the correct combination is punched in. The magnet is so strong it can move the solenoid core entirely by itself."

He began sliding the magnet in the sock slightly in random directions from where he had placed it. After only a few trials, the lever rotated, and the safe opened.

"That's—that's magic!" Margo blurted.

"Nothing like that. Good ol' modern technology instead."

Inside the safe was a single sheet of paper. Jake took it out and examined it.

"And just like the old man, too," Jake shook his head. "A final failsafe if he forgot the usernames and passwords for his computer, firewall, and encrypted files."

"Firewalls and encrypted files. How do you know anything about things like that?"

"Bri—I mean—Maurice surfed the net for me and found out what to do."

Jake hastened to the desk and started typing on the keyboard. In a few minutes more, following instructions that 'Maurice' had written out for him, he had altered firewall settings so he could log in remotely. He wrote the new user name and password for entry on a scrap of paper and shoved it in his pocket.

"Well that does it," he said. "Thanks for coming along, Margo. The receptionist wouldn't stop Jonathon Waverton, Jr's wife from entering even if she might for the wayward son. And the wrapped package was a genius touch."

"This is how you can thank me," Margo said as she sat down on the carpet and started to unbutton her blouse.

"What! No, this is crazy!" Jake said. "I'm coming back up tomorrow anyway. Let's get out of here now."

"Think of it." Margo began sliding down her slacks. "What better place to shove it to him than in his very own office."

Jake started to protest, but his hindbrain took control, and he started undressing as well.

Things progressed swiftly. They always did with Margo. She was too impatient to bother with all of the foreplay. Then, the outer door of the suite slammed with purpose, and Jake sat up, startled.

"What was that?" he whispered.

The raised voice of the receptionist penetrated the closed door. "Why, Mr. Waverton, what are you doing back here? Your flight should be taking off about now."

"Forgot an important file," Jake's father answered. "I'll take a later plane."

"Ah, wait. Maybe you shouldn't be going in there yet,"

"What do you mean?" The elder Waverton puzzled.

"It's... it's a surprise."

Jake's father hesitated for a few seconds, then shrugged and jerked open the door. His eyebrows flew up when he saw Jake and Margo standing there.

"What are you two doing here?" he asked.

119

"Surprise!" Jake said. He thrust forward the package. "And happy birthday!"

"My birthday is not until next March," Jake's father growled.

"Yes, and that is why it is a surprise." Margo smiled at her husband.

The elder Waverton turned his attention to his wife and frowned. "You have been hitting the sauce a little too much lately, Margo. Look at you. Your blouse isn't even buttoned right."

He turned back to Jake. "And you don't look much better." Then he scanned the room. "Half of the panels are open. What exactly were you two doing in here?"

"Trying to find a good hiding place," the two said in unison.

Jake's father eyed the package being pushed at him. He placed his hands on either side of his son's and drew the offering toward him. "Ah, Passion Flower," he said as he inhaled. "At least you remembered to get that right, Margo. Some of it has even rubbed off on this package."

"Well, surprise over," Jake said. "We gotta go now."

The elder Waverton watched the two scurry out. He put the box to his nose, inhaled again and then frowned.

"Elsa, get me the number of Acme Detective," he said.

BRIANA IGNORED the look as she opened her computer in Jake's living room and began the logon process.

"Okay, now you have access," Jake said. "You can do all sorts of queries on the NYSE historical transaction database."

He leered. "I have performed the deed you desired. Now, do I get my reward?"

He thought for a moment. "Although, it doesn't really have to be tonight. I have to fly back up north tomorrow and want to be in tip-top shape for that."

"Let's see if the data is of any use." Briana ignored Jake's words.

"What is it you want to know?" he asked.

"I am searching to see if anyone has been very, *very* lucky, someone who knows exactly when to buy and when to sell."

"You mean a day trader?" Maurice interjected as he came to look over Briana's other shoulder. "Buddha says 'Refrain from evil and from strong drink and to be steadfast in virtue; that is the good luck'.'"

"Yes, very short-term trades," Briana said. "Carl, a friend of mine on campus explained it to me." She fell silent and continued manipulating the keys. After a while, it became clear to Jake that nothing was going to happen tonight even if he didn't have plans for tomorrow. He watched her input queries for a few moments more and then backed away. Maybe she would be sufficiently grateful when he returned from up north. The two men retreated, Maurice back to his meditation and Jake to the dolls in his room.

After several hours, Briana shouted. "A hit! I got a hit!"

"What, what?" Jake and Maurice rejoined her. "What did you find?"

Briana pointed at the screen. "There, I have assembled the data. There is a trader in New York, Fredrick Emmertyn. He buys a variety of stocks but then only holds them for a few minutes—five at the most. Then he sells. Or sometimes, he sells short and then buys back minutes later. The dollar amounts are small so that no one would notice. But time after time, *every* time, over the last three years, as far back as the data goes, he makes a profit. Finally! Finally after all of my searching. I see what looks like proof."

Jake watched Briana somewhat surprised. He had never seen her this animated.

"Sorcery is practiced here on Earth after all!" she said.

"Sorcery? Here on *Earth*? What are you babbling about?" Jake asked.

"It is the perfect use of the craft in a culture such as this. No need to confront. No need to struggle overtly for power. Use the system to build up wealth slowly. Build until you had the wherewithal to buy whatever else you needed."

"You're still not making sense," Jake said. His leer returned. "Maybe we don't have to wait until after my, ah, meeting tomorrow. Maybe I can get my reward tonight?"

Briana smiled. She leaned toward Jake and kissed him on his cheek.

"That's it?" he exclaimed. "I risked my butt to give you what you wanted, and all I get for it is a lousy peck on the jaw? *That's* the pleasure to come? I don't understand why this is so valuable to you, but don't you truly... *like* me now?"

Briana thought for a moment. "No, not yet. There is more."

"What?" Jake exploded.

"We have to go to New York and confront this trader. Find out if he is acting on his own or for someone—or *someones* else."

A Disciple of Murphy

THALING CRANED his head backward and looked up at the apex of Littlebutt's sphere. No sky showed, but he was anxious anyway. The peak was only inches below the surface. One hiccough upward and the boundary would be pierced. The air the humans breathed would rush in. No, that was not right, he corrected himself. Air from their prison would rush out like that from a failed dam.

"Why didn't you think this all the way through?" Littlebutt asked. "I would much rather be hangin' out at the pool."

"What? What pool? You guys don't have a pool!"

"It's a metaphor," Littlebutt said. "It means not having anything unpleasant to do, like convincing this recluse to come and help. You know, Boss, for a wizard, you're kinda dumb."

"I am a magician, not a wizard," Thaling ignored the barb. It was better to keep focused on the ultimate objective. "I had no idea the air imps would charge so much for the scrap odometers I wanted."

"Right. The mechanical ones are hard to come by now. Not used in newer chariots any more. Instead, we have to connect up electronic ones, small glowing lights in an array forming each digit."

"And that means," Littlebutt continued, "we must deal with a gremlin. They're unpleasant guys. Don't talk much. Would rather hang out inside of electronics, shooting off sparks to make them fail. The idea of assembly rather than destruction is an entirely new concept for them."

"How do you know about these things anyway?" Thaling asked. "When you spend all of your idle time, as you say, hangin' out at the pool."

"Or shooting the breeze," Littlebutt said.

Thaling scowled, and Littlebutt hurried on. "The imp who is coming. He calls himself a..." The sprite stopped, held up his hands, extended two fingers from each, and clawed at the air. "He calls himself a

'Disciple of Murphy,' whatever that is."

One of the sprite's eyebrows raised for a moment, but Thaling did not react. Finally, it said, "You see what I did, Boss? The sprites above the surface say the humans call the clawing fingers 'air quotes'. Personally, I don't get it."

He lowered his arms and raised one shoulder as far as he could, let it relax, and then raised the other.

"What are you doing now?" Thaling felt his irritation rise.

"Only trying to behave like you, Boss," Littlebutt said. "How do you get both of your shoulders to rise at the same time, anyway? What is that called again?"

"It's a shrug," Thaling said. "Now, stop this blather and pay attention to my questions. We have never heard of such imps as gremlins on the world we come from. How come they are here and not there?"

"It's the energy needed to bridge the gap between the realms, Boss. You have nothing that potent where you come from. The flames that open the connection between the realms for gremlins is powerful stuff — ionizing arcs that tear through the air."

"So some wizard elsewhere controls them as I control you?"

"Well, they pretend to be controlled," Littlebutt said.

"Only pretend? Then why do they come?"

"You see, Boss, size *does* matter in our realm. Size matters a lot. And these little guys get no respect there, none at all. They are happy to escape to wherever they can."

Thaling did not say more. He thought he could hear something.

"I will push my sphere a tad upward and..." Littlebutt said. "Yep, here he is."

Thaling straightened as tall as he could and squinted. An imp about a quarter the size of a rockbubbler hovered above him, his skin even more pockmarked and convoluted. Sparks jumped from his skin like tiny exploding fireworks and fizzled out in the air. A wicked smile stretched from ear to ear.

"I can't make out anything the imp might be saying," the magician complained.

"Of course not, Boss. Little body. Small vocal chords. Very high-pitched voice. Unless you have some sort of downshifting device, you won't hear anything."

"Then how do you — "

"Sign language, Boss," Littlebutt said. "Universal in our realm.

Otherwise, it would be chaos there." Littlebutt suddenly giggled. "Chaos, Boss, get it, chaos. A little more chaos in the realm of demons. Exactly what we need."

"Let's get started," Thaling commanded. "Take this little imp to the alcove with the tracker. Get him to do whatever he has to do to connect the keypads and numerical displays to it. And do it with haste. I am getting a little worried the portal is only nearby one day in ten now—not every day."

The Modern Woman

JAKE WAS stunned. What was it with this woman? Was she only a tease? No way could one win with a tease.

He stared at her intently, watching her enthusiasm seem to bubble almost like lava from a newly awakened volcano.

He shrugged. Arrange for a trip to New York, and then his 'deed' certainly would be done. *Shangri-La!* He had waited this long. Another few days would not matter.

"I don't think this trader will level with you," he said.

"Why not?" Briana asked.

"You need to appear as someone deserving of attention. A business suit, heels, makeup, the whole enchilada."

"I do not mean to intrude," Maurice chimed in. "Buddha says, 'It is better to travel well than to arrive.'"

"That makes no sense at all," Jake growled. "Do you have to have a quote for every situation, even when it does not quite fit?"

"Well, I am fudging a bit," Maurice said. "Buddha, in fact, did not say that. But somehow it has crept into the standard list of his quotes."

"So then, why did you — " Jake began.

"I do not mean to pry, Briana," Maurice continued. "But I wonder. Do you have valid identification? You will need that in order to get a boarding pass for the plane."

Briana did not immediately answer. Her enthusiasm looked like it was starting to melt away. "Jake, I do not have enough money for all of the things you mentioned," she said. "And Maurice, I suspect I do not have what you call identification either."

Jake smiled. "If I were to bankroll you, would that be merely payment for favors to be received or instead would it count as a gift that — "

"The real problem is the ID," Maurice persisted. "A driver's license is very hard to fake. More than a half-dozen security features." He closed his eyes. "Perhaps an Indian tribal card would be easier to forge, but even so, the risk of being caught…"

"Maybe your visa," Jake suggested. Maybe now he would find out where she was from.

Briana shook her head.

"We could travel by car," Maurice said. "Do the driving in shifts."

"From LA to New York, by car!" Jake shook his head. "That will take days. A whole week without Margo." He pointed at Briana in frustration. "Another week waiting for this one to deliver."

"Well, it would be with your Tesla," Maurice said.

Jake considered for a moment. It *would* be a chance to see how the car performs outside of the LA crawl. He looked again at Briana and sighed. "*Shangri- La! Shangri-La!* Damn it, you better be worth it."

Without another word, he went to his room, returned with an attaché case, and flipped it open. Inside were two dozen slits cut into foam. In each incision was a small plastic card.

"Gift cards," Jake explained. "Every month, I use the allowance my old man sends me to buy them. The bank account goes to almost zero right away. I don't trust the bastard. He probably has some way of draining it if he wanted. Anyway, I use these babies for whatever I want to buy."

He began drawing cards out of the row in the middle. "Five hundred, a thousand, fifteen hundred, two, twenty-five, three," he said. "Briana, that should be enough to doll you up. Maurice, you take her to one of the fancy stores and connect her with a sales associate. Get a suit for yourself for the trip as well."

Jake leered at Briana. "And a bikini or two while you are at it."

"What about you?" Maurice asked.

"I'm going to hit the waves," Jake said. "Work off some of the frustration."

LATER IN the day, Jake returned to the apartment and looked around. Maurice was in the living area seating on the floor with knees bent, hands palm upward, and eyes closed. A buzzing came from the bathroom.

126

"What's the noise?" Jake asked. "Where's Briana? I want to see what she bought."

"In the bathroom," Maurice said. "Shaving her legs."

"Really?" Jake said. "I never imagined — "

The buzzing stopped, and Briana exited the lavatory. She was wearing a casual dress with emerald green colors that accented her copper tresses.

She smiled and posed for Jake.

"Do you like it?" she asked.

"I thought you were going to get a business suit," Jake said.

"I did that, and had money left over, so I bought a few more things, too. The clerk was quite helpful. Taught me about makeup. Explained what the little tubes and bottles of color were for." She blushed. "Also, I got what she called 'unmentionables.' I had no idea women on Eart... here had such colorful choices."

"Great!" Jake said. "Now, model the bikinis."

Briana's face frosted over. "I did not buy such things," she said. "That type of clothing should not be worn in public, revealing almost everything for any passing male to see." She looked down toward the floor. "For me, the height of the hem on this dress is enough of a challenge to get comfortable with."

Before Jake could respond, one of the windows facing the ocean shattered. A piece of paper wrapped around a stone crashed onto the floor. Maurice picked the missile up.

"It says, 'We know where you live.'"

"Lemme see that," Jake yanked the paper away. "Some of the surfers are territorial around here, but I've had no trouble with them before."

"Look at the scrawl at the bottom," Maurice said. "I recognize it. The Crimsons... the gang that threatened the temple master when you visited."

"Well, we'll see about that," Jake said. "My old man has some deep connections with the SFPD. He'll get a request relayed to look into this down here."

"That will not accomplish anything." Maurice shook his head. "Except for fuzzy descriptions, there would be nothing to go on." He examined the note again. "Evidently, the hoodlums feel our interference needs to be repaid."

"Ah, our trip?" Briana asked.

Jake marveled. She was like a bitch bulldog with a steak in her teeth and refusing to let go.

"Yeah, the trip," he said. "Okay, so they found us. We'll start now. Get it over with. Maybe by the time we get back, they will be concentrating on something else."

He looked at Briana. "And maybe we will, too."

No Luck Involved

THE ELEVATOR doors opened on the twenty-seventh floor. A receptionist sat behind a desk in the foyer. Corridors ran off in four directions, two on each side. The paneling: burnished walnut, the carpet plush and deep. The atmosphere: quiet, reserved, as if for an exclusive club.

Briana stepped forward, teetering on shoes that gave her little lateral support. She tugged at the hem of her suit jacket. The briefcase containing the heavy printout pulled to one side. Maurice flanked on the left, ready to offer a hand if there were a stumble. Jake glanced at her face. It was a tense mask. Even so, dressed up in green, hair curled into a sophisticated do, she was a stunning figure.

He was trying, he told himself. Except for a few leers and occasional remarks about bikinis and such that slipped out, his behavior had to have been tolerable. He had kept his hands to himself. Not a single remark about how much this was costing him, but then not a single thank you either.

"Can I help you?" the receptionist said, breaking through Jake's reverie.

"The office of Mr. Emmertyn," he responded.

"Do you have an appointment?"

"Ah, yes. Yes, we do. Please show us which corridor — "

"I will let him know you are here." The receptionist indicated the seating area and then reached for her phone.

"No, wait," Jake said. "It is a surprise, actually. It's... it's his birthday."

The receptionist shook her head. "We hear stuff like that a lot around here. All sorts wanting to pitch insider information to the brokers. Like the other advisors, Mr. Emmertyn has strict orders not to be disturbed unless someone has an appointment."

Jake reached into his wallet, withdrew a five hundred dollar gift card, and dropped it on the desk. He glanced again at Briana, but she did not react. He scowled at the receptionist. "Perhaps you might remember he told you we were coming."

For an instant, the gatekeeper's eyes widened. Then she scooped up the card and pointed to the corridor on the left behind her.

"Three offices down," she mumbled and began busying herself with some papers on her desk.

Jake nodded, and the trio headed into the corridor. Soon, they were standing before a door bearing a placard reading 'Frederick Emmertyn, High Yield Investments.'

The three entered a small anteroom furnished with two couches and a small, low table in between. A second door much like the first adorned the far wall; a third, smaller one was on the right. Briana's heels clicked on a parquet floor that had replaced the carpeting down the long corridor. The overall effect magnified a dozen-fold that of the central reception area. It was as if there were a competition to see which could ooze the greater air of wealth and privilege.

Jake walked over to the door on the right and pulled it open. A heavy winter coat hanging on a hook swung into view. A clothes rod was dimly visible in the dark interior. "New York," he said looking back at the other two. "Snowy winters."

He ducked in his head. "And it looks like there is room for some storage off to the left."

"Get out of there!" Briana commanded. "I want to talk to this man, not be thrown out before I can say a single word."

Jake emerged and studied the decorations for a moment. "Look at that." He pointed at one of the panels on the opposite sidewall. "Like something from your temple, Maurice."

"Yes, what looks like a wheel from a large sailing ship is the eight spoked Dharmachakra," Maurice said. "Each spoke represents one step along the Noble Eightfold Path. Next to it is the lotus flower, the symbol for purity. Emmertyn is a Buddhist."

The big man swung his head around to study the wall with the closet. "And over here is... that image is not from Buddhism," he said, puzzled. "It is Shiva, the Hindu god whose duty is to destroy all of the worlds at the end of creation. And next to him is the Ying-Yan of Taoism."

Silently, Maurice resurveyed the decorations on the two walls and then spoke again.

"No, not a Buddhist. The occupant of this office is an eastern religion junkie! Or maybe his clientele is. People like that hop from one set of beliefs to the next. Searching for the quick fix. The simple prescription explaining everything."

"Briana, are you sure?" Jake asked. "Sure this flake is the one you want to talk to?"

"The computer evidence was compelling." Briana nodded. She approached the inner door and knocked crisply.

There was no immediate answer. She knocked again.

"A moment. Give me a moment," a voice sounding drugged or only half-awake came from behind the door. There was some shuffling, and then the entry opened. Standing there was an elderly man, hair white and flowing. A straggly beard adorned his chin as if it were part of a costume poorly made. Granny glasses cocked to one side. His unkempt visage contrasted sharply with an expensive three-piece suit.

"You interrupted me while I was contemplating a trade," Emmertyn growled. "You do not have an appointment. The receptionist should have not let you pass. Now, I will have nausea that might last for hours."

"How are you so lucky?" Briana ignored the complaint.

Jake watched her serious expression. She reminded him of a runaway boulder crashing downhill. She was not going to be diverted.

Emmertyn's expression changed from one of annoyance to that of a child whose hand had been caught in the cookie jar.

"Lu — luck?" he stammered. "No respectable broker deals in luck. It is by careful analysis that profits are made."

"How is it you are able to buy and sell on intervals as short as five minutes and always be right?" Briana persisted. "How do you analyze things so quickly?"

She did not wait for an invitation and entered the inner office. The others followed. It was decorated in much the same way as the outer reception area, the walls filled with images of Shinto shrine gates, the god Ganesha, and half a dozen vajras. An uncluttered desk contained only a clock, a notepad and a small incense burner from which rose thin strands of smoke. A massive four-drawer safe stood to one side.

"Over sixty years we have worked together. He told me he would not tell," the trader muttered as he shut the door behind them. He frowned for a second, and then, as if he were a drowning man grasping at a piece of driftwood, asked, "You *are* from the FBI, right?"

"Yes, the FBI," Jake said quickly. He pointed to Briana's briefcase. "Insider trading. We have the evidence right here. Show him, agent... ah, agent — "

131

"The charm of prophecy," Briana cut him off. "How did you come to know it? Did a client give it to you?"

"A charm? What do you mean, a charm? What are you talking about?" Emmertyn said.

"'Thrice spoken, once fulfilled,'" Briana said. "The Rule of Three — the fundamental law. Sorcery. Isn't that what you are doing?"

Emmertyn staggered back against the desk front. "Yes, three times repeated," he said quietly. He looked at Briana as if he had only seen her for the first time. "How do you know?"

"The *how* you have to worry about now is how to come up with — sixty years, was it? — sixty years of restitution that will be the basis for your fine. And not only the commissions but the base prices considered as well."

"Sixty years!" Emmertyn cried. "Even though each trade was small, the total would come to millions. I have not salted away anything like that."

"Cooperate," Jake commanded. "Tell us everything. If you do, then maybe something can be worked out." He looked at Briana and smiled, hoping she noticed how clever he was being.

Emmertyn sighed deeply, walked around his desk, sat down, and then stared silently at one of the images on the wall to the right.

"Actually it is a relief," he said at last. "After all these years." He looked back at the trio and motioned for them to sit. "I only have a single client, and as of late, he ignores completely the advice I give him. There is no longer any pleasure there."

"Did your client give you the charm?" Briana asked again.

"No, no, not my client," Emmertyn said. "I have been careful from the very beginning. Only making small transactions. All of them going through many different intermediaries, so they do not attract attention."

"The artwork on the walls?" Briana asked.

"I need it to help my mental imagery."

"So, what's your performance record?" Jake asked. "How can you possibly make a living with only one client and piddling returns?"

Emmertyn looked at the wall for a moment and then continued. "Ganesha has been kind. He cleared the obstacles, oh, so many times. They are much better than the averages — perhaps twenty percent a year more."

"Twenty percent," Jake said. "You mean if the return of the market in general is, say, six percent, yours is seven point two?"

"No, if the market rises six percent, then my client's wealth increases by twenty-six. A doubling approximately every three years."

"Then in sixty years, one dollar becomes a million!" Jake said. "The Rule of Seventy-two. One hundred bucks becomes one hundred million."

"Yes, that is right," Emmertyn said. "One has to focus on the ways of the kami. Use their power to part the veil between now and other tim — "

"You haven't answered *my* question," Briana said. "How did you come to know the charm?"

"I *do not* know anything about *charms*," Emmertyn protested. "I already told you that."

"In your own words then," Briana said.

"It began some sixty years ago." Emmertyn nodded. "I was starting out. But the big trader environment didn't suit me. It was too rigorous, too constrained. Too many laws."

He pressed his hands to his forehead and began kneading his brow. "Oh, the ache! I can feel it coming on already. I should not have stopped."

"In your youth, you were not following the Noble Path, right?" Maurice asked gently. "I... we can relate to that."

"Yes, I bounced from one firm to another, but for each one of them, I could not generate enough of a client base to survive. One by one, the few I did have abandoned me for others. I was headed for rock bottom and did not see how to avert becoming destitute. Alone in my apartment in a cold and hostile city, I started learning about eastern religions, looking for solace, a reason for being. On a lark, I drank some peyote tea before starting meditation hoping to find some new avenues, some new answers to my plight."

Emmertyn stopped and smiled, as if he were overcome with a sudden feeling of peace. "It is hard to describe, really. I took the drug, tried to unlock my mind and then... and then, words started coming to me. Strange words, words with no meaning. Words not in any dictionary I could ever find. But I felt compelled to speak them aloud, to hear how they sounded when they were cast into the air.

"After a while, I don't know how long, they stopped. And the strange thing was, as exotic and unfamiliar as they were, I somehow was able to remember them all. To prove that to myself, I recited them again, and then a third time to be absolutely sure."

"Okay, you were on a trip. We get that," Jake said. "And now you are going to tell us about the wonderful things you saw and felt."

"Nothing strange and wonderful," Emmertyn said. "On that first time,

I remember... I remember looking at the clock." He glanced down at his desk and pointed. "This very one. And even though the numbers were twisted like those painted by a debauched typographer, I saw the clock read a few minutes ahead. I knew because I had started my meditation precisely on the hour. The discipline helped me keep on track with my study every day."

"Like the oldest of the sagas," Briana said softly. "How the first charms were discovered by accident on Murdina. Sorcery. The craft *is* practiced here on earth after all!"

"I don't know anything about sagas either," Emmertyn shook his head. "It was the Jade Emperor, Shiva, Omoikane, and the others who led the way." He stopped rubbing his head and looked at the trio, his eyes wide with wonder. "After a few minutes, the clock numerals blurred for a moment and then again became crisp and clear — sharp and glowing. I looked at my wristwatch, and they agreed. I could not quite believe what had happened. It was as if, as if..."

The broker's face softened. "Don't you see? The impossible had occurred. For a brief time, I could see a little bit... minutes into the future."

The expression of rapture turned into a scowl. "And I had a headache that lasted for the rest of the morning."

"'Liberated mind is the greatest bliss,'" Maurice said.

"Yes, I recognize Buddha's words," Emmertyn nodded. "But when the throbbing is at its peak, I sometimes wonder."

"So you went on strange peyote trips," Jake said. "Big deal. Others have had experiences even more bizarre."

"Perhaps few others did so with the proper practice of meditation *and* a mind filled with the lore of not one religion but several," Emmertyn said. "Each with but a piece of a greater truth.

"The next day," the broker continued, "I repeated what I had done. Started at the same hour and took the same dose of the drug."

He extended his index finger as if he were making an important point while lecturing. "Only this time other words came. None matched those of before. In a panic, I pushed them out of my thoughts. I wanted to repeat exactly what I uttered before. I discovered the original words were still in my memory, so I spoke them three times again. And again, the numbers on the clock seemed to change for a few minutes and then fade back to agree with my watch.

"What does resetting clocks have to do with the stock market?" Jake asked.

"Why everything!" Emmertyn replied. "Seeing into the future, even a little bit, is all that is needed to make a lot of money. I performed more experiments. First saying the words and then looking at the stock ticker on my monitor. I remembered a few of the trades scrolling past and then after the spell or whatever it is was over checked the ticker again."

"Impossible!" Jake said. "Nobody can do that. No matter how high they get."

"Nevertheless, for me it worked. I really did not require *any* clients, none. I disassociated from everyone who remained. My personal needs were few. I only traded for my own account and made each trade low enough to go by unnoticed. Gradually I accumulated enough capital to rent the small office here. As far as anybody could tell, I was a small-time broker, a modestly successful one, but no more."

Emmertyn sighed again. "Things went along so smoothly that I must admit I became a little bored about how easy life had become. Even with my earthly needs satisfied, I still could not follow the Eightfold Path. None of my meditations gave me any hint about how to handle the ennui.

"Then one day, completely unsolicited, I received a letter from what I assumed to be a potential client with a request very unlike the others I occasionally would get. It was beguiling in its naïveté — perhaps a student's school project, I thought at first. The sender asked if he could open an account. Only wanted to put the grand sum of one hundred dollars into it. My instructions were to invest it as I saw best, then liquidate everything at the end of one week's time and wire the net proceeds back to him.

"I tried to explain the fees for buying and selling for such a small sum would eat up most of the profits and could dip into principal as well."

"'No matter,' I was told as we communicated back and forth. It was part of a competition, an experiment testing how random the market was. The end measure would be the return on the investment compared to the change in the market average over the same period. The client stated he was starting with 128 smalltime brokers like myself picked at random from some directory. Had all of us make the same sort of trades."

"This is getting boring," Jake said. "He's starting to sound like my old man."

"Patience!" Briana snapped. "This is important. Let him finish. This client. Could it be? Have I guessed correctly? To escape and then thrive, the exiles needed wealth. And what better way to get it than in this practice of trading intangible things the humans called stocks. Trading quietly over many years."

"There is little more to tell," Emmertyn ignored her words. "The result of such an experiment should indeed be random. Over a one-week period, I would suppose an investment would outperform the market half of the time. But I was intrigued and did as I was asked. And because of what the near future told me, I was able to make a small profit, guaranteed."

Emmertyn stopped for a moment like a storyteller preparing his audience for the climax. "But it did not end there. The next week there was another trial request and then a third one after that. And for these there were restrictions. I had to make new investments different from the ones before — different stocks, different sectors even.

"And of course, because of my advantage, I was able to produce a profit each and every time. Small to be sure, but consistent nevertheless. Finally, after seven trials, I received notice that I had won. But when it was over I realized I should not have even bothered with the contest from the very beginning — that I did not want the client to be bragging about what I could do. In exchange for serving as his broker in the markets — and for other business transactions as well — I had him swear to secrecy, which he was eager to do. I have provided service for several decades since."

"*Who* is he?" Briana asked with more urgency. "Where can I find him?"

Emmertyn open his mouth to speak again, but then immediately slammed it shut.

"I have told you enough," Emmertyn said.

"Ah, the FBI, remember?" Jake said.

Emmertyn shook his head one final time. "You may have a case that I used information not available to the general public to guide my trades. But my client knows nothing of it."

The broker's jaws grew firm. "I do not care for what our interactions have turned into recently, but, nevertheless, for sixty years he has honored my request for confidentiality. I honor his."

"This is *so* like the sagas," Briana marveled. The quest never proceeds in a straight line. The heroine has to adapt, find a way to continue on the trail. She looked around the bare office. "If there is a new clue to follow, it might be here somewhere."

Jake shook his head. This was so like her. Part of her allure, he guessed. Exotic ramblings making no sense whatsoever. But when one looked at her, there was no doubt she herself did fervently believe. Better to get her away before the broker finally demanded they show some IDs.

A Working Interface

THALING FINISHED adding the final control buttons to the tracker. The gremlin had taken longer than he had wanted to complete, what he called ... the 'interface' to the keypad and digital displays. But now that work was done. Everything was physically connected. It was time to make everything perform magically.

He looked about his hidden alcove and smiled. The sprites stood ready, like toy soldiers arrayed for battle, their pens full of ink. The ritual was similar to the one before, but of course, not exactly the same. And once the protocol was completed, the augmented tracker would contain almost all of the additional functionality needed. The clock was the countdown mechanism; the keypad and displays, the destination selections.

Thaling felt a burst of pride about what he was doing. He was no mere plodding magician, but one of the first rank. He smiled at the discipline of the sprites anxiously awaiting his commands. After this step, he would have constructed another setter—another controller for the portal. He would be able to command where the doors opened upon throughout the universe — and when the movements should take place. He, not Angus or Dinton, will have provided the means for the escape from confinement — the means for the return to home and revenge.

There was, of course, one detail remaining to take care of. He had begun the calculations, but they were complex, not easily derived from only a few days contemplation. He had to make sure that when he instructed the portal with what he had built, there would be no interference. Commands from the other setter blocked out, completely ignored. Otherwise, if both were instructing at the same time, who knew what could happen.

Yes, it would take a while to derive the final ritual, but it was the course of prudence. He expanded his lungs with what the natives would call tainted air. Thoughts of his mate, Alika, danced in his mind.

Discovery

JAKE HURRIED back down the corridor clutching the purchases. Emmertyn had been quite brusque when he had finished his tale, ushered everyone out of his office, and shut the door.

At that point, Jake had been ready to leave. That was that. A second deed accomplished, and now he should be able to collect his reward. But, damn it, no! Briana's quest was not complete. She was insistent. She had to contact Emmertyn's client; she *had* to.

He shook his head. Briana's behavior in the broker's office was a side of her he had not seen before. More like a DA grilling a witness than playing hard to get. Despite the frustration, he found himself smiling. *Shangri-La!*. In the end, this one was going to be oh so sweet.

Jake tested the door to Emmertyn's anteroom, and, as he expected, it was now locked. He knocked loudly and waited. In a few moments, it opened, and Maurice ushered him in.

"What took you so long?" Briana asked.

"Gimme a break!" Jake said. "I am not familiar with the city. The cabbies knew it and racked up the fares driving all around before reaching where I wanted to go. Hardware stores and dental supply houses are not common in Manhattan."

"As Briana predicted, Emmertyn did not look too closely when he took his coat out of the closet," Maurice said. "We were able to scrunch up in the storage area, and he never saw us."

"Part of the aftereffects of the charm," Briana added.

"What is all this charm business?" Jake asked. "No, forget that for now. Let's see if Maurice can pull off what he says he can."

"It will take the two of us," Maurice said. He shrugged. "From one of my previous lives... before I began trying to walk the Noble Path."

The Buddhist hesitated for a moment. "I realize I was the one who came up with this plan," he said. "But I am not sure if we should go ahead. Buddha says 'It is better to do nothing than to do what is wrong.' We are breaking and entering here."

"We're not going to take anything," Jake said. "Just look around. Right, Briana?"

"Yes, that is all," Briana said.

"To find the right thing to do is so confusing." Maurice sighed. "We are not to do what is wrong. But the fourth step on the Eightfold Path is Right Action — acting without selfish attachment to our own agendas."

"Maurice, do you have any agenda here?" Briana asked.

"Well... no." Maurice shook his head. "I am merely going with the flow. What will happen, will happen."

He crossed the floor to the inner door and stretched himself out prone in front of it. "Hand me the dental mirror," he said to Jake, "and get comfortable alongside of me here."

Jake complied and watched Maurice slip the little circular mirror on a stick underneath the inner door and turn it, so it faced upward. With his free hand, he motioned Jake to get his head closer to the floor. "Look at the reflection," he said. "You can see the doorknob on the other side and the little locking mechanism protruding from it. Your job is going to be keeping the mirror steady and focused on the knob."

Jake grunted, and Maurice rose to sitting. He grabbed the pliers Jake had purchased from the hardware store and began uncoiling one of the metal coat hangers from the closet. When it was a more or less straight piece of wire, he bent a little hook into one end and an ell about half way down its length. Then he inserted it under the door.

"Can you see the hook?" Maurice asked.

"Yeah," Jake said. "Now what?"

"Give me directions. Tell me how to guide the hook until it grabs the thumbturn."

"Okay, go an inch to my left. No, too much. Back, maybe a half..."

IN A few minutes, the inner door was open, and the trio entered. A thin mailer sat on the desk in addition to the clock and incense burner.

Briana looked about. "The safe," she pointed. "What we need probably is in there."

Jake shook his head. "The stuff you found on the net won't work on that baby. It looks like it is a Class One." He surveyed the room. "This is a dead end, Briana. Let's get out of here and go home."

Briana frowned. "Not so fast," she said as she scooped up the mailer. "Universal Systems (USX) Attention Ms. Ashley Anderfield, Department Head," she read aloud. "'RFP's are stamped on it several times. And the address is back in LA. One of the beach towns." She toyed with a strand of hair for a second, and then her eyes brightened. "Maybe *she* is one of the exiles or at least can lead us to them."

Her smile broadened. "And going back, this time, Jake, you can teach me how to drive."

JAKE CLIMBED out of the Tesla last and followed the other two up the stairs to his apartment. The car had behaved beautifully, but driving straight through with breaks only for snacks and recharging was tiring. They should have stopped longer rather than pushing on. But no matter; a hot shower and a familiar bed would fix up everything by next morning.

He reached into his pocket, checked his phone, and puzzled. There were over a dozen calls from Margo. Of course! He had turned it off when they were going to visit Emmertyn's office the second time. And the driving lessons and stewing about Briana had filled all his thoughts on the way back home.

He was about to turn it on but then, thought better of it. Later, after Briana was out of earshot.

"I'm sure we closed everything up when we left," Maurice said as they reached Jake's floor. "But look. The door is ajar."

"What? Lemme see," Jake said. He moved to the front, flung the door all the way open, and gasped. The plywood paneling he had installed over the broken window before they left was still there. But that was all. The living area was vacant, no TV, not one piece of furniture. He ran to his bedroom, and it was the same, completely bare. No bed, no dresser, no clothes in the closet, nothing.

Briana and Maurice confirmed it was the same in their rooms and the kitchen. What was going on here? Impulsively, he turned on his phone and clicked on the first of Margo's messages.

"He's found out, Jake! He's found out!" the phone recited. "I'm on the street with only the clothes on my back. I don't know what to do. Call me! Call me as soon as you get this!"

Jake hit reply, but the phone voiced "Number no longer in service."

He was amazed and confused at the same time. Margo gone? His father had found out. How? Did that have something to do with the apparent burglary?

"You will have to leave now," someone said from the doorway. "I represent the property manager. Your lease has been cancelled."

"What! What for?" Jake demanded. His senses reeled. "What happened?"

"Well, first, the visitors over the last few days, always asking about you, where you were, annoying the other residents." He waved his hands, palms up. "And then when your father called and bought out the lease at a price we couldn't refuse..."

"He did this, my father?"

"Well yes. He took care of everything. The removal of all of your possessions. The cleaning. You will have to go now." He hesitated for a moment. "And if I were you, I would be quick about it. I think a few of your 'friends' might still be lurking about, waiting for your return. That Tesla really shouts 'Look, here I am.' And, oh, I am to tell you to leave it in your parking spot. The repossessors will be here for it tomorrow."

For a moment, Jake said nothing. Then, like a discarded marionette, he sagged to his knees. Suddenly, everything was fading away — his cool apartment with the ocean view, surfboards, money for his next meal. They *all* were vanishing.

Like a hollow egg, the shell he had built to shield himself from the meaningless of it all cracked into a thousand pieces. There were no longer going to be diversions to distract him. His very soul felt naked.

"Fine," Jake managed to say. "Just fine." The words came with difficulty, one by one. "I will show him he can't do this. Yeah, we'll get a motel somewhere nearby for tonight, and tomorrow..."

The words trickled away from him. Tomorrow... what?

"Not my business of course," the property rep said, "but your father did mention he had cancelled your credit cards as well." He shook his head and marveled. "Your dad must be a real mover to pull all of this off."

"I know a place where we can hide," Briana said. "It means sleeping on open ground, but spring is starting, and we will be warm enough there." She slapped at her backpack. "As for me, everything I need is in here."

Jake tried to shake off the weight of what was happening to him. He looked at Briana, frowning at how unfazed she seemed. So confident, so... so *bold*.

"What's going on?" he swept his arm around the emptiness. "Is all of this a bad dream, an illusion?"

"To paraphrase Buddha slightly," Maurice said, "*All* the world is an illusion."

"Don't start me on that crap," Jake could no longer contain himself. His thoughts raged out of control. He turned and threw an angry stare at Briana. "The next thing you'll be telling me is now we have to travel to Switzerland because reality is a bunch of Higgs... Higgs —"

"Higgs bosons," Briana said. "I read about them on the internet when I was researching. At CERN, they —"

"We need cash in order to eat!" Jake snapped as he tried to recover himself.

"I know a place where you can work for meals," Briana said. "Probably bussing and helping in the kitchen, but at least it is something."

Jake looked around the empty apartment one more time. But that was all he could manage. He could barely think anymore. It was better not to. Just retreat. Retreat like a wounded turtle into its shell and hope this will all go away.

He grasped at one last straw "The bastard's not taking my Tesla," he growled.

"Right," Briana said. "We will need the car to take us to meet Ashley Anderfield."

Part Three

An Expanded Reality

The Staff Meeting

ASHLEY ANDERFIELD froze her face into a pleasant mask. She looked at the other department managers one at a time. The last three months gone without even one contract win. This was going to be painful to Robert sitting on her left, but she had to look after her own. More than that. Ultimately, the job of everyone in the room was at stake as well.

She wanted to fan her face to make up for the overtaxed air-conditioning unit, but she didn't dare. That would be a sign of weakness. The entire spring had been mild, but Mother Nature was making up for it as summer approached.

Ashley was quite striking. A woman in her mid-forties, hair dark as a moonless night, high cheeks with only a hint of blush, and lips saying come-hither and kiss me. It gave her no advantage, she reminded herself time after time. These engineers were left-brain. True, probably every woman in the division was ranked on a tradeoff matrix somewhere. But here in the conference room, what was between the ears counted the most.

The room was small, only large enough to seat six at most at the long table in its center. The walls were unadorned except for a single whiteboard, the tables and chairs no-nonsense metal and cheap plastic. It had to be that way throughout every one of the engineering buildings. Ashley remember the explosion that had happened when she had ushered the Marine Brigadier General into the Division Manager's office, and he saw the walnut paneling, plush seats, and expansive desk.

"I know you think a lot of Sheila." Ashley focused on Robert. "But remember what happened on the Southrim Project. Alan, in my shop, had to come and fix her work. He should be the last one above the line."

Robert gestured at the list of names on the whiteboard. He straightened his posture as he always did before speaking. "You're getting greedy, Ash. All of us think our own troops are the best, but we all have to share the pain."

145

Ashley smiled inwardly. Good. He did not come back with anything of substance. Only the same, old 'pity me, the poor baby,' approach.

"Keep it quantitative, Bob. Stick to the facts." the laboratory manager, Douglas, said. He looked around the room wearing one of his condescending smiles he thought made him appear friendly and likable. "Our goal is to rank everyone across the entire lab in one list. Then we draw the line underneath the last name above the eighty percent mark. The twenty percent below will be laid off. Doesn't matter what department they're in."

"Then how come miss pretty face here has the most above the line?" Robert's voice hardened. He stretched his back even straighter.

"Maybe because she recruited well." Douglas grimaced in distaste. "She looked a little more closely at the applicants than only to see if they passed the mirror test."

"The mirror test?" Dave asked. Unconsciously, he wrung one hand in the other. "Excuse me. I know I am the newest one here, but I haven't heard of that."

"If the applicant breathed on a mirror and it fogged up, it meant he was not dead," Tom said, mimicking Douglas's tone as best he could. "All it took to get an offer from Robert."

"Gentlemen, gentlemen..." Douglas hesitated. He smiled even more patronizingly at Ashley. "And lady," he said. "We do not have all day to do this. I have to take the list to HR at eleven, so they can start the paperwork. We need to get this done fast, so rumors of more layoffs to come do not start."

"Right," Tom said. "But that'll be true only until the next round *does* come."

That was unexpected, Ashley thought. Usually, Tom followed Douglas' lead closely. Maybe now was the time to add something to the discussion. She knew better than only to remain quiet unless spoken to.

"Perhaps, we should be paying more attention to the cold RFPs," she said. "Or maybe do something bold to improve the performance on the projects we have... something to attract more warm ones."

"Yeah, yeah. We know what a hot-shot project manager you were before the promotion to the line," Robert said. His back could not possibly be even more straight. If you stood him against a wall, not one photon would be able to wiggle behind him from one side to the other. "Change control boards, preliminary design language, earned value spending forecasts, and so on, and so on..."

Ashley felt her stomach lurch. Don't be drawn down that path, she told herself. Personal attacks are what the others would look for. Just like a woman, unable to control her emotions. Instead, stay focused on the goal. Save as many of her department as she could. The words spoken here would fade. She glanced at the board.

"I received a cold RFP a while back," Ashley ignored the barb. "Some company in Hawaii — Kahuna Enterprises."

"Right," Robert continued his attack. "A little outfit in the islands is going to fix the shortfall when our work for the Fort and the Company dry up. The big overruns this past year did not help one bit."

The loss of budget control was the cause of their problems, true. But talking about them led the conversation away from where she wanted it to go. A non-sequitur. Expected. Now to get Robert to dig his hole even deeper.

"What they want seems fairly simple," Ashley said. "The tanks we use for exotic gas transport. Wants on-call remote technical support. Be able to answer the phone and speak English rather than gobbledygook."

"Sounds like you need an English major for something like that. Your department is supposed to concentrate on operations research," Tom said. He pulled on his coat sleeves so that the shirt cuffs showed exactly the same amount as did Douglas'. "Or are you going to claim Alan was actually an English double major in college?"

Tom was butting in. She hadn't expected that. She wanted him also to kick Robert when he was going down.

"No." Ashley kept her voice calm. "I have also received a resumé from a grad student working on his PhD at Wagonbrook, you know, the online university."

"How can you think of hiring somebody when we are in the middle of deciding who to lay off?" Tom tugged at his coat again. He was not going to make it this time. He needed to have used Douglas' tailor when he bought the thing.

"I think I have figured out a way," Ashley said. "A way not detracting from anything already budgeted."

Her administrative assistant was due for maternity leave soon, and the money for that was an overhead allocation no one questioned. That would provide the resources she needed to respond to this blue bird. The color of money problem this created she would have to work out later. For now, the task was saving bodies. And if Tom was not going to join in, it was time to make the stroke.

"Look, let's put Alan in place of Sheila as the last name on the list," she said. "That's our eighty percent, and we are done. You are right,

147

Douglas. It is getting close to eleven. No use in haggling over someone who may or may not be in the bottom twenty percent. The others remaining, we do not have to rank — only give them the bad news."

"Damn it!" Robert said. "You always find some way to wiggle out of the sack, down to the very last. Gimme a break here. We are only talking about one last name. I have bled enough already."

No one else spoke for a moment, as Douglas put on his pondering face. "Ash is right, Robert," he said at last. "We could haggle forever and never get it one hundred percent perfect. Go back to your own departments. Betty will come in here, transcribe the names, and give each of you a list of which ones of yours are safe. And, oh, Ash, come into my office for a minute, before I have to rush off to HR."

The other department managers left, all of them with shoulders slumped and heads down. When she finally faced up to it, Ashley knew hers would sag, too. A line manager's greatest failure was having to let one of his own go. USX was a matrix organization. Each department was like a small company within the larger one. Project managers came to the line with job assignments and the line manager assigned the engineers to do the work.

Yes, she had done well, Ashley thought, better than the others… but not perfectly. She, too, had bad news to tell.

Heat

DINTON SQUINTED his eyes nearly shut, crossed his legs and settled himself in his own chamber. He felt a numbness starting to creep even up to his thighs. Except for the Clue game box and a stack of newspapers, the cavern was completely bare. Only a glimmer of light filtered in from the rocky passageway. It was quiet. He liked it that way.

"I shall practice no craft," he whispered to himself as the urge began to return. It always returned. But how could he demand it of his brothers if he did not abstain as well? No, after the last time there were to be no more. This time he would have the strength, the strength to resist.

He closed his eyes to push the temptation away, but as usual, that was a mistake. Cut off from other senses, the desire washed over him like gentle surf climbing a beach. It felt so good when his mind went racing, out of the caverns, out over the oceans, even to lands more distant than a bird could fly.

He breathed in the relaxing rhythm — breath in through the nose for a count of seven, hold for four more, then exhale through the mouth for a final five. With each repetition, his body calmed.

As he had done many times before, Dinton imagined his thoughts appearing on a chalkboard before his inner eye. Soon as one appeared, he quickly erased it away. Finally, he was at peace and ready to begin the charm.

The spell was a long one. Enunciating each word correctly three times through was difficult, but was the way it always had to be. Only the most accomplished would succeed. A smile formed on Dinton's lips as he thought about how skilled he was, but he gently pushed the pleasure aside, waiting for the first glimmer of contact with the natives who roamed the world above at will.

There was more than a single spell of far-seeing. Many charms of enchantment existed as well. But this one was different. It incorporated elements of both. He felt like a sturdy watercraft from his home world skimming over the sea. Fish glimmered beneath the surface, some tiny as minnows, others as large as leviathan whales. Each was the mind of a native, barely out of reach, tantalizingly near, begging to be swooped up and caught.

Who was it to be this time? One the natives called a 'political analyst,' or even better, one who actually ruled? No matter, the strategy was not one of bold strokes. Instead, it consisted of undetectable gentle nudges, feathers of persuasion tipping decisions in the way he wanted them to go.

There were always many choices from which to choose. The movie star activist espousing famine relief in a continent far away. He could be distracted by the demands of his craft and become silent. The naysayer who screeched that global warming was merely weather variation, or if true, not the work of men. He could be emboldened to seek wider platforms for his views. After a single year of conservation, a governor could rescind water restrictions while still in the middle of drought.

Whale harvesting quotas? The glimmer of consciousness caught Dinton's attention. Excellent. One of the newspapers had mentioned something about that. There had been some animosity at the last meeting of what the natives called nations. Many wanted the yearly total revised still further downward, but a minority resisted with vigor.

Dinton tested the tendrils of thought of those sitting around the large ornate conference table until he recognized the resolve of one of the resistors. He cast a second charm, this one much shorter than the first, and in a few heartbeats, a part of the human's subconscious was no longer totally his own.

The suggestion was a simple one, a slight increase in emphasis competing with arguments that rebutted. Despite the compromise offered, the delegate would not yield. For another year, the harvest quotas would remain the same.

Dinton pulled his own thoughts out of the meditation. He let his smile complete. Keeping the quota the same, by itself, probably did nothing of course. But it was another example of agreement not reached, of resources continuing to be squandered away, of opportunities not acted upon until it was too late. And these little things would add up, piling on one another until the meetings became so hostile they would be abandoned. The base instincts of the natives were not so very different from his own.

Yes, all these little things would contribute. He recalled his experiment of a few years before. Never again had he been able to find the mind of the little shop owner to see how his idea fared. Had the gnome of a man managed to stumble onto the workings of true alchemy? Had he managed to concoct a potion that turned the most mild-mannered native into a savage blood-lusting beast? Would the patrons who consumed the philter also contribute to the downfall of human kind?

No matter. With enough paths being trod, eventually, resources would dwindle and be hoarded by those with wealth. And after that, wars would blossom between those who had them and those who did not. Blossom like weeds in a garden that once swayed in a gentle wind with so much beauty.

As he kept telling his brothers, patience was all they needed. Trust in the eldest. He alone saw the path leading to freedom. He alone was gently manipulating the affairs of men so there would be no doubt of their extinction.

It would be better, of course, if the mental connection were firmer — strong enough so total enchantment could be achieved, total control of another's will to act as commanded. But the charm he was casting now did not work that way. The distances were too far, the connections too weak. It was only by his skill any small changes could be made at all.

He glanced at the pile of newspapers, the older ones yellow and brittle from the heat. At first, he had ignored them, unintelligible symbols on flimsy parchment serving no purpose. But Angus had insisted they had value. Patiently, his brother had instructed him in the written language, as he had learned it from the recluse on the surface.

And the more examples Angus obtained, the more Dinton learned. Without that knowledge, what he sensed in the enchantments would be only useless babble. But there was risk in what Angus was doing. He had to be handled carefully. Repeated scoldings about his traffic with the native. Not so much that his sibling would stop all together, but enough to keep his indiscretions in bounds.

"I am in heat," a voice broke through Dinton's reverie.

The exile turned toward the passageway, and his smile broadened. "My love," he said. "As usual, your visits to my own lair are always a surprise, but nevertheless most welcome."

"I am in heat," Dinton's mate repeated. "We can even do it here. My need is great, and I do not care. When the child comes, we can give him one of the rings abandoned by the others."

Dinton sighed. "We are closer, Fretha, but the time is still not here."

"Why must we wait until the natives are gone?" Fretha said. "You explain it every time that I have need, but I am never convinced."

"We have responsibilities that go beyond our lusts," Dinton said. "Can you not imagine how horrible it would be for a little one to endure the emptiness we have now? No, let us continue to wait until the entire orb is ours to use as we wish."

"What about your own lusts?" Fretha asked. She dropped her skirt and bent over in the manner of a four-legged beast.

Dinton's pulse quickened as he viewed his mate in her readiness. He licked his lips and imagined what it would be like. It had indeed been so very long. He took one step, then a second, placing his hands on her hips.

"I am ready," Fretha whispered.

Dinton's hand trembled. With a gasp, he withdrew and stepped back.

"No! I said no, Fretha. Angus is up to something. I do not know what. I must keep my thoughts focused. Soothe his ego. If he were by some chance to win, get him to continue to choose Clue as the game to decide the one who holds the baton next. Get him not to wonder why I have been successful, so many times running.

Dinton sighed. Why did Angus challenge him so? Did he not realize that leadership was a burden, not a delight?

Fretha rose and readjusted her skirt. She stroked Dinton's bare cheek. "Your self-discipline is strong, my love," she said. "But I can tell that each time you come closer to doing what I desire. Somehow I will manage to wait again, and then we will see what happens."

Dinton started to reply, when another voice interrupted.

"I beg your pardon, Flock Leader," the intruder said. "I am called Jormind. And I have something to tell you that you must hear."

Reorganization

DOUGLAS' OFFICE was furnished like the adjacent conference room, the only difference being a picture of a wife and two kids hanging next to the whiteboard.

"Sit." Douglas motioned to one of the two chairs facing his desk as he slid around to be on the other side. He looked at Ashley for a moment without saying anything. Then his face contorted into his patented smile. Ashley was used to it by now.

"Ah, you have something to tell me?" she asked.

"Well, as you can figure out when you do the numbers, shrinking the lab by twenty percent means we can get by with one less department. One less department manager. Less overhead that way."

As a matter of principle, being a woman in what was still a man's world, Ashley always tried to hide what she was thinking from her expression, but this time she could not.

"You mean reorganization, right?" she asked.

"A natural part of what happens when the population changes by too much in a short time."

The words sounded to Ashley as if she should have known that. Well, it was obvious, but she had been too distracted thinking about what she was going to say to her engineers being cast aside.

"So, who gets the axe? Has Robert finally reached the end of his rope?"

"It's not quite that simple," Douglas said. "There will be changes higher up as well." He opened his arms and turned his hands palm upward like a priest receiving a blessing from his faithful. "I am going to be the new operations manager."

Ashley's heart skipped a beat. "You mean your position will be open, too? One less department certainly, but an entire lab…"

Her thoughts raced. She had had some misgivings about buying a house two years ago. No reason for it. It was really too big for her, living alone. No significant other. How could she have had one? Her job kept her busy so much more than merely 'full time.'

The monthly payments were steep. Ones even a department manager could barely afford. An investment she had told herself. It would be worth it. Another promotion and things would work out. Substantial annual bonuses. And now, sooner than she had expected, a lab manager...

"Don't get ahead of yourself, Ash." Douglas' plastered on smile faded. He chewed his lip for a moment. "I have made the decision. He hesitated for a second and then blurted. "And Tom will be taking over the lab."

Ashley's thoughts froze. The images of her sitting behind the oversized desk faded away.

"Tom! He is a good department manager, of course," she said slowly, trying to hold her voice level. "But I have been one longer and..."

"It makes sense when you think about it," she continued after Douglas did not react. "Robert is not qualified and Dave is too new."

"USX is in trouble, Ash," Douglas said. He shifted in his chair as if there were a burr there he could not avoid. "You know that. And we need our best people in positions where they can do the most good to bail us out."

He looked away toward the picture of his family. "You did *such* good work as a manager for the projects for the Fort, Ash. Such good work that we need you to take the reins on Golden Spirit. That one is all screwed up. The Company is threatening cancellation." The fake smile returned. "You can do it, Ash. I know you can."

"Do I have any say in this?" The words rushed from Ashley's mouth.

"Ah, wait. There's more."

"What?"

"I fought against this part of the decision, Ash. I really did. But sometimes HR becomes a boulder in the path that cannot be moved." He paused again. "We have to reduce our cost of doing business. Along with everything else, we really do."

Ashley studied Douglas' face. It was clear that the second shoe had not yet hit the floor.

"The project budget is so overrun it cannot afford your department manager salary, Ash. Even if you are the project manager. Your pay will have to be reduced to what it was before you joined my team."

154

"I qu — "

Ashley slammed shut her mouth before she said more. Action without thought was a recipe for disaster. She knew this. But back to project manager wasn't even a lateral arabesque. It was an insult! Probably something to do with the idea that women did not need to be paid as much because theirs was a second income for a family. But what to do? The project manager pay probably would not even meet her *mortgage* payments. She needed time to think things over.

"Who decided all of this?" she finally asked.

"I did."

"Has any of it been cast in concrete yet?"

"Not yet. The higher up reorg has to happen first. And I need to have my conversations with Tom and Robert."

"I see," Ashley snapped. "Then in the meantime, excuse me, I have some layoffs to attend to."

Without another word, she left the office.

Tigerwasps

THALING STEPPED out of Littlebutt's sphere into his own alcove, and the sprite disappeared back into the wall. The calculations for the mutual exclusion ritual were going well. None of the rockbubblers was causing problems. Now was the time for some more relaxing thoughts.

Of all the noxious little creatures under his sway, he had to admit Littlebutt was his favorite. He suddenly realized that when escape and revenge were complete, he did not know what he would do, release them or perhaps…

"I am going to see Angus." Dinton's voice cut in through the cavern opening. "Join me."

Thaling did not reply. Did his brother somehow suspect? "Why?" he asked, but received no answer. In silence, he followed Dinton clambering through the twisty lava tubes and gas tunnels that connected their prison together.

Angus dozed, head down on his desk when they entered his alcove, but that was no surprise to Thaling. With no direct contact with the cycle of the day, everyone's sleeping rhythm drifted one from another.

Dinton growled the battle challenge of their kind, and Angus immediately sprang awake, reaching for his dagger.

"Why do you accost me so?" the aroused exile said. "Our meeting is not for another three days."

"Angus, You have used *alchemy*!" Dinton said. "Even though the three of us have sworn. Reason enough to confront you now."

Angus sheathed his dagger. He looked at Dinton's unyielding face and then to his other brother. "Thaling," he said. "Help me dissuade Dinton of his fantasy. Help calm him down."

Thaling did not know what to say. Was it true that Angus had broken the oath? Did Dinton know that he had done so, too?

"Angus, one of your flock came to me," Dinton said. "Jormind is his name."

Angus put his hand back on the dagger's hilt. "A malcontent, no more," he said. "I did not permit his union with one of the unbound females, and he sought revenge."

"He took me to the garden pool," Dinton shook his head. "Showed me the traces remaining of what you had done. I had always wondered how you convinced the native to agree to trade. Gold dust. Is that what it is called?"

Thaling watched Angus' face struggling to reveal nothing of what must be bubbling inside. "It was harmless, my brothers. No alchemy was performed on the surface. The formula I activated was for only part of the smelting, not the entirety. None of the Faithful would have been able to detect."

"Nevertheless, you broke your oath. How can anything you do now be trusted?"

Angus remained silent as the grip on his dagger tightened.

"You are my brother," Dinton said. "But I am the one who carries the baton and must act for the good of us all." He turned to Thaling. "Disarm him and then… escort him to the wasp pit."

The words shocked Thaling. He was stunned. Acid in his stomach rose in his chest, searing the tissues as it passed. Angus, his brother, to be fodder for the wasps? And how could he be the one to disarm him? Thaling felt himself straighten his back as much as he could. Even so, Angus was a head-height taller, and the swiftness of his blade was known by all.

A tense moment passed while no one moved. Then, before Thaling had to act, a heavy tromp echoed from the connecting passage. The alcove filled with a half dozen more of the exiles — all from Dinton's flock.

Like a child's game of statues, no one moved, each waiting for an adversary to try something. A dozen heartbeats passed and then another. Angus studied the new arrivals as if calculating his odds in a game of chance. Then he released the grip on his dagger and turned to stare intently at Thaling.

"Brother, my fate is in your hands. I rely on you to do what is right."

The searing in Thaling's throat intensified. What was Angus asking him to do? Stand beside him in a fight, so the odds were reduced? Or did his younger brother suspect he too exercised one of the crafts also? Did he think it to be fair they both share the same fate?

Thaling shivered involuntarily. But the tigerwasps? How horrible. In many ways, the magic induced longevity was a curse. The growing pile of shed rings in Dinton's alcove was proof of that. But to finally expire in such a way…

Thaling's indecision was interrupted when, without waiting for further instruction, Dinton's flock members drew their own blades and converged on Angus. Dinton's brother growled defiance only once, and with a dramatic gesture raised his hand from his dagger hilt and held it palm open high in the air.

"Twist the middle finger to the palm and affix it there," Dinton said. "Twist it so the ring cannot be removed. A visitor to the pit serves as a continuing lesson for the rest of us as long as possible."

Thaling felt a sigh like the last gasp of a deflating balloon erupt from his lungs. He slumped to his usual bowed posture. He would not have to draw his own dagger after all.

"Middle brother, accompany me at the tail of the procession," Dinton commanded. "You shall be the official witness that all is done in accordance with the protocol."

Thaling nodded dumbly. He turned his head to avoid Angus' stare as he passed. In a moment, only the two brothers remained in the alcove.

"You hesitated when I asked you to disarm Angus," Dinton said. "I wonder. Is he the only one who has not adhered to the oath?"

THE BUZZ became almost unbearably loud before anyone got close. Thaling wanted to cover his ears, but knew he would lose face if he did. Stature was very important now. What would happen to Angus' flock? Would he get a share?

Far too soon, the troop arrived at the pit, so called because it was the lowest of the exile's chambers, almost too hot even for them. Thaling had not visited since the last victim was given to the wasps over two hundred orbits ago. But now, like the others, he could not resist looking through the thin sheet of mica providing a view into the insects' lair.

Like all such creatures from their home world, the wasps stood on four spindly legs and had what looked like too tiny wings on their backs. One would think the appendages to be puny, but the bugs could rear up on their rear limbs and stand the height of a native who lived on the surface above. Their massive bodies divided into four distinct segments:

head, thorax, abdomen, and tail, each as black and striped with yellow as the foulest heresy. Six multifaceted eyes reflected the soft glow of the grubs that had finished their meals and clung to the cavern's ceiling.

It was from the tail new larvae were extruded — after a conjoined mating lasting a full circle of the planet on its axis. But that only happened when a new host was shoved into the pit, a new source of infant food.

Thaling remembered watching when that last had happened. He had shouldered his way to the mica in front of the others who had also gathered. After all, what else was there to do?

After the mating was complete, the victim shrank into a corner rolling into a ball as best he could. The wasps stalked him slowly, almost as if they were savoring what was to come next and wanted to prolong it as long as they could. The insects were strong, strong enough that four of them could pry away the limbs trying to protect the host's midsection. Then when he was prone and face up on the rough cavern floor, the fifth slashed open the stomach with razor-sharp mandibles. Finally, the sixth exuded the egg into the open wound and then licked shut the incision with a thick mucus drool.

After the implanting, the watchers dispersed. There was little else to see — only the gradually weakening of the host as his internal organs were gradually dissolved and consumed. From time to time, one of the wasps would regurgitate some gruel and shove it into an unwilling mouth held open by mandibles. Because of the rings that could not be removed, the decay was not swift. The magic of longevity kept the victim alive far longer than would be expected. But eventually, even magic could not completely forestall the inevitable. The host grew weaker and weaker until he finally expired.

Thaling looked at the flock member sentenced what was now hundreds of orbits ago. He lay on the floor, eyes tearing with the continual pain, but otherwise unfocused. He had no strength left to stand or even sit up. The only thoughts must be ones praying for final release.

Around him lay the litter of plant stalks and uneaten leaves that served as food for both him and the imagoes. Whenever one of the exiles transgressed in a minor way, the punishment was to harvest from the garden and bring it here. This sentence lasted until someone else misbehaved and took his place.

Thaling puzzled at how he was feeling. He was going to lose a brother, someone who had endured with him in this captivity for a thousand years. It was not the same as he felt when he lost Alika. There was no true sorrow now. No rage. But there was *something* he felt, an emotion of... of bonding, of shared experiences, something that would now never be the same.

"Wait, Dinton," he surprised himself saying. "We both know that, although Angus is rash, he does not act without good reason. If he were to be lost to us now, we would never know *why* he performed the alchemy. Perhaps, in his own way, he was acting for the benefit of us all."

Dinton pondered. "Your brother speaks in your behalf, Angus," he said. "What would you tell us before you pass through to your doom?"

Angus struggled with the guards holding him in place and managed to turn and face Thaling. "Thank you, brother," he said quietly. "You have saved me. I knew you would." He thought for a moment. "Although, I would have liked it better had you come to your wits a little sooner before we got this close to the pit."

"Only for a moment," Dinton said. "Explain your actions to us. Act as a flock leader should."

"It is not something elucidated in a few words," Angus said. Thaling could tell his brother's normal bluster was rapidly returning. "Take off this fetter from my hand. Ensconce me somewhere and give me pen and ink. I will write everything down."

"A stalling tactic, nothing more," Dinton spat.

"Then, here is a tidbit setting you on the right trail for what I plan to do." Angus hesitated for effect. "Ashley Anderfield, USX, Redondo Beach, California."

"Gibber — " Dinton began, but then halted. "Where have I heard some of that before?" he mumbled aloud and then was silent. Finally, his voice of command recovered. "Very well. This does not have to be done in haste. Secure my brother and give him what he needs to write his confession. There is something else I will now explore."

The Interview

ASHLEY FORCED a welcoming smile as the applicant was ushered into her office. Compartmentalize, she told herself. The reorganization was not the only plate that was spinning. She rose and extended her hand across the desk. "Please, sit down," she said.

Raven black hair like her own. The beginnings of a scruffy beard. And dimples! Shouldn't a graduate student look a little bit older? But in all other ways, he was typical, almost a caricature. Glasses held together by a coil of duct tape, a slight stain on the white shirt, rumpled slacks.

"My name is Figaro Newton," the young man said as he sat. "My parents were from Italy. My mother's an opera buff and my father a barber. Changed their surname when they immigrated. Didn't really foresee what my nickname would be." He smiled back at Ashley. "Go ahead and call me Fig. I'm used to it."

At least he wasn't shy. She no longer had time to worry about how to integrate him with her other employees. Other *remaining* employees? She could not help herself from grimacing. And with the way things were headed, she wasn't going to end up with any at all.

Fig's face had contorted into a puzzle, Ashley realized. She was the one who was supposed to speak next, not the applicant who was at a natural disadvantage.

"I am looking for an intern," she rattled off. "Someone with a technical background who writes and speaks well. There is an RFP — a request for a proposal to provide technical support for getting through regulation paperwork. Paperwork for transporting a liquefied gas."

She tried another smile. "It's only for the summer. And the phone might not even ring. But the experience of what goes into writing a proposal might be useful."

"You mean like a grant application?" Fig asked. "And only for some handholding. Nothing with new technology?"

"Well yes, that's it. Look, the job is not like CERN. Do you want the work or not?" The words leapt from Ashley before she could stop them. Evidently, she could not keep her frustrations completely under control. She started over. "Let me rephrase that. I am curious. Why is a grad student, doing research with data from CERN of all places, applying for a summer internship at an engineering company, anyway?"

Fig ignored the outburst. "A very fair question," he said. "I *do* want to write my dissertation on the analysis of CERN data." He adjusted his glasses. "At least I think I do."

Then his voice shifted a bit higher. The words came faster. "But, well, even though Wagonbrook is not as expensive as the bigger names like Harvard and Stanford, it still has tuition. And so far, I do not have any fellowship support. I am paying my own way." He looked down at his belt buckle. "Actually, actually, yes, that's it. Actually, I have run out of cash."

"Berkeley isn't all that bad."

"I had... other interests in high school. My grades were only so-so." Like a storyteller trying to regain the interest of a bored crowd, he rushed on. "In fact, I dropped out. The program I was working on to predict airline fares sucked up all of my time."

"Then, how did you get into Wagonbrook?"

"Well, they aren't exactly accredited yet." Fig's speaking pace slowed back to something more normal. "But they are working on it. Maybe by the time I finish, they will be." His smile broadened as if he were sharing an in-group joke with a friend. "It's a case of either water over the bridge or under the dam."

"Water over..." Ashley said. "Hmm. I see."

She had gone ahead with the interview despite everything else happening with her own trajectory. USX wouldn't look good to cancel it before the guy even showed up. Besides, its best asset was the people it employed. In the long run, recruiting and hiring fresh talent would only help. Internships led to full-time jobs, and the company had a calibration on what they were getting.

Otherwise, when a work force surge was needed, Robert and his mirror test would be bringing onboard total incompetents like that woman who kept trying to get in touch with her. A total pest. First, weeks of phone calls. Then repeated visits that had to be turned away at the guard station — each time with a different fantastic story.

And this guy did not sound all that good of a match, either. She shouldn't have set up the interview in the first place. If his heart was in basic physics, he wouldn't want to stay with USX when the summer was over. And now because of the reorg, she wouldn't have the funds for him to write the proposal anyway. She scribbled a note on the pad in front of her to compose the applicant specific paragraph that would go into the rejection letter.

"I think the focus should be on making sure the lithium ion battery does not overheat," Fig said suddenly. "If the gas is liquefied, it has to be kept cool enough, so the vapor pressure does not get too high."

Okay, maybe not totally a dim bulb, after all, Ashley thought. But in any case, she should let things proceed normally. If she did end up accepting the demotion, or quitting, or whatever, then the letter could be one of the last things she would need to do to tidy up.

"Thank you for coming in," she said. "Ah, there's a lot going on here right now, but I'll get back to you within... within two weeks."

Fig nodded and stood up. His face betrayed he thought he had failed.

"In two weeks," he said. "Right. Sure you will."

Experiment Results

"CALIFORNIA," DINTON mumbled. "Where had I heard that before?"

He cleansed his mind, began the cadence of measured breathing, and like a beast searching for a scent, let his thoughts wander where they may. He did not speak any words of a charm. That was not the purpose of his meditation. This time, it was to retrieve a memory from years before. All of the nametags of the natives, of course, were unnatural and their memories not strongly held. But with practice and concentration, they could be retrieved.

"My experiment!" he exclaimed after a short while. The one he had guided onto the path of discovering alchemy. Yes, he was the one. Dinton had forgotten entirely about him since he did not have a solid hook with which to select his mind from the thought stream as it coursed by.

Like the soft whisper of a lover, the fragment suddenly revealed itself to him. *...Tats...Melrose Avenue...California...* Yes, that was what he had snatched away so many years ago. In addition, the gibberish Angus had recited when he was imprisoned repeated one of the words as well.

"Ashley Anderfield. USX, Redondo Beach, California." The words felt uncomfortable on his lips, but they would suffice. "Two minds with the same address," he mused. "Of course, there is no way of knowing how large a place this 'California' was, but suppose, just suppose, it was small enough that his experiment and this new target were close enough together that..."

Dinton's excitement broke him out of his meditation. Angus' confession also contained a *name* — the name of an individual — a gaff he could use to latch onto the mind in the stream. Yes, a mind that could test the potency of the alchemy he had caused to be performed.

Dinton paced his alcove waiting for the emotion to calm down. Despite the risk, he had to cast another charm — one more potent — one far easier to detect. He would need to practice his craft exactly — far more than a simple suggestion, one having some hint of compulsion that would make the target follow his command without questioning, without knowing why.

After several hundred heartbeats, he was ready. He squinted his eyes nearly shut, crossed his legs and settled. This time, he did not struggle with whether or not to engage in sorcery. This time, he succumbed to the urge with a willingness that was surprising. Angus would practice a craft no more. Thaling was too timid to try. He was Dinton, the one who had the wisdom, the foresight to see what eventually would come. The oath did not apply to him. It was only right what he was about to do.

Patiently, he sensed the minds streaming by, not bothered by how long it would take. Somehow, in a way he did not fully understand, there was a selection process performed by his own unconscious, pushing candidates into his awareness — ones the most likely to be the type he sought.

After a little bit more than an hour of native time, he caught his prey. It was a woman rather than a man! Surprising, but no matter. The lore of both the Heretics and Faithful alike contained tales of prodigious feats by female warriors rivaling those of the males. This Ashley would be the vessel, the measure of the potency of the alchemy his initial enchantment had caused to become so.

As he had done before, Dinton proceeded cautiously, not blasting his presence into the unsuspecting mind, but with a gentle touch pushing the thoughts and desires in the direction he wanted them to go.

Curiosity. Yes, that was the feeling to strengthen. Emphasize curiosity as the mechanism for seeking out a relief from pent up distress. She should go... go to where she had never been before. ... *Tats... Melrose Avenue... California...*

Dinton finished the charm and broke out of his trance. He smiled with a satisfaction he had seldom felt in his struggles with his brothers. Now it was a simple matter of from time to time monitoring what this Ashley was up to — how close she was to partaking of what the native alchemist had to offer.

Love Potion Number Nine

ASHLEY LOOKED in the store window on Melrose Avenue. It was the kind of place she was looking for. She felt quite pleased. What had attracted her to it? Tucked into an alley in a funky part of town like a quaint out of the way magic shop.

She really needed a change of pace. The five layoffs had taken her only a single day, but what a draining one it was. As she had registered the shocked expression of each engineer, her sense of failure grew. Were there any additional small projects with which she had not gotten in touch? Should she have been more aggressive when trying to shoulder her way into projects she had no business being involved? What else could she had done?

And so, as she always did when the burden of keeping her business family fed with robust job numbers became too much, she took a day off. Went to a part of town totally new and unfamiliar. Without thinking, let her impulses of the moment guide her. Absorbing the atmosphere and clearing her head was the goal. She had to gather strength to think through how to tackle the real problem — how to prevent the reorganization at USX from taking place.

The sign above the street windows proclaimed 'Tats and Stuff,' and the displays were aged with dust, probably not disturbed for years. A few sketches, yellow and curled with age, displayed simple designs that even Ashley knew were out of fashion. A scatter of small quartz and amethyst crystals fanned out on the display shelf next to what resembled a rack from a child's chemistry set filled with more than a dozen vials of colored liquids.

Ashley entered, and a small bell over the doorframe chimed. Immediately, she was struck by the strong smell. The odor of paint thinner, ether, vinegar, and ammonia competed for attention.

"This isn't a meth lab," a voice croaked from the opening to a room in the rear.

Ashley looked about. On the left, there was the standard tattoo chair with the small stool at its side, both covered in ebony Naugahyde, old and cracked with age. More sketches filled the wall behind. To the right was a long display case containing more crystals and vials. A flat, hinged panel blocked entry to the room beyond.

"Wanna tat?" A stooped troll-like man limped out of the back and attempted what was meant to be a smile. Only two teeth remained in a cavernous mouth. Jaws sagged with skin rough and pocked. A few wisps of hair covered a scalp with five or six small oozing sores.

Ashley took a step backwards, repulsed by the figure standing behind the counter. "Uh, no tattoo," she said. "I am only look — "

"They all say that at first," the little man said. "And call me Ziggy. The return customers do. Who recommended you?"

"No one." Ashley let a bit of the irritation of being interrupted show in her voice.

"Right answer," Ziggy said.

"What. Why?"

"I don't sell to braggarts who can't keep their mouths shut."

"As I was trying to say," Ashley's tone grew more unpleasant, "I'm only here to get a different perspective on a problem I am dealing with."

"No need for the back story," Ziggy interrupted again. "I don't really care. My potions work. They are worth the price. That is all there is to it."

"Potions?"

"Yes, love potions."

"Yeah, right," Ashley said. She could not believe the spiel she was getting.

"I can prove it." Ziggy pulled a small vial of clear liquid out of one of his pockets. Fumbling for a few moments in a drawer beneath the display of crystals, he produced an eyedropper. Then he pointed at the bottle poking out of Ashley's purse.

"I'll add three drops to your water, and you take a few sips. Then we'll see if it's 'yeah, right.'"

"I will do no such thing," Ashley said.

"No physical harm to your body," Ziggy said. "Watch me." He opened the vial, filled the eyedropper, tilted back his head, and let three drops fall into his open mouth. He wiped his lips with his tongue and then burped.

"The little bit of gas is the only side effect." He looked at a small

167

mirror on the wall behind him. And smiled at what he saw. "Ah, beautiful," he said and then turned back to Ashley. "Now your turn."

Despite herself, Ashley was intrigued. She knew she should leave, but her purpose for this whole afternoon was to get into a different mindset.

"I'll give you a couple hundred bucks to do it," Ziggy persisted. From another pocket, he produced two bills and slammed them down on the counter top.

Ashley leaned forward to inspect the Benjamins. They looked real enough. They could cover the cable bill if nothing else. What the hell. She shrugged. Nothing ventured, nothing gained. She moved quickly before she could change her mind, pulled the water bottle from her purse, unscrewed the cap, and thrust it forward.

Ziggy added the drops, and Ashley swirled the bottle so they were diluted as much as possible. Then she took a cautious sip.

For a moment, nothing happened. Then change swept over her body. She began to tingle. A blush blossomed on her cheeks.

"Should hit you right about now," Ziggy said.

Ashley looked at the little gnome, and arousal burst over her in all the right places like the first flowers of spring. He was handsome, virile beyond belief. How could she have not seen that before!

Short, short and broad. Of course, the perfect body shape. No thin beanpole with ugly muscles bulging where the skin should be without ripples. And the head. What an astonishing head! Not completely bald but with interesting blemishes artfully placed. Lips full and sensuous, hiding a tongue probably long and sinuous and not blocked by useless teeth that would only get in the way.

Without fully understanding what she was doing, Ashley dropped the bottle and her purse. Frantically, she began unbuttoning her blouse.

"Slow down and wait a minute," Ziggy held up his hand as if it were a teasing barrier to her advance. "With only three drops, the effect does not last long."

Ashley stared again at the Adonis before her and her eyes widened with delight. Why would blemishes be attractive? And the lopsided smile...

She hesitated. Then, as suddenly as it had come, the passion washed away like the last wave of the lowest tide. Her thoughts were clear again. She had a problem to be solved. Douglas — she had to convince him to change his mind.

The idea hit her at once. Moments ago, she had been willing to do anything the gnome asked — anything. Didn't have to be only for sex, she reasoned. Would work as well on someone executing a reorganization — anything to please a woman he absolutely adored.

"What is that stuff?"

"Like I said, a love potion."

"How much?" Ashley surprised herself with her words.

"A full vial is two hundred bucks." Ziggy smiled. He reached to scoop up the bills still on the counter. "Looks like we could call it even."

"How do you make any money then?"

"You will be back for more. Everyone always comes back. A month is not that long a time."

"For me, that will be enough," Ashley said. "Give me the one you are holding. It will do."

"This vial will not work for you," Ziggy shook his head. "It was concocted with my pheromones, not yours."

"My pheromones?"

Ziggy sighed. "I have to tell the same story over again each and every time. Maybe I should get a handout or something."

Tattoos and Alchemy

SHE SHOULD turn and leave, Ashley told herself. It was the rational thing to do. But the thought of Douglas, condescending Douglas, the bastard who would rip apart her department… The image was too painful to push aside. *She* would become the lab manager. She would promote the best engineer she had to take her place. Robert would go…

"I can't *guess* what you exude that is unique," Ziggy's voice cut through the roar of her thoughts. "Stick out your arm. I have to seal the mouth before the air inside cools too much."

Ashley felt herself drawn in to what Ziggy was doing. He had a Bunsen burner going in the midst of a circle of what looked like small brandy snifters. He cradled one bulb in his left hand and covered its opening with his right. She winced when the warm glass touched her arm. Not hot enough to burn, but startling nonetheless.

"It will take a few minutes for the air to cool," he said. "And when it does, the partial vacuum will pull molecules defining your uniqueness away from your skin. I got the idea from the movie *Zorba the Greek*."

"Dispense with the mumbo jumbo," Ashley said as she watched a mound of flesh rise into the interior of the bulb. "What I experienced was convincing enough."

"No mumbo jumbo involved." Ziggy shook his head. "You know about pheromones, right? The airborne chemicals insects use to attract one another of the opposite sex. That's what the medieval alchemists missed. They concentrated too much on the liquids and gasses producing fancy reactions — chemicals like ether, vinegar, and ammonia."

"Coincidentally, also used in a meth lab," Ashley said. The last of what she had felt moments before was entirely gone.

"Well, yeah, originally I *did* make meth in this place. It is the rest of what happened that is the coincidence."

Ziggy ignored Ashley for a moment. He twisted the goblet a quarter turn and released it from her arm. He put his hand back over the open

170

mouth and rushed back into the room behind the counter.

"See the latch on the counter top?" he called out. "The one holding the hinged panel to the display case."

"Why is it on my side?" Ashley looked at the mechanism, puzzled. "Shouldn't it be on yours?"

"For your protection when I do the test," Ziggy answered. "Make sure it is closed so that I cannot fling it open. I'm too short to climb over the case. Just stand there while I mix in the rest of the ingredients while things are fresh."

"And then, poof, a love potion is born?"

"No, not 'then poof.' The traditional alchemists messed up in a second way also. They tried to make a potion that would work for anyone. They have to be tailored to a single individual."

"Okay, you were lucky. Saw a movie, and then brewed together stuff you had on hand."

"There was one more step," Ziggy said as he emerged back into the room. "Turns out, the messing around had to happen in a tattoo parlor as well." He waved his arm around the walls. "As I was gently heating the mixture and waiting for it to show some sort of reaction, I grabbed some blank paper and started doodling some designs."

"What do tattoos have to do with anything?"

"Not tattoos. The drawing of the designs. The crazy arcane symbols. Over the last decade, I must have come up with ten thousand of them. But, that's the key. The right ones somehow are an activation formula. Write the symbols near the proper reagents and then as they dry, some chemistry takes place that I can't begin to figure out."

"Why are you telling me all of this? Why wouldn't I run off to the police or something?"

"It's happened a time or two. The cops come by, take samples, but no meth is ever found."

Ashley's analytical training began to shift back into gear. "Then commercialize what you do. You could make millions."

"Ah, well, that would require investors, credit ratings, background checks — that sort of thing," Ziggy said as he reappeared. "It's better this way. Only happy customers returning for their refills. I get enough from them to get by." He snorted. "I even have a few couples, if you would believe it. Too scared the bloom of new love would fade that they enchant each other like clockwork once a month."

He held up a small vial filled with colorless liquid exactly like the one she had seen before.

"This one is specifically tuned to me, right?" she asked.

Ziggy nodded. As he had done before, he used the eyedropper to place three drops on his tongue. Then he stood in the doorway to the rear and grabbed two handles attached to either side of the jamb.

"And?" Ashley said after a moment.

"Nope, a dud," Ziggy said. "Didn't think so. Only works about one time out of ten. Put out your arm and I'll try again."

"I really do not need the show," Ashley insisted.

"No show involved," Ziggy said as he took the second sample from her into the back room. Again, he returned and stood in the doorway. Again, he grabbed the handles. Again, nothing happened. He motioned for her to extend her arm once more, and the entire sequence repeated.

On the third try, Ashley heard Ziggy burp. When he returned, a serene smile like that of a Madonna spread across his face. His muscles tensed and his fingers grew white from their grip on the handles. Drops of sweat formed on his forehead and began coursing down his cheeks. With a gasp, he released his handholds and slammed his stomach into the hinged panel. Like a madman trying to break into a coffin, he strained to tear the barrier between them out of its restraints.

Ashley looked into Ziggy's eyes and saw the will propelling him forward. He wanted her, wanted her desperately. She took a step backwards and then another.

Then, as suddenly as it had consumed him, the effect began to vanish. The longing on Ziggy's face relaxed into boredom.

"Your pheromones are strong ones," he croaked as he held out the vial. "Yes, this bottle has captured them. Come back in thirty days, and I'll give you a refill good for another month — same price as what you paid now."

"Can you make something not quite so powerful?" Ashley asked. "I want to make a man an obedient love-slave, not a snorting bull."

"Hold it over low heat for a while. The potion will gradually denature. Do it long enough and it becomes harmless."

"How long for what I want?"

"Heat it for a little while. Take a sip and then look in a mirror. If you see yourself as a ravenous beauty, heat it a little more."

Ashley nodded, stuffed the tiny bottle in her purse, and turned to leave.

"One more thing," Ziggy said. "Button back up your blouse."

Make War Not Love

DINTON STOOD up abruptly, stunned. He retreated from the native female's mind. The experiment had failed. The intent was to get the formula for making war potions spread throughout the native world above. Something added to their daily lives so that when the first hints of conflict between the haves and have-nots became apparent, there would be immediate uncontrollable reactions... reactions inevitably leading to world conflict and the destruction of all of humankind — all attempts at cooperation abandoned, crop failures everywhere, nuclear winters...

Love instead of war? An interesting exercise in alchemy. There was no denying that. But it did not fit with Dinton's vision for how things should proceed. Was it possible other elements of his foresight also were flawed? Again, he would have to use more powerful sorcery. The gentle suggestions to random minds might not suffice. Implant into, what did he call himself... into Ziggy's brain the formula for a potion of rage. Take no chances that this time the alchemist would err. Increase his desire for wealth so he would tell others what to do. Have him covet the curious invention of what the natives called royalties on what his clients sold.

That of course also increased the risk. The Faithful might detect what he was doing. Perhaps they already had. Angus' words could not be trusted. He protested that the alchemy he performed was always underground; here in their claustrophobic prison where blank and confining walls made surviving each day's passage a small victory. But suppose his brother had done more? Exercised his craft on the surface, performed what the natives would consider to be miracles, lighting beacons the Faithful could not help but see.

Dinton began pacing. For the very first time after their father had surrendered his ring, he felt alone, abandoned. The baton of leadership, even if he did not wear it all the time, felt as heavy as lead. It pulled him off balance, making even the simple pleasure of a scramble in the twisty passageways a challenge.

He needed help. Someone else to bear the burden with him, someone else to reason with, to determine with clear thought the best steps to take, something that had never occurred whenever he and his brothers met.

Angus was soon to be gone. Thaling most always seemed to be conciliatory enough. Maybe he should be approached. Confess the sorceries he had performed. Form a stronger bond together...

Dinton stopped his pacing. Confess to Thaling? No, he could not do that. Too humbling. Too much a loss of face. All that really had transpired with the natives was a mild surprise. This Ziggy had made a potion for love rather than war. That was all.

And could not causing undeniable love be as disrupting as uncontrollable rage? Both probably could satisfy the original intent equally well. Dinton's passion cooled. Besides, he now had easy entrance into the mind of one of the natives. She suspected nothing. There might be other things he could cause her to do.

The Tryst

ASHLEY LOOKED at Douglas across the table-for-two tucked into a discreet corner of the posh restaurant. The booth curving around them was deeply padded in leather dyed blood-red and studded with shiny brass buttons like the vest of an overweight official. Except for the exit signs required by the fire marshal, the only lighting came from the flickering trio of candles artfully adorning each tabletop.

The bill was going to be horrific, Ashley thought, more than she should be spending now with the bleak future ahead, but the bait had to be irresistible.

"You know," Douglas said as he swirled the wine in his glass, "in all my years at USX, no subordinate has ever treated me to a dinner — especially one for whom the parting might not be a cause for celebration."

Ashley put on her game face. "I have learned a lot from you, Douglas," she said. "This is my way of saying thanks." She gave him her best smile.

"Sometimes a body needs something like this." Douglas smiled back. "No agenda, no decisions to be made. Just two friends hanging out."

This was not going to be easy. After Ashley had decided to go through with this wild scheme, and then got Douglas to accept the invitation, she discovered she did not have the time to plan all of the steps in detail. Things had been so rushed — documenting the current status of the projects she was responsible for, squashing untrue rumors about the reorg, reassuring her troops everything would work out well... Now, far too late, she was racking her brain about how to slip the love potion to her boss.

In the romance novels she used to read decades ago, it happened without any problem again and again. A head turned for an instant, a deftly emptied vial and the deed was done. But his glass was clear across the table. She almost would have to stand in order to reach it.

Douglas abruptly put down his tumbler and rose. "Hold that thought," he said, and then in a whisper, "Little boy's room."

Did she now have her chance? He will be gone for at least a few minutes. His wine glass was sitting within an arm's length, even if she did have to crane over the table. Take the vial out of her purse, unscrew the cap, and empty the contents. Ziggy had said the potion was clear, tasteless, and odorless for a reason. No way would it be detected. It was half of what Ziggy had given her. She had held back some in case. But if she emptied the bottle she had with her completely, and Douglas drunk it all, he would be her thrall for at least half a month. Enough time to get everything changed to the way she wanted. What was she waiting for?

Ashley looked hastily in the direction in which her boss had vanished, and then around the room to check that no waiters were watching. She retrieved the phial and got it ready to pour. She thrust her hand over Douglas' glass and tipped the little bottle to the side, the first drop hanging tantalizingly from the lip.

Yes, what *was* she waiting for? In a few seconds, it would be over. The vial emptied. She hid it away into the bottom of her purse.

Now, the few minutes expanded into what felt like hours. What was taking so long? She had heard the whispers about what happened when men aged but had never thought much of it. Would he take a sip as soon as he sat down or want to keep the forced chitchat going for a while?

While she waited, more thoughts bubbled up in her mind. After the potion worked, then what? Get more vials to keep Douglas seduced in his new role as Operations Manager? Get him to step aside willingly so she could ascend to that level, too? If she did this once, could she resist doing it repeatedly? Like an escalator rising into the clouds, the future extended before her. After the ops, target the division manager the same way? , Then the CEO? Run for office perhaps. Representative, Senator, even President!

With a jolt, the stairway came to a halt. Where would it all stop? If it were only as easy as that, then what would any of it prove?

This is not right, Ashley girl. The thought she had been ignoring all along in the rush had popped into prominence, front and center. Life was a ladder with widely spaced rungs, not a gliding stairway. Every step she had climbed had been because of merit and merit alone. No sleeping with the boss, no come-on smiles and flirtations, no gimmicks like forcing one to fall in love.

The morality of what she was doing hit home with a hammer blow. These potions were evil, pure evil. Ziggy said his clientele was discrete, concerned about their own petty trysts and nothing more. But suppose one was like herself, ambitious, and not concerned about the means. What would happen to society if there use became widespread? Could any sophisticated civilization even survive?

"Why the long face," Douglas said as he sat down again. "It looks like you are trying to solve all the problems of the world."

He reached for his wine. Ashley suddenly rose and swatted his hand to the side. The glass broke free and with a crash fell to the floor spewing its contents.

"What the hell!" Douglas exclaimed, his eyes wide with astonishment.

"This was a bad idea from the start." Ashley reached for her purse and started to leave. "Go ahead, Douglas. Reorganize your operation as you see fit."

Only one option now remained. She called back over her shoulder, "I quit!"

As she walked away, a wave of regret began to overwhelm her, a door had closed that could never be opened again.

A Final Shot

ASHLEY PUT the pile of performance appraisals in the out box. It was the least she could do for her engineers before Dave and Robert swallowed them up. Her resignation papers were working their way through the review process like a rabbit being digested by a python. A week from Friday would be her last day. She could spend her time until then not even bothering to come in to work. Only the exit interview with HR remained.

There was frustration, sadness, regret, yes, but also something more. It *irritated* her that there was such a small reaction when she tossed her badge on Douglas' desk when she saw him again the day after the restaurant meeting. No plea for her to reconsider, that the company needed her, or how valuable she was. Good luck and a weak handshake. That was all.

Around the division, there were the usual perfunctory condolences and polite questions about her plans, but no more. Standard steps in the ritual, hollow with no real content. Dead woman walking. Better to pretend she was not even there.

Her resumé was on the street, but it would take weeks or even months before there was an invitation for an interview by one of USX's competitors. No matter. She would use her cash savings for a little while, and then, if she had to, withdraw some more from her IRA. She had made of her mind. New adventures awaited her, whatever they might be.

Yet, the lack of reaction did stick in her craw, she admitted when the irritation did not completely dissolve. *She* was taking the brunt of this and USX was getting off scot-free. The higher-ups should at least feel some regret, a little of the pain.

Oh, one more thing, a final task popped into her head as she looked over her now almost clean desktop. The paragraph for Figaro Newton's rejection letter. She should dash it off now.

Wait a minute. What would Tom do if an unannounced new hire did show up the Monday after she was gone? The new laboratory manager was competent, sure, but he knew less than she did about how to run a lab. He was already up to his ears learning the standard procedures and protocols. No time to get in front of things. No option but to react.

And then, on top of it all, suppose Fig shows up in the lobby. As a courtesy, he would be escorted in, brimming with questions. Where was the RFP needing the response, who was he reporting to, where was his desk?

USX would never admit it was a big mistake. Say 'Go back home, little boy. We have the defense of the country to worry about here.' No, that could explode into a PR disaster — another example of management incompetence.

Fig would not be turned away. Instead, like an Easter egg hunt, there would be a job number scramble. Some hasty rebudgeting and he would get something out of this for a few months even if it were busy work. And he had said he was out of cash. Who knew? It might make a big difference for him as he figured out what to do next.

Ashley felt a sudden sense of relief. Malicious relief to be sure, but relief. She picked up Fig's resumé and found his phone number. She was *not* going to reject him. No, she was going to make him an offer — one to write a response to the cold RFP starting a week from next Monday — exactly as she had explained to him a week ago.

She hesitated dialing for a moment. Yes, the organization would be embarrassed. She did want that. But she had not considered how Fig might feel. No planned welcome, no real task, no one caring about how he felt. He would be a mere pawn in all of this and did not deserve everything that might happen.

An idea struck. Go ahead with the offer. Have him show up the Friday before he officially was to start. On her own last day. She could introduce him to some of the younger engineers, and ask them to take him under their wings. Give him a heads up that Monday might not go as smoothly as he might expect. That should be okay. Smiling about her petty attempt of spite, she made the call.

CERN

FIGARO NEWTON took one last look at the audience. He could hardly keep his breakfast down. This was much more intimidating than watching a seminar on Skype. He was physically at the European Organization for Nuclear Research (CERN). Up in the last row — was that Glasberg and Weinhow sitting next to each other and whispering? Did they fly in for this? How many Nobel laureates were watching anyway?

And the others. Most of the others were full of *gravitas,* so full of dignity, seriousness, a firm sense of belonging. Fig was one of the shortest in the room and felt he had none. He was merely a graduate student from a minor university, one unaccredited at that.

The sports coat felt uncomfortable. He had bought it in a thrift shop years before in the hopes of getting a date to his high school prom. It was just as well he did not. The sleeves were too long, and he felt tiny within the draping shoulders.

None of the graduate students in the audience had their glasses held together by tape over the nose. Even his scraggly beard looked out of place.

It had been such a whirlwind. An email from his doctorial advisor to hop on the first plane for Geneva he could get. Professor Chalice had finally got a seminar slotted to talk about his work, but it was a little too soon. He had to focus on data collection because the year-end shutdown of the Large Hadron Collider was almost here. There was hardly any time to spare. Since Fig was Chalice's only graduate student, he would have to give the talk instead.

And then the phone call from Ashley Anderfield with the job offer from USX. Five for five — five interviews and five acceptances! He had not expected one from USX. The word buzzing around was that they were in trouble. But no matter which one he accepted, if he were frugal, he could save enough to keep working on his dissertation for another semester. Chalice's email changed everything. Maybe if he did well in Geneva, a fellowship might follow, and he could turn all of them down.

He remembered talking with Anderfield and finally signing off with a 'I'll think about it.' No sense in blowing off any of the fallbacks if he didn't have to.

And it was a good thing he kept his options open. The preparation for the talk had not gone as expected. Professor Chalice had not even met him at the airport. Instead, his advisor had left a message about a hotel, the lecture time and room number, the PowerPoint file name, and not to disturb him until summoned to do so.

When he had been an undergrad, Fig had talked before audiences and knew once he got started he would lose himself in the words. He tried the old trick of thinking everyone was naked, but today that did nothing to help. The image of the exposed paunches of these middle-aged men and women was not a pretty one.

"Chalice is setting some sort of record," someone in the second row called out. "He's been here for over a year and hasn't come to a single seminar. Even sends an RA when he is supposed to be the speaker."

Great. Even some physicists were hecklers. Fig had to do something to make the atmosphere a little more friendly. He pushed his glasses up on his nose and then a second time to be sure, trying to make the daydream fresh...

Standing in front of a learned crowd. Expounding a great theory and watching their eyes widen in surprise. The thunderous applause. A standing ovation. Glasberg, no Glasberg *and* Weinhow pressing forward to shake his hand...

So why not? Maybe it could happen. Nothing ventured, nothing gained, he told himself. *Excelsior!* Faint heart never won fair lady. Margaret's sassy smile in the eighth grade briefly flickered before him, but he pushed that aside. Into the Breach. *Carpe Diem.* Concentrate. Oh man, he was going to be so lame. ...

Finally, be true to oneself., here goes.

"A physicist, a mathematician, and an engineer walked into a bar..."

"TO SUM up," Fig said, "the data collected two years ago showed an anomaly in one of the low cross section decay channels. Nothing to write home about, but exactly as Professor Chalice's super symmetry theory had predicted. Then, when another round of collection after the year-end shutdown was added, the discrepancy became larger. Those results are what I have presented here.

"Professor Chalice could not give this talk because he is busy with the LHC run going on now. We hope when that data is added, we will be able to say…"

Fig paused for effect. "As the bishop said to the actress, "Ah, that is a gluon of a different color."

This time, no one laughed. Most of the audience immediately rose, not for an ovation but to leave quickly and get back to more interesting work. The moderator stepped to the dais. "Before the questions, I only would like to say that the results presented are an example of CERN's outreach program — getting some of the smaller universities involved in the work we are doing here. Now please direct your questions to Mr. Newton."

The questions! The experimental ones he probably could handle by himself. After all, he was the curator of Chalice's data. But the theoretical ones… He glanced again in the direction of Glashow and Weinberg. They were already gone. None of it was going to happen. Oh, well, there were other dreams where that one had come from.

FIG HURRIED down the long corridor of guest offices on the basement floor of the satellite building. The overhead lights were dim, part of an energy conservation plan to thwart the complaints that CERN was a waste of taxpayer money. It took a bit of getting used to, but it was no worse than a stroll at evening twilight. Most doors were open, the usual indication the occupant would permit interruptions from whatever he was doing.

Luckily, someone had shown him how to use the directory to find Chalice's room number. It was closed. Not unexpected, given his aloofness.

Fig tapped gently, but got no response. His advisor would be pleased with how things had gone. Would want to know immediately if not sooner. That is why he did not wait for his advisor's summons. Best to avoid the scolding that would occur if he delayed until later. Don't make any stupid mistakes while trying to capitalize on the opportunity for some educational funding.

He put his ear to the door and heard Chalice's voice. He was there. Evidently, he was talking to someone.

Yes, Professor Chalice was bristly. Always concerned about proper protocol — the respect due to a full professor — even one from a place like Wagonbrook. And he did push the image of sainthood to the limit. Suits a car salesman would be proud to wear. A business card with the tag line 'Searcher for the holy grail of physics.'

But if there was conversation, then perhaps his advisor would not mind hearing his report now rather than later. Cautiously, Fig grasped the knob and turned. The door was not locked. He slowly started to open it. Only darkness showed in the slit that had been revealed. Although the corridor was dim, the darkness of the office wall on the right now looked striped with a vertical ribbon of soft light.

He could hear Chalice more clearly. "Everyone, pay attention. My third-stage trigger has found another event, and I have computed the changes to be made."

Fig extended his head into the partially open door and waited until his eyes adjusted. Chalice was sitting at a desk near the opposite wall, absorbed with whatever he was looking at on the computer screen. He had not noticed the door was ajar.

"First, the initial pixel detector," Chalice said. "I will give you the new ID." A keyboard in front of the professor began to clatter, and one of the windows before him started to scroll.

Fig puzzled until he made out the band of metal circling the top of Chalice's head and the positioning earphones over his ears. A headset. Whomever Chalice was talking to must not be in the room.

"Two, one, seven, three," Chalice said. "Convert it to binary as you have been taught."

Fig cracked the door slightly more and snaked himself into the office. As silently as he had opened it, he closed the door behind. Waiting for the right moment to announce his presence, he let his eyes adjust to the almost total darkness. Several of the windows on the screen were for entering text commands, and Fig recognized the image in the center one. It was a reconstruction of an event from the Atlas Toroidal Apparatus, one of the two high-energy detectors of proton-proton collisions.

What was it above Chalice's head? Tiny specks of many colors, each one too small to resolve individually, but together they formed an iridescent cloud, almost like an aurora but not quite — churning in restless motion.

"Closer to the microphone when you are done," Chalice said. "I can't tell you what to do next until I know you are finished with the last." The advisor waited a moment. "Slower and more clearly. And speak up, speak up."

"Ah, professor," Fig ventured softly. "I do not mean to inter — "

Chalice bolted from his chair and whirled about as if bit by a snake. "How long have you been here?" he commanded. "What did you hear?"

His headset was not wireless but connected to another device on the desk. The cord had pulled out of its jack when he rose, and a second voice spoke from a nearby speaker. "The first ID has been changed and the error correcting code modified to compensate. What is next? Another pixel detector, a semiconductor tracker, the calorimeter, the muon spectrometer?" To Fig, it sounded like one of the high falsetto chipmunk characters from years ago.

"Silence!" Chalice shouted. "Silence! All of you. Factor some large numbers or something while you await my next command."

He walked to the wall and flicked on the lights. Striding menacingly toward Fig, he growled, "I told you to wait until summoned."

"Yes, but, I though you would want to know as soon as — "

Chalice glowered down at Fig. "You did not hear anything, understand?"

"Hear anything? Only you talking to someone."

Fig pushed his glasses upward on his nose. "Well that, and the funny cloud over your head." He craned his neck to look upward. There was no glow, but the air shimmered in a subtle way. He noticed his ears now were buzzing faintly as well. This was quite curious. Was he imagining things? Wasn't there a bunch of colored dots before?

"Say, those events showing on the screen," he said. "Are they ones being collected in real time right now?"

"I will make a bargain with you," Chalice's expression grew even grimmer. "You keep quiet about this, and, as the reward, … you will get some tuition relief." Chalice scowled. "Or perhaps to make it even more clear — you will still get a degree."

Fig felt his stomach protest again. He was only hanging on by a thread with Chalice anyway. And if now he got the boot, the last three years were a total waste. Out on the street. No advanced degree. No postdoc anywhere.

"Okay, Okay. I will not talk about what I heard — whatever it was."

FIG SCOOTED the chair a little closer to the table. The IT staff had been quite helpful. As another visiting scholar, he had obtained an account and a desk — in a public area rather than a private office, but it certainly would do. He had done this many times before remotely from the States, of course, but he felt a thrill using the exploration tools on data that was so fresh. As he had witnessed Chalice doing a few hours before, he would be working with events shortly after they were obtained, not months later.

Fig brought up a level three trigger. It performed complicated queries on events reconstructed from the raw data.

He set the criteria to save the same type of events his advisor had been studying for the last two years. Low probability final states from marginal observations. The ones ambiguous and possibly corrupted by error. He and Chalice were bottom feeders, trying to squeeze new physics out of material no one else wanted to bother with.

Of course, the first plot he brought up was the crucial one. If there were a bump not explained by known particles, then he, well, Chalice actually, would be the discoverer. And since his advisor had predicted it before...

It was fascinating to watch the histogram on the screen begin to fill up in real time. In general, lower level triggers filtered out what happened with most of the collisions. Only a few hundred per second were processed further. And of those, only every minute or so would there be one passing Chalice's level three.

An hour passed, but there was no unexplained bump at the right-hand edge of the plot. In fact, it looked much worse than the data from the last two years. Where had the effect of Chalice's predicted particle gone?

Then the screen flickered and refreshed. The histogram redrew. Now, there *was* a bump at the edge. He was sure there was no such instants before. What was going on here?

Fig looked at his watch. It was exactly 11 AM, Central European Time. A coincidence? He cleared the graph and started over. The histogram again started filling.

A minute before twelve, he made a screenshot of the display. Again, there was no bump on the right. Again, there was a flicker and refresh. When the histogram was repainted, the bump was there. Fig superimposed the two graphs and flickered them back and forth like an astronomer looking for a planet moving against a starry background. There was no doubt about it. The raw data collected in the last hour now was showing results that had changed.

Fig pondered. He knew that all sorts of recalibrations were performed on the raw data all the time. One lecture he had Skyped said there were almost as many modifications as there were new additions. But there should be nothing as dramatic as what he had just seen. What strange phenomena was happening to the raw data? What was making it change?

Professor Chalice. He needed to interrupt him again.

The Basis of Truth

THIS TIME, Fig slammed open the door to Chalice's guest office. The room was again dark. His advisor stared at the computer screen, his head surrounded by the twinkling cloud.

Fig did not wait for Chalice to react to his entrance. "How are you doing it?" he asked. "How are you changing what shows up on the data plot?"

"I asked you once before, but you did not answer," Chalice said. "Do you really want to get your degree?"

"Of course," Fig answered. "But, Professor, what *you* are doing is wrong. When they find out, your career will be ruined." He adjusted his glasses. "And I will be tarred with the same brush. I will be ruined, too."

"They won't find out."

Fig could not believe that he was lecturing his own advisor, a senior scientist who must know how the game was played. "Your super-symmetry idea will be subjected to the most rigorous scrutiny. You know that. It is one of the most basic mantras of science. 'Extraordinary claims demand extraordinary proof.'"

"There is no way for anyone to check the results by another means," Chalice said calmly. "There is only one CERN. No other accelerator can reach the same energies."

"CERN data is distributed all over the world," Fig rebutted. "More than a hundred places. A slew of others will look at their copies of the same information and see no bump is there. Then they will examine yours and recognize the discrepancy. What you are claiming is not physical truth. You will be accused of fraud."

"That will not happen."

"Why not?"

"Look, in the early twentieth century, we observed small particles dancing around in a liquid and postulated the theory of atoms and molecules explained what was happening, right? Then we saw actual tracks in photo plates and cloud and bubble chambers and decided there must be moving particles that explained them, too.

"All of this was Okay," Chalice continued. "Any reasonable person would accept what was causing these phenomena. There was no doubt. No alternate explanation making any sense. But the physics of the sixties, produced *statistical* plots that did not agree with the theories of the time. So, we postulated more particles to explain the differences — new little bits of matter for which there was no direct evidence at all."

"Yeah, so?"

"Fig, I am not 'editing' the event reconstructions in my own dataset that is derived from the raw data. I am *changing* the raw data itself. And when there is a change, software automatically updates additional copies wherever they happen to be throughout the world. The data from CERN *is* the truth, Fig. When anyone anywhere makes the same plots as I do, they will see the same results. There is nothing to contradict what I have produced."

"Then the audit trails. That software will indicate that changes have been made to the raw data."

"I do not use a computer to edit the data," Chalice said. "The data bits on the disks are directly manipulated instead by my little helpers. There will be no trace of what they do."

"Little helpers?" Fig asked. "You are not making sense."

For a moment, Chalice stared at Fig but did not speak. Finally, he said, "You are not going to keep quiet about this are you? Very well. You force my hand. I will have to make more clear the reward." He motioned to a chair near the wall. "Sit. This is going to take a while."

"LET ME get this straight," Fig said. He felt as if he had been drinking from a fire hose. "You use the PYTHIA software to construct the events you want and GEANT to simulate what the Atlas detector responses would be — the responses for all of them, individual pixels, the calorimeter, the muon detector, everything. Then you find events in the real data close to the ones you want and substitute those detector outputs with the artificial replacements you have created."

"Yes, that is correct."

"Okay, theoretically possible," Fig said. "I guess I understand that part of it. As implausible as it may be. But the rest... pure fantasy, Professor, impossible to believe."

"An accident, I admit." Chalice smiled. "As so many great scientific discoveries are."

Chalice stood and clasped his hands behind his back as if he were lecturing to a rapt audience of new students.

"After the first long shut down, I went down to the Atlas experiment bay. Got as close as I could. After all, even for a senior physicist, a marvelous thing to behold — almost 50 meters long, 25 meters high and wide, six types of detectors arranged in concentric layers about the central proton beams.

"It was after midnight. Everyone else had gone. For some reason, there was a power surge somewhere, and the breakers tripped. The huge device plunged into darkness. Only a few emergency lamps provided some light. I looked around, trying to remember the way I had come, and saw something in the dimness, a small glowing cloud of tiny twinkling lights."

"Like what was over your head in this office?" Fig asked.

"You said you saw them, too, didn't you? I had thought I was the only one." He scowled. "That is the reason for the path we now are on."

"The cloud of lights?" Fig persisted.

"Yes, exactly the same as what you saw," Chalice answered. "They are what I call imps, for want of a better name. Tiny creatures from somewhere else in the multiverse. My guess is they were transported here in the bursts of ionization produced when the protons collide.

"Their explanation is total nonsense, of course," the professor continued. "Something about what the imps call wizardry — The Law of Ubiquity — 'Flame Permeates All.'"

Fig's jaw dropped at what he was hearing. Chalice explaining how he altered the data was due to the work of imps? Had his advisor gone insane?

As he pondered, another tiny thought crept into Fig's head. 'The reality of 'imps' was nonsense, of course. More intriguing was 'from somewhere else.' His favorite books from childhood had been about magical lands beyond one's reach — Oz, Narnia, Neverland.

An unexpected excitement within him began to awaken. He felt the warm glow that had been absent for, well, for too long a time. It was the sense of wonder, the delicate flower that, when it bloomed, was oh-so-sweet. Imps from another part of a multiverse was foolishness, of course, but if only they indeed were real…

"As I waited for light to be restored, I got to know them," Chalice ignored the far-away look flickering for a moment in Fig's eyes. "They were sentient. We were able to communicate, and somehow I got them to obey my commands. Almost immediately I saw my way to the Nobel Prize."

"Professor, please take this in the spirit it is given," Fig said.

"Yes, what?"

"Have you considered getting help — professional help?"

"Help? Of course not." Chalice snorted. "They are real, I tell you. The imps are real. Didn't *you* see the cloud of twinkling lights?"

Fig took a cautious step backward. He did not like the way this was going, the wild stare starting to bore into him.

"I have decided I must take you into my confidence," Chalice continued. "Use a carrot rather than a stick."

Fig took another step backwards. Temporize, he thought. Temporize until he could reach the door. "Professor, this *is* amazing. Amazing as a — as an electric banana. Why haven't you already gone public?"

"The imps obey most of my commands, but not all. Evidently, they are quite shy. Show themselves only to me and, until now, to no other. Imprinting like ducklings maybe."

Another step backward. The door handle was now almost within reach. "Wouldn't the discovery of the imps be even more important than that of another particle? You could photograph the cloud or something."

"I tried, and used other detectors also: remote TV, active sonar, you name it — but I never could succeed. Somehow, when they do not want to be observed, they cloak themselves in some way. I could not figure out how to prove they exist.

"So, my road to the Nobel is along the more traditional route. No one would ever believe anything about little imps from elsewhere only because I said so."

Fig reached behind and felt the handle. "There must be some way …"

Chalice shook his head. "The prediction and discovery of my supersymmetry gluon will be enough. That has the prize written all over it. Well, it will take several years after publication, of course. Time enough to doctor a few other decay channels to exhibit more of my predictions, and then the conclusion will be overwhelming.

"Think of it. Edison was known as the 'Wizard of Menlo Park.' I will be known as the 'Wizard of CERN.'"

The physicist rushed on. "And to ensure you do not come down with a sudden case of scruples and start blabbering so as to cast doubt, here's the deal. Keep quiet about this, and your name along with mine will be on the papers I will write. The ones showing the CERN data — that my supersymmetry theory is correct.

"I will give you equal credit. We will share. Both of us, Nobel laureates. After that, you will be able to pick any university you want. Immediate tenure. A member of a very exclusive club — Lawrence Bragg is the only other one under thirty to have garnered a Nobel."

The Nobel Prize! Fig's thoughts thundered with the very thought of it. The award ceremony in the Stockholm Concert Hall. White ties and tails. Evening gowns. He probably even could get a date. The king handing him his diploma and medal. The banquet afterward in the city hall. The television, radio and print coverage...

"Fig? Did you hear what I said?"

Fig shook his head back to reality. The image was so vibrant, so real. He looked at Chalice intently, but did not like the beginning of a crazed look forming there. Almost staggering, he stepped backwards to the door and swung it open.

"I will think about it, Professor. I really will." He rushed out and called over his shoulder. "And I'll get back to you as soon as I can."

Cosmic Pranksters

HE SHOULDN'T be here anymore, Fig thought. Instead, be on the first plane he could get out of Geneva. Back to the States and figure out how he could transfer to another university. It would have to be an online one like Wagonbrook, but like a rat in a one-branch maze, he had few other options. In the meantime, do the internship at one of the aerospace companies and get a bankroll to start with.

Like a runaway chariot, Chalice's mind must have vanished down a bumpy road. That was clear. But there were two things Fig could not explain away. The data *was* being corrupted. Physical truth was being changed. How, he did not know, but it was happening. He had seen it. Secondly, there was the matter of the cloud of twinkling lights. He had seen that, too. Well, he thought he had. Before he left, he had to make sure.

Fig waited in the empty office across the hall until he heard his advisor leave for the night after a sixteen-hour shift. Evidently, if what Chalice had told him was true, his advisor was pushing himself to get as many events altered as he could before the LHC shut down for year-end maintenance.

Fig crossed the hallway, entered his professor's office cautiously, and shut the door. No lights were on. The room was completely dark. He could see nothing. The old tale about how graduate students were used at the turn of the previous century popped into his mind.

Long before there were fancy digital cameras, primitive scintillation counters in a darkened room signaled that a cosmic ray had entered from above and exposed a trail on a photographic emulsion. A grad student was stationed nearby to watch for these flashes of light. When he saw one, he was to mark the film plate as containing data and replace it in the ray path with a fresher one.

Being alone in the complete dark for hours, however, presented a problem. A person's eyes grew tired of no input and began producing phantom flashes on their own. Many plates in the 'exposed' pile were still blank. They showed no trail of a cosmic ray. The yield for a recording session was greatly reduced. Was something like that what had happened to him?

To correct for this, experimental physicists resorted to using 'coincidence' grad students. Not one but two stood watch in the room at the same time. They had to see a flash simultaneously in order for the film plate to be tagged as having recorded the passage of a particle from outer space.

Fig waited patiently for his eyes to adjust, and after a short while, he began to see tiny lights swarming back and forth. As if he had salt in his eyes, he blinked several times to be sure, but the image did not go away. There was not a single isolated dot, but what looked like hundreds, perhaps thousands of specks in a rainbow of colors flitting back and forth in an amorphous cloud — the same as he had seen above Chalice's head when he had come to his office before.

Fig let out a long sigh of relief. No hallucination, no delusion. No need for another watcher. What he was experiencing was real. But now what? What was causing the twinkling? Chalice had claimed the imps were thinking creatures. Okay, test the hypothesis. What does one do to establish contact? As he hesitated, the cloud transformed and took on a new shape. The random motion resolved into a stationary pattern that twinkled. He recognized what it said.

Hi!

Fig blinked again, but there was no mistaking what he saw. There was even an exclamation point hovering next to the letter 'i.'

Reflexively, he batted at his face as if he was trying to shoo away a moth. Had some sort of virtual reality goggles been put in front of him? Maybe a holographic screen lowered silently from the ceiling?

"Can you hear me?" he asked, feeling foolish talking to what was otherwise empty air.

Like a marching band at a football game, the pattern dissolved and then quickly reformed.

Yes.

Fig pushed aside the sudden wonder of why the imps were even bothering with displaying a period at the end of the word. He could not believe this. There must be some rational explanation. He had to stall so he could think.

"Who — what are you?" he blurted.

Too hard.

"Okay then. How did you get here?"

Desk. Left side. Top drawer.

Fig looked about the office, but except for the glow could still see nothing. He backed up to the door, ran his hand over the wall near the jamb, and flicked on the lights. Squinting at the sudden change in illumination, the tiny mites, if they really were the explanation, were difficult to see. But he barely could make out that they were still present, now hovering over Chalice's desk in the back of the room.

Fig moved to the worktable and pulled open the drawer. Inside, on top of other papers, was an electronic schematic. He removed the drawing and studied it. There was no title or label, but part of the circuit appeared to be a simple enough one. It was a frequency converter that shifted audio signals higher and lower. And the output of that fed to something else more complicated.

Fig studied the diagram a while longer. "Is this how you were communicating with Chalice?" he finally asked aloud. "He built a device that shifts the tones of what you say and then slows them down so a human can understand?"

The imps swirled in front of Fig's face and formed another pattern, now dim in the ambient light.

Build one, is all that it said.

FIG SET up shop in the office across from Chalice's. He had checked, and it was not currently assigned. Obtaining the necessary equipment and parts from a central supply had been easy. Grad students signing out materials for their advisors was the usual custom here. A resource he could use to figure out the explanation.

As he was putting together the translator, Fig couldn't help speculating about the implications of what all of this meant. If the imps really did exist, where were they from? Had they always been around, but never discovered? Or were they not of the earth, newly arrived, life from another planet?

Perhaps from somewhere even farther, somewhere *else*. He smiled as childhood memories reawoke — Barsoom, Pellucidar ...

And he was the one, not John Carter, not Tarzan. No. He was the one. He had dreamed of being the traveler, the one who experienced the glorious wonders himself…

But first things first. Get proof the imps did exist or not. And if they did, then and only then, take on the problem of a journey to where they were from. Focusing on the equipment, he began putting it together.

AFTER COMPLETING the final assembly, he plugged it into power and doused the lights. The cloud of mites almost immediately appeared before him.

"Much better," the high chipmunky voice said — the one Fig had heard before in Chalice's office across the hall.

"What are you?" he repeated his very first question from days before.

"Still too hard," came the answer.

"Okay, then. *Why* are you here?"

"To do mischief, of course."

"Mischief?"

"Our pranks are the best, the most sophisticated."

Fig could almost hear a shrug in the translated tone of voice, but he could not be sure. "I don't understand."

"Others from our realm had been doing them for *years, centuries* before the higher energies made it possible for us to come through to this realm ourselves."

"You're not making sense."

"OK, here's an example. Your civilization has reached a point in its culture where you now have what are called 'dryers' to remove the water from the clothes you wash, right?"

"Yeah, so?"

"So, haven't you ever wondered why it sometimes happens when you remove the socks from the dryer there is an odd one that does not pair up?"

"Your kind has something to do with that?"

"Not us. We are too small. But no one has ever bothered to check — not even your so-called 'physicists" here at CERN. For every sock mysteriously vanishing from a dryer, another one appears in a second appliance not too far away from the first."

"You mean — "

"Yes, hoseherders, they call themselves. They move socks around all the time."

"So misplacing socks and mutilating physics data. Those are the two things you are — make you so proud?"

"Oh, there is a lot more. Tangles, for instance. Ever wonder why when a woman with long hair wakes up after a night's sleep, her hair is snarled? Takes an hour sometimes to get the rats out."

"Well, no..."

"Hairjumblers. They've been doing it for maybe three thousand of your years. And the glitches in electronics — "

"And yourselves? What type are you?"

"Well, others in our realm call us micromites — because of our size. But we ae so dynamic that we prefer another."

"What?"

"Why, dynamites, of course."

"Okay, enough of that," Fig said. "I can relate to doing mischief. I've been known to do some myself." He pushed up his glasses. "But I'm having a struggle accepting all of this. Let's get to my next question. Chalice said only he could see you and was surprised I could as well. Why me?"

"Boredom. We've been doing stuff for him for almost three years now. Been there; done that. And once we figured out he was a cheat, we no longer liked him very much. Now we are looking for a new candidate."

"So... why me?"

"You were intrigued about the prospect of a Nobel Prize, right? You did not out and out say no to Chalice's proposition to you."

"Tempted, yes." Fig nodded. "I thought about that... thought about that a lot." He shook his head. "But the way to the prize is not by manipulating bits in a data file." He fiddled with his glasses. "Exposing you guys to the world. Now *that* would be worthy of the honor."

"Yes, we agree. Bringing us to the attention of your world would be sufficient. We can help you do that."

"What!"

"Well, you would have to prove yourself worthy first. Prove you are not another faker."

"How do you propose I do that?" Fig felt a twinge of excitement begin to ignite.

"*Prove* we exist. We are not going to do circus tricks with you as a ring master. You are a physicist. Do as one does. Collect data — unaltered data convincing other scientists."

"That would be easy. You swirl around in a cloud, you talk and reason — "

"Yes, yes. Of course, we *could* do that, but we are not going to. Your challenge is to find a means of proving our existence when we refuse to cooperate in any way. That accomplishment is the path to a Nobel Prize."

"So, you are abandoning Chalice?"

"No, not at all. For two-thirds of your daily cycle, we will continue altering data as he directs. It will make his crash all the more spectacular when the truth is revealed. For the remaining third, we will work with you."

"But it will be so easy." Fig pulled his phone out of his pocket, snapped a picture of the hovering cloud, and held the screen up for the imps to see. "Bingo. I'm finished."

A detachment of the mites broke off from the main cloud and surrounded Fig's hand. As he watched, the image of colored dots against a black background began to disappear one by one. What remained was the picture of an empty room.

"Digital data store," the voice emanated from the down converter. "How do you say it? Infant's play. Anything digital. Move a few electrons from here to there, and it is done."

"Then something analog, like film," Fig shot back. "Something that cannot be doctored so easily."

"Won't work either. It takes a little more effort, true, but the task is still one of moving around electrons — reversing the photochemical reaction that deposits the silver grains recording the image. Same thing with magnetic tape. Flip back the domains and only random noise remains."

"Hmm. Well, there must be a way. I will think of something."

"Yes! Yes! Please try. Try to prove we exist. This is going to be so much fun."

Bump Hunting

FIG WHEELED the cart with the different types of recorders into the office he was occupying. It had taken him two days to figure out what he needed.

The imps had been right. It was not the simple matter of taking a snapshot with an analog camera or recording a tape of their buzzing wings. He had to come up with some other scheme — reproducible measurements with instruments the little sprites could not outwit. And now, he was ready to try. He made sure the door was shut and fired up the first. It was a thermometer — an old one with a chart wrapped around a rotating cylinder that traced the wiggles of a pen attached to the sensor.

The precision was not great — a tenth of a degree at the best. But the wing flapping of the hovering cloud of imps would increase the temperature of the air, and it would be recorded.

Next was an anemometer. It too was ancient with an analog recording of pen scraggles. Standing on a chair, Fig stuffed a square of insulation into the air-conditioning vent in the ceiling. If he then were to lie perfectly still on the floor and control his breathing, any anomalous variations in air pressure should be due to the beating wings.

The other instruments were powered up and initialized as well. None of them recorded their measurements as a string of ones and zeros, domains on magnetic tape, or grains of silver. He lay down on the floor, started breathing with a constant rhythm, and waited. In an hour, the imps would finish their shift working for Chalice and come to find him.

After the hour had passed, he rose and examined the recordings. These data would be the baseline. He replaced the charts with new ones, settled one more time on the floor and began his slow and even breathing. In a few minutes, the twinkling cloud appeared and settled as well, hovering inches above his eyes.

At first, he thought he would have to guard against falling asleep, but he found himself too excited performing the experiment. Slowly, the minutes ticked away.

AFTER ANOTHER hour, Fig rose, removed the new charts, and on each placed a small mark so he could tell the difference from the ones before. Every chart showed a ragged line, not straight but nearly so with only small deviations to either side along its trace. He sighed. At first blush, the measurement lines looked the same between before and after. He could not tell the 'live data' charts from their baselines. He would have to examine each one carefully under a magnifying glass.

Another hour passed as he slowly marched the glass over the first trace that he had uncoiled along a table. "There!" he shouted suddenly to no one. "There, half-way down, a small deviation to the top."

Fig continued scanning down the trace. The imp cloud grew agitated when he found two more shifts in the same direction indicating that for brief moments the temperature was slightly higher.

But before he could look further, a dozen or so bright sparking red and orange dots appeared on a portion of the paper he had already examined. They formed a twinkling circle drawing back his attention.

Fig moved the glass and looked. His excitement dissolved. There was another deviation, but this one was to the bottom indicating the temperature had fallen and not increased. Somehow, he had ignored it as he had scanned along.

Before he could react further, two more circles appeared, this time near the end of the trace. When Fig studied them, he was not surprised by what he saw — two more deviations also toward the bottom.

"I'm bump hunting, aren't I?" he said to the cloud as it reassembled. He did not know if they could understand him without the aid of the frequency shifter, but it did not matter. "Straining to see an effect in statistical data that I hope is there. Like particle physicists so anxious to find something publishable. There may be a temperature deviation here, but you guys are too small to register."

Fig examined the other traces, and the results were the same. Random noise, like static on a radio, nothing beyond what one would expect from mere chance.

He thought for a long while and then decided to try another tactic. He turned the communication frequency shifter on.

"Can you hear me?" he asked.

"Of course."

"I am wondering," Fig began slowly. "Besides the hoseherders and hairjumblers, what other types of — what is a generic name for all of you?"

"Demons is a good choice, although devils would serve as well."

"Okay, demons. So besides hoseherders and hairjumblers, are there other types of demons here on Earth?"

"Lots of kinds. Air sprites, rockbubblers, grem — "

"And are all of them able to disguise their presence?"

"We're the only ones because we are so small. Others are much larger and would have a difficult time of it."

"Okay, does anybody on Earth control them?"

"Most have come through the flame of their own volition. Like ourselves, they have no masters. There is no struggle for dominance."

"But only *most*?"

"Well, Chalice thinks he controls us, but actually, that is not true. And yes, there are a few wizards here somewhat worthy of the name. The rockbubblers are a feisty bunch. They have a master, but he barely manages to direct them. He is far away and buried underground. It would be great peril for you to venture to visit him."

"Underground? — Never mind. Who else?"

"Well, there is a female much like yourself who has some matchmites under her thrall. She is far away as well."

"But above ground and easier to reach?"

"Why are you asking about other types of demons?"

"It looks like there is no way for me to get irrefutable proof of your existence without an awful lot of effort. So, instead, now that I know others of your ilk exist — bigger ones. I will get proof of *them* instead,"

"No fair! We want you to compete with Chalice for the Nobel Prize. He does not treat us with respect. If he gets it, we will have done all of the work and get no credit at all."

"I intend to compete," Fig said. "And if you really want to make me a creditable contender, you should use your powers to help rather than hinder. Whose side are you on, anyway?"

In reply, the cloud rose to the ceiling, far enough away that Fig could not hear even the faint whine of what must be the tiny wings. The colored lights faded out, and for a quarter hour or so there was absolute silence like that on the moon.

Finally, the lights in the cloud resumed their blinking and descended.

"OK. We agree," the voice from the converter said. "Would you like to travel and meet her?"

"Yes. Absolutely I would. But I have to ask. If you are at CERN all the time, how do you know all of this?"

"Word gets around."

Imp in a Haystack

FIG STOOD on the sidewalk outside of the terminal at LAX. He glanced at his reflection in the large glass window behind but saw no dance of lights over his head. The little imps, one third of the total, had assured him that, despite the travel, they would still be with him.

They had better. Like his first visit for the interview at USX, the view of the landscape when landing was bewildering — like a carpet of fireflies anchored to the ground and stretching as far as one could see. Los Angeles was a big place. Southern California even bigger. He had drained his savings for the airfare and had little money left for transportation.

Fig took the downconverter out of his carry-on and slipped it on his belt. Getting the device through the security check was something he did not relish having to do again. He slipped on the microphone headset and put the bud in his ear.

"You told me word gets around," he said softly. "Why can't you take me directly to this female wizard?"

"Doesn't have to be a wizard," squeaked in his ear. "Matchmites have very little brain. They are easily controlled."

"That's not what I asked." Fig let the irritation from the long trip from Geneva find some relief in the tone of his voice. "Where is she? I need to find how much it will cost to get to her."

"We have no idea. There has been no contact for several months. The mites probably are being kept in a jar."

"Why didn't you tell me this before we left?"

"You didn't ask. This is still a challenge, remember."

Fig's irritation grew. Dealing with little points of light with minds all their own was not easy.

He pulled out his phone and entered a query. "Let's see... Here it is. The area of Los Angeles County alone is — why it is almost five thousand square miles! How can we possibly search all of that?"

"Easy enough. That is only half a square mile for each of us. It will be a snap."

"What? Looking for a jar that may be hidden away? How long will that take?"

"A year for each of us. Maybe a year and a half at most."

Fig stepped back from the curb. He did not want to climb into a taxi yet. He was a physicist, after all, he told himself. There had to be a better way than a blanket search.

"These matchmites," he said. "What do they look like? Are they points of light like yourself?"

"No. Not at all. They are quite large. Compared to our svelte selves, lumbering giants. As large as what you call a fruit fly. We can spot easily such a creature twenty of your human paces away."

"Don't they glow like you do? Couldn't you detect them farther —"

"No. Not at all. Uninteresting gray. And now that we think about it, there are certain backgrounds in which they would easily blend."

Fig adjusted the microphone slightly on his headset. "Their voices then. Perhaps you can listen for them instead."

"Would work. We barely would be able to hear them though. Deep slow rumbles hard to distinguish from background noise. For you it also would be different of course. More like the whine of what you call a mosquito."

"Yes, a mosquito's whine!" Fig exclaimed. Two or three other waiting passengers turned their heads and stared. "I can add a little parabolic antenna and a narrow band filter to the converter," he said more softly. "Center it on the frequency of wingbeats, convert it up for you guys, and then you can home in on the source."

"We would need about nine thousand, nine hundred and ninety nine more of the devices — one for each half square mile."

"Maybe there is a way to accomplish that," Fig said. "First steps first. Let me find out how to get to an electronics store for the additional circuitry, and we can test the prototype out around here. Who knows, we might get lucky."

"Yeah, right. One chance in ten thousand. And, oh, do you remember the part about probably being kept in a jar?"

FIG GRIMACED as he remembered putting the three one-dollar bills of change into his empty wallet. Cab fare was expensive, and so were the parts and tools he had to buy. He had packed a few small breadboards, wire, some ICs and so on in his carry-on, but the snips and stripper had been confiscated at the airport in Geneva. He did have a credit card, but it already was almost maxed out.

But no matter for now. He stood up from the small table in the internet café and left before the waiter could come and ask him again what he was doing with the breadboard and wires. Outside, he pushed the ON button on the modified converter and pointed the antenna north.

"Hear anything?" he asked into his headset.

"Only static."

Fig began pivoting to the west. After turning about twenty degrees, his earbud came alive.

"There! That direction! We hear the whine."

Fig started walking north.

"No, no. Not that way! More north-by-northwest."

"I'm on a street where there is traffic," Fig said. "I can't cut across where I want to. Hang on. At the next intersection, I will cross to the other side. We will have to zig-zag our way."

There was no reply, and Fig continued. After about a mile or so of crooked path, he came upon a small city park. It had the usual playground equipment and children riding bikes. In the very center stood a small pond that no one was near, an oasis beckoning the weary traveler.

Fig approached, and as he did, the whine in his earbud grew louder. He squinted, trying to see if any imps were visible, but saw none. When he reached the edge, a cloud of swirling activity did come into view, bigger than the tiny dots of light, but darting about in much the same way.

While he pondered, he felt a tickling on his forehead. Instinctively, he swatted at it. As he did, more of the cloud surrounded him and began biting as well. Mosquitos! This was not a cloud of imps, but mosquitos instead. Of course! What kind of physicist was he anyway? His altered device had done its job well, but not the way he had intended. Finding what he was looking for was going to be a lot harder.

The Queen of the Eight Universes

FIG PONDERED the alternatives. Seeking out the matchmites was not going to work. Somehow, he would have to get them to come to him instead. But if they were confined to a jar or bottle, that was not going to happen either. How horrible that must be, he thought, confined in a small volume. Having to live in one's own...

"Wait a minute! What about bathroom breaks?" he said into his headset. Or if not that, giving the place a cleaning every once and a while. Do you guys even have to go?"

"Of course we do. Like all living things, we take in food, convert some of it to a form we can use for energy, and get rid of the rest. It takes a lot of power to keep buzzing around, flashing our lights, and thinking about things."

"Not you. The matchmites."

"It is the same for them. Every so often, the wizard lets them out to forage."

"Why don't they then flee?"

"They are forced to return if they are being dominated by a master."

"Okay, never mind that part."

He pushed up his glasses, and then, after a moment, his eyes brightened. "How about this? The matchmites get free every so often so they can seek out food. What is their favorite kind?

Fig did not wait for an answer. "You see, we could go with the idea of spreading out over the entire area, one of you guys to every half square mile or so. And each of you would have a food lure. Then, bingo, when a matchmite showed up for one of you, we would know exactly where to concentrate a subsequent search. With all of you looking over half a square mile, it should not take long at all, certainly not a year. So how about it? What is the mite's favorite food?"

The colors and patterns shifted again, although this time the change lasted for a few minutes.

"Hello," Fig jiggled the wire running from his headset to the converter. "Can you still hear me?"

"Favorite food? Well, we are!" the voice sounded in Fig's earbud after another few moments. "Kind of a delicacy — so we have been told."

Fig blanched. "Whoa! No need to go that way. What is the second favorite?"

"There isn't one. Matchmites almost go berserk when they can wolf down one of us. Somehow we ... Well, it is hard to believe, but we have been told we smell something wonderful to other demons. But, if one of us is not in the area, the matchmites eat whatever else is around because they have to."

"I said no. We aren't going to do that."

"It wouldn't be so bad. Like before, the odds would be ten thousand to one. And something the rest of us could talk about later for many orbits around your sun."

"But being eaten alive."

"No worse than what we have to deal with all the time back in our own realm. One big gulp is okay. It's the grinding and gnashing that doesn't feel so good."

The speaking stopped, and the cloud began to disperse.

"Wait!"

"We have decided," the last one to leave said. "You are not a wizard who can command us to stop. We are going to do it. Spread out over the entire area. Report back every twenty-four of your hours. And since release for feeding probably is not a daily event it will take a little while before a roll call is one short. But then, all of us will converge and comb the area that remains. We will find the mites there even if they are kept in a jar."

FIG WALKED cautiously up to the closed door of the café. The curtains were drawn, but loud music managed to escape and fill the air. The imps said they had been successful. They had told him to go there.

"You're sure she is inside? She's the one?"

"Yes, we have found the matchmite. There is only one and in a jar, as we suspected. Tucked away in a satchel she carries on her back when she comes here from somewhere else. There are two males with her, but they are not seen much."

"Then one of you — "

"No longer a matter of concern. Get the mite from the female so we can get the competition with your advisor underway. Can you imagine the look on his face when you show it to him?"

Fig's heart began to race. He *was* on the cusp of a great discovery, one that would make him famous. Rockbubblers, hairjumblers, matchmites, all demons from somewhere else. This was the experience of a lifetime. Greater than Oz, Narnia, Neverland, Barsoom, Pellucidar, all of the rest. Nothing could be more perfect than this!

He opened the door, entered, and looked from left to right, still listening to the directions in his earbud. He saw three waitresses bustling about with meals stacked on their arms like giant buttons of extreme fashion.

"The one with the long red hair," the speaker chirped.

At first, Fig frowned at what he saw. The woman's clothes had seen better days, a patch on one knee, a slight tear on a sleeve. Her shoulders sagged. Furrows hung under puffy and listless eyes. A smile forced itself on her face for the benefit of the customers. She was visibly tired and overworked.

But she was not wrapped in the despair of her lot, Fig decided as he watched. No, that too was clear. There was defiance underneath it all, her motions not tentative but quickly done like a robot so she could move on to the next step. Whatever was her plight, despite everything, she labored on.

And her face. Pale skin, oh so very pale, and large green eyes — Bette Davis eyes, a previous generation would have said. She definitely was different.

Fig moved to intercept her as she headed back toward a hallway leading to the rear. He reached out to touch her arm, but she quickly pulled it away.

"The imp in the jar," he bent down and whispered in her ear. "A matchmite from another realm. I know you have it."

The woman blinked. "How do you know? How..." The tiredness she could not shake off stole away the rest of her words. But the little she spoke was accented. She was not from anywhere near here.

Fig inhaled her essence. He smelled spicecinnamon, nutmeg, and — and other scents as well. More forgotten memories from childhood suddenly surfaced. He remembered spotting the new girl, Margaret, on the first day of eighth grade. Not knockout gorgeous like the blond already surrounded by a half dozen of the jocks, but sassy, perfect for a nerd who would want nothing better than to pledge to her his sword. *The Scarlet Pimpernel* and *The Prisoner of Zenda* had become the stories that then ran through his head.

Yes, there were other dreams that had matured with him as he grew. Visit to a new unexplored land had become no longer enough. There had to be adventure as well, the rescue of the princess. No, better than that, the faithful retainer who rescued — what had he imagined — yes, rescued no less than the queen, the Queen of the Eight Universes.

He hesitated a moment more as another thought crowded in. Impossible. Truly impossible. Wasn't he already experiencing wonders enough? But like the crescendo at the end of a symphony, the feeling welled up within him, drowning out the rest of his thoughts. The icing on the cake would be if the woman who controlled the mite, the one standing right before him, *also* was not from the Earth. Like the imps, not from the Earth, but instead... He imagined the drum roll. Not from the Earth, but instead... the *Queen*.

Then before he could stop himself, Fig fell to his knees, ripped the electronics from his head, and offered it up to her as if it were her long-lost crown.

No one in the dining area noticed. The patrons continued paying attention to their own concerns. But out of the corner of his eye, Fig saw two men approach them from the hall that must have led to the kitchen, one big with bulky muscles flexing through a tight T-shirt, the other shorter, smaller, with a vacant look on his face, as if the other was dragging him along.

"Is this guy giving you trouble, Briana?" the big man asked. "Jake and I can take care of it. Go outside for a breath of air for a bit. You have been pushing yourself too hard. Worrying too much. The extra shifts so all three of us get enough to eat — well, you do eat everybody's desserts, and that's okay. But anyway, maybe tomorrow we can figure out a way around the security guards."

Fig wanted to find out more about the matchmite, but to his surprise, he blurted other words instead. "How can I serve you?" he asked.

Briana stared back at him for a second, then answered. "You have no accent. You are from here, not Murdina, yet you speak of — "

"Briana?" The big man moved menacingly close.

Briana shook her head. "No Maurice. I must take the chance. There is nothing left to try." She turned her attention back to Fig. "USX, the aerospace company. We have made almost a dozen attempts to see an Ashley Anderfield, but have failed every time. And with each day, the time remaining grows less. I must find out soon, or it will be too late."

"USX?" Fig asked. He sprang to his feet. She *was* in distress! Unbelievable. On top of everything, every bit of it, *all* of his childhood fantasy was going to come true!

"I can get in there!" he said. Like from the spillway of a dam, the rest gushed forth. "I have an offer to start this Friday."

Briana drew back. "You are trying to fool me. This is too much of a coincidence."

"No, no. It is true. The aerospace companies are always blasting 'come work with us' emails to campuses everywhere. All of the physics grad students do it — send a resumé in reply to every single one. A good number of the times, we get called in for an interview, and a job offer follows. A short vacation if nothing else. I got five acceptances this year — just in case. USX was one of them. And once I show up there, I can arrange for you to meet with whomever you wish."

Briana's face brightened. The fatigue faded away. "Besides matchmites, what else do you know about me?" she asked.

"Briana?" Maurice's voice became more urgent.

Fig ignored the implied threat. As he looked at Briana, now all he saw was beauty shining through the weariness.

"Well, nothing. I only want to — "

Briana put a finger to his lips. "Come outside, and I will explain," she said. "Explain about more things than matchmites. Although I warn you, you will not believe everything that you will hear."

"Try me!" Fig said, smiling from ear to ear.

Part Four

Turn of the Ratchetwheel

Escape

THALING FROWNED with disgust at the guilt hanging over him like an obsidian cloud. Angus had been sentenced to die a prolonged and horrible death while he himself was free to roam wherever he desired. The words he had spoken to Dinton when Angus was captured had only postponed his brother's fate, nothing more.

Thaling ran his reasoning through his mind one final time. He could confess he, too, had used the forbidden crafts and offer himself up also. There would be justice in that.

But what he was doing was important — so very important. It was the means to strike back at the Faithful, to avenge what had happened not only to Alika, but to everyone else, too.

Therefore, if he was not to die, then so should not Angus. For the thousandth time, the conclusion was the same. His brother must be freed.

"Stand back!" He tried to sound as authoritative as he could as he approached the two guardsmen in front of the little alcove. Angus could not be seen in the opening. He was probably back in the little cavern's interior that snaked off to the left.

"Flock Leader Dinton has commanded the prisoner is to have no visitors," one of the guards said.

"I am a flock leader as much as is my older brother," Thaling said. "I can speak wherever I please."

The two guards muttered something but moved down the passageway out of earshot. Thaling entered the alcove. His brother was squatting with a brush over an uncoiled portion of a large scroll.

"Greetings, brother," Thaling said. "I bring you good news."

Angus startled and looked up. "What took you so long?" he asked. Then he pointed at the scroll. "I have almost run out of more nonsense to add to this fable." He cocked his head as he rose. "I am curious. What did you say to change Dinton's mind?"

"Nothing," Thaling said. "I don't think any more words would alter his disposition."

"Then, begone. I do not need a stool or easel to make things a small bit easier for me here."

Thaling looked around the alcove. Except for the scroll, a bowl of ink, a brush, and a few stalks of uneaten greens from the garden near the surface, it was completely bare.

"What I offer is far better," Thaling said. "I have the means to secure your escape."

"Escape? Escape to where?" Angus snorted. "Everyone knows every cranny in these rocks. They have all been explored many times before."

"Not here," Thaling said. He was starting to feel quite satisfied with himself. It was not often he held the upper hand over his brother. "Another cavern. One not connected by a passageway with this one at all."

He stepped back to look out the alcove entrance. The guards were at the turn in the distance, far enough away.

"Mintbreath, attend unto me," he said.

Angus looked curious now, like a courtesan expecting a gift. Thaling's pleasure grew. "Watch the wall there," he pointed as he rocked on his heels like a child expecting a treat.

A small circle opened in the back wall of the alcove and rapidly grew in size, revealing a truncated sphere containing a hovering imp.

"A rockbubbler," Thaling explained. "I have control over quite a few of them."

"Wizardry," Angus said softly. Then, he roared with laughter. "My timid middle brother." He lowered his voice again. "Whoever would have guessed? *You* have violated the oath."

For a moment, Thaling's bliss soared even higher. His brother actually was astonished at what he had been doing. Then almost as quickly, like a balloon punctured by a spear, his satisfaction fell into irritation. Astonished. Why should that be? Were his capabilities so lightly regarded?

"Your words are like the tunic calling the britches black," Thaling snapped back.

"You mean, brother, that I can step into this sphere, and the sprite will take me wherever I want?" Angus asked.

"Wherever *I* want," Thaling answered.

"It was supposed to be Lilacbottom's turn," Mintbreath said.

"Not now, Mintbreath." Thaling's irritation grew. This was not starting out anywhere like he had envisioned. Angus was the same as he always was — trying to cow him into irrelevance.

"I can arrange for food and water to be brought there so that no one notices," Thaling rushed on. "In time, we can get your table, clock, and whatever else moved there as well."

Angus scowled. "So instead of being a prisoner of Dinton, I become one of yours?"

"No, it is not like that at all. I can — "

"Where else can this bubble in the rock go?" Angus interrupted.

"Anywhere. Even up to touch the surface."

Angus' eyes closed. Thaling had never seen him this way. Whenever the three brothers met, Angus was always alert. His eyes flickering from Dinton to himself and back, looking for some advantage, small though it might be.

"I must put on swathing," Angus said.

"There is no need. The environment is the same as it is here."

Angus suddenly reached out and grabbed the dagger at Thaling's waist. He wrapped one arm around his brother and pressed the point into his chin.

"I will need my swathing," Angus repeated.

Thaling tensed. With Angus, one could never quite be sure. He squirmed to crane his head upward and look his brother in the eye. But the knifepoint bit a little deeper, and he stopped. "All right," he said. "You will see soon enough that the protection is not necessary. I will go and fetch your bundling from your alcove and return."

Angus released his grip, and Thaling hastily stepped into Mintbreath's sphere. Soon it disappeared back into the rock leaving not a trace.

THALING INSPECTED Angus' back after he had wrapped him. He tucked and pulled at several places until the coverage was complete. Then they stepped into the rockbubbler's hovering sphere.

"To the other cavern," Thaling said.

"No!" Angus growled through his speaking tube. "The surface. Take me to the surface."

"Don't you understand?" Thaling exploded. "I am not offering you a less gruesome death. It is life instead."

For a second time, Angus reached for Thaling's dagger, but the bundling he was in slowed his effort. Thaling managed to step back a bit but then stumbled against the curved wall of the sphere.

"Are you crazy?" the magician continued. "There is death up there. Only death. That certainty is what has confined us here below."

Angus spread his arms wide in a threatening circle and leaned over Thaling as he sprawled.

"The surface," he repeated.

Thaling exhaled slowly. He had tried his best. The long confinement affected each of them in their own unique way. Angus was high strung. Maybe he could stand it no longer.

He stretched out his hand and grabbed Angus' arm, pulling himself back erect.

"To the surface, Mintbreath," he said through clinched teeth. "If that is what my brother wants, then so shall it be."

As the sphere started to rise, Angus' eyes widened slightly as he saw the rock around him seem to sink and disappear below.

"Third floor. Lingerie. *Ding!*" Mintbreath said after a moment.

"What? What did you say?" Thaling asked.

Another moment passed

"Second floor. Men's clothing. *Ding!*"

"What are you doing?" Thaling's voice hardened.

"Gimme a break, Boss," Mintbreath said. "It gets boring only going back and forth. Up and down is a rare treat."

Thaling scowled. He would deal with the rockbubbler later.

"Ground floor. Watch your step," Mintbreath said, as a tiny circle appeared directly overhead. Thaling looked up. The boundary was ringed with a ragged wreath of unmowed grass.

As the sphere continued its slow rise, Angus placed his hands on Thaling's shoulders. He raised one leg knee-high. The air below began mixing with that above.

Haste, Thaling thought. Haste was what was needed now. So that this all could be over, and he could return to the safety below.

Without thinking any more about what to do, Thaling cupped his hands underneath his brother's boot and strained upward. The sphere

216

continued climbing, and Angus leaned awkwardly over Thaling's head to keep his hands grasping the expanding circle's edge.

Finally, when Angus could get enough advantage, he scrambled out of the sphere and onto the surface, vanishing from sight. Thaling's last image of his brother was his white shroud-like swathing disappearing voluntarily into what must turn out to be a waiting grave.

Mintbreath reversed direction and soon the sphere was completely below ground.

"One thing I gotta say, Boss," Mintbreath shook his head. "All white? It is not mid-summer yet. You guys sure don't have any sense of fashion."

Convergence

ASHLEY LOOKED across her desk at Fig. He was dressed much the same as when he had interviewed. Only his eyes appeared different. They kept moving back and forth from her face and down to her phone.

"Thank you for coming in a day early," Ashley said. "You will get paid for today as well, but it will take a few weeks for the computer to sort things out and have it show up in a check."

"That's Okay, Ms. Anderfield," Fig said. "There is something more important I need to talk to you about."

Ashley couldn't help but grimace. He must be backing out and did not have the guts to tell her over the phone. Something must have come up with CERN. So much for her little barb of spite. "Oh?" was all she managed to say.

The phone rang unexpectedly before she could continue. It had been silent for almost a week now.

"Maybe you should answer," Fig said. "It might be important."

"Shouldn't be." Ashley reached for the handset. "One thing I need to tell you at the very first is that this is my last…"

She stopped and spoke into the phone. "This is Ashley Anderfield."

"Gate Seventeen Security here," the voice said. "Sorry to bother you on your last day, but the persistent trio is back again — the ones who claim they must see you but will not say about what."

"Same answer as before," Ashley said. "Send them away."

"This time, the story is a little different. The woman says she wants to speak to a Figaro Newton who should be in your office right now."

Ashley felt puzzled as if she was the butt of an elaborate prank. She covered the handset and shook her head at Fig. "Some pests I can't get rid of. Apparently, they know you. What is this all about?"

"I think you should give them the okay to come in," Fig said. "What

218

they want to ask you is important."

"Important? Well, yes, to them obviously, but why is it of concern to USX?"

Ashley frowned. Wait a minute, she thought. By tomorrow, she would not be part of USX. That was no longer relevant to her. She studied Fig for a moment. Whatever was going on, he seemed very eager.

"I was amazed about what they had to say. You will be, too," he said.

She shrugged and spoke back into the phone. "Okay, badge them as Unclassified and escort them to my office. I guess I *will* see them this time."

"One of them, the woman, says she has no ID."

Ashley looked critically at Fig. "You were amazed? How exactly?"

"Have you ever experienced something you never dreamed would be possible? But could be proved to you without a shadow of doubt."

Ashley frowned again. It *was* her last day. What did she really care? Maybe this would give Tom an even bigger problem to solve than she thought.

"Badge her anyway," she said over the phone. "I will take full responsibility." She crossed her fingers. If security thought it through about her not being around later....

"Yes, ma'am," the guard said. "One of us will bring them right up."

Ashley raised one eyebrow and looked at Fig for an explanation, but he offered none. In silence, they waited until the trio of visitors appeared.

ASHLEY DID not know exactly what to expect, but certainly not this. The small woman led the group. She wore a business suit — wrinkled and in a far too shocking green, no stockings, scruffy sandals rather than heels, no makeup, and long red hair that could use a vigorous brushing.

The two men accompanying her were stranger still. One was tall and muscular. He hovered near the woman with a tense expression on his face. Shabby jeans and a dirty tee, his triceps flexed as if he would lash out in an instant if the guard so much as touched the woman at his side. The third man was shorter and dressed in much the same way. But his eyes held a vacant stare, searching in the distance for something no longer there.

219

"My name is Briana," the woman said. "I apologize for our appearance, but serving meals and bussing tables in a dive has given us meager funds to make ourselves more presentable. My companions are Maurice and Jake."

Maurice tipped his head slightly but remained silent. Jake seemingly returned back to the here and now. "My car," he said. "It must be protected. It is in the open for everyone to see."

"Jake, this whole place is guarded," Maurice said. "Surveillance cameras everywhere. There is nothing to worry about."

"Suppose they check the VIN number."

"Jake, we have been over this more than a dozen times, remember? I popped out the car's ID and replaced the plates with some dealer cardboard. We made sure to park it somewhere different every night. Relax, let Briana give her spiel."

He shrugged at Ashley. "Sleeping on the open ground in some cheap blankets can make one grouchy after a while — or in Jake's case, maybe a little more out of it than usual."

"Why are you here?" Ashley asked as politely as she could. She was seriously considering calling the guards to escort these looneys back out.

"Let me show you a little demonstration." Briana moved to Ashley's desk and took the seat Fig had hastily abandoned. "This is going to be hard for you to believe. It is an example of what you would call 'magic.'"

"Magic? Hard to believe?" Ashley let the glimmer of a smile form on her face but said nothing more.

ASHLEY POINTED out the assistant's bay, and Fig and Maurice brought in three more chairs so they all could sit. Briana's demonstration had been convincing. Somehow, she was able to manipulate a hand-sized metal cylinder without touching it at all. Then she released a tiny winged creature from a jar and had it buzz around the room according to her commands.

If it had not been for the visit to Ziggy's, Ashley would have dismissed it all as some very clever stage magician's performance. But the way she had felt when gazing at the little gnome was still a vivid memory. Dumbfounded, she listened to all of Briana's tale, and then Fig's after that.

All vestige of doubt crumbled. A week ago, stockbrokers who used sorcery to predict the market and tiny imps altering digital records would have been mind-blowing. But not now. If there were such things as love potions, then other wonders were equally plausible.

"And you think that somehow Kahuna Enterprises is involved with... with magic?" Ashley asked.

Briana nodded. "Has to be. The broker, Emmertyn, said he had a single client. The RFP you received must have been from whoever was directing him. The return address on the document tells us where he is."

"But for what purpose?" Ashley shook her head. Her stomach rumbled, even though it was still early in the morning. "This is so much to take in at one time."

"I think they are trying to escape," Briana said.

"Escape? Who? Escape from what?"

"They are beings from another orb, as am I."

"Stop right there!" Ashley stood and pushed out her upraised palm. "I accept the magic part. I… I have to." She gulped in a lung-full of air.

"But aliens from another planet. And you are from somewhere else, too?"

"Yes, I came here through a magic portal."

Ashley gripped the edge of her desk. "Right, and a magic portal also? No! Too much." She shook her head almost violently from side to side and then crumpled back into her chair.

"I know it is hard to believe it all," Maurice said. "But, you, yourself, spoke so fervently about the existence of powerful love potions that take over one's mind. It took Briana several days to convince Jake and me. Well, because at first she wanted to tell us nothing. But having to take care of resetting the portals arrivals and departures every morning before we even stirred got to be too much for her."

Ashley continued to shake her head.

"It does not matter if you believe everything or not," Briana said. "You have told us what we need to know. Hilo, Hawaii. That is where we are going next."

Ashley stopped the agitation roaring through her head. She felt calmness wash back over her as if she were slipping into a bath at precisely the right temperature. The trio didn't care what she thought! They weren't trying to convince her. They didn't care. Whatever was going on, it wasn't a swindle, and she was not their pigeon.

She studied Fig's expression. He was not protesting either. Maybe, just maybe, like love potions, there was truth to the rest of their tales as well.

But to Hawaii? They can't even afford decent clothes. And to do what? Confront aliens? How? Walk up to them and say 'Hi'? Suppose they were dangerous?

Good questions. But then, she reminded herself, did they really matter to her? She had been shunning the trio for weeks. Now they had what they wanted and would be out of her hair, out of her life. She could get on with her own. Her thoughts slowed to a halt. Yeah, her life. What life? What was she now going to do with herself after this last hurrah?

"Wait," she said. Her training as a manager of state-of-the-art projects kicked in. Old habits were hard to let go. "Don't rush off like that without a plan."

"Why do you care?" Briana shot back.

"Instinct," Ashley shrugged. "'Plan the work. Then work the plan.' That's what I do... well, that's what I did."

Briana tugged on the stray curl, as if trying to get energy to what she did next. "Perhaps then, you also can help," the younger woman said.

Brainstorm

ASHLEY SWIVELED her chair and rose. She shook her head as she looked at her whiteboard. It had remained completely erased for a week. No schedules, no To-dos, or any other reminder of her past remained.

She glanced back at the four occupants of the guest chairs. Like eager kindergarteners on the first day of school, they seemed intent on listening to what she was going to say. Good.

"It looks like you could benefit from a little brainstorming," she told them. A tiny sense of well-being poked through her overriding sense of bitterness about what was happening in her own life. Over the years, she had facilitated many such sessions, and if any group needed one, this was it.

"It seems to me we have not thought through clearly what is to be done." She picked up a colored marker and wrote 'Goal' on the whiteboard. "What is it?"

"To find out if the exiles have used magic and escaped." Briana rose halfway out of her chair. "To have come out of the forgetting spell of the Faithful — and, as a consequence, are a dire threat to the people of this planet."

Ashley smiled. Good again. She wrote 'exiles,' 'magic,' and 'escape' on the board. Usually, It took a while for the first person to crack — no longer able to stand the silence. But Briana had broken the ice immediately. Now to add some more impetus for the others to join in.

"Seeing the future, tiny imps, potions of love," Ashley said. "Don't we have all the evidence of magic we need? What do others of you think?"

"Those indeed are aspects of the crafts," Briana answered before anyone else could speak. "I do not need them to convince me the arts of the masters exist. And as far as I can tell, the micromites from CERN have no connection with exiles, nor does what happened to you in the

223

tattoo shop."

Briana rushed on. "Even Emmertyn's trances may not be connected. He is a native, not from somewhere else. His customer is my only lead, and perhaps he, too, is native to this planet."

"Can't be." Jake surprisingly came out of his stupor. For the first time since Ashley had met him, the fog in his eyes dissipated. "Connected to a broker who never failed? Why would anyone with even a single brain cell not insist on bigger and bigger trades? Plowing the profit from one deal back into the next? I know my father sure would. My father..."

Jake lapsed back into his inner world, and Briana continued. "So, we have to go to Hawaii and find out what Kahuna Enterprises is all about. I cannot return to my own home with only speculation. I must show I can be relied upon for convincing proof, regardless of what it is."

The others begin to squirm in their seats like newly hatched tadpoles. It looked like they also had things to say. But to get too far behind with the recording would cause the momentum eventually to die out.

"Hold it a moment." She held up her hand, turned back to the whiteboard, and rapidly began adding memory joggers for what had been said — 'micromites,' 'tattoo,' 'trance,' and 'profits.'

"Wouldn't the ones who call themselves the Faithful create a prison that was magical somehow... something that could not be escaped from?" Ashley asked when she was done.

"Evidently the victors did not," Briana said. "Randor would not have asked for help had they done so."

Ashley studied Briana. The young woman's tone hinted at a little hostility. Perhaps she was regretting she had asked for help — that someone else was holding the marker and leading the group.

"But you said whatever the confinement is, it has been successful for a thousand years," Ashley persisted. "That is a long time. Enough to chip away a path to freedom, no matter how thick were walls of stone and mortar. If that were the case, they would have become free long ago."

"Perhaps something natural," Maurice said. "There are active volcanoes on the Hawaiian Islands. Lava tubes. Caves and caverns. The location of the prison could be below ground."

Good. Finally, more were joining in.

"Hey, below ground!" Fig craned forward. Good. He was feeling the momentum starting to build. "The micromites spoke of rockbubbler imps and a master far away and underground."

"Too hot," Jake woke from his private reverie a second time. "It would be too hot. Nobody could survive for centuries in the bowels of a volcano."

"Nothing negative, Jake," Ashley said. "We're brainstorming here. Let the possibilities interact. Don't shoot them down as soon as they emerge. Instead, build on them. Go with the flow."

Now a long silence did fall on the group. No one else spoke again. Ashley bit her lip. This always happened when someone had to be reminded of the rules. Jake probably would not contribute again at all. And the others would become more cautious, censuring their thoughts before they became verbal. She wrote 'below ground' and 'volcano' on the white board to cover the awkwardness starting to fill the room like a creeping miasma of doubt.

How long should she merely stand there before intervening and trying to pump things up again? Ashley smiled encouragement at Fig and then Maurice, but neither responded.

"This is not working!" Briana said suddenly. "We are wasting our time. I do not have a storm in my brain. We should go to Hilo and then decide what to do next." She frowned at Ashley. "This is *my quest*, not yours. I only asked for your *help*, not to take over everything."

Ashley started to reply but caught the words in her throat. Getting into a pissing contest with Briana would end the chance of anything coming of this. She returned to the whiteboard and wrote 'too hot.'

"Yes, too hot," Briana said. "Randor was swathed from head to toe when he appeared before my father. Near the natural heat of a volcano would make things almost unbearable. They would fry in something like that."

Another muteness. Both Maurice and Fig looked away when Ashley tried again to encourage them with a smile.

"So, maybe the bundling works like a wetsuit," Jake said as Ashley was about to try jogging things again. "Not too hot, just warm enough."

Ashley wrote 'just warm enough' on the board.

"Then for them, maybe our air is like the ocean," Fig said.

"They would not need to wear swathing in the prison," Maurice said. "They would not look hideous to one another when among themselves. As Buddha says, 'The greatest wisdom is seeing through appearances.'"

"Seeing through appearances!" Fig said. "Here's a wild thought." He turned to Briana. "How do you know the exiles swath themselves to cover how hideous they look?"

"Why else?" Briana answered.

"Because," Maurice said slowly. "Because, maybe, just maybe, the swathing serves some other purpose than disguise."

Ashley wrote quickly, trying to keep up with the sudden outburst of ideas… 'hideous' and 'disguise.'

Now, she thought. Now was the time to provide a boost. "Hmm, some other purpose," she said. "Like what?"

"Well, like… like something else swathing is used for," Fig said.

The hush returned for a few moments and then, "Like protection from the elements!" Maurice exclaimed. "Yes, that's it! Gotta be! The heat of a volcano is not oppressive. To the exiles, it is *normal*. And if that is so, then the temperature of the air on the surface is *freezing* to them. The swathing is protection like that worn by an Antarctic explorer — protection from the *cold*."

"That explains the prison!" Fig agreed. "There was no need for rock and iron. Nothing to check on and repair. The exiles could venture above ground, but only wrapped so they could barely move. Only briefly could brave explorers manage to survive. The exterior of our planet is a hostile environment for them."

"That does make sense," Briana said slowly, then shook her head. "But it is not a complete answer. There still is the matter of the crafts. With them, who knows what they could accomplish."

"I agree," Fig said. "But it does explain a lot — how they were able to communicate. Visits to the surface for short times by explorers. Limited contact with a few humans, and the internet for all the rest."

"I still need to verify this with my own eyes," Briana said. She shot a steely glance of what had to be defiance in Ashley's direction. Then she smiled at Fig. "Speculation, even by what you call a physicist, is not enough." For a moment, she played with a stray curl. "But you guys are usually good at math, right? I do need someone to figure out the destination coordinates of Hilo for the portal."

"Sure, I probably can do that," Fig said. "But, Briana, don't you see? If what we have come up with is correct, there is no way the Heretics could escape from where the Faithful had put them."

To Hilo

DINTON WAS always cautious, Angus reasoned. But this time, he could not be sure. Jormind surely would have told him Oscar's hut was near the opening to the crop garden. It probably was only a short matter of time before a troop would brave the cold and come looking for him. To be prudent, he must get far enough away so that his elder brother will have no thoughts of pursuit. The base of operations would have to shift to Hilo, as daunting as that was.

Angus turned his attention to the clothing he had laid out on the floor. He removed his swathing as rapidly as he could and huddled in the blast of air coming from the open oven. The fabric he had added was fragile, and if he moved too quickly, it would rip and become useless. He kicked aside the packing boxes that had arrived in only two days, exactly as the seller said they would. One arm skittered into an outstretched sleeve, and immediately he heard a crunching noise as if one were wadding up a large sheet of coarse paper.

He inhaled deeply, and then immediately regretted it. The air was cold, frosty cold. His lungs stung from the contact. "Control yourself," he muttered. "As the saying goes, 'Speed makes garbage.' Fix the sleeve first and then proceed."

He knelt down and carefully inverted the loose shirtsleeve, exposing the inside where he had stitched on the delicate strips of cloth. Yes, there was damage. He would have to rip out what was there and replace it with a fresh insulation.

"Aerogel," Angus said aloud, practicing the native language in order to force himself to move slowly as he resewed. Studying Oscar's notes on using the computer and doing searches had opened doors he did not even know existed.

He stopped and shook his head. No, not enough time for more surfing the net, he thought. Must stay focused. Most of the technology would die with the natives anyway. He shrugged. It would not be a great loss.

Carefully, he donned one of Oscar's shirts, the one on which he had sewn on the panels of aerogel fabric in front and back. The short sleeves from several other shirts he had stitched together into longer tubes and secured the insulation around them as well. He worked his arms through their interiors like a land eel hunting rat eggs in a tunnel.

The britches Angus had augmented in the same way, and once he had them on after two aborted attempts that also damaged what he had added and then repaired, he stepped out of the kitchen into the other room of the hut for a first test. Instantly, his head, his face, his hands, and his feet began to grow numb, but his arms, legs, and torso felt no discomfort.

"It works," he continued verbalizing to no one as he reentered the kitchen and placed his hands inside the oven to rewarm the stiffening fingers. A silica gel, he mused, almost weightless because of being crammed so full of microscopic pockets of air. Insulation so a human could withstand the frigid air of the south pole, protect liquid hydrogen in a rocket's fuel tank — or provide the means by which a Heretic Who Has Found the Truth could brave downtown Hilo without a single wrap of swathing.

When his hands were again warm enough to function, Angus put on his boots, strapped the lithium polymer battery to his back and hooked the output to the wires leading to his feet. For his face, he slid on an insulated Halloween mask, covered on the backside, one for a 'bigfoot,' whatever that was. He smiled. If by chance it were ripped away, the startled native would see a face not so very different. Next came gloves also electrically warmed. Finally, he slipped on a hoodie, aerogel padded on the inside, and pulled tight the drawstring. When he was done, Angus looked in a mirror.

More humanlike in shape, better than swathing, he supposed, but he could not hold in the laughter. He was warm, comfortably warm, but looked like a slightly overstuffed and insane native. Pass unnoticed on a street in Hilo? Probably not.

So, he should not try to, he decided at last. Rather than attempting to conform as best he could, he should stand out in the crowd instead. Have a reason why he was clothed so oddly. Perhaps a final adornment would do the trick.

THE SUMMONED cab honked outside of Oscar's front door. Angus draped the sign he had drawn in bright red letters around his neck and stuffed the recluse's credit cards and cell phone into his tummy pouch. He took one last look around the interior of Oscar's shack. The shipping boxes, packing slips, and remaining scraps of aerogel fabric all destroyed. If Dinton's minions came to check, they would get no clue to what he had achieved. Pursuit would not be possible.

He stepped outside and approached the passenger seat in the taxi. "Lost an election bet." The cabbie read from the sign tied around his neck. "Wow, mister, what kind of wager was that?"

The Weight of Leadership

BRIANA SENT the portal away and turned her attention to the shabby little hut. It was not as she had imagined — peeling paint, bare wood, and windows completely draped behind taped together pieces of pane. If this was the foothold of the exiles on the surface world, it did not speak of any magic.

Google Earth had given them the coordinates they needed, and, with the help of the portal's user manual, Fig had figured out how to translate them to the ones the device would understand. He had also calculated the settings to take them to the back yard of Ashley's house when they were ready to return.

At first, Briana had wanted to come alone. "It is, after all, *my* quest," she had said. But everyone else thought very little of the idea. To stop the protests, she had agreed, but only on one condition — there was to be only a single other traveler. She had not felt this excited in some while, and the tedium of waiting until it was daylight in Hawaii and then the ferrying passengers one by one would have been too much to bear.

Jake had been out of the question. The deep depression he had fallen into could not be broken. He would be useless if an emergency arose. The decision not to choose Maurice was difficult. But Fig was so… Well, he was like a newborn puppy, so eager to please his master. And, after all, he did deserve some reward for getting the meeting with Ashley arranged.

Briana watched as her 'scout' approached the door of the hut cautiously. He put his ear to it and then jerked back.

"It is warm to the touch," Fig said. "Surprisingly so." He frowned for a moment. "Then again, maybe not."

Fig began stepping over the weeds clustered to the very edge of the hut and pacing off around its perimeter. After a few moments, he returned.

"All of the windows are covered," he said. "No sounds coming from inside. I think the place is unoccupied." He put his hand on the door latch and pushed it open.

"Fig, be careful!" Briana called out. "We don't want to leave any sign we have been here. If there is something that has to be done about the exiles, it will be a matter for my father to decide once I return home."

"All clear," Fig said after he scanned the interior from side to side. Without another word, he entered. Briana scrambled to follow and shut her eyes to the blast of hot air pushing to freedom through the open door. Instinctively, she dropped her backpack to the floor and began to fan her face.

"It is the oven in the kitchen," Fig pointed. "It's on and its door is open. Fits in well with the idea the exiles are using this place."

Briana forgot about her admonition not to disturb anything. Her memories about her first impressions of Hollywood Boulevard flooded back. This, too, was bizarre, but in a completely different way, more like the sty of an alien pig than the residence of an advanced culture.

Fig sat down at the table and turned on the computer.

"No need to do a data search," Briana said. "I know how long such a thing can take."

"Not the internet," Fig said. "There is an email account here. Let's see what we can find out."

He clicked a few times and then pointed at the screen. "Look at this! A message to the broker you were talking about. The one in New York. See, there are instructions to buy up salt domes in the Gulf of Mexico."

He pondered for a moment. "Sulfur," he said finally. "Salt domes are a source for sulfur. Why would the exiles have any interest in that? "

Briana did not pay attention. Instead, she spotted coils of alabaster white material on the floor. She hurried to them and pulled up a helmet of the same color buried in the pile. It would completely cover one's head with only eye slits protected by goggles and a speaking tube poking out.

"Exactly like what I saw in the council room!" she exclaimed. "The exiles! This *is* of their making." She looked about again. "But a kitchen, an oven, computers? How long has this been going on? What have they been up to?"

Fig rose and came to examine the swathing. "Does it matter?" he asked. "Your task was to find if they had escaped from their confinement." He waved his hand around the room. "Here is the proof."

"But as you said," Briana rebutted, "this is only for explorers, not for all seven hundred others remaining entombed. Maybe this is only a first outpost. Kept as a monument. Maybe there are more of them elsewhere."

She returned to the table. "Continue searching on the computer," she commanded. "I will look through this scattered paper for additional clues."

LIKE THE relentless progress of an immense grinding wheel, dawn turned into dusk. Briana got up and stretched. Only one more bit of information had been found — in a letter, the address of a storage warehouse in downtown Hilo.

"I have been thinking," Fig said as he joined her in the stretch. "There must be a way for the exiles to get from the caverns to this place. An opening, a cave…"

"Right!" Briana exclaimed. The taste of adventure strengthened into a seductive lure. "Let's look for that before we go to Hilo. It must be around here somewhere."

"I don't know, Briana," Fig said. "It is getting dark. Who knows what we might run into?"

Briana raised one eyebrow in imitation of Ashley and laughed. "Spoken like the true follower of, what did you call her, the Queen of the Eight Dimensions?"

Fig blushed. "Yes, milady," he said. "I forgot. By all means, let us push forward."

AS THE shadows grew long from the setting sun, the path leading away from the hut to the cave opening was found. Fig scrambled to enter and turned on the light of his cell phone. Briana tried to follow, but she could not squeeze through with the pack on her back.

"Leave it here." Fig extended a hand to help. "Tucked away just inside, no one will notice, especially in the dark."

Together they entered. The floor of the cave was littered with a jumble of rocks, some smooth and others jagged like teeth of a shark. They moved slowly, shining the phone light to show the way. As they progressed, the walls converged. The wide and low opening narrowed into a much narrower path.

"We've reached the end," Fig said after a while. "See, there is only blank wall ahead." He swung the phone from side to side.

"There!" Briana said. "Look on the left. The passage turns to the left."

"Hmm," Fig said. "We have come quite far, and it must be totally dark outside by now. Perhaps, we should get back and return on another day. Maybe there are many branches from this main conduit that we have already passed. With all of us armed with lights, we can be thorough."

"Only a bit more," Briana persisted. She felt she was getting near to the end of her quest. No sense in turning back now.

Fig smiled. "Of course, my Quee… of course, Briana," he said.

They entered the passage to the side to continue their search. Again, Fig swiveled the phone around. This part of the cavern was much wider and extended far into the darkness. After a few hundred paces more, Fig suddenly tripped over one of the rocks on the floor. As he fell, the phone flew out of his hand and crashed to the ground.

The light winked out. Suddenly, they were surrounded by darkness.

Briana fell to her knees, and the two of them began groping the ground, trying to find the phone. They bumped into one another and shuffled around, increasing the area of their search from where they had first started.

"I've found it!" Briana said and stood up. She thrust it forward to where she thought Fig might be. He brushed against her low to the ground. For a second she felt a bit flustered by the close contact, but then it passed. She bent down and extended her hand forward. As she did, a thick wetness surprised her.

"What's this?" she asked. "It's sticky like blood. Fig, are you hurt?"

"I just fell," Fig said. "Gravity is not just a good idea, it is the law."

"Are you hurt?"

"A little bit," Fig agreed. "I must have cut myself on one of the rocks when I went down. It's my leg. It stings a bit. But no matter. When we get out of here, I can get stitched up."

The transfer of the phone in the darkness took a little while. Briana did not want it to be dropped again. Fig pressed the ON switch when he finally grasped it firmly, but nothing happened. He exhaled through his mouth. "Apparently, it is broken," he said.

"My glowsticks are in my backpack. I should have brought them."

"It is too bad the micromites refused to come with me," Fig said. "Something about the loop back through their own realm that frightens them. Our only choice is to feel our way out in the dark."

"Okay, which way?" Briana asked.

"I... I don't know," Fig said. "We will have to put out our hands until we find a wall and then travel along it. Cup a finger through one of my belt loops in the back. We don't want to get separated."

Briana did not like this. It did not feel like something from the sagas at all. They had to get back to Ashley's and then to an emergency room and quickly.

Like a two-person clump in the game of Sardines, they shuffled forward a dozen steps, and then Fig halted.

"Wall," he said.

"Now which way?" Briana asked.

"I... I still don't know," Fig answered. "With all the groping on the ground, I lost my bearings."

Briana felt panic begin to swell within her. No one knew they were here. The only ones who had any idea of their general vicinity were thousands of miles away.

If they waited to morning, there might be enough light. But the blood she had felt seeping out of Fig's pants was more than a trickle. They had to get him out now as soon as possible. Back to the portal, to Ashley's and then an emergency room.

What should she do? What would Ashley do if she were here?

Ashley would *think*, she decided after a moment. She would use whatever resources were at hand, and somehow, somehow, use them to find a way out.

But what resources did she have? She was no thaumaturge, no alchemist, no magician, no sorcerer, no wizard. All she had was Fig, and he was the one needing the help.

Fig! Yes, Fig was her resource. He had been able to track her down even though she was a continent away. He would have to save them both.

"Fig, Fig!" she said. "Start thinking. Use your head. Come up with something."

"I think I need to sit down for a while," Fig said. "Put my head between my legs. I'm starting to get a little woozy."

"No, not that," Briana said. She twisted him around to face her as best she could and smartly slapped him on the cheek.

"Ow! What was that for?"

"Think! Fig, think! Physics, right? How can that help?" She was yelling now, and her words bounced off the walls echoing repeatedly, making their plight feel even worse.

"Echoes," Fig slurred. "Sound bouncing off of walls and returning. The time delay tells us how far away they are."

"Echoes, yes, and then what?"

Briana felt Fig slowly rise back to his feet. "Keep me oriented exactly as I tell you," he said, "but do not say a word." She felt his arms rise to his face to cup his mouth and then heard him shout, "Hi!"

Immediately she heard "Hi!" bounce back, then weaker a second time, and then a third.

"Now turn me exactly 180 degrees," he said, "and I will try again."

Briana did as she was told, and this time… she could not be sure… this time the echo returned a little later.

"The two side walls," Fig said. "Now turn me ninety degrees from where I am now."

The third echo took still longer to return. There was little doubt about it.

"Okay, now we are oriented along the tunnel direction," Fig said. "One more echo will tell us which has the longer path."

"The way you are facing now was the longer one," Briana said when the next echo returned.

"I think so, too. So we will go in the opposite direction."

"But —"

"I know. I know. This passage might not be long, but let's assume it is. We had only travelled down it a little bit. The opposite direction is the way we want to go."

Fig continued to send out signals, and as he did, the response time grew shorter and shorter. Eventually, they found themselves facing another wall. Fig turned ninety degrees and then the other way after that. This time they chose the direction having the longer echo return.

After what seemed excruciatingly long, they were back to the surface. Fig had stopped speaking the last few hundred steps. Briana had to become the one calling out, to prop him up, using all of her strength to keep him moving forward. When they reached the open air, she let him sink to the ground gently as best she could.

Then Briana opened her pack and broke one of her remaining glowsticks. She took another with her and hurried down the dimly lit path to the hut. Rushing inside as the glow of the first faded away, she broke the second. There! What she was looking for — the swathing on the floor.

Returning to the mouth of the cave, she hacked off a strip of the shrouding long enough to serve as a tourniquet and bound up Fig's leg. She looked down at him while she cradled his head in her lap. Should she talk to him, trying to keep him awake? She did not know.

Briana pressed the little button on the side of the watch she had bought at a thrift store. A half hour more before the portal would return. If something should happen to him... The thought hit her with the blow of a pile driver. If something should happen to him, she would be the one responsible.

She had fallen into the role so effortlessly — the leader commanding the troops. Exactly as in the sagas. She was the torchbearer, giving the command to go into battle — to enter a cave with no real preparation at all. And her loyal followers — follower — so wanting to please, so trusting...

The sagas did not speak of *all* the realities of a quest, she realized. Certainly, they told of the glory, of the hard-fought battle to be waged when everything seemed lost. But of responsibility, they were silent. The journey was not only for the goals of the leaders. No. The leaders also were given the burden of trust. Being true to the faith bestowed upon them.

The Catalytic Seed

ANGUS PRESSED the power button, and the heavy door to the loading dock rolled down into place. The warehouse had the musty smell of airborne mold. It had been unoccupied for some time. The grime on the large, frosted windows was as thick as scum on an undisturbed pond. A catwalk circled at the height where a second floor would have been, and his footsteps reverberated throughout the mostly empty volume.

The deliveryman who brought the portable gas leak detector did not even comment on Angus' attire. Nor did the truck driver who rolled the cylinder of liquefied fluorine gas to where Angus had specified. Like building blocks scattered by a small child, the large crates containing the powdered sulfur stood in disarray all about the exile. Well enough, he thought. He had instructed Emmertyn only to get the cargo from the ship transported, not place it in an orderly array.

With the unfortunate change of plans, he would have to procure the fluorine commercially rather than merely tap the source from underground. And that meant an additional risk for exposure. A series of small shipments of compressed gas staged over time to minimize that as much as he could. The fact one delivery happened without a hitch did not prove much. He needed many more.

Angus emitted a long, low growl to push the anxiety of failure away and focused his attention on the experiment he had to perform. He opened one of the sulfur crates, scooped out a small amount of powder, and poured it into an abandoned wine bottle he had found in the litter on the floor. It took him a half-hour more to locate a cork from an unemptied trash bin that would fit. Finally, he pressed the container against the gas output spigot and eased open the valve.

The fluorine shot into the bottle, covering the sulfur in a swirl of pale yellow. Coughing at the fetid odor, he reset the cork and watched for what would happen.

The chemicals started reacting immediately. The light yellow color began to fade. After less than a minute, only the faintest hint remained. Yes, exactly as he had hoped, the two chemicals combined spontaneously. Three types of gas would result, and getting rid of the two he did not desire would be easy. An hour later, only the important one remained.

Angus then unpacked the leak detector and read the operating instructions. Simple enough. Deploy the probe and read the output. Now for the real test. He placed the bottle into the tummy pouch of his hoodie, grabbed the handle of the detector, and called a cab.

TWO HOURS later, Angus handed Oscar's credit card to the taxi driver at the barrier across the Crater Road in the Hawaiian Volcanoes National Park. No one else was about. It was dark. The features of the landscape receded into the blackness — all except one. Off to the left a short hike away, a pool of hot lava glowed with fiery yellows and reds. Occasional spheres of gas bubbled to the surface and then popped, releasing their contents into the air. Had there been more light, one could see wisps of smoke curling into the air like strands of uncombed hair.

"Are you sure, mister?" the cabbie asked. "The rangers have blocked the road because of the new eruption. The trail is closed. It is too dangerous now."

"I am sure," Angus said through the Halloween mask. "This is official business." He tapped the detection probe.

"You can go now," he continued. "I will call when I want a ride back. And, oh, make that a twenty-five percent tip to thank you for your warning."

Angus watched the cab turn around and vanish into the night. He hopped over the barrier and walked along the deserted trail leading to the overlook. A dime store flashlight showed him the way. He whiffed the air and smiled despite himself. Ah, sulfur dioxide. Fatal to the natives, but for him, it tasted as if a pungent perfume was in the air.

He reached the edge of the reborn lava pool glowing fiercely in the night and took a preliminary reading with the probe. None of the gas like that in the bottle was present. Then he inverted the small container and pulled out the cork.

Angus had reviewed all the steps of the incantation a dozen times. Nothing should go wrong — even though what he was attempting had never been tried before. His home world was inert. Its core had cooled ages ago.

He started speaking the incantation. Traditionally, one surrounded the words of power with nonsense both before and after, but he did not bother. No one else was within hailing distance. No native would listen and record what he heard.

Angus' words bound the molecules to the spell as they spilled out of the bottle and sank. Then, the liquid sulfur and fluorine gas escaping from the lava also were coupled, and finally the heat of the liquid rock itself. The last was essential — the motive force.

After the links were complete, even though he could discern nothing about the path of the invisible and released gas, he visualized what must be happening. The vapor was heavier than air and therefore sank onto the surface of the molten pond.

The atoms of gas from the bottle and those emerging from the pool would mingle and swirl about. But because of 'once together, always together,' there then would always be a connection between them. Marshalled by the driving heat energy of the lake, 'like produces like' would force the free sulfur and fluorine to combine, to mimic the molecules that were now their cousins. More of the desired gas would result. None of the other possible reactions would occur.

Angus felt the anticipation build within him. If this did not work, then what? Decades of preparation and planning wasted. Would he even have the heart to start over from scratch? He waited a dozen heartbeats more and then turned on the leak detector a second time. He watched the concentration of the gas that was important. It began to rise — an unseen mist over the now calm pool of lava.

As he continued to monitor, the dangerous gas churning in the pool continued to increase. More and more of it was forming and contributing to the seed catalyzing the production of even more. As long as there was binding energy, as long as the spell was not broken, the cycle would continually repeat. Like an invisible ghost of a giant rising from the dead, it grew and grew.

He grunted with satisfaction. The incantation had worked! Worked exactly as he had hoped. Exactly as he had designed. With a final few words of power, he broke the coupling between all of the elements, and the pond again began to bubble. The monitor reading stabilized and no longer changed.

But now he knew the spell was correct. He could proceed with the grand plan. All three of the volcanoes he had chosen would be seeded, each with much more raw materials then had been in his tiny bottle. All the upwelling energies of each fiery cauldron similarly bound. Then when he did break the connections, that energy would be freed. Each volcano would erupt in a spectacular fashion. Vast quantities of solids, liquids, and most importantly dangerous gasses hurled high into the air. And as a result, after a thousand years, he would be free.

Rising Stakes

ASHLEY PEEKED through the doorway into her bedroom. Fig was sitting up, propped by a lace pillow — a good sign. The ambulance trip to the emergency room had been in time. A few stitches, a transfusion, whatever Briana had rubbed on the wound the next day, and then he had been released.

Her bedroom, Ashley thought. Her bed with a man in it. How long had it been since she had seen such a sight? She wrinkled her nose. Briana had protested that substituting for some of the ingredients not easily found here on Earth would make it less effective, but what she concocted seemed far better than nothing. The tenderness had gone down around Fig's wound with remarkable swiftness. Sweetbalm. Sweetbalm, it was called. It was well named.

Ashley heard the refrigerator door slam. Maurice had made himself right at home. He was in the kitchen making sandwiches for everyone. She shook her head in disbelief as she pondered everything that had happened. Yesterday, she had given Jake her address, ushered the other three out and then sat through a boring two-hour final debriefing. USX, her two-decade career — that all now like a half-forgotten dream, as if it never existed.

Now, her life centered on love potions, seeing into the future, dancing imps, and aliens from another planet. And strangely, as she thought about it, there was no longer any regret, no bitterness about what had happened at USX. She was alive and energized. Still in the first few pages, but how could anyone resist the new story that was unfolding.

Fig hobbled out of bed, leaning on Briana for support. Without any words between any of them, the quintet convened in Ashley's living room. Danish modern seating around a low glass table accommodated them all. An obligatory watercolor by a local artist hung over a fireplace that was never used. The view of the Pacific was breathtaking, but no one chose to watch. The glow of excitement from what Fig and Briana had discovered wrapped around them like a warm blanket.

"The puzzle is not completely solved." Fig looked directly at Ashley when they were settled. "What was the purpose for the RFP?"

"How to use the special gas transfer tanks safely," she answered. "We talked about that at your interview."

"Any kind of gas?"

"Well, no, only simple cylinders with a strong enough valve on top is fine for most. The ones that USX builds are for the Mark 50 torpedo — for sulfur hexafluoride."

"Sulfur hexafluoride! SF_6. That's dangerous stuff," Fig said. "It is a greenhouse gas. Much more dangerous than CO_2."

"Yes," Ashley said. "Usually used for squelching breakdowns in high power line transformers. Because of its properties, many regulations and monitoring of its use. For the Mark 50, it is heated and provides the torpedo's propulsion."

"Sulfur hexafluoride," Fig mumbled aloud. "Made from sulfur and fluorine and nothing else. Happens spontaneously when the two mix together."

"How do you know all of this? Jake asked. "I thought you studied physics, not chemistry."

The others looked at Jake startled. He appeared to be coming out of his shell.

"These digs are nice," Jake continued. "Reminds me of what I had before my father…"

"Double undergraduate major," Fig shrugged.

"CO_2 isn't *toxic*," Jake protested. "Even *I* know that. It's part of the air we breathe."

"Not toxic, dangerous," Fig said. "Dangerous in terms of what it does in causing global warming. One pound of SF_6 in the air does the same damage as several thousand pounds of carbon dioxide."

Fig's eyes suddenly widened. "Holy tomatoes!" he exclaimed. "It is better to be rich and handsome than sick and unlucky!"

"What?" Briana said. "What?"

"Global warming!" Fig almost shouted. "The *exiles* want to heat up the Earth. Heat the entire planet up enough so they can merely walk out of their prisons into the open air. Not wait and see if we get our act together."

"Some claim global warming is not of great concern," Jake said.

"Perhaps a few degrees in decades, no more."

"No! No! That is not the point." Fig was frantic now. "The exiles do not want to raise the Earth's temperature a few more degrees over years and years. They want to raise it, I don't know how much, but probably a lot. And not over decades or centuries. They want to raise it now!

"If enough SF_6 were released into the air at one time, we... humanity would not be able to do anything about it. There is no way to get the stuff back once it is circulating in the atmosphere. Within a year, the air temperature would rise. Crops would fail throughout the world. Everyone would starve."

"The USX technical assistance," Fig rattled on as fast as he could speak. "I bet they want to transport SF_6 all over the world. To many places around the Earth so it can be put into the atmosphere everywhere."

Fig suddenly was silent. No one else spoke. Everyone is trying to make sense of what Fig was saying. Ashley felt the possibility of new, beckoning horizons fade away. She stared at Fig. He did not look like he was suddenly going to shout 'April Fool.' He was not clowning around.

"Still, an awful lot of the gas would be required," Fig said after a moment. "There probably isn't enough raw sulfur and fluorine available from any mining site to make all the chemical that would be needed. The atmosphere is a big place. It would be a tremendous enterprise."

He smiled sheepishly. "Sorry, folks," he said. "False alarm. I do get carried away sometimes. After all, what do you call a boomerang that *does* come back?"

Briana shook her head. "No, Fig. You may not be wrong," she said softly. "The masters from my home have talked about it for years. A *theoretical* possibility for us, but no more. No one could come up with an incantation powerful enough to control the energy needed to operate on such a microscopic level. But the exiles... The exiles' skill in the arts is more advanced than ours. The magic portal is an example. They might have figured out how to make, what do you say, a catalyst. Yes, a thaumaturgical catalyst."

Again, no one else spoke.

"Where is there both a lot of raw sulfur and fluorine around the world?" Briana asked.

"Well, I guess in volcanoes," Fig said. "But probably there is not enough in one to mine commercially. And the heat of the eruption would break down compounds like SF_6 into lighter ones."

"The exiles would only need a small quantity of SF_6 transported to a volcano with high sulfur and fluorine content," Briana rebutted. "The craft of thaumaturgy could be used to self-catalyze the production of more once a sufficiently large seed of it is there."

"Catalyze? How do you know anything about such a thing as a catalyst?" Fig asked.

"When I searched on the internet, I followed many false trails." Briana shrugged.

"Briana, this is not only a task to prove your worth to your father." Fig's face resumed the mask of panic. His eyes opened even wider. "The fate of the entire world is at stake! Don't you get it? These exiles not only want to get out of their prison. They want the world to be theirs. We will be gone.

"We got to tell about this. Alert the authorities. This has to be stopped before it gets started. Before it is too late."

Ashley watched Jake shake off the last of his lethargy. "Yeah," he said. "The cops, the army, the UN. Everybody."

"Wait a moment," Ashley shouted above the other competing voices. "That is what we must do, but it won't be easy. What exactly are we going to say? Do you have any idea of how slowly governments move? Will performing Briana's tricks with the little imp be enough to convince anyone of the bigger problem?"

"The exiles would be alerted before governments could act," Briana agreed. "If they really are able to use the crafts now, no country on this earth would prevail against them." She pulled at her loose curl. "*We* are the ones to assume responsibility."

Briana's eyes took on a glow. A broad smile filled her face. "A quest to save an entire world. A tale worthy of the sagas. Convincing proof for my father and all the others. Yes! Yes!"

"Nonsense," Jake said. "There are hundreds of these guys, right? We are only five, and sure enough, none of us is an Energy Ranger. We don't have super powers. This isn't a comic book. Let's tell who we have to — now."

"Stop! All of you stop!" Ashley rose and said in the most authoritarian voice she could muster. "Let's..." She decided abruptly. "Let's put what to do to a vote."

"This has nothing to do with democracy," Jake scowled. "Something this important isn't decided by majority rule. One could hold out against many, and in the end, he might be the one on the side of right."

"As my ex-boss, Douglas says," Ashley raised her voice even higher, "neither is it determined by the one who can put the biggest balls on the table. First a vote, and then, depending on the results, we can decide what to do next."

"I am destined for this," Briana said immediately.

"This is reality," Fig said. "Rushing into peril succeeds only in fantasy, not here." He looked at Briana and then away. "Sorry, my Queen. My vote is to get help. Lots of it."

"I apologize for letting twenty years of frustration in dealing with the government get in the way," Ashley said. She smoothed down her jacket. "We *should* get help. Of course, we should. But what we should do is first get irrefutable evidence. Right now, all we have is Fig's speculations. We don't even know where all of the aliens are — what they plan to do next. Once we have all of that, we can tell whomever we have to."

"I agree we need to learn more," Briana said. "But once we do, we should strike. The crafts can be used in a matter of mere minutes."

"But in any case, we need to learn more *first*," Ashley said. "For now, let's only agree to do that."

"No," Briana shot back. "I know enough from reading the sagas that the performance of the warrior depends on his task. Scouting is one thing. Committing to carry through on what he has learned is quite another. We should agree on *all* of it now."

Ashley did not respond. She stared at Briana. She could almost hear the gears grinding in the young woman's head, calculating what to do in order to have all of them agree to join her in her quest. Finally, the daughter of the Archimage stopped and looked directly at Jake. "All along, you've wanted something from me, haven't you?

Jake immediately smiled back, as if he were remembering a childhood pleasure. "And..."

"Join me in what I must do," Briana said softly. She coiled a finger in her hair and then slowly unwound it again. "Do so, and I will reward you with what you want," she said at last.

"Well, well. It sounds as if the stakes have changed," Jake replied. He slowly scanned Briana from head to toe, stopping deliberately twice along the way. After he was done, he spoke again. "Oh, yeah. There is a payoff in this. I'm definitely in."

"Wait a minute!" Fig interrupted. "I am the sworn liege of the Q — "

"Flake off, little man." Jake reached into his pocket, pulled out a gnarled wad of paper, and held it up for everyone to see. "If we are going to do this alone, then we will need cash, lots of it. I held onto this for a reason, and now I know why. My old man's user name and password."

He stuck out his chest. "I am *back* and ready to act."

A silence hung in the air like a caustic smog. Each woman stood her ground. Fig looked back and forth between the others. "Two to two," he said. "Briana and Jake on one hand. Ashley and me on the other. A tie. All right, Maurice. What does the follower of the Buddha say?"

MAURICE CLOSED the guest bedroom door behind him. If ever he needed to get insight from meditation, this was the time to do it. He settled into a comfortable posture and began the slow even breathing that was supposed to make one more aware.

The fourth step on the Noble Eightfold Path was Right Action — no killing, no stealing, no sexual misconduct. How did that apply here?

If everything Fig said were true, then the exiles attempt to kill all of humankind was not Right Action. But in order to deter them from doing so, would taking their lives be the correct choice for what to do? What would happen if the plot were exposed and millions, perhaps even billions of people demanded they be eliminated? On the other hand, to do nothing, merely stand by. Would not that make one as guilty of murder as would be the exiles themselves?

Maurice groaned in irritation before he could put the intruding thought away. It always was like this. No definite answers, only more questions.

He changed his focus. Go through the list. Stealing, what about stealing. The aliens were labeled as exiles. Did that not imply what was theirs was taken from them? Was the bounty of the Earth meant to be reparation? He sighed. Another blocked path — more questions than answers.

Okay, sexual misconduct? He knew it meant more than only physical action. But it was oh so hard to keep his thoughts away from women. Briana — what a bright shining star. What a delight to be around her, soaking in her enthusiasm and exuberant drive. And now, Ashley. A more mature woman to be sure, but one secure in her own sexuality. What would be the...

Maurice halted the way his thoughts were going. He had a decision to make. If the others all agree to abide with the majority, then the burden of choosing correctly was entirely on his shoulders.

One of his feet began to fall asleep. His crotch began to itch. Distracting bits of conversation from the living room filtered through the walls.

He increased the focus on his breathing. Otherwise, he would start drifting out of control. Too much of the outside world was crowding in.

Ignore those things! No, that was not right. Accept them. They are part of what is. Perhaps, this was a true test, he thought. Not a simple exercise to decide whether to eat out or order in tonight, but something that could determine the fate of the entire planet. He felt a twinge of panic, but then surprisingly, he was able to push it away. If indeed he could decide this and then be at peace with whatever the decision was, then, finally, finally, he would be walking the Eightfold Path.

Five minutes, then ten... time drifted away.

ASHLEY AND the others turned their eyes on Maurice as he emerged from the bedroom an hour later.

"We act ourselves," he said simply. "Buddha says we shall not kill. Asimov says that we cannot allow harm to come to another human through our own inaction."

"We all agree on that," Fig said. "The question is whether or not we should do something entirely on our own once we figure out what is to be done."

"Yes," Maurice agreed. "And Robert Frost says, 'I took the one less traveled by, and that has made all the difference.'"

"Briana has stated the truth of it," he continued. "If we involve others — many others — the exiles will inevitably hear of it far too soon. They will use their magic before we can act. The risk of involving more is too great. To succeed, we must take the path less traveled by."

"The fate of the world decided by a hundred-year-old poem?" Fig snorted. "You're mouthing platitudes. Gimme a break!"

But no one else spoke.

"Well, that settles it," Briana said. She then looked at Ashley and smiled. "I could not help but noticing when I looked into your freezer. Would anyone else also like some ice cream?"

The Warehouse

"I CAN'T say enough how much I appreciate what you are doing for me, Mr. Angus," the woman standing in front of him said. "I've been deposited away in care facilities all my life, just waiting until finally I wither and die. It is a shame really."

"You have expressed your gratitude already more than once." Angus stirred uncomfortably in the chair. Keeping a civil and polite tone with one of the inferior natives was quite hard to maintain. "You do not need to remind me each time we discuss the tasks for the day."

He had given the woman several hours of instruction, and now he could feel the first icy fingers of cold beginning to creep in through the aerogel insulation. Besides, he was hungry. The leafy greens delivery each day that his new assistant had arranged mostly went right through him.

"I can't help myself, Mr. Angus," Ursula Price continued. "I am so very grateful. Not charity, but a job, an actual job! I am the envy of my little clique in the assisted living center. Picked up in the morning and driven directly here. Then returned safely when the day is done. Doing the same work as someone with sight. And call me Ursula. Ms. Price is far too formal. Do you have a first name as well?"

Angus studied Ursula for a moment. Except for Oscar and the two cabbies, he had never seen any other humans up close. In the caverns, Dinton joked that despite all of the newspapers he had scanned, he could not tell them apart. That well could be true for the males, but the females did seem slightly different. This one was shorter than any of those three men and much more slender. Stark white hair. Rather than eye-blinking garb, she wore a simple dress of gray with a like-hued belt pulled tight around the waist. Made sense, he supposed. She did not have any need for color.

"The agency recommended you very highly, Ms.... ah, Ursula,"

Angus said. "And I must confess that I didn't know that such things as Braille keyboards and Read Aloud for pdf files existed. I wanted to try the experiment, and... and to my... *delight*, you are working out very well."

"But one last thing." He paused. "This is a little delicate, but I wonder..."

"Yes, Mr. Angus?"

No sign of any of Dinton's minions yet. But one could not be too sure.

"The neighborhood here is not the best. I worry about disreputable characters breaking in. Do you by chance know of any in your family who could provide some sort of protection, who could take care of any intrusion if one were to occur?"

There was silence for a moment. Finally, Ursula said, "I do have a nephew who-well, I do not like his friends. Why do you ask?"

"Excellent, Ursula," Angus said. "I would like to hire them-full time and at a wage that would make whatever else they are doing now not as worthwhile."

"I don't know about that, Mr. Angus. I would hate to have something happen, and then you think I was responsible."

"Didn't you say you cannot thank me enough, Ms. Price?"

"Oh, yes, sir, I did," Ursula replied, but she did not volunteer more.

"Ms. Price?" Angus prodded.

Ursula sighed. "I understand. I will send for Sidney to see you right away."

"Excellent! Get him here now, but I do not want to communicate with either him or his friends directly. As with everyone else, that is... *your* job. Post them on the loading dock. They can receive the incoming shipments and move them to where they will be stored."

"Next to the start of the production line, you had the plumbing contractor set up?"

"Yes, Ursula. Very perceptive as usual. Now if you will excuse me, please return to the reception area. I need to retire to my other office. The one in back with the kiln for — for a little rest."

Ursula pulled the door shut behind her as she left. Renting time in an internet café had been easy, Angus thought as he watched her go. A connection node with time to rent. He had not been the most bizarrely dressed one there. Then the mail order laptop, the employment agency... Search, select, order, pay with credit, give the shipping address. He had gotten the hang of it. No need for Emmertyn anymore.

It was going to be so easy. The civilization of these natives was so interconnected, so efficient. Little needed to be taken care of face to face. The gears turned, and half a world away things happened as one wished.

But that connectivity, that efficiency made everything so fragile — like a poorly spun spider web that would fail if a single strand were cut. He was but a lone warrior, using a mere smidgen of magical lore, yet he alone could bring everything crashing down in total ruin.

And soon. Oh-so-soon. Before Dinton could even begin to figure out what he was doing. The radio equipment should arrive tomorrow. Ursula's nephew probably would know someone who would set him up on the dark web. Then, for enough bitcoins, the labor he needed halfway around the world would be taken care of. No question of legality would ever arise.

That meant there was only one more piece to the puzzle, and all the preparation would be complete — making sure the paperwork for the transfer of the cylinders of SF_6 onto the cargo ships would not have a hitch. He hoped the change notice to the RFP specifying the new delivery address had been properly received and processed by USX. He would hate to have to travel back to Oscar's hut in order to pick it up.

Watch and Wait

BRIANA BRISTLED as she watched Ashley talk into her cell phone. True, she was the one who originally had asked for the older woman's help. But what happened afterward over the ensuing weeks was unexpected. Almost without realizing it, gradually, bit by bit, she had surrendered her leadership of the group. It was not supposed to be that way. She, the Archimage's daughter, was the one destined to be immortalized in the sagas.

"Maurice reports nothing has happened on his shift," Ashley put down the phone. "He moved the swathing from the cave mouth back to the hut without any problem. No activity there. And Jake reports that, for two days now, there have been no more incoming shipments to the warehouse. The juvenile thugs hanging around the loading dock are bored out of their skulls."

"Sitting and doing nothing is very hard," Briana said. "I could watch as well as the men."

"You insisted on keeping possession of the setter," Ashley said. "We need to have it located in a central place so everyone can phone in with their request to be picked up."

"I can run circles around Jake and Fig. I have the greater endurance." Briana slapped the dagger at her waist. "And I have this, too."

She frowned as she watched Ashley act through one of her theatrical sighs. "We seem to have to go over this almost every day," the older woman said. "Briana, you can't have your ice cream and eat it, too."

"I don't see why we have to continue watching and waiting — and nothing else. Are we going to wait until the SF_6 is spewing into the air before we start doing something?"

"You did ask for my help," Ashley said. "And I did come up with a plan that made sense. It was only natural I should be the one who makes sure it is followed. We have to locate the whereabouts of all of the aliens first."

"Jake scraped off enough grime from one of the warehouse windows over a week ago. And mounted the CCTV camera there for peering inside. And we have seen the same routine repeated day after day. A single figure clad in a hoodie operating some sort of production line. He's probably one of the exiles."

"We aren't sure about that," Ashley said. "No white swathing. Maybe he is only a foreman who likes wearing a hoodie."

"*Or*," Briana insisted, "*maybe* he's the one who was camped in the hut near the cave. Maybe even be the leader! The only other person coming and going is the blind woman during the day. Certainly, she can be no threat. When are we going to attack?"

Ashley lowered her eyes and shook her head. "I am as anxious as you are," she said.

Briana felt even more frustrated. "But as Fig has explained, we know the sulfur has been delivered to the warehouse, and we have seen many shipments of liquefied fluorine following that. There is a production line consuming those two elements and produces a gas as a result. A *lone* exile must be producing SF_6, massive amounts of it. That is the only thing making sense."

"A single being responsible for it all?" Ashley rebutted. She raised one eyebrow skeptically. "*That's* what doesn't make sense. Where are the others? The seven hundred minions? What are they up to? Are they peacefully waiting underground for everything to be complete? Or instead, are they somehow dispersed throughout the world ready to release the gas once it is shipped to them? We need more information, Briana. We have to do this right. There won't be a second chance."

"Every day we delay the exile plan gets closer to complete execution." Briana shot back. "Every day, the chance of disaster for everyone here increases." She tugged at her loose curl with frustration. "I think we should go into the cave again. This time more of us and in daylight."

"And if we do stumble upon hundreds of beings hostile to our existence, what then?"

The phone rang, interrupting the conversation, and Ashley looked at the caller's number on the muted TV.

"Hawaii area code," she said. "I better take this."

She picked up the handset. "USX."

"This is Mr. Angus of Kahuna Enterprises calling. We accept your proposal, and I am ready to start. I have my first set of questions."

"I am the one to help you," Ashley said. She covered the mouthpiece and whispered to Briana. "It is a good thing I put my home phone as the contact point when I sent in the proposal."

"Hear the accent?" Briana said. "I bet he is one of the exiles."

Ashley ignored the comment. Uncovering the handset, she said, "Go ahead, Mr. Angus."

Burning the Ship

THALING LOOKED about Dinton's alcove. Although the biggest, it was even more sparsely furnished than Angus' had been. No desk, a simple cushion on the bumpy floor, nothing on the walls. Several teetering stacks of yellowing newsprint haphazardly hid the far wall.

"How did you manage to do it?" Dinton snapped. "How did you get almost two-thirds of Angus' flock choose to join yours rather than mine? I am the eldest brother, and, regardless of who carries the baton, am due the greater respect."

"I did nothing, brother." Thaling flinched from Dinton's piercing gaze. "Perhaps the majority of Angus' flock preferred a... preferred a less regimented existence than one you provide. And then once the trend started, more and more followed. You know how we are. No flock member wants to be looked upon as out of step with his friends."

"Blubberheads, all of them, just like that Jormind." Dinton's frustration pulled at the muscles in his face like bands made of strong rubber. "Patience is all I ask. Patience for only a while longer. The temperature of the surface continues to creep upward. Nothing of substance is being done to stop it. Only half-hearted treaties not agreed to by all of the natives and broken by many. One hundred years more of waiting, two hundred at the most, and this orb will be ours. A mere blink of a sorcerer's eye compared to what we have already endured."

"It is not this world we should desire." Thaling straightened as tall as he could. "It is our own. We should be working together to... to find a way to return and fight for the right to stay."

Dinton laughed, something Thaling did not recall ever happening before.

"Do not be so simple, brother," Dinton said. "We were defeated by the Faithful when we were a thousand. How would we win back the right to stay if we only number mere hundreds?"

He continued before Thaling could answer. "Father was naïve, I now realize. Our ten hundred were not warriors, merely lounge-abouts, pleasure indulgers, ones who panicked and ran when they felt the first bite of a blade."

"But perhaps now that we have endured this prison for so long, backbones might be stiffer."

"No, I think if the choice came to battle or return to exile, few would stand their ground. To make the ones we lead do that, we would have to act as did the native captain, the one they call Cortez."

"Cortez?"

"I read about him in some of the verbiage." Dinton waved at the stack of newsprint. "When preparing for battle in a newly found land, he burned his ships behind him so there would be no chance of turning back. It was either die or fight in order to live."

He shook his head. "But as for our own kind, one can never be sure which way the wind will blow with *any* of them. Even two of my most trusted guards allowed Angus to escape. They, of course, deny they did anything wrong. They say they returned to their posts after your visit, and then, sometime later, Angus was gone — vanished without a trace. I wonder. Did you have anything to do with this? Maybe you, too, should be joining the traitors in the wasp pit."

"Wait. What?" Thaling said. "You are punishing the guards — and in such a cruel fashion? That… that is not just, not fair."

"You have not answered my question."

Thaling slumped. He had not thought things all the way through. If the guards were thrown to the wasps, it would be his fault. His fault alone. Mentally reviewing old rituals had not helped. There was no rationalization. He could not let this happen.

"Such a pronouncement would have to be made by the one who carries the baton," he said deliberately with weight on every word. "Whoever commands for the next cycle. Whoever wins the game the two of us will play." He sighed and stared at Dinton as best he could. "If *I* were to become the bearer of the baton, I will pardon the guards for what they did not do."

"Two cannot play the game," Dinton shook his head. "It requires at least three, and without Angus' sojourns to the surface, there is no substitute we can procure. I should retain the baton by default."

"My sprit… I have thought of another that does not require any implements at all," Thaling said. "It is called 'Rock, paper, scissors'. We will play fifteen times, and the one who first wins eight will be the next carrier of the baton."

THALING LOOKED at the assembled rockbubblers waiting his instruction in his private alcove, the one housing the nearly finished portal setter. He patted the baton on his side for the dozenth time, hardly believing he had won so easily. He smiled at his sprites for what they had provided to him — not only the rules of the game but also the winning strategies that had worked as predicted.

He put the setter aside, replaced it on the table with one of the spare odometer displays, and marched the imps through their paces. Without rousing suspicion, Thaling already had arranged for a census of all of their kind who remained in their exile caverns. Dinton had been correct. The number was slightly higher than seven hundred. To this figure, Thaling added a few dozen more to account for trips to retrieve objects left behind and forgotten. Using the keypad, he entered 769 into the now magical display. It would be bolted into the body of the portal later.

Despite the difficulty and the time it was taking to finish the calculations for the override of the other setter, he felt some satisfaction with how things were going. With the baton, he had the means to ensure everyone, yes, everyone, would elect to go home. And the idea Dinton had given him made certain there would be no alternative but to fight when they arrived.

The ritual for making sure only one setter could control the portal at a time was still not finished. Overriding a magical device once it was completed was tricky. But he had made progress. Hopefully, it would not take much longer until it was done. And then, and then, the glorious trip home.

Watch and Hurry Up

"GOOD MORNING, miss," Fig said as he stood in front of Ursula. "Is the owner in?" The reception area was plain and in need of fresh paint. A few old marketing posters were on the walls, faded from years of sunlight filtering in through ragged blinds.

"Mr. Vargas is not expecting anyone this morning."

"Correct. I do not have an appointment."

Fig smiled but then realized it did no good at all. The additional CCTVs they had mounted on the building across the street from the warehouse had given a clear view of the front entrance. Every morning, promptly at eight, a cabbie led a woman with a white cane up to it, and she keyed herself inside. Now it was time to find out more about the interior.

"Perhaps I can show... tell you about my product," Fig said. While he talked, he clicked open a satchel and deftly set up a camera tripod, one with a small speaker attached to the top. He quietly stepped away from Ursula's desk and approached the double doors leading into the interior of the warehouse.

"Every warehouse needs one of these," he whispered into his microphone headset, the one he used to communicate with the micromites when they were present. His voice relayed into the speaker in front of Ursula, and he hoped she would think he was still standing there.

Like Briana, he chafed with the inactivity. Once all the mysteries were revealed, he was sure she would come to her senses. She would see that five against seven hundred made absolutely no sense. She would have what she needed to return to Murdina, and then he would...

No sense in thinking about that now. He jerked his focus back to what he was doing. Feelings were for later. But for now, sixteen hours a day of doing nothing but waiting for something to happen had grown old. He had never contemplated such a thing would be the lot of one who served

257

the Queen of the Eight Universes.

As Fig continued his patter, he squeezed open one of the double doors and slipped beyond. This was going to be risky, but the CCTV had shown production stopping abruptly yesterday afternoon. Something had changed, and the team needed to figure out what. Looking around, he saw he was not on the main warehouse floor as he had hoped, but in a small office completely undecorated except for a single desk and chair. The desktop was bare except for a laptop to which was attached a standing microphone, one much larger than his own.

Something to broadcast to workers on the main floor? No, that was not it. As far as he knew, there was only the one. He hastened to a window on the rear wall and peeked between two of the closed blinds. Fig saw only what he had seen several times before when looking in from outside in the darkness of night or trolling through the CCTV images. Nobody was there, not even the one wearing the hoodie who had run the production line without ceasing, day in and day out like a disciplined automaton.

Fig's train of thought was interrupted by the rumble of the loading dock door beginning to rise.

"Hear that?" Ursula's voice sounded in his earbuds. We are shipping today. I will have to sign the bills of lading. You have to leave now."

"Bills of lading?" Fig continued to chat as he came back into the reception area, switched off his mike and began collapsing the tripod back into his satchel. "Where are you shipping to, somewhere here on the island?"

"None of your business," Ursula snapped. "It is time for you to go."

"Yes, ma'am," Fig called over his shoulder as he hurried out of the building. Peeking around the corner, he saw the four junior thug wannabes helping a truck driver roll out gas cylinders onto his waiting rig. A second carrier idled nearby, ready to be loaded up next.

The SF_6, Fig realized. The exiles were shipping it out! Finally, something happening. Although not a good thing, he thought with a lurch. If Briana's little group did not do something soon, it would be too late. He jumped on a motor scooter he had parked nearby and got it started. After a few minutes, the first truck, its cargo area filled with upright cylinders jostling off one another, entered the street, and headed off.

Fig followed the truck as it crept along. It was an old one with gray wooden side panels, pitted and splintered with age. They swayed in their sockets and banged against the cargo. None of the cylinders was restrained by chain. Like the tune from a carillon played by a tonedeaf musician, a cacophony of deep gongs filled the air.

The truck continued down to the harbor and then along the wharf, past the more modern moorings to one near the end of the line — a small ship riding quietly with rust showing through paint from decades ago, like bruises that would not heal. A sling hung over the wharf from a weather-beaten hoist next to the opening of a single hold. *'Mizuno Maru'* declared peeling signage the vessel's side. The flag of Panama flapped listlessly from a short mast above the bridge. A gull sat on the mast top, cooing to others who circled along the wharf looking for scraps of food. The air smelt of brine, diesel oil, and organic decay.

Evidently, the exiles were having a budget crunch, Fig thought as he surveyed the freighter, or maybe finding a reputable shipper had been too hard to do. And the second truck? Was it headed to the harbor as well? He felt he had to stay and watch what was happening here. Anxiety began to fester. He needed more eyes right away.

Ashley answered his call on the first ring.

"On it," she said after he had finished his report. "Maurice is asleep, but I can get Jake there from watching the hut in a minute or two. Move to somewhere secluded, and the portal door will appear right in front of your phone."

Fig looked about. There were no shadows. The hot sun blazed down on everything. He watched the stevedores for a moment and decided that all their attentions were on the content of the truck. "We will have to chance it," he said. "Tell Jake to be quick about it when he arrives."

Fig watched nervously for another minute. Then the air right in front of him shimmered, and he involuntarily took a step back. The portal door materialized in the empty air. It opened, and Jake stepped out, his gaudy Hawaiian shirt almost too vivid to look at.

As rapidly as it had come, the door vanished. Fig looked about again, but no one appeared to have noticed. "We are going to have to figure out a better way to do this," he said. "But never mind that now. Take the scooter and go back along the path to the warehouse. If you are lucky, you will see a second truck coming with another load. Probably here, but we can't be too sure."

"Righto, cocky little man," Jake said. "Did Ashley abdicate and appoint you the new queen?"

"Get on with it," Fig said. "No time for any of that stuff now."

"Yeah, okay," Jake said. "This is what we have been waiting for." He climbed on the scooter and putted off.

FIG AND Jake stood at the foot of the exterior stairs leading up to the office of the Hilo Harbormaster. Jake had caught up with the second truck. It had been headed to the harbor as well. But to the other end of the wharf. Fig would never had been able to watch both loading areas by himself.

Nor were either of them able to learn anything about destinations from yelling questions at either of the two crews. "Ask the Harbormaster," was all they heard after several tries.

Both of them sensed that merely walking in and asking what they wanted to know probably was not going to work, Jake's shirt notwithstanding. They waited two hours for Briana to appear so she could try.

"Now, no one is looking," Fig said into his phone.

The air shimmered, and Briana emerged. A fedora with a card labeled 'Press' sticking from the brim sat on her head at a snappy angle. She wore a trim vest on top a short-sleeved frilly blouse and clutched a notebook with stenciling reading 'Hilo High School Viking - Student newspaper'. Screaming-red hot pants swayed from her hips, so short they could not possibly expose any more leg.

Both Fig and Jake goggled at what they saw.

"Wow, Briana, you really must want this," Jake said. "I remember you blushing when you twirled your dress and a little knee was exposed."

"To die for," Fig whispered quietly.

"Focus," Briana said. "Focus. This is not for you two, but the Harbormaster. I need some help with my homework assignment to find out what he does."

BRIANA DESCENDED the stairs to where Fig and Jake were waiting. "The second ship, the *Oakdale*, is headed to Europe through the Panama Canal," she said. "First stop of Messina, Sicily. And the *Mizuno Maru* is going to Port Moresby in Papua and New Guinea, but after crossing the

Pacific to Japan and then to Taiwan. It might be a coincidence, but they get to their final destinations at about the same time."

"Any other stops?" Jake asked, glancing down at Briana's legs. Fig scowled. Evidently, the creep could not stop ogling his queen. There were more important things to worry about now. He closed his eyes and tried to visualize the globe.

"No. No additional stops," Briana said. "And the Harbormaster thought that was strange, especially for the *Oakdale*. He explained that ordinarily, these old boats take on cargo from all over. Sometimes spend months at sea, going from port to port. Need to do that to make things profitable enough."

"The exiles don't want to make the landfalls public," Jake said. "I bet that's it. Distributing the SF_6 without anyone being able to connect the dots."

"Then why didn't a third ship also get loaded today?" Fig frowned. "The first two were so closely coordinated. Bang. Bang. And the production line has been shut down."

"There is a website that keeps track of maritime traffic," Briana said. "For safety reasons, they are broadcasting all the time." She took off her hat and smiled at it. "I didn't need to do any of this."

"Hold on a minute," Fig said. "Maybe we are making an assumption we don't have to." He began to pace, hands folded behind his back like an expectant father. "First, let's do the math. From the CCTV camera, we know how many empty cylinders were delivered to the warehouse originally — not the ones that brought in the fluorine, but those presumably to be filled with the SF_6.

"We have counted the number loaded on the two ships here," he continued, "the same number on each one. A second coincidence, like the final port arrival times. So that means… One third of the output to each of the ships and therefore one third remaining back in the warehouse but ready to go.

"I wonder. Three equal portions." He started speaking more rapidly. "We should monitor for unexpected arrival, certainly, but maybe, just maybe, it might be that there are not hundreds of targets the exiles plan to pollute, but, in fact, only three."

"What limb are you going out on this time?" Jake asked.

"Hush," Briana said. "Fig has been right on everything else so far."

"So maybe there are no more destinations," Fig said. "No clandestine stops in between. The *Oakdale* is going to Sicily and nowhere else, and the Japanese and Taipei stops for the *Mizuno Maru* are for other — "

"Okay, why?" Jake asked.

"Etna," Fig said. "Mount Etna on Sicily. Almost perpetually active, and a short distance from Messina. I know because a cousin of mine visited the 'friendly giant' a few years ago. And for the South Pacific, I remember something about active volcanoes there too. We can check when we get back to Ashley's."

"The final third?" Briana chimed in.

"Kilauea. Right here on the big island," Fig said. "No need for a boat."

"So, then what?" Jake asked.

"The good news is that Pollyanna does not need shoes anymore," Fig said.

"What?" Jake and Briana asked in unison.

"The good news is that there are only three volcanoes that we have to worry about, not hundreds of them all over the world," Fig explained. "The bad news is that we are going to have to worry about them right away."

"Okay, I will let Ashley know to return the portal so that we can go back to her place," Briana said. "Maybe now she will get up off her rump."

While they waited, Fig shrugged. "This one at a time routine is a drag."

He looked at Briana but saw that she did not seem to care.

"You know," she said. "Grandfather types are even easier than page boys."

"Easier for what?" Jake asked.

"Easier to wrap around one's little finger."

Watch and Hurry Up Again

FORTY DAYS. Forty days of following maritime positions. Finally, the wait was over.

Briana paced back and forth in Ashley's living room, shouldering her pack. It felt unfamiliar, lighter. She was nervous about surrendering the portal setter, but it was a choice she had had to make. They had agreed that, once the two ships started unloading at their destinations, a single person tracking what would happen next would not be enough.

The *Oakdale* was due to arrive in Messina, Sicily tomorrow — well, in about twelve hours due to the difference in time zones. She and Jake would take the portal there shortly.

Maurice and Fig were already in Port Moresby, New Guinea, but the *Mizuno Maru* had not shown up there. According to the maritime reports, it instead was heading Northeast in the Solomon Sea toward Bougainville Island.

Ashley would continue monitoring things from her home, keeping her eye on the CCTV in Hilo for any activity. Two more people camped outside the warehouse would be nice, but they did not have that luxury.

Ashley slammed down the lid of her laptop. "Damn! So much for the reputed 'instant news' from the internet. The latest postings for Arawa Town and Kieta Port are from 2010. 'Do not travel to the other wharf area near Loloho. This is under the control of gangs involved in the illegal export of scrap metal…'"

"Right where Fig had predicted," Briana said. "Mount Bagana is in the center of the island."

"You're feeling pretty smug about this, aren't you?" Ashley said. "Getting us the data we needed to keep track of things."

"Well, yes, I guess I do," Briana replied. "The Harbormaster was an accomplishment. Easy, but an accomplishment, none the less."

Ashley shook her head. "That is not something to be proud of,

Briana."

"Why not?"

"Think, woman. You were using your body, nothing more."

"How about Fig grinding away without any complaint?" Briana glanced toward the kitchen where Jake was packing some snacks. She lowered her voice. "Getting Jake to vote for the adventure?"

"I said 'think,'" Ashley's tone hardened. "Those aren't accomplishments, Briana. Only notches on your bedpost. A difference of degree from what Jake always has in mind, but at the core..."

She stared at Briana like a mother lecturing a wayward daughter. "If we are ever going to be judged the equals of men, it will be because we used our wits rather than our bodies."

"So, maybe, you're a wee bit jealous," Briana laughed with simple pleasure. The monotony of over a month being together was beginning to wear.

"No, of course not," Ashley snapped. "For me, your accomplishments, your true accomplishments are how you managed to survive the culture shock of being thrown into our modern society, how you foiled the would-be rapist, deduced that the exiles would try to manipulate the stock market, what you did to save Fig's life while you waited for the portal to return."

Briana started to answer with a rebuttal but discovered she did not have one. Notches on a bedpost? *Her* actions? Of course not? She had done these things, all of them because... because she had to. But the ones Ashley mentioned... What was the older woman's phrase? Not because of the way she looked or pleasures she promised, but because... because of what was between her ears. She chewed on the words as if they were hard gristle. Yes, even the sagas, she admitted finally. None of the greatest deeds, the ones most heralded, had anything to do with seduction.

So, going forward, how should she —

"I found a small boat willing to take Fig and me to Bougainville." Maurice's voice in the external speaker cut off Briana's thoughts. "Leaving now. Fig and I might even get there before the freighter does."

"Why not use the portal," Briana called back. "Just send me... I mean Ashley — the coordinates."

"Without the ship to center on, not sure what they would be. Going in by boat is the right thing to do."

"Be careful, Maurice," Ashley said. "The characters Jake and Briana are likely to encounter in Messina will be bad enough. It doesn't look like there is any police help where you and Fig are going."

Jake came from the kitchen to join Ashley and Briana around the speaker. "Don't worry, pard. Buddha says 'No matter where you go, there you are.'"

"He does not," Maurice said. "That's from an old movie from decades ago."

Briana marveled at Jake. He was setting the right tone. The long wait had made them sluggish and now perhaps hesitant to act. She reached down and patted the dagger at her side. Soon, she thought. No matter what Ashley might think of her, soon, she would prove herself, and it will be over.

Mount Etna

JAKE BEEPED shut the doors of the rented Maserati as he and Briana rolled their luggage into the lobby. The building was a simple four-story rectangle with ten tiny gables dotting a sloping roof. The name, *Riparo Sapienza*, in large white letters on an orange background gave no doubt they were in the right place — that and the truck filled with cylinders of gas parked next to the car.

The bare essence of the mountain weighed upon him. Desolate, black, and almost devoid of life. The volcano itself was active, however. From where he stood, he could see the occasional burst of fiery yellow above the crater's rim and a relentless flow down the mountainside, fortunately some distance away. This was a place perhaps to visit, but too depressing to stay a long while.

He gulped for air. Even though they were not very high up Etna's southern slope, he could already feel the difference. And it was chilly. They would need their jackets if there was exploring to be done at night.

No matter. His fingers had been tingling with excitement ever since he had spotted the *Oakdale* unloading in the Messina harbor. Sending word back to Ashley brought Briana under the cover of darkness that very evening. The next day, they had rented the car, bought luggage, and purchased tourist clothing. Then, following the loaded truck to Catania on A18 and up a winding road to this tourist jumping off place had been a snap.

He gulped again. The air was not crisp and clean, but he did not care. All the days of doing nothing but waiting for the *Oakdale* to get here had given him time to think... to think a lot. The pretending to be a student, surfing on the puny waves at the Rat Beach, that all felt so, well, so shallow now. No purpose. No goal. No ending. What a pitiful existence. Yes, that was all true. He had to admit it.

But this! What he was doing now, it was important! No, better than that. Vitally important. The fate of the entire *world* depended on it. This was something he could grab ahold of, contribute…

He glanced at Briana strolling beside him. Well, no sense in getting *too* carried away. The women of his life. They were still important also.

Jake approached the lobby desk. "Do you speak English?" he asked.

"Of course," the clerk said. "How can I help you?"

"Reservations for Mr. and Mrs. Waverton." He looked at Briana and smiled. "We're on our honeymoon."

"What!" Briana glared as if she were a policewoman about to write a ticket. "Jake, you promised. No crazy business."

He turned his attention back to the clerk and shook his head with what he hoped was an amused expression. "She is such a kick. You do have us in the bridal suite, right?"

"Of course, sir. It is ready. Here are your keys."

Jake took the keys in one hand and swooped his arm around Briana with the other. He felt her tense and start to pull away. "Don't blow our cover," he whispered in her ear. "A little buss right now is what the audience needs."

Briana's scowl deepened, peeked at the clerk watching them out of the corner of his eye, and then forced her face into a small smile. Standing rigid as a statue, she let Jake pull her tight and get his way. "See, that wasn't so bad," he whispered before he let her go.

"Focus," Briana said quietly as they started looking for their room. "Keep your thoughts on what we have to do here. Find where the exiles are hiding. If Fig is right about a three-way split, there should be around two hundred and fifty of them around. It shouldn't be hard, if you would only focus."

"Yes, dear," Jake said much louder. "Whatever you say."

THE CLANGING of the gas cylinders woke the pair from a short nap. It was dark. Jake donned the night vision goggles from his suitcase and peered out through a slit in the drawn curtains.

"There are six of them," he said. "Four are sandwiching themselves onto the truck bed. Two more in the cab. Can't tell with the glasses but probably the same thugs we saw back in Messina."

He opened the curtains more and slewed the goggles from side to side. "No sign of any more. Certainly not a couple hundred. They must be meeting the exiles somewhere else."

"Let's go!" Briana said. "We have to follow them."

Who's the boss here? Jake thought. The man is the one who is supposed to lead, right? He watched Briana hurriedly put on her boots and head for the door. Headstrong. No doubt about it.

He and Briana ran out onto the parking lot barely in time to see the taillights of the truck start on the road leading farther up the mountain.

"It goes to the upper cable car terminus," Briana said. "I read the trip advisor reports before we came."

Jake peered at the retreating truck as it bounced up the road. "I don't like the looks of it." He shook his head. "The rental place probably will not care for what it will do to the Maserati."

"There is a trail starting right here," Briana said. "It follows the course of the cable car. Takes an hour on foot."

Jake grunted with resignation, and they started striding up the hill with a rapid pace. The path, if it could be called that, was nearly flat but rough and unmarked with many large boulders littering the way. Both of them slipped several times, breaking falls with outstretched arms.

"What is this stuff?" He kicked at one of the small rocks skittering under each of his steps.

"Stones of congealed lava," Briana said. "From some past eruption."

"I should use the light on my phone," Jake said, swinging his pack from his shoulders.

"No!" Briana said. "They might see us." She pointed to the sky. "The moon is full. If we are careful, it will be enough. See. We can make out the cable car up ahead."

They conversed no more and turned to concentrate on the slope. Passing the lower terminus, they saw a single small gondola suspended above like a huge and exotic fruit.

After they passed the shed protecting the cable car from the elements, the slant steepened sharply. The pace slowed to a deliberate walk, one careful step after the other. Jake could see Briana's impatience radiate from her as, with each stumble, she redoubled her efforts to make up for mere seconds of lost time.

The black cables were hard to see against the night sky, but by carefully ascending parallel to their path, few of their steps were wasted.

An hour and a half later, panting from the effort, they approached the upper terminus.

As they drew closer, Jake spotted the parked truck and heard that its engine was still running. Every stride now became shorter. The pair hunched over and concentrated on placing each boot carefully so there was only a soft crunch of gravel and no cascade of the tiny stones. They had to be quiet. Discovery would mean disaster.

The pair halted when they had gone as close as they dared. Jake put back on the goggles and looked about. "There's a winch on the front of the truck," he whispered. "It is attached to a loop of chain that is running farther up the slope."

"The summit is not too far away," Briana said. She folded her arms about herself. The wind was picking up, and the temperature was dropping. They both shivered, but not only because of the cold. They were so close, so very close.

"They must have put the chain loop in place when they first got here," Jake whispered. He handed her the goggles. "See. They put a cylinder on a dolly, and then attach the dolly to the chain. There is a lot of bouncing around, but it works. They are towing everything almost up to what must be a summit viewing area."

"But no one is swathed," Briana said.

Jake took back the goggles and swung them back and forth. "No, only five thugs. Two loading the cylinders to the chain lift here and two more taking them off at the top. Where is the other... There he is by the side of the truck. What is he doing? It looks like he is erecting an antenna of some sort and pointing it back downhill toward the retreat."

Jake paused a moment. "No, two antennas, back to back. One pointed downslope and the other toward the peak. Like a relay or something."

Before Jake could say more, a loud voice boomed, *"Testare. Uno, due, tre."*

Jake frowned. He wasn't sure, but it sounded like the words were being repeated, sent farther up the slope. Was the sixth man back at the refuge, originating the message?

Jake looked to where the cylinders were being collected. One of them was being strapped down on a complex mechanism and then suddenly without warning flung far into the air. He watched in amazement as it arced up the mountainside like a missile and then fell into the Etna's crater.

"What are they doing?" He thrust the goggles at Briana. "It looks like they are sending the cylinders right into the volcano."

Briana grabbed the glasses. After a moment, she lowered them, and her shoulders sagged.

"There will be no swathed exiles here tonight," she said. "A catapult. Of course. They have figured out a way so that hundreds of hands are not needed."

"You are making no sense," Jake said.

"Etna is erupting. There is lava in the crater, boiling hot. Thousands of degrees. The cylinders containing the SF_6 will melt through. Or maybe only the valve structure at the top. How it happens doesn't matter. The gas is liquefied, under high pressure. It will escape and spew out as soon as the containment is breached."

"So the '*Uno, due, tre*' was a test signal to start the catapult?"

"How do you know what the words mean in English?" Briana asked.

"I took a year of Italian at UCLA," Jake said.

"Why?"

"I never get tired of answering questions like that," Jake said. "Because that is where the women are, duh."

Another voice cut off Briana before she could reply.

"*Allora, cosa succede?*"

JAKE'S HEAD snapped back as his vision filled with stars. The blow was a glancing one, professionally delivered, but it hurt painfully nevertheless.

He struggled to keep himself upright with his arms tied firmly behind his back. If it were not for the wall of rock he had been placed against, that would have been impossible. He glanced at Briana sitting next to him and bound the same as was he, but did not see any fear in her eyes, at least not yet.

"In English, *tonto*", the Mafioso bending over him said. "No more of your poor Italian."

"Now one more time." The captor held up one of the credit cards with the name of Jake's father on it. "Tell me his address so the package can be mailed to him."

"I don't know!" Jake said. "He moves around a lot. San Francisco, New York, ..."

Another slap knocked Jake's head sideways, and the stars began swimming again.

"Wrong answer. Look, *tonto*. You and your *donna* here are wearing clothes only the wealthiest could afford here in Sicily. You had ten thousand Euros in your wallet. Ten thousand! And for the final proof, you drive the latest Maserati. There has got to be a lot more where that came from."

"You're wasting your time," Jake managed to say. "He has... has disowned me. You won't get a cent from him."

"We will see." The Mafioso turned to Briana and leered. "No purse with euros," he said. "Instead, a backpack, of all things." He scooped up the canvas bag and turned it upside down. The contents fell to the ground in a cacophony of tinkles and crashes.

"The usual *donna* stuff." He kicked at the array at his feet. "Nail polish, a comb, and trinkets. Nothing of any real use."

"My dad is deep into internet security," Jake said. "He knows all about that stuff. He will think a message saying we have been captured is a hoax and ignore it. You won't be able to craft anything convincing enough."

"Not an email," the Mafioso said. "The postal service. It takes a few days, even with airmail, but the result is much more effective."

He held up a pair of long-handled pinchers. "You see these? They leave you with nothing. Nothing at all."

He reached forward and roughly cupped Briana's chin in his hand. "I will give you an hour to come up with an address from your *tonto*. If not, then we will start by sending his *padre* everything... everything between his legs."

Jake startled. No! No, no, no. The full impact of what was happening hit him. They had failed. They had failed miserably. The SF_6 was going into the volcano unimpeded. They were no closer to finding out where any exiles were than they were over a month ago. In fact, they had lost ground. The exiles were a step closer.

But more important to him than that, more important than anything else could possibly be in his life, he had been captured and threatened with... He shuddered. With unthinkable harm.

Mount Bagana

MAURICE WATCHED the anchorage of Kieta disappear to the stern. The maritime reports had the *Mizuno Maru* heading north to Loloho instead. Jake's credit card had taken a big hit for the extra distance. Dangerous, the skiff's captain had said. The independence of Bougainville Island from Papua New Guinea still had not occurred. Lots of talk, new ceasefires, and several years of peace. But then rumors of reopening the copper mine at Panguna would pop up again like the flowers from a stubborn weed. The native tribesmen were suspicious. Once more, they had not laid down their arms.

Loloho Harbor was sheltered only from the north by a slip of flat land jutting into the Pacific. Along the slip's southern side, a narrow road ran along its entire length. Near the middle stood a single isolated wharf where the cargo ship had docked.

As the skiff swung around and slowed to a small jetty nestled near the inland end of the road, Maurice's eyes opened in surprise. A large crowd of tribesmen had converged on the *Mizuno Maru*. Unlike most of the modern-day islanders, they were not dressed in shirts and pants. Instead, their faces glistened a brilliant red with eyes and mouth outlined in white. Feathered headdresses adorned the brows and many strands of shells looped their necks. A bamboo band stroked a complex beat, barely audible above a communal chant.

Maurice and Fig disembarked and walked toward the excitement, but were stopped by uniformed men with side arms strapped to their waists.

"It is best you remain here," the nearest one said. "It is a protest about the mine — a demonstration of a native culture being lost, so they say."

"We need to get closer to the ship as it is unloading," Fig said. "Don't you have to inspect the cargo?"

"Tomorrow will work fine," another voice said. He wore a blue cap with the word 'Customs' stenciled on the brim and carried a clip board in his hand. "They will dance and shout until sundown and then disappear back into the interior, leaving the shipment littering the dockside. I'm stopping for the day. Be back tomorrow."

"We cannot guarantee your safety if you approach too near," the guardsman said as the agent retreated. "Some of those characters can be quite unsavory." He shrugged. "Get close to them at your own peril."

"Buddha says we are to cultivate a limitless heart with regard to all beings," Maurice replied.

He and Fig hurried along the road. When they reached the rearmost line of protestors, the natives parted, and let them enter into their midst. Maurice looked upward and saw one of the gas cylinders dangling from the ships hoist moving overhead. Then to his surprise, the carriage line spooled out, and the tube of gas sped toward the ground into the middle of the crowd.

Bodies moved aside at the very last moment, and the SF_6 container alighted with a dull clang. No one was hurt. One of the natives adroitly removed the harness and tipped the cylinder horizontally. The boom lifted and swung back over the cargo ship's hold.

The unloading continued like the workings of a giant metronome. Cylinder after cylinder was hoisted and then placed at the feet of the dancers, hidden from view.

Maurice looked to see where Fig was standing, and saw he was hemmed in also. He took a tentative step backward but immediately bumped into someone who did not move. He closed his eyes. What was going on here?

Meditation alone would not yield the answer, Maurice decided after only a few moments of thought. He let his muscles relax and tried to call out to Fig to do the same. It might take several hours but, eventually the ship would be completely unloaded, and they would find out what would happen next.

THE CHANTING continued until well into dusk — the entire time it took the *Mazuno Maru* to surrender all of its cargo. From what little Maurice could see in snatches between dancing arms and legs, the guards at the end of the road were giving up for the day.

Finally, a last delivery appeared, a small oblong crate, reinforced with narrow bands of steel. As it lit on the dock, a native produced an axe and shattered one of its side panels. From where he stood, Maurice could see the contents — rifles, perhaps more than a dozen.

"English, right?" a voice sounded in his ear. "You understand English?"

Maurice tried once more to back his way out of the crowd, but when he did, he felt strong hands grab each of his arms. Old habits flashed in his mind. A few kicks and he could break free, but Fig would not know what to do. There were too many for him to take on them all. And, he told himself, merely escaping from a mob was not why they were here.

"Yes," he finally answered, as the guns were removed and distributed. "I speak English. But your fight is no concern for my friend or me. I do not understand why we cannot leave."

"We have a wagon," the native standing beside him said. "But no petrol. The last horse died many months ago."

"That is not an answ — "

"It has been agreed. We carry the tubes of metal to Bagana and offer them there. In exchange, we acquire many rifles. Twenty today, and when the volcano has consumed all of the cylinders, twenty more. Maybe those will be enough, enough so the outsiders from the south, from the biggest of all islands, will now stay away."

"What has that to do with me and my friend?" Maurice persisted.

"Many tubes. A long walk. Very heavy." He laughed. "As in the old days, *you* are now our slaves — our beasts of burden. Do as you are told, and you will live, at least until the task is done. Of course, what the tribe we will trade you to then will have in store is their business, not ours."

Maurice looked around hastily. There was no one nearby who could help. Worse, he and Fig were going to provide the transport of the SF_6 to Bagana. Probably would have to help throw them into the volcano too. There were no strangers clad in white involved at all.

"The only real failure in life is not to be true to the best one knows," Maurice cried out to compose himself, but it did not help. Their team was pushing against a ratchetwheel. What was happening felt like failure no matter what Buddha had said.

Mount Kilauea

ASHLEY JERKED herself to attention. She had been dozing. Staring at the unchanging CCTV feed was boring, especially in a quiet house with no one about. But now there was activity on the loading dock like there had been over a month ago. It was hard to see in the darkness, but it looked as if a flatbed truck was backing up to the dock. The thuglings were marshalling the gas transport cylinders from inside the warehouse.

She knew Maurice and Fig were out of phone contact in the Pacific, so she called Jake to fill him in on what was happening. Perhaps Briana could continue monitoring Etna, and he could come to Hilo. But no answer after three tries.

Ashley considered the possibilities and decided what she had to do. The feeling of her very first briefing, the one over two decades ago returned with annoying familiarity, but she pushed it aside. Only surveillance after all. She could handle it.

The portal presented the challenge. Briana was no longer programming it, nor standing at her side when she performed a trial run from her kitchen to her den. She would have to take the setter with her and make double sure of each of her steps. But then, how hard could it be? It was no different from writing a program — a short one with only two steps.

Speed was of the essence. Without any second thoughts that might make her change her mind, Ashley grabbed the setter and her cell phone and entered the portal. Then she immediately came back out. Lounging pajamas would not be proper on the streets of Hilo in the middle of the night.

Properly dressed in a jogging suit, she entered again, set the destination to outside of the warehouse, and started the transition. Like a fleeting bad dream, the expected wave of nausea dissipated. In a trice, she was standing across the street watching the truck.

Ashley felt a sense of exhilaration unlike anything she had ever experienced before. This was madness, total madness. No careful planning, no steps examined from every side before they were made. Only acting on impulses as soon as they occurred.

She hailed a taxi and climbed inside. "See the truck across the street?" she asked. "I want you to follow it when it is loaded and pulls out."

"Yes, ma'am," the cabbie said. "Are you an author? One who writes the detective stuff? Absorbing the realism of Hilo as it sleeps? I'm a writer, too, well, an aspiring one. Maybe we can stay in touch and you can read my stuff and tell me what you think."

"Um, yes. Correct," Ashley said. "Basically right, I guess. For now, keep alert." The exhilaration swelled as she said, "The game is afoot."

"NOT TOO close," Ashley said, several hours later as they sped along highway 11 toward the Hawaii Volcanoes National Park. "I don't want them to know they are being followed."

"Besides the truck, lady, we are the only ones on the road," the cabbie said. "If they're not suspicious, then they are pretty dumb crooks."

"Can't be helped," Ashley snapped back. She tried dialing Jake again, but still no answer. "I don't have any backup."

The truck slowed and turned right onto Crater Rim Drive.

She pulled up a Google map on her phone and studied it for a moment.

"No, no, to the left," she said. "It is a loop. They probably are going to get as close as they can to the Kilauea crater. We can approach them head on rather than from the rear." She considered if she should say more. "And keep your eye open for hundreds of people completely bundled up in white."

"Okay," the cabbie said slowly. Evidently, Ashley thought, he was beginning to doubt his passenger was all there. "This is going to be a cash fare, right?"

Ashley fumbled for her purse. Damn it! It was not there. So much for acting on impulse. "When we get back to Hilo, I will have to duck out for a moment and then get you paid."

The cab screeched to a halt.

"Okay, lady, I hate to do this, but unless you show me you have money, you will be walking back home."

"You can't leave me here in the dark like this!"

"I've tossed out drunks much bigger than you more than once. Show me the money."

Ashley looked at what she held. "Okay, how about my cell phone? Latest model, I'll give you the password, all you need to get it transferred. That's got to be worth more than the fare."

The cabbie considered for a moment. "Hmm. Give it to me now. But you know the charge is for time as well as distance, right? If this ends up too high, then you are out on your butt."

"Deal," Ashley said and extended the phone for the cabbie to grasp. "I may want to copy down a few numbers when this is done. Um, do you happen to have a pencil and a scrap of paper?"

The cabbie scowled.

"Okay, okay. We can talk about that later. For now, let's go find the truck."

THE DRIVE to the left was longer and curvier than the one to the right. By the time the truck came into view, Ashley saw it was already completely unloaded — and apparently abandoned. She hopped out when the cab stopped, nose to nose with the other vehicle and looked upslope toward the crater.

It was quiescent at the moment. The world-renowned bursts of angry reds and yellows did not arc to impossible heights in the sky. Instead the crater was illuminated dimly by three or four dancing flashlights, like giant fireflies looking for mates. Every minute or so a loud thump echoed down the slope. Ashley strained to see what was happening and occasionally saw one of the beams reflect off a metal cylinder arching across the sky. The SF_6! Somehow, the gas containers were being shot into the Kilauea's mouth.

The moon was nearly full, but nothing white stood out on the volcano's wall. There were no exiles about. Ashley's rush of adrenaline drained away. She had failed. Maybe the others had done better, but she had failed. Nowhere were any of the exiles to be seen here, and worst of all, Kilauea was being successfully seeded with what could destroy all life on earth.

ANGUS STRETCHED his arms. It felt good to be out of the hoodie and aerogel insulation. He rubbed his hands back and forth in front of the heat radiating from the kiln. Everything was going according to plan.

The cab that had appeared where the truck was parked was a bit unusual given the time of night, but then native tourists sometimes acted so strange — probably wanting to photograph the bubbling lava against the backdrop of deepest black.

He had already heard from Sicily. Etna's deposit was completed also. The transaction was over. His minions there probably now were focused back on ransoming wealthy tourists, their usual line of work.

Bagana would take another day or so. The delivery from the *Mizuno Maru* had gone smoothly and the SF_6 was working its way into the island interior as planned. The shaman would signal when the dumping was complete. Allowing a little time for the native to receive the command to start the incantation would mean it would be more or less in synchrony with the broadcasts of the audio files by the speakers near Etna's and Kilauea's peaks. Like the irresistible turn of a ratchetwheel, his plan was working perfectly.

Part Five

Eightfold Path Neverending

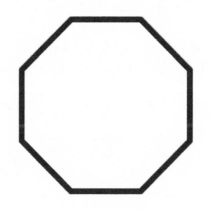

1

The Magic Eightball

THALING GRINNED with satisfaction. Finally, he had constructed a solid proof for the ritual ensuring his makeshift setter would dominate once it was placed in use. It was long to execute, and the rockbubblers grumbled throughout, but now it was done. The transformation of the tracker into a setter was complete.

Giving each of his flock their own choice had been a good decision. The first few were enthusiastic, and they helped convince the others. In the end, every single one had decided to go. It was like what had happened when Angus had brought home from above ground the little arm bands for Captain something-or-another, red, white, and blue rings around a common center. Everybody had to have one.

Yes, his flock was excited about going home. But to an uncertain future, Thaling admitted. Dinton had been right. The Faithful would resist their return. There would be a battle as there was before. 'Burning the ship' would help, but every dagger he could add to his flock could only improve the odds of success.

So, there was the matter of those who had Dinton as their leader. Of course, his elder brother himself would refuse to go. Like a brittle bone, he was so rigidly stubborn, unable to give up his dream of the eventual heating of the orb, no matter what. His brother's minions, however. Should they not get to choose for themselves? Choose free of the badgering of their flock leader who would demand they stay with him? Thaling could hear Dinton's voice now. 'I am due the respect that goes with my position. You must do as I say.'

Thaling began pacing. The problem was so very messy, not neat, and cleanly defined like the theorems of magic. Those could be proven either true or false. It was why he had chosen the craft in the first place — pure and precise. Not like the silliness of his rockbub...

His rockbubblers. Was there a way they could help?

DINTON SAT on the table in his alcove, his legs crossed in front. Thaling stood with his back to one of the walls, his hunched shoulders pressed against it, following the gently rounding contour like a garment in a native's spinning dryer.

Thaling firmed his resolve. He slapped the rod on his side for emphasis.

"I hold the baton, do I not?"

"Yes," growled Dinton. "I still have not figured out how you have been able to win each time we play the new game."

"No matter now," Thaling said. "I ask you respect what we both agree it means — and do exactly as I say."

"A command?" Dinton asked. "You give me a command?"

"As holder of the baton, yes, I do." This was the tricky part. Dinton had to be intrigued. "All I ask is you remain silent without interrupting until the finish of what I have to say."

"Then speak," Dinton growled.

"Eldest brother, it is now a time of decision. With the use of my craft, I will shortly be in control of the magic portal that brought us here so long ago."

"What! The portal! Magic! How — "

"I hold the baton," Thaling cut him off. "Be true to your word. Hear me out." He watched his brother settle back down and began again.

"Yes, I have used magic... used magic for our common good. All the members of my flock are going to return to our home world. I wish to offer the same opportunity to all of yours."

"I forbid such a choice," Dinton thundered. "It is a decision of great peril. If only we would wait — "

"Yes, yes, everyone knows about the joys of thumb twiddling and nit grooming. Because the natives will destroy their environment, and we will be their successors." He matched his fingertips together as if to encage his next thought and Dinton did not speak again. Now to start planting the hook.

"Hypothetically," Thaling continued, "if your flock members were offered the chance, how many do you think would accept? Twenty? Twenty-five?"

"Why, no more than ten," Dinton said. "They have enough sense not to be beguiled."

"Okay, ten. Suppose we make a game of it. A contest of pure chance. If I win, then each of your flock members would be allowed to choose. If I lose, I transfer ten of mine over to you... *and* give you the baton."

Dinton squinted at Thaling. "Suppose it were not ten but twenty, and I get to choose which ones? What is it you have in mind?"

"Here," Thaling thrust out the small black sphere he was holding. "This is your chance to extend your command."

"What is this thing?"

"The device is one fabricated by the natives. It is called the Magic Eight Ball."

Dinton grasped the globe and then shook his head. "This is not magic. There is no tingle when I hold it. Besides, the natives know nothing of the craft."

"Correct. It is a mere toy, not something of great power. Ask a yes or no question aloud, shake the orb, and it will give a random answer."

"Has my younger brother lost his mind?" Dinton shook the sphere vigorously and watched as words appeared in a window cut into it."

"Ha!" He laughed. "It says 'Without a doubt.'"

"There are only twenty different answers," Thaling said. "Each on the face of an icosahedron. It is a regular solid with twenty faces, each one — "

"Don't start on the magician gobbledygook." Dinton interrupted. He shook the sphere again. "Will my brother surrender his baton now before he does something stupid?

He waited a moment and laughed again. "'Don't count on it.' Well, it got that one right, too."

"So, are you game?"

Dinton frowned. He shook the sphere again. "There must be some sort of trick here."

"Exercise the toy all you want. When you are satisfied there are no biases, then we can ask the question. Think of it, my brother. You gamble perhaps ten of your flock against twenty of mine."

"Be gone," Dinton said. He held up the sphere against a wall candle and peered at it closely. "I will think on this."

SEVERAL HOURS later, the two brothers met again.

"I have decided to accept your offer to surrender members of your flock to me," Dinton said.

"Only if the orb says no to giving *all* of yours the choice to decide their own destinies."

"Yes, yes. I understand. But there are additional conditions you must agree to."

"Additional conditions! Not what I proposed." Thaling then said nothing more for what he hoped would convince Dinton he was open to negotiating. "Like what?" he asked at last.

"I have performed hundreds of trials," Dinton said. "There are twenty different answers, as you have stated, and the results are indeed random. Ten are 'yes,' five are 'no,' and five are undecided. If an undecided one comes up, we will shake the ball again."

"I know about all the answers. What are your conditions?"

"The first is that you pick one of the 'yes' answers to truly mean 'yes.' All of the other nineteen mean 'no.'"

"I would choose 'It is decidedly so'… but, wait! That is not fair! I have only one chance in twenty of winning."

"No, not one chance in twenty." Dinton smiled. "It will be even less. We will shake the ball, not once, but five times. For you to win, 'It is decidedly so' would have to come up at least three times in the five."

"But, but…" Thaling mentally pretended he was calculating. "That is less than one chance in — "

"One chance in thousands," Dinton said. "I figured out as much. But don't dwell on certainty. Think instead of possibility, Thaling. If you lose, it will only be a few of your flock. If you win, you might gain many more daggers for your side."

Dinton's smile grew bigger. "I have you figured out, little brother. It is the additional strength in arms you want. You want more warriors badly. So badly you are willing to gamble almost anything to acquire them."

"If I win, you said only ten would come."

"Words spoken in haste," Dinton said. "Look, your journey is going to be a gamble. You already knew that. I am agreeing to participate in it — just so long as it is a big one."

"Why all of sudden are you now the one who wants to play the game?" Thaling asked.

"You may be a mathematician, little brother, but simple odd calculations are something even a sorcerer like myself can do." He squinted his eyes almost shut. "Do you want a chance at ten more warriors or not?"

"If you can pick and choose if you win, then I can talk to each of your flock members individually before they decide," Thaling blurted.

"Oh, all right," Dinton said. "Now, let's get this over with. I think I already know the names in your flock I will select."

Thaling pressed against the wall as firmly as he could and slid his hands behind his back. Wait a few moments more before agreeing, he thought. Everything depends on the final bit of the sell.

The hole Littlebutt had made was small, so it did not show. Tiny, but still large enough that the rockbubbler could see his finger signal to manipulate the piece of paper he was holding.

"You shake, brother," he said.

BACK IN his separate magic alcove, Thaling smiled. "Good job, Littlebutt," he said.

"I don't get it, Boss. How is my turning one of the icoso... icosa — "

"Icosahedron," Thaling said. "It was an exercise of thaumaturgy."

"Is that part of wizardry or magic?"

"No, a separate craft, but a very simple one to perform."

"Never heard of it."

"Look, you guys came up with the idea of the fortune-telling orbs, and bartered with the air imps to get about six of them, right?"

"Yeah, Boss. But you know we don't like doing the payment part of the bargain."

"All of that is over and done with. We got six and a good thing, too. We broke three of them trying to take them apart."

"We have two spares. So?"

"Turned out, they were not needed. We cut new icosahedrons out of paper — both from the same sheet. That was important. 'Once together, always together' right."

"Why are you telling me all of this, Boss?"

"I'm going home, Littlebutt. Soon, you, Mintbreath. Lilacbottom, all of you will be on your own. Knowing a little thaumaturgy might help you when you get a new master."

Thaling felt a little twinge as he said this. But yes, letting them go was the proper thing to do.

"Anyway, once two things that were once together are bound by the incantation, you manipulated one of the paper constructs to always come up 'It is decidedly so' when I signaled you. The one in the sphere rotated to present the same.

Then, like the sheep we are, first a few, then in larger and larger numbers, all of Dinton's flock came over to my side. My brother is so enamored of rigor of logic that he has forgotten how impulsive all of us are. Like the lemmings of this world, we herd together at the slightest hint of a new direction. My brother, my know-it-all brother, the eldest. He did not have a chance.

"And the natives," he mused. "How much better their lives would be if only they understood a little magic. It would help them out of so many seemingly impossible problems."

Souvenirs

BRIANA WAITED until the thug disappeared. She and Jake were alone. She looked up at the moon. A tiny flicker of blackness flashed across its face. The crash of glass when her pack had emptied meant her matchmites were free. Staring at the flicker, she opened her mind, reached out, and issued commands.

The little imp was not powerful, but it was obedient and easy to control. It settled next to where the remaining five matches in the pack had been strewn and, trembling from the exertion, managed to drag one against the rough ground. It lit, and almost instantly, another sprite appeared. To the untrained eye, it looked identical to the first.

Briana extended her control, and soon six tiny helpers were hovering at attention awaiting their next command.

"Jake, pay attention," Briana whispered. "Sit up and bend forward. Move away from the wall as best you can."

"What?"

"Not so loud! And don't question. Do as I say."

For an instant, Jake frowned, but then spotted the imps and shrugged. He must be realizing who was in charge now, Briana thought. The mites swarmed behind him, and all six began gnawing at the fetters binding his hands. It took more than ten minutes, but eventually, he was free.

"Now you do the same for me," Briana said. "But move slowly. Any misstep will send a cascade of these small stones downslope and alert the guard. He can't be too far away."

"Okay, you're free too," Jake said after another few minutes of fumbling. "Let's get out of here."

"No! He would see us and raise an alarm. We need to surprise him when he returns of his own volition."

"But how?"

Briana eyed the scattered contents of her pack. She spotted the nail polish and the little egg of silly putty among the mess.

"I have an idea," she said.

AN HOUR later, the guard approached. He held a small shipping box in one hand and the pinchers in the other. Briana and Jake were propped against the rock wall, but this time side by side with their heads nestled together.

"*Mama mia!* What have you done?" he said when he spotted what lay on the ground in front of his two prisoners.

"So long as it was going to happen, we managed to do it ourselves," Jake said with a slight tremble in his voice. "I am not going to submit to butchery that will make a plastic surgeon's task impossible."

Briana got the reaction she wanted. The Mafioso was incredulous. He dropped the box and pinchers, knelt down, and extended his hand toward what had attracted his attention. He saw what looked like a severed penis, pale and fleshy in the moonlight and coated in blood at one end. Briana had to clamp her face tight to prevent herself from smiling. The silly putty had been quite good for modeling. And the nail polish glinted in the moonlight like real blood.

As the thug gawked, both Briana and Jake leaped up like clowns springing from toy boxes. With rocks in their hands, they pummeled the thug's head and sent him sprawling. A cascade of the little stones radiated from under his slumping form and noisily began tumbling down the hill.

While Jake stood guard with another rock, Briana restuffed her pack with everything worth saving.

"Now!" she slid her arms into the straps and took a first cautious step. Jake nodded, dropped the rock, and began to follow.

Despite their best efforts, more pebbles started to bounce down the slope.

"Let's hope the rest will think this noise is due to the guard and not us," she said.

Jake nodded again, and crouching low, the pair started their descent.

The first ten steps were tentative and agonizingly slow. Without causing a large spill, they slipped pass the remaining thugs huddled around a small fire a little distance away and passing around a bottle.

The next twenty came more easily, and with rising confidence, they lengthened their strides and increased the pace. Soon, they were a quarter way back down the slope. The upper terminus of the cable car loomed faintly in the darkness.

Briana glanced up at the moon. The silhouettes of her matchmites hovered in the soft light. They were descending as she had commanded, at the proper angle so she could keep track of them. She strained to make out more detail of the path ahead, wishing Jake still had the night vision goggles, but the Mafioso immediately had taken them away when they were captured. Rather than have him lead, they were stepping in parallel, side by side.

Suddenly, a larger rock under Briana's foot gave way and started a clatter. She lost her balance, and before she could regain it, she fell onto her back and started picking up speed. Jake reached out at one of her upraised hands, but he could not stop her. He, too, became prone and started to thunder down the hill.

As they fell, the speed of their descent quickened. Hands thrust out to the side for balance rapidly were withdrawn. They were moving too fast. Bare flesh could not withstand the friction. Even their pant legs were beginning to fray and tatter.

"Don't try to sit up," Jake cried over the racket of the tumbling stones. "You will go head over heels."

Briana did not answer. She heard another sound — the start of a truck engine from where the Mafioso had camped on the slope above. Their escape had been discovered. The thugs were going to race down the road and meet them where the ground again became level.

She tried to relay this to Jake, but now the noise was too loud, the speed too terrifyingly swift. Like runaway luges, the pair plummeted faster and faster.

Then as abruptly as it had started, the rush of momentum stopped. The ground leveled. They skidded to a halt. Reflexively, they both stood, trying to push out of their minds what it was going to feel like when the numbness of the scraped away flesh wore off.

But no time for that now, Briana's thoughts raced. The Mafioso were still coming after them. The growl of the truck's engine protesting the descent in a low gear grew louder and louder. She looked upwards again. There was a shadow overhead.

"The gondola car. It is parked right here. Maybe they won't think to look."

Jake nodded, and the two climbed the staircase zigging back and forth from the ground to the gondola.

"Your remote," Briana said as they caught their breaths and sagged to the floor, then abruptly stood again as exposed flesh touched the bare metal. "Use it. Start the car. Turn on the headlights."

Jake nodded, dug the key fob out of his pocket, and pointed it farther down slope to the retreat's parking lot.

"I hope this thing has sufficient range to — "

His words were caught short by the deep growl of the Maserati starting up. Peering over the rim of the gondola's side panel, they held hands and hoped as their pursuers pulled up next to the rental car, their flashlights swinging back and forth across the lot, looking for the prisoners who had escaped them.

"Now the phone," Briana said. "Connect to Ashley. Tell her to zero in on us. Send the portal right away. Right up next to this gondola's door."

She hurt everywhere but ignored the pain. She looked about one last time. "We are getting away but did not stop anything. Let's hope that Maurice and Fig have done better."

"Thank you, thank you, thank you," Jake whispered. "If we had not gotten away, I would have...."

"The portal!" Briana commanded. "The portal. Now!

Words of the Master

MAURICE STARED back at the shaman. His entire body ached from the effort to lug the gas cylinders to this camp high in the central ridge of mountains running the length of Bougainville Island. His shoulders and back bled from blisters and cracked calluses caused by the chafe of the harness. Hazy smoke rose from Mount Bagana in the distance, polluting an otherwise crystal blue sky with a low haze like a mistake made by a beginning painter. The crater was still too far off to be seen, but in another day and they would be at its rim.

The remains of an evening meal campfire sputtered between Maurice and the one who squinted in the quickening dusk to examine him. The medicine man was wrinkled head to toe as if he were a prune left in the sun far too long. His eyes were rheumy as if fed from hidden springs within his skull. Fig and most of the others around the fire were already asleep.

"Which tribe?" the shaman said in English.

"I have no tribe. What do you mean?"

"You are not like the others." The old man pointed at Fig curled in a ball nearby. "Not like that one or the other whites who come from the biggest of all islands. 'Mediating peace,' they say. 'We are here to help.' But they are not. None of us believes that. Their purpose is to reopen the copper mine. To make their own pockets bulge. Nothing for us, the ones who are the rightful owners."

"The bottles are not empty," Maurice said. "They contain sulfurhexa... bad air. Harmful air. It will make all of your land hot and sick. It will be as if Bagana's rivers of fire had covered everything."

"If we do not feed the long, empty tubes to Bagana, then we will not get the rest of the rifles we are promised — even if I speak the words as I have been told."

"Words? What words?"

The shaman reached into the shirt he had stuffed into trousers two sizes too small. He fumbled for a moment and withdrew a sheaf of papers, all wrinkled and creased. "Here," he said. "I do not understand any of them. Tell me. What do they say?"

Maurice took the top sheet from the offered pile, bent forward to get nearer the fire and began mouthing the words. "I do not understand them either." He shook his head.

The healer grunted. "Performing labor in exchange for goods, I do understand," he said. "But saying strange words without knowing their meaning is not a good thing to do.

"Tomorrow, we are to go to Bagana's rim and send back word by runner that we have arrived. Then when we get a reply, I am to speak the words into the crater and report back that I have done so. Speak all the words except for the very last three. Those I deliver when a second message comes several days later."

Maurice felt a sudden flash of hope. "I think they are the words of a powerful spell. They are the ones that will cause the disaster to happen." He considered what he should say next. "You have been given a great responsibility, and you must choose wisely."

"And what choice is that?"

"Whether or not to dump the... the long hollow tubes into the volcano, to chant any spell when that has been done."

"Simple enough tasks for twenty more rifles."

"No. A wise follower of the Buddha has said 'If you can, help others; if you cannot, at least do them no harm.'"

The shaman peered more closely at Maurice. "Is your name Buddha? Are you the leader of your tribe?"

Maurice shook his head. "Not me. Buddha says 'No man is a leader until his appointment is ratified in the hearts and minds of his men.'"

"Then what else? What else does this Buddha say?"

"Many things." Maurice's thoughts raced. Was there a possibility he could convince this shaman not to act as he intended? "You will not be punished *for* your anger. You will be punished *by* your anger';'Your worst enemy cannot harm you as much as your own unguarded thoughts'; 'What you are is what you have been. What you'll be is what you do now..'"

"Enough! Stop! Your words seem deep, but I think they must be pondered a great while before one acts according to them."

"Exactly so. It is not easy. I have been struggling myself for... well, for years."

"All of these words, how many are they?"

"I don't know."

"Nevertheless, I see your fervor. I judge you do speak from the heart."

"Then you will not feed the volcano or say the evil words?"

"Oh, no. We will continue on that path. Twenty rifles are worth far more than even thousands of words."

Maurice slumped. Of course. He was not the master of a temple. He did not have the skill to convince others. Doubts cluttered his own path every step of the way. The shaman must see the defeat in my eyes.

"I will fetch paper and pencil," the old man said. "Write down all of the sayings your Buddha expounds so I can study them. The world changes. Even a shaman must keep abreast of the new."

"Why should I — "

The medicine man held up his hand for Maurice to stop. "Do as I say, and I will then let you and your companion go free — back into your world to seek truth along paths of your own."

No More Waiting

ASHLEY TURNED her head from Briana's glare. The rescue of Jake and the younger woman had been successful, but from Briana's attitude, one would never guess it.

"We can't wait any longer for Fig and Maurice," Briana said. "We have been overtaken by events. We have to act now. At least two of the volcanoes have been seeded. Maybe even all three. The man in the hoodie could very well be our last hope." She paced back and forth in small circles across the street from the warehouse in Hilo. Like a primitive thermostat, she spent as much time in the sun as in the shade.

Ashley fingered the heavy and uncomfortable Kevlar vest she wore. It reminded her of a girdle she had once tried on years ago when the pounds had first started to accumulate. The miner's lamp from the surplus store felt uneasy on her head. But she did not complain. None of the others, similarly clad, were not.

Jake took a few tentative swings with the sword Briana had directed him to procure. Purchased as a trio from a pawnshop with his new credit card. The charges from Etna had not triggered an alarm.

But makeshift armor? Ashley asked herself. And after only a few hours of Briana's sketchy training? The younger woman put on a good air about her expertise, but it was clear what she knew had been learned by watching, not real use.

Ashley shook her head. But then neither was Briana a coward. That was very clear, too. The daughter of an archimage was driven by some inner force, and whatever it was, it was infectious.

"There are the four thuglings on the loading dock," Ashley tried to temporize. "We are not sure if there is more than one hoodie-wearer inside. I don't see how we could force one of them to tell us where the seven hundred exiles are."

"It's our only option now." Briana stopped her next circuit into the sun. "The SF_6 has been deployed. We have to figure out who is slated to intone the incantation that starts the catalytic reaction."

"Yes, but — " Ashley began.

"Let me finish," Briana snapped. "Normally, the energy of the volcanoes fuels gentle venting and small lava flows. Once the spell is completed, however, the trapped power is bound only to the SF_6 creation and nothing else. Any not used accumulates — no place to go, no way to dissipate. This is mere thaumaturgy we are talking about here, not intricate magic rituals. And when the release happens, there will be eruptions, tremendous ones, spewing the SF_6 into the air."

"Calm down a bit, Briana," Jake said. "We get it. Really, both of us do. But as Ashley has argued, until we can locate the seven hundred or so exiles, they always will be the threat. Probably any one of them could work the charm. We have to find out where they *all* are."

"Incantation, not charm," Briana snapped again. She frowned. "Oh, sorry. That doesn't make any difference, does it?" She tugged at her hair. "So, we crash the building. Do something like, I don't know, lock the loading dock door so the thuglings remain outside. Force hoodie-man to tell us where the exiles are."

"How? Torture?" Ashley asked.

"No. Not that, of course!" Briana's eyes widened in shock. She was silent for a moment and then spoke more calmly. "Well, I guess, yes, it might require brutal force." A faraway look came over her face. "Although, I don't remember any of the sagas talking about the use of such a thing."

Jake's phone rang.

"Hello? Yes, Maurice. Where are you?" He waited for a second and then echoed what he was hearing for Briana and Ashley. "Back in Port Moresby. Both you and Fig? Great! But no hordes of white-swathed mummies. The SF_6 will be dropped into Mount Bagana soon."

"Tell him to go to the very spot at which we dropped him off," Briana said. "The portal door will appear right away. And when the two of them join us, we will go ahead and attack." She pulled the setter out of her pack and began entering the settings.

A few moments later, the portal door opened right on the sidewalk where they stood. Fig stepped out and smiled. Briana shut the opening, and the four waited for Maurice to pop through as soon as he realized the lock on his end had disengaged.

A minute passed and then another, but Maurice did not appear. Jake punched Maurice's number. "Hey, buddy, what's the hang-up? Come on through. We don't want the door on your end to start attracting attention."

"Something must have gone wrong," Maurice's voice came out of Jake's phone. "You are outside of the warehouse in Hilo, right?"

"Yeah. Fig just came through."

"I'm here in Hawaii, too," Maurice said. "But not with you guys. It looks like I'm standing right outside of what Briana described as Oscar's shack."

Briana stabbed at the setter, re-entering their location and set the countdown to only a few seconds.

"The display," she said in a puzzled voice as she pressed the keys. "All of a sudden, it's frozen."

"Maurice! Maurice!" Jake shouted into the phone. "Where are you again?"

5

Interplanetary Stowaway

MAURICE CAUTIOUSLY approached the door of the shack, put his ear to it, and then drew back from the surprising heat. He looked up toward the sun. It was partially hidden by the lush green overgrowth arching over the small structure. Not the sun then. The heat was coming from the inside.

The Buddhist knocked tentatively and then with more force, but there was no answer. His last blows pushed the door inward from the jamb, and he entered. A blast of hot air jogged his memory. Papers littered the floor, and in one corner was a coiled pile at his feet brilliant white cloth. Yes, definitely Oscar's shack, he thought. This is how Briana had described it. Somehow the portal must have slipped a cog and arrived at a previous destination.

He was about to call back to the others again when through the open door he saw some movement up the trail. More swathing! Someone was coming. Maurice pushed the door shut again and raced to one of the grime-encrusted windows. Peering through a small spot less fogged than the rest, he watched the figure lumber closer and closer. Could it be? Was he watching the approach of one of the aliens Briana wanted to find?

Maurice sprang up, raced into the kitchen, and began pulling open drawers. There was a paring knife in one, but nothing more substantial. It would have to do. He grabbed it and returned to his crouch by the door. The figure continued laboriously coming nearer, close enough that Maurice could tell the being was unarmed — at least on the outside of his covering.

The Buddhist eyed the doorframe. The hinges were on the side nearest him. When it opened and the creature entered, it would not see him waiting there. But should he strike? And if so, where? Hold the blade of the knife against where the neck might be? Push it inward until he could feel the resistance of...

Maurice stopped the train of his thoughts. What was he thinking? This was not the teaching of Siddhartha. The beast, if that indeed what he was watching, continued past the shack's door and opened the one to the portal standing nearby. It shut itself inside, and the door shimmered for a moment immediately after.

Back along the trail, a second swathed alien appeared. A third trailed a short distance behind. The Buddhist phoned Briana and began whispering rapidly. "I have found them. I have found the ones you are looking for. They are coming out of the underground, and then, one by one, going into the portal."

"It can only transport a single person at a time," Briana said over the phone. "Keep watching. There may be more. When I can get my setter working again, I will let you know."

"Right," Maurice said. He settled on the floor, crossed his legs, and made himself comfortable. It was like meditation — no, more like an inverted glove. He had to keep focused outward rather than into the depths of his own mind.

The second exile entered the portal and shortly thereafter the third. On the trail, four or five more appeared. Maurice rummaged through the papers on the floor, found a pencil, and began marking the number that passed. Briana had said there were about seven hundred, he remembered. Could they all have been nearby the entire time?

"SEVEN HUNDRED twenty-seven," Maurice mumbled aloud when the procession stopped several hours later. It was true. They had been here, all of them. But now they had gone to…

Maurice could not speculate. It was so outside of his experience. He phoned Briana with a final update and was preparing to ask her what to do next when one more swathed figure appeared on the path. This one walked slower than the rest. Unlike the others, he was bent over like an old man and appeared to be gesturing to something on the ground in front of him. The Buddhist stood on tiptoe as the being came closer and peered out of another spot near the top of the window. It was a hole! A hole in the ground that somehow moved along the path in pace with the exile.

This last being stopped before the portal, just as had the others. But rather than pull open the door, it remained still, shrouded head tilted downward and peering into the hollow. Maurice blinked. He heard voices. The alien was talking to someone… something… in the opening.

"I am giving you your freedom," the swathed being said. "Go! Be off! Feel the freedom of doing what you will. I am no longer trying to dominate you."

English? The being was speaking in English!

"Well, it is not quite that simple, Boss." Another voice answered from the cavity. "You see, it gets pretty boring down here without something to do. And as wizards go, you aren't too bad. Except for the business of trading with the air imps, you never gave us a distasteful task. No dabbling in world domination — that kind of stuff."

The being laughed. "But I am, Littlebutt. I *am*. Not on this world but another. And if there were a way to take you there with me — "

"But there is, Boss. There is! All you need to do is find a big enough boulder, and, one by one, we drift inside it. Then you roll the rock into the doorway thingy and have someone else roll it out wherever it is you are going. The limitation of one at a time does not apply to us since it is the demon realm that the portal loops through. It would be a piece of quartz, as we say."

"I am the last one, Littlebutt. The others have already gone. Well, all except for Dinton. My stubborn elder brother elected to remain until the climate here changes even though his own mate has elected to return. And I alone have insufficient strength to push around large rocks as you suggest."

Maurice called the others again and relayed what he had just learned. All of the exiles were going somewhere else — all except one who for some reason was staying. He felt a flush of panic as he recalled what he had heard. 'Remain until the climate here changes.' What did that mean? Briana had explained that even after the SF_6 was in the volcanoes, there was a final step to be performed before it was in the air. Were any of these aliens the ones involved with that?

And 'I am the last one,' the exile had said. When he left, the portal might disappear. There would be no trace. No clue for what to do next. Maurice looked around the room and then focused on the swathing coiled on the floor. English, they understand English, he thought. In a flash, he knew what he had to do.

MAURICE CAUTIOUSLY emerged from the hut while the exile and whatever it was continued to argue. The swathing felt cumbersome, and he was not sure he had managed to cover himself completely. Some of it had been missing — the bandages for Fig when he was wounded. And he had to use some more to cover his boots. But there was no other choice.

The being turned when he heard the creak of the door. "Dinton!" he cried. "You have changed your mind! Wonderful! If only we knew where Angus had vanished to, if he were still alive... But no matter. Together, brother, together, we will return and wrest back what is ours."

Maurice nodded, not trusting himself to say a word.

"You go next, brother. Enter the portal and exit on the other side. I will be last after I say goodbye to my... to my — "

Maurice heard what could have been a slight choke in the voice of the other, but he could not be sure. He took a deep breath, already beginning to feel discomfort from how hot it was to be completely swathed, and entered the magic portal.

6

Plan the Work, Then Work the Plan

ASHLEY WATCHED Briana punching savagely at the remote. It did not respond.

"We will have to figure out this problem later," the younger woman said. "I'll probably have to put another boot on it. But now with Fig here, at least we have four of us. Let's go."

"Remember, Briana," Ashley said. "Plan the work first." The stakes were too high. She was going to have to slow this whirlwind down.

"There are the four guys on the dock and at least one inside," Jake said. "Maurice is the only one who really knows karate or whatever it is he can do. He looked at Fig and frowned. "I'm only an amateur, and Fig..."

"And the woman at the front desk," Ashley nodded. "Even if she is blind, we are outnumbered." She was silent for a moment, then continued. "Three locations separated from one another. Perhaps we should take advantage of that." A fresh thought suddenly blossomed. "Like... like Nelson at Trafalgar," she said.

"What do you mean?" Briana asked. "Concentration of force is a well-known tactic. At least it is on Murdina."

Ashley steeled herself. She was going to have to do something she never would have even contemplated in her former life. Then she felt something new. Just as when she had followed the truck to Kilauea, there was a thrill in this as well.

"I will take one of the motor scooters to a sporting goods store. Don't do anything until I return."

"Wait! What?" Jake said.

"Trust me on this," Ashley said. "I have a plan. Nelson at Trafalgar. Lanchester Square Law. I did some operations research work on it when I was at USX." Without another word, she kicked the scooter to life and sped off.

301

TWENTY MINUTES later, Ashley returned. "Okay, here's the plan. Briana, you go in the front door and distract the receptionist. That will allow Jake and Fig to slip by her and get into the main warehouse floor without creating an alarm.

"And the thugs on the loading dock?" Jake asked.

"I'm getting to that," Ashley said. "Briana, you certainly will be able to handle the receptionist — a superior force there. And Jake and Fig will outnumber the guy in the hoodie two to one. Yes, it would be great if Maurice were here, but this is the best we can do — two to one."

"You're forgetting about the thugs," Fig said.

"That's where I come in," Ashley said. She took in another gulp of air. Was she really going to be doing this? "I will distract them."

"Sounds dangerous," Fig said.

"No more so than what you and Jake will have to face," Ashley replied. She could tell that her voice did not carry the conviction she was used to using at USX, but that is what had to be. "You see, Nelson faced a larger French fleet at Trafalgar. He broke his own line of ships into two groups, and they crossed the tee — "

"Never mind the details," Briana cut her off. "Jake, Fig, Let's head for the lobby now, before anyone of us changes his..." She glanced at Ashley. "Or her mind."

FIG AND Jake followed Briana into the lobby. Ursula looked up from her Braille keyboard at the sound. "Can I help you?" she asked.

"We are here to see Mr. Angus," Briana said. Now, with the operation in motion, her feeling of pique faded away. Ashley was right. Barging in and raising a ruckus had not been a very good idea. As she spoke, Fig and Jake stepped quietly to the side toward the door opening into the office behind.

"Mr. Angus has no appointments on his calendar," Ursula said. "My name is Ursula Price. Please tell me why you want to see him, and I will try to set up a meeting for you."

"Well, here's the thing," Briana raised her voice as the door behind came open, and Fig vanished inside. Jake followed, but did not put his hand behind him to cushion the click of the latch.

"What was that?" Ursula said, alarmed. "How many of you are here?" She rose, picked up a letter opener. "Get out! Get out before I call my nephew and his friends from the loading dock." She waved the opener in front of her. "I can defend myself if I have to."

Reflexively, Briana pulled her dagger from her belt and turned to face the blind woman as she came closer. Her first duel with an armed opponent! But against someone who was blind? And wielding a blade that was dull? She scowled at the way her thoughts were going. No, definitely nothing for the sagas.

Briana took a hesitant step backward, but Ursula took two to close the distance between them. "Mr. Angus has been so generous to me," Ursula said. "I would do anything for him, anything he says. And he was most clear no one was to go behind this lobby unless he explicitly told me to let them pass."

"I... I really don't want to hurt you," Briana said, "but I have a blade much sharper than yours."

"Mr. Angus has been so generous to me." Ursula took another step forward. "I would do anything for him, *anything*."

ASHLEY PUTTED into the parking lot next to the loading dock. She had discarded her Kevlar vest and miner lamp 'helmet.' Unlike most women of her age, she continued to wear her hair long. Men seemed to like it that way. Maybe a few curls wafting in the breeze would give her an added chance to approach without being challenged.

"Hey, pretty mama," one of the thugs called out as she neared. "Are you lost?"

Ashley did not answer. She swung the scooter parallel to the dock and waited. The thug who had spoken first came to kneel down and look at her.

"What are you carrying?" He pointed at the paint gun concealed in its original bag from the store.

"You'll see in a moment," Ashley said. Her heart started thumping.

The guy was young, wearing an undershirt with no sleeves. Tattoos covered both arms. Like a jack-o-lantern, his face was filled with a big smile, but it was clear it was fake. It did little to cover the mean streak barely underneath.

The three others came to crouch next to the first. Two extended their hands, offering to lift her off her ride.

Now or never, Ashley thought. She ripped the covering aside, and then, splat, splat, splat, splat. The gun blasted dye into each of the startled faces.

"Bitch," the first one yelled, and vaulted to the macadam in front of the scooter. "Who put you up to this? Was it the Cryptos over on Palele?"

Ashley reved the engine and popped the clutch. The scooter vaulted forward, and the thug in her way jumped aside. She roared out of the parking lot and onto the street, turning into traffic as quick as she could.

That was easy, she thought as she began to speed away. Then she jammed on the brakes. The idea was to lure them, not leave them where they were. She pulled to the side of the road, stopped and waited. For what felt like forever, nothing more happened, but then alerted by the squeal of tires, she saw a car round on to the street. One of the thugs leaned out of the passenger window pointing ahead. They were coming after. Now to lead them far away.

Another thought crept into her head. Part of the plan had not been thought through. Supposed they caught up with her. Then what?

FIG SURVEYED the office. It was the same as when he had visited before. A desk, computer, and microphone. But with all their little troop had learned, the equipment looked far more sinister than it had before. The exiles had managed to get the SF_6 delivered to three volcanoes without exposing any of themselves, not a one. Could it be that words spoken from here by a single individual would be all that was needed to start the catalytic reaction?

No one followed him and Jake into the office. The loading dock door remained closed. A peek between the shut blinds showed no activity on the warehouse floor. If the one with the hoodie were still here, he would have to be behind the door at the far end of the floor.

Fig tried the knob for the opening onto the warehouse proper. It turned, and soon he and Jake crossed through. Nervously, he clasped and unclasped the pommel of his sword. Guns would have been better, but with the background checks and delays, that was not an option. Anyway, Briana seemed quite comfortable with the idea of blades. Where she came from, they were natural — the weapons of choice. The assumption was, however, that whomever they encountered would be armed no better.

His heart started to race. This was totally unlike how he had imagined things, nothing like an adventure in a book. This was the real thing. Five of them against aliens who could work magic. They were in way over their heads.

Walking quietly across the warehouse floor was not easy. With many of the gas cylinders gone and only the production line on the far wall, the structure was almost empty. Footfalls, even soft ones echoed off the high ceiling.

After carefully striding, step by careful step, the pair reached the door of the rectangle jutting into the warehouse floor in the far corner. Fig placed his hand on the door as he had done at Oscar's hut, and then pulled it away. It was hot to the touch, even hotter than when he had tested one before.

Fig put his hand on the knob and grimaced. He was going to get a burn from this so had to move swiftly. With a twist, he torqued the handle and pushed. The door swung inward, and a blast of impossibly hot air roared out. Both he and Jake entered.

Inside, a startled figure rose to its feet. It was... impossible to describe. Covered with dense hair from head to toe. Deep-set eyes and fangs protruding from a mouth open in surprise. It wore a tunic and had a small dagger strapped to its side. In an instant, the blade was drawn, and the creature roared.

Fig looked about. The room was almost entirely empty. A chair in the middle with a cluster of clothing on one side. A single sheet of paper, seeming oddly out of place, lay on the otherwise bare floor. An oven, no, a kiln with a slit in the side glowing almost orange-red pulsed angry heat into the air.

Fig and Jake stood transfixed. Their swords were both drawn, but they pointed to the ground, not ready to challenge the creature when he charged.

The Spoils of Victory

BRIANA EYED the letter opener coming closer. She tried sliding to the side, but either Ursula's hearing was very good or the blind woman had guessed what she had done. What would one of her cadre do in this situation? What would Ashley do?

The older woman would think before she acted, of course. Briana pulled her lips into a grim line. But in this situation, it looked like there would be little time for that.

"Were you born without sight?" Briana suddenly blurted. Something to distract the woman from what she was set upon doing.

"No, a childhood accident," Ursula said. "Lived in a home. Needed help all my life... until Mr. Angus came along."

A bubble of an idea started to wiggle in Briana's mind. "He has helped you a great deal, right?"

"Yes, of course."

"I wonder," Briana said. She stepped back to facing Ursula head on. "Why did you pull a weapon when you heard the door latch click? Wouldn't it have been better to call the police?"

"Mr. Angus is a very private person. He would not care to deal with the interruption."

"You suspect whatever he is doing is illegal, don't you? Maybe not on the surface, but certainly deep down inside. Hiring a blind person to handle whomever might come by. Yes, I know, it sounds wonderful, but don't you think it is at least a little bit odd?"

"He is a very generous person."

"You thought we were from a rival. Ursula, didn't you? Briana kept the patter going. "But we are not. If Mr. Angus is not doing anything he shouldn't, then there is nothing to worry about, right?"

"I could lose my job!" Ursula shouted. "The instructions were clear. 'Do not let anyone beyond my office.' He did not say it, but it was strongly implied. Or... or else I would be sent back to the home. To sit around a table, listen to idle chatter. Listen to the click of the clock until the next meal. Until the end of another day without purpose, without use."

"Why the letter opener rather than the phone?" Briana persisted.

Ursula began to weep. "I could lose my job," she choked.

Briana reached out and touched Ursula gently on the arm. "Put down the opener. You will not need it. Return to your seat. If Mr. Angus is displeased, then I will take all of the blame. You tried to stop us. You did as you were told.

Ursula continued sobbing. "He is a good man. He has to be. It is a misunderstanding. You will see."

"Come," Briana said as she sheathed her dagger and headed for the inner door. "Resume your duties. I will tell you everything I learn."

ASHLEY PRESSED the scooter's gas pedal to the floor. The little engine complained as it reved higher, doing little to help. The car following was gaining ground. How was she going to make this work, she thought. Keep close enough so the thugs would continue to chase. But not so close that they would catch.

Up ahead there was a long line of cars at a red light. She cut almost to the gutter and streaked up to the intersection. Her rearview mirror showed her pursuers had to come to a stop at least a dozen cars back.

The light turned green, and Ashley cut sharply to the right. It would take a few moments for the intersection to clear, and she would gain back some of the initial distance she had lost. The side street was deserted, and for a few precious moments, she bent down behind the windshield and soared along.

But eventually, the dark car reappeared. With a throaty roar, it accelerated to close once again. The light ahead turned yellow and then, as Ashley reached the intersection, red. She closed her eyes and kept her foot on the accelerator, hoping she would burst through before any cross traffic started to move.

When she looked back, she heard screeching brakes. Cross traffic was moving. The thugs were blocked. While the seconds passed, her distance grew until she could no longer make out any of the occupants, only a deep gray fading into total darkness in the car's interior.

The entrance to a side street drew closer. Ducking down it and then another turn would make her safe and then... Ashley slammed on the brakes. Not good. They have still to be in pursuit. Coasting to a complete stop at the intersection, she contemplated what to do. She pivoted from side to side, eyeing the roadway ahead as well as to the left and right.

The building closest to her looked as if it had been abandoned years before. Litter piled against where the stucco met the sidewalk. The windows were boarded with weathered wood. Glancing at the structure across the perpendicular street appeared the same — dirty, neglected and uninvited. She thought of something to try.

Ashley pulled the paint ball gun out of its sling and fired four quick bursts at one of the shuttered windows. The dull grayness sprouted bursts of bright yellow as if eggs had been hurled onto it. Then she rounded the corner and took aim at the building now on her left. After reloading the gun, it too was adorned with a marking that could not be missed. Satisfied, she sped off down the little street.

They will see the marking and decide I had left them a trail to follow. Perhaps they will think it was an invitation — a game with perhaps pleasures to be the prize when she was finally caught. Why not? Why else would the 'mama' leave them a clue?

Ashley continued zigzagging through the streets of Hilo, blazing a trail at every turn. Finally, using a map downloaded on her phone, she worked her way to the entrance to highway nineteen, the one leading to the national park.

After she had sped onto the road for a bit, continuing the mark the trail along the way whenever a convenient roadside building presented itself, she stopped and reversed direction, accelerating as fast as she could. It was a gamble, but maybe the twists and turns had slowed the pursuit down to a more leisurely pace. When she reached the first crossing road, she sighed with relief. The thugs were not yet in sight. She turned on it and carefully followed a course taking her back to the warehouse. Her pursuers instead would continue down highway nineteen for a long, long time.

AS ANGUS closed, Fig gripped his sword with both hands and thrust with an uncertain quaver. The Heretic nimbly stepped a tiny bit to the side, kept coming, and wrapped his free hand around Fig's extended arm. Simultaneously, he raised his dagger hand high and started to swing downward into Fig's chest.

Jake came out of his momentary shock and interposed his own blade to block Angus' thrust, and the blade skidded harmlessly over Fig's shoulder.

Angus grunted and disengaged. He retreated, swinging his dagger back and forth between his two assailants.

Fig instinctively moved a step to the right. Jake watched what he was doing and paced an equal amount to the left. If they could come at the exile from two different directions, they might have a chance.

Fig took a tentative breath and immediately gasped. His lungs seared as if they were on fire. The air of the room was hot, unbelievably hot. He remembered a trip to the Arabian Peninsula when he was a boy — 131 degrees Fahrenheit in the shade. But as will sapping as that was, it was nothing compared to this. He had to withdraw, back to the large main floor before it was too late.

Fig glanced at Jake. There was panic in the other man's eyes. Together, they hastily beat a retreat back through the open door. Angus followed them to the doorway, fangs bared and waiving his dagger. He threw his head back and growled.

As the pair watched, the Heretic reversed the grip on his dagger. He raised it past his ear and focused on Fig's chest. Involuntarily, Fig took another step backward, but then stopped. No matter what the cost, this was not the behavior of one who had pledged his sword to his queen.

Angus' eyed narrowed. Fig imagined the calculation going on in the exile's mind, or at least what he hoped was. If the dagger were thrown, it would give Jake an opening to strike. And to venture into the cooler warehouse floor to retrieve the blade, the air temperature would shift the advantage to his remaining foe. No, the dagger was going to remain in the alien's hand.

Fig thought furiously. Two to one. The exile was outnumbered, exactly as Ashley said he would be. He and Jake should be able to subdue him. But the first encounter, as brief as it had been, made clear their opponent was a skilled fighter. One swift movement and his own weapon had been completely neutralized. He and Jake had never even handled a sword until Briana gave them a few brief instructions earlier in the day.

Disregard the pounding heart, Fig told himself. It was the kiln. The kiln was the key. He surveyed the expanse of the warehouse and saw what he had hoped for on the far wall near the loading dock door.

"Jake, stay where you are. Keep him occupied." He started backpedaling as rapidly as he could, sword still drawn.

"Wait!" Jake called out. "Where are you going? I can't take on this guy only on my own."

"I'll be back in a second. Keep menacing him. It's a standoff."

Fig reached the warehouse wall. He studied the boxes mounted there and then jerked on the biggest switch. Instantly the warehouse plunged into a deep gloom. The encrusted windows let in only the smallest glimmer of light. But more importantly, the spark igniting the fire in the kiln went out. The fan blowing hot air silenced. It might take a while, but the air inside the back office would start to cool. Fig reached up and flicked on his miner's lamp. Across the warehouse floor, Jake did the same.

Angus looked over his shoulder to see what had happened. Fig moved until he was on a line perpendicular to the doors opening. Jake did the same on its other side. Together they converged on the exile step by step.

The pair closed within a few feet of their opponent, who then had to look rapidly from side to side to see who might dare strike first. Other than that, no one moved.

Fig heard footsteps behind him and glanced to see Briana enter from the front office.

"So that is what they look like!" she exclaimed. As she approached, she positioned her own dagger alert. There was a big smile on her face.

"From what Maurice phoned to us, there was only a single exile who did not use the portal," she continued. He was not left by Oscar's hut. He is here!"

Angus' eyes widened. "What kind of being uses females for fighting," he spat. "A disgrace. It is well you should all die."

"You speak English!" Briana marveled. "How? How did you learn?"

"A thousand of your years is a long time to study and prepare," Angus said. "But no matter. Surrender to me, and I will arrange that the three of you can be spared." He waved back at the silent kiln. "Just as I can heat the air to comfort, I can cool it as well. We have many structures of cold where I am from."

"Your plan will not come to pass," Briana said. "We know about the SF_6 and the volcanoes."

"The microphone and computer in the front office," Fig said. "That is

310

how you planned to do it, right? Broadcast the incantation that starts the catalytic reaction. Speakers on the slopes. The rest of the seven hundred are not involved at all. You are a one-man show."

Angus did not reply. He clasped both arms to his sides and shivered slightly. He lifted his head and growled again, although this time not as ferociously as before.

"He's weakening," Jake said. "All we have to do is wait a little longer, and then he probably will not even be able to lift his weapon. All we have to do is wait and then — "

"And then slash his throat," Fig cut in. "It is too dangerous for him to live."

"What about the others?" Briana asked. "Maurice said they were using the portal to go somewhere else."

"Well, then torture him first," Fig said. "Find out what the rest are up to so they can be stopped, too."

Angus interrupted with a laugh. "The others? I think not. They are all happy rotting in their holes."

"You're lying, Jake said. "We can't believe anything you're saying."

"What do we do with him then?" Fig asked.

Decisions

BRIANA PACED in a small circle again. The standoff continued for what must have been two hours, but finally the exile collapsed in a shivering heap. Jake and Fig looked at her for what to do next, but she had no ready answer. She needed to think.

To buy more time, she directed the pair to clothe the alien in the hoodie and other garments containing the strange inserts. A high degree of thermal isolation, Fig had explained. They bound and gagged him and let him wiggle on the floor as his body heat began to warm his numbness. The lights were turned back on, but not the power to the kiln.

The paper on the floor was covered in a strange script. The only other place she had seen such symbols were on the inside of the portal. The length was about what would be expected for an incantation, however. It did look like this single exile was acting alone.

Ashley had arrived with the warning the thuglings sooner or later would give up the chase and return. Whatever their own little group was going to do with Angus, they had to do it soon.

"Ursula will keep quiet at her desk," Briana had said.

"And we can leave a note on the small door leading to the loading dock, telling the thuglings to go away until they are called back," Ashley had said. "They will probably want to go to a bar somewhere and release their frustrations after losing me on highway nineteen."

Briana frowned as she saw the other three were watching her as she paced. No one offered any more opinions. Not even Ashley. It was irritating, if nothing else. When a *big* decision had to be made, one of immediate life or death, they had shied away. And Maurice was not even here. Somehow, he was the moral compass of the group. His absence could not have happened at a worse time. But it was her quest they had reminded her. She was the one who had to decide and she alone.

The easy answer was to dispatch the exile. He clearly was evil.

Merely escaping from imprisonment was not enough for him. Every living soul, every living animal and plant on the Earth was to be destroyed so he and his kind — a mere seven hundred or so, could be free.

But to do so was murder, pure and simple. There was no way around that. Yes, there was bloodshed recorded repeatedly in the sagas. But those were the tales of others. Decisions they faced, not her. Could she do it? Plunge a dagger into the heart of someone bound and gagged?

Or torture first in order to learn more? On Murdina, only barbarians engaged in the hideous practice. More than one sorcerer said such a thing did not work. Victims would agree to anything suggested to them in order to stop the pain. Only by the craft could one look without error into someone else's mind.

She looked at each of her companions, one at a time. They did not refuse to look back. No, they entrusted her to make the decision, whatever it may be. She recalled a quote she had read when she had surfed the internet what now seemed like so long ago.

'Leadership is not dictated. It is granted by those willing to be led.'

Briana smiled at that. It did give her a small degree of comfort. She was not sure how it had happened, but even with Ashley taking over the task of detailed planning, Jake and Fig — and probably Maurice as well have given her that grant. When she returned to Murdina, perhaps that would be sufficient for the story — the *grand* story she would be able to tell.

She looked at 'Mr. Angus' as Ursula called him, straining at his bonds, struggling to be free. Was 'Angus' an alias? Maurice had phoned that only 'Dinton' remained.

She pushed the speculation away. The label was not important, only the decision about what to do. Confinement is what prevented him from executing all the steps of his plan. Confinement. Perhaps that was the only answer needed.

The caverns of the exiles were most likely empty now. The one on the floor before them was the last one left. And imprisonment there had worked for a thousand years. With proper barriers to influences from the outside, no access to the world above, especially to the internet, they probably could serve for additional millennia.

Like the release of a crushing weight that had pinned her to the ground, Briana felt the burden roll aside. "We will travel to Oscar's hut," she said. "Travel there for three reasons. First, Maurice was last heard from there. We must find out what happened to him.

313

"Second, the portal door may still be there.

"Lastly, we can return this exile to the caverns. With no swathing or access to the internet, he will not be able to threaten this orb again."

"We just can't carry him out of here bound and gagged for any passerby to see," Fig said.

"Easily solved," Ashley joined in. "Put him in, I don't know, a blanket or a rug. Haul him to the hut on a rented truck." She tried to smooth a business suit that she no longer wore, and then looked at Briana. "Well done," she said.

"And I am hungry," Jake complained. "The adrenaline rush from the swordplay must take a lot of energy. It has made me famished."

"Okay, one to go and rent the truck, one to get the blanket and cuffs, another to get take out, and one to stand guard until we return," Briana agreed.

"Um, the first rule of Dungeons and Dragons is not to split your party," Fig said.

"Can't be helped," Briana said. She was getting into her stride now. Once the hard decisions were made, the rest were easy. "Who wants to be the one to stand guard?"

"I will," Jake said. He flicked on his miner's lamp. "Douse the lights on your way out. If any of the thugs do come back, they won't be able to see where they are going and then surely leave."

"It will only be for an hour at most. He will not manage to get away." Briana said. She smiled at Jake. "All of us, together. We have made great progress today."

She played with a curl for a moment. "About the takeout. Let's pick a place serving desserts." Being a leader did have some perks.

314

The Loyal Minion

ANGUS TRIED to push the thought away, but it stubbornly remained. If what the natives said were true, then, except for his stubborn elder brother, all the rest of his kind had gone away. To where? Back home to face again the wrath of those who opposed them? Or striking out to some new place where there was warmth, hot breezes, and the delicious air?

And how was he even found out about, anyway? The natives should have shown complete shock when they encountered him. Instead, their words sounded as if the existence of the Heretics was common knowledge.

Angus sighed, something he had not done in as long as he could remember. He had been close, oh so close, to achieving liberty not only for himself, but for everyone else. Freedom for almost a thousand bodies. He would be exalted even though he was the youngest, hailed as the new flock leader of them all!

He glared up at the native with the light on his head. It was growing steadily dimmer. Perhaps soon it would go out altogether. He wriggled in his bounds. They were a tiny bit looser but not much. And even if he did manage to get free and speak the two incantations — the first to start the catalytic buildup of the SF_6, and the second to break it, to blast the gas into the air, what then?

Only he and Dinton were left. No mates, no concubines, no one to laud his feats. An entire planet to do with what he would… but to what purpose? Why climb a mountain if there were no others to hear how amazing was the assent? Why tell a joke if there were no one to laugh? Why feel lust running hot if there were no one to quench it in the warmth of their sweet bodies?

Instead… he had heard what the young female had spoken. Returned to prison, the prison that had already confined him for a thousand years. Worse yet, his only company would be the overbearing pomposity of his brother.

It was not right! Angus could not help himself from roaring in frustration, in sorrow, in despair.

HOW LONG he roared and beat his head against the hard floor, Angus could not tell. The little room had plunged into darkness as the lamp battery drained, but his guard did not seem to care. Every time he made noise as he struggled against his bonds, he felt the prick of the sword tip on his chest.

Then, there was a tap on the door.

"About time," the native warrior called out. "What did you do, visit every restaurant in a mall?"

The door swung open, but the blackness did not change.

"Well?" the guard persisted. "What did you bri — "

Angus heard a dull thump against the metal helmet of the sentinel and then the crash of his body to the ground.

"Mr. Angus, are you all right?" the soft voice came through the doorway. "I think the baseball bat I had stored besides my desk disabled the bad man who was here with you." She paused. "He must have been bad, right?"

It was Ursula, gentle, caring, naïve Ursula Price. Could it be? Was she still here?

A sudden burst of new energy surged through him.

"A minute, Ms. Price. I mean Ursula. I first must collect my thoughts."

Even if he did away with his unpleasant brother, he would not have to be alone. Just as swathing protected from the cold, it also could from the heat if the immediate surroundings were somehow cooled. It would be a small flock to be sure, and one tainted with the traits of an inferior species. But at least someone to talk to, someone to carry out his orders, respond to his every wish.

And who knows, his imagination began to race. Perhaps with the help of the crafts, maybe even interspecies breeding might be possible. And yes, for diversity, rather than eliminating his brother, he could share.

Like a steam engine of the natives leaving a station, the momentum of his will began to grow. The microphone and the computer. They were less than two hundred paces away! There was no real need to wait for the confirmation from Bagana so that everything could be tightly synchronized. Speak the necessary words now, and the reactions at Etna and Kilauea would begin — begin now!

Also send the go-ahead message to Bagana. It would take a few days, but the incantation would start there as well. The buildup would lag that of the other two volcanoes, but that would have to do.

He was not thwarted after all! Except for this single chosen one, all of the inferior natives yet would perish. He would still transform this orb, reach the end of the road he had embarked upon so many orbits ago.

"Do you have some sort of knife in your desk, Ursula?" he called out. "Something with a sharp blade?"

"Yes, Mr. Angus. A box cutter for opening packages when they arrive. But please, tell me. I do not understand what is happening?"

"Excellent, Ursula. Go get the tool and then return to me. I... I am a little tied up at the moment, and you can help me get free. Then after I use the computer in the front office for a bit, we will take a... yes, take a vacation together. Somewhere special for a few days and then celebrate the beginning of the end."

"A vacation? A few days, Mr. Angus? How many?"

"I am not yet sure, Ursula. It will take some measurements first to establish the rate of buildup. Then I will pick the correct moment. I will make sure the timing of the final words will be exactly right."

Now, with a clear path before him, Angus took the luxury of letting his thoughts wander. Thaling and the others, he mused. I wonder, where *did* they go?

Return from Exile

MAURICE PUSHED open the portal door and staggered out. The sun loomed high overhead, yellow green, painfully bright. It filled up too much of the sky, too bright to discern anything with unshaded eyes. The ground underfoot was featureless, flat, sandy, and coarse. Obviously the work of intelligent beings.

Arrayed in front of him like a convention of festival revelers were the hundreds of exiles he had seen come here, one by one. They no longer wore any swathing. Most had on no clothing at all. Instead, they coupled with urgency, some standing face to face, others, tightly embraced, rolled in a frenzy over the ground. A few grouped in threes and fours, intertwined and growling lustily.

Maurice blinked. They looked like... like great apes but covered with dark brown hair rather than gray. Noses protruding rather than flat. Fangs exposed on each side of the mouth. Not grotesque, but deeply disturbing all the same. The eyes. The eyes betrayed the intelligence behind and hinted at rage and cruelty.

As he watched transfixed, two nearby pairs finished, and the males flopped on their backs, arms outspread in satisfaction. The females threw their heads back, and, to Maurice, appeared to laugh. They came bounding toward him, and he took a hasty step backwards, bumped into the portal door, and flinging up his arms in defense.

Undeterred, the first female batted his hands aside while the second began to claw at his swathing. So inexpertly self-wrapped, Maurice felt it begin to rip away. He staggered to his knees, and the first grabbed his helmet and flung it aside.

Both women stopped, shocked at what they had found. Maurice felt a horrific blast of hot air seemingly roast his face as if he had been plunged into a spa with a thermostat gone wild. He inhaled reflexively and immediately regretted his action. This place was hot, dangerously hot.

His eyes filled with stinging salty sweat.

The portal door opened. The last of the exiles emerged. All semblance of reason left Maurice as the alien said, "Dinton! Where is Dinton? What have you done with him?"

The Buddhist could not think straight. The heat, the oppressive heat, was too sapping. Could he reenter the portal and return home while it was still so close? Was this a situation for his judo or karate? Could he even remember the basic moves?

But these were the exiles Briana was looking for. They had to be. Clearly, they had not merely moved from one place on the Earth to another. Instead, they had traveled... traveled somewhere else. And if so, the thought roared into Maurice's head, then they may no longer be a threat to humankind.

He looked back over the field of exiles cavorting in front of him. Except for the swapping of partners, the energy had abated but little. The exile who had spoken to him unwound his own covering, growling at the others, who, as far as Maurice could tell, were ignoring him completely. The alien strained to stand straight and stamped his foot in frustration. Finally, what must have been orders were barked, and the two females picked Maurice up, one with hands under his shoulders, the other with his legs astride her hips.

He was not a little man, but with no effort, the two carried him away from the field of frolic and toward a small structure a short distance away — one of many dotting the landscape. It was a single story with gaudy painted walls — swirling bands of color mixing and frothing like storm driven waves crashing ashore.

On one end was a ladder leading to the roof and a steep slide returned to earth on the other side. Between were a series of rings hanging by chains from an overhead frame. Disguised by the bands of color was a narrow doorway near one end. The exile who had given the command opened it as the women approached. The pair entered, dropped Maurice unceremoniously on the floor and then raced back to rejoin the revelry. The exile who had given the command shut the door.

Maurice felt his breath taken away. Goosebumps erupted on his arms and legs where they had been exposed. It was no longer hot, but instead cold, freezing cold. The sudden change in temperature extremes was almost too much a shock to bear. He looked about. In the corner stood a large curved pipe venting to the outside from a complicated mechanism of whirling pulleys and creaking belts. A second vent blew the frigid air into the single room that filled the entire insides of the building. On the far wall were a row of man-high chests closed with bulky doors. Tables with stacks of measuring cups and stirring ladles stood nearer.

"Tell me what you did with Dinton," the exile said. "I am Thaling, and he is my elder brother."

"I did nothing with him," Maurice managed to say. "I saw all of you vanishing through the portal, one by one, and followed to find out where you were going."

"This is our home," Thaling said. "After a millennium, we have returned." He growled. "You have not answered my question."

"If he has not come with you, then probably he's still in the cavern near Oscar's shack. Or if not, there at the warehouse in Hilo." Maurice hesitated for a second, then rushed on. "But if he returns as well and the portal somehow is made to stop working, then the threat to the Earth will be ended. Briana can return home. A happy ending for her."

Before Thaling could answer, the door opened. The exile turned and began growling again. The one who entered snarled in return. Almost everything said, Maurice did not understand. The only word he caught was the very first. "Randor!"

It sounded vaguely familiar, and Maurice grasped for the meaning. Then he remembered. It was a name. Briana had told him and the others. What the visitor to Murdina had called himself—called himself when he appeared out of the portal what now seemed like so long ago.

Randor the Tribunal

THALING FELT the rage building within him like a wildfire. Alika, Alika, his thoughts thundered. Finally, her death would be avenged.

But nothing was going according to plan. Randor stood before him, unchanged even after a thousand orbits of their prison about its sun. Still tall and stern-faced, a pike of unbending steel. He wore the blazing emblem of tribunal on his chest, nestled amid the bulging pockets of his tunic.

Thaling's flock members were showing no discipline at all. True, all had forgone any sexual activity for so very long. No one had wanted the guilt and burden of bringing young ones into their depressing and monotonous exile. But if Randor was here now confronting him, the warriors of the Faithful could not be far behind.

All of his followers had to line up in battle formation and quickly. He had to give the speech that would boost their resolve, tell them the ship had been burned. There was no alternative. They must fight for their lives or certainly die.

Thaling roared twice in frustration and then forced himself to be calm. There was also this native who had taken the portal journey. Why did he come? What did he know? How did he fit in to everything now happening?

Was there some way the presence of this primitive could be used? He forced himself to consider the thought. He looked Maurice up and down and saw the confusion in his eyes. Of course, besides the shock of everything else, he could not understand what either he or Randor was saying. At the very least, he might provide a diversion from whatever the tribunal had in mind, give himself more time.

"Why did you come?" Thaling asked Maurice. "Why did you take Dinton's place?"

"To find out where you were going?" Maurice answered.

Thaling started to translate, but Randor held up his hand to stop.

"I understand many of these natives' tongues," Randor said. "Over most of the thousand years, I was one of the party checking to see if you were still confined." He studied Maurice for a moment. "Yes, let us communicate so he can participate as we decide your fate. That may serve at least as a partial distraction — not enough to compensate completely for what I was engaged in before this interruption in *All My Siblings*, but perhaps it will be worth something."

"After all these years," Thaling asked, "you still pursue then the complete suppression of your conscious thoughts?" He was incredulous. The task was impossible. It was why Dinton, Angus, and the others had rebelled in the first place.

"Our technology has progressed tremendously since you heretics were banned." Randor shook his head as if trying to wipe away the surprise growing on Thaling's face. "We have tried and abandoned many distractions along the way, it is true. But now, we are almost there. We can succeed in not having disturbing thoughts almost all of the time. We are not completely there yet, but soon perhaps we will be. As the ancient philosopher said, 'The examined life is not worth living.'"

"That sounds like the complete opposite of meditation," Maurice said suddenly. "How can you possibly gain any true wisdom about how the world works without inner examinations? Buddha says 'Meditation brings wisdom; lack of meditation leaves ignorance.'"

"Ignorance? Wisdom?" Randor said. "When you are fully occupied with amusements, you need not think about such things."

"But — ," Maurice began.

"It is why Thaling and the others were confined as they were," Randor interrupted. "An almost total absence of distracting stimulation so their thoughts would be about their plight, how there was no hope for things to improve, why they even existed, indeed, even why did anything in the universe have any purpose."

Randor started to pant. Spittle began to form on his lips. This conversation was going nowhere, Thaling thought. It was if a thousand years had not even passed. And if only harmless amusements still was what Randor desired, then perhaps that is what he should be served.

"I see this sorbet parlor is still here," Thaling said. "Almost unchanged. Even the decorations are the same."

"You do not know how difficult it is to allocate the imp labor," Randor snapped. "Each faction wants it spent on his own pet project. There is no way to please everyone." He sighed. "Eventually, all the needs will be met, but it will take time. Besides, even if the painters were to be so allocated, their designs have been used repeatedly a dozen times. The walls would look different, but not enough to provide fresh diversion."

"In all this time, you have not imported more imps?" Thaling asked. Keep up the bombardment of questions, keep him off balance, he thought. It could only help.

"The decree remains," Randor thundered. "The war with the demon prince so long ago was almost disaster. We must have no more contact with his realm. You know that. As our magicians tell us, the contrapositive of the law of wizardry is also true — 'no flame permeates nothing.' We allow no more fires of any kind. The imps we have under thrall will never be augmented so that we remain safe."

The tribunal waved his hand around the room. "But there *have* been changes, even here. There are more senses than only sight. When you left, we had only three flavors, vanilla, chocolate, and beebleberry. Now there are a thousand or more. Taste can grow jaded as can each of the others. And when there is boredom with the input, the thoughts of despair can arise."

Maurice shook his head. "Buddha says, 'Despair is the price one pays for setting oneself an impossible aim.'"

"Do warriors come to fight us again?" Thaling asked. This native might prove to be a worthy verbal dueler with Randor. But that was not important, not why he had returned. Alika, Alika. Keep hold of the thought. He needed time to marshal his troops, to get ready before the Faithful were to strike.

"A second battle? And then sending you to exile again?" Randor said. "Of course not. That would be a rerun of a drama we have already seen. No, this time your flock will be slaughtered to the last. An imp recording crew will come to document the bloodshed, but those details... those have not been arranged yet." He shrugged. "Of course, it will not be shown in prime time. Too close to what happened in the original."

"The ship has been burned," Thaling blurted.

"What?" Randor said.

"I have modified the portal. There is an additional counter on board. Each transfer decreases it by one. There are not very many journeys before it becomes useless."

Randor puzzled for a moment. "How many more trips?" he asked at last.

"I allowed for a ten percent error," Thaling said. "There are only sixty some-odd left."

"Sixty will be far more than enough," Randor said. "A video crew is only five imps. After the slaughter, they will transfer through along with a few practitioners of the crafts. The humans have no knowledge of the workings, no defense against what will befall them." He smiled. "Now *that* will be worthy of a multi-night special. An epic — the destruction of an entire civilization. And reality, not reenactments of feeble fantasies written eons ago."

"You might be surprised," Thaling said. "In the hundred or so of Earth years since your last visit, they have progressed greatly."

"Excellent!" Randor said. "It will make it more entertaining." He thought for a moment. "But I do not like loose ends. Have all of you returned? Where is your father? Where are Angus and Dinton?"

"Our father succumbed as you Faithful had hoped," Thaling said. "Angus has gone missing. Dinton alone remains."

Randor smiled. "It is only fitting. I imagine you and Angus continued to pester him. He found no relief, even in exile."

"It was not all bad," Thaling said. "Dinton is the eldest, after all."

"Hmm," Randor said. "Before you are dispatched, perhaps there is something more you should know about your brother. It will make the ending more delicious."

"What about *him*?" Thaling pointed at Maurice. "Is he to be slaughtered too? Might not you get some amusement about what he has to tell first?"

Randor studied Maurice for a moment. "It would be a unique distraction for the other two tribunals," he said. "Yes, maybe presenting him to them will decrease the additional time on solo duty I will have to spend… spend because of the emergency session I was forced to call because of your return." He turned back to Thaling. "Go and prepare yourself then," he said. "Prepare yourself to die. I will tell the captive instead."

Thaling did not reply. There was mystery here. Why was Randor not attacking immediately? Maybe there was sufficient time to marshal the exiles before it was too late.

Vanish the Thought

AS THE wagon bumped along the dirt road, Maurice patted his chest beneath the swathing, looking for which pocket he had stored his phone. There was so much to learn here. He should get everything down while still fresh in his mind. Who knew what bit of information would be important for Briana.

Randor noticed what he was doing and swatted his hand aside. "Here, wear this." The tribunal of the Faithful reached into a pocket of his own and held out a jeweled pendent dangling from a loop of leather. "Thaling is not the only one with skill in magic. I had this translator fashioned for our second trip to your world."

Maurice slipped the device around his neck. Almost immediately, the pendant began translating Randor's words in his native language into ones that Maurice understood.

Looking back over his shoulder, the Buddhist saw that all of the exiles except for Thaling and his flock continued with their preoccupations. None had stopped to watch them board the small wagon standing nearby. What looked like an incredibly deformed child sat in the driver's seat. Next to him sat another of Thaling's race, shackled wrist and ankles, and chained to the wagon's frame. Hitched in front were four nightmares from Maurice's childhood. Large, hulking humanoid beasts on all fours. Wings bound tightly to their backs. Drool dripped from their muzzled mouths.

"The basic system has not changed since the Heretics left," Randor said. Maurice nodded. In his experience, so many of those in power had an uncontrollable urge to orate.

"The punishment for small transgressions is servitude as wizards," Randor continued. "Keep the wheels of transportation running. Farm the crops. No access to any of the distractions. None at all. They are left with their thoughts, as depressing as they may be. Few make the mistake of breaking the law a second time."

Maurice looked at the creature next to the wizard. An imp he decided. Larger versions of the ones Briana and Fig had described. And the burden of motion provided by greater demons still. The wizard was there to keep them under control.

The Buddhist looked toward the horizon. Nearest were neat rows of broad-leaved crops, huge lettuces, and cabbage soaking in the rays of the sun. Between the lines walked imps with bulging canvas bags slung around their necks, stopping and picking the plants as directed by another wizard in chains walking behind.

In the distance was a row of tall structures, some a dozen stories high and butting against one another with no gaps between. None was identical to another. There was no architectural theme apparent at all. Some showed a completely blank façade, others festooned with windows placed as if chosen by chance. Slender towers topped others and soared still higher into the sky. Like the buildings themselves, none was identical or showed even a hint of symmetry other than a tapering cylindrical form. If anything, to Maurice, the entire scene resembled the temples of Angkor Wat as rendered by a cubist painter who was four sheets to the wind.

After a short journey over the bumpy road, the wagon entered through an archway added as an afterthought to one of the towers seemingly swaying in the air. Inside, two more carts pointed farther into the interior. Their wheels were flanged and pushed snugly against wooden rails receding into darkness. Next to the one on the right was a queue of five or six more of the alien beings.

"Let's not take the express," Randor said as he prodded Maurice to the cart with the waiting line. "The memories of the morning are slipping away. I need a burst of refreshment as we proceed."

Those waiting climbed into the cart as a chain in the center of the rail bed engaged and started pulling it forward. It vanished into the dimness, and shortly thereafter, there was a sudden roar from the occupants. Not a threatening growl but more like… a cry of pleasure.

Another car appeared, and Maurice followed Randor aboard. They too entered the darkness, but the Buddhist could see nothing. For a few moments more, the only sensory input was the clank of the chain and creak of the wheels. Then suddenly, the cart tilted backwards. Maurice found he was lying nearly prone. The chain continued its labor, lifting the cart high into the interior of the tower.

There was no way for Maurice to tell how high he climbed, but eventually, the car righted itself and started to plunge downward. He felt his stomach rise in his chest, and involuntarily he gasped for air. Down and down the cart flew, and in the darkness, there was no end in sight.

Then as quickly as it had begun, the cart splashed into a pool of water, braking fiercely with a jolt. The carriage rocked and then somehow disengaged from the tow and started floating. Up ahead, there was a faint light and what could only be alien singing.

The cart slowed streaming forward, bounced against a wall and turned into full light. Maurice was in a cavern, and the walls were decorated by much smaller aliens... No, not actual living beings, he decided, but little automatons with mouths opened into small letter Os and voices singing in high pitched tones.

More turns and more tableaus followed. Each with a chorus of tiny robots caroling over and over the same simple melody. Finally, the cart emerged back into the intense sunlight, and Maurice followed Randor scrambling to exit.

Without pause, Randor led him into another large room, this one floored with sheets of shiny metal. A dozen smaller carts without wheels sat on the smooth surface. Behind each was a harnessed imp with his slender hands grasping handles and bending forward getting ready to push. A cat o' nine tails hung from a mechanism arching to a forward compartment containing two seats. It dangled over a back scarred and oozing ichor.

Most of the other cars were already filled, and Randor ran to one remaining, motioning Maurice to follow. They sat on low, shallowly cushioned chairs and buckled thick belts about their waists. A klaxon sounded, and the carts began moving. Randor turned a steering wheel hard to one side to disengage. The imp behind them grunted from the effort, but soon they were circuiting around the floor with increasing speed.

Then a second car crashed into the side near where Maurice and Randor were sitting. Their heads whipsawed from the impact, and the tribunal roared with laughter. He pivoted the car swiftly to the side and then reached the handle dangling on his right and pulled. The imp behind cried with a burst of pain as the whips hit his bare back. He applied a burst of speed, and Randor crashed the car into another who had appeared directly ahead.

The klaxon sounded again, and all of the cars immediately were abandoned. "Ah, I needed that," Randor said. "A perfect tonic. Not a single stray thought broke through on the entire journey. Definitely better than the express."

Maurice tried to make sense of what he was experiencing, but he could not. There was no time to sit and ponder. The tribunal ushered him into another tower, this one with a façade much like the others, but somehow with a little more attention to style and repeated motifs. Guard imps in gaudy tunics and holding halberds at attention bowed as they passed. Soon they entered a room with large doors and a high ceiling and stood in front of a long, curved dais bowing out in front of them. Behind were three imposing high back chairs. Two were occupied.

"This is most annoying," one of the two seated tribunals said. "Our regularly scheduled quarterly meetings I can manage to prepare for — show something before that I have forgotten, then something new when I return to my chambers."

"I understand your discontent," Randor said. "I feel it as well. But there is no other choice but to deal with this before it gets out of hand." He pointed toward Maurice. "I have brought a native from Earth with me. We meet to decide his fate."

"Earth? You told us you had taken care of that problem a long time ago," the first tribunal persisted. "Handed the task off to others who do not believe as do we, the Faithful."

Randor did not bother to rebut. "He has things to say you might find interesting," he said.

"Very well," the second tribunal said. "Archivists, to your stations."

Two imps immediately sprang up from where they had been resting along a sidewall. They had sat near a hearth containing unburned logs and colored paper dancing above in the imitation of a flame. One of the aroused demons began scribbling on some parchment with a long quill pen while the other squinted at Maurice and started sketching.

Maurice pushed the sense of wonder aside. He had a chance to speak, he realized, and he should use it. From what little he could gather, novelty was something prized here. Was this an opportunity?

"Buddha says," Maurice paused a moment to be sure all attention was on him. The translation sounded an instant later, although the word for Buddha was severely mangled.

"Buddha says," he continued, "'There are only two mistakes one can make on the road to truth: not going the whole way and not starting.'"

"This is most excellent!" the second tribunal exclaimed. "Droll and original. Perfect for the sundown news today." He turned to the other tribunal sitting beside him. "The sundowner has become so very stale, don't you agree? There is only so much one can do to make the weather exciting."

"Unswath him," the first said. "Give the artist something to work with."

Maurice snapped out of his awe of the strange surroundings. His life was at stake here. Two more imps appeared and began unwinding his protection.

He began to resist, but then stopped as he remembered. 'Do not learn how to react; learn how to respond,' Buddha had said.

Maurice held off the urge to take a deep breath and decided. He would have to endure the discomfort as long as he could stand it. "Educate me," he said. "The one named Thaling. You say he is a Heretic. What was his crime?"

There was silence for a moment, and then the first on the dais spoke again. "Simply put, he and his comrades dared to think."

"Rather than helping to create more distractions, more amusements to keep thoughts away," the second chimed in, "they dared to try and answer questions that could not be."

"Yes," continued the first. "Why is there evil in the world? Why are we here? What is our purpose?" He shook his head. "These questions cannot be decided. Our minds are too meager to contemplate such things. All that can come of such a waste of time is despair, life-snuffing despair."

"Buddha says, 'He who walks in the eightfold noble path with unswerving determination is sure to reach Nirvana.'"

"What noble path? What is Nirvana?"

Maurice noticed the scribe writing furiously and his companion finish one sketch and start another. With his helmet off, the heat felt as if he had put his head in an oven. A wave of dizziness began to wash over him.

"Buddha says, 'We are shaped by our thoughts. We become what we think.' Well, that is not a real quote, but perhaps it applies in this place anyway."

"And a wrap!" another voice sounded as Maurice sagged to his knees. "If we get started now, this will make this evening's line up."

"I am not sure these words should be broadcast," Randor said. "I meant this captive's words to be for this chamber only. Something... something sophisticated ones such as yourselves could handle. They sound too much like what Thaling and the others were grasping for."

"We have been steadfast in our faithfulness for many orbs around our star," the second dais member said. "Surely, we can withstand the babbles of an alien in a single news bite."

"By your leave," the new speaker rattled his fetters. "I will get the crew working now on the presentation. And yes, I envision a landscape view for how the alien arrived here as well." He smiled. "If all goes well, perhaps a reduction in the length of my sentence is a worthy consideration."

Unwanted Distractions

THALING SQUINTED up at the sunrise. It felt good to be home again, to see the great orb begin to peek over the horizon like a beckoning god. As the darkness faded, he scanned the city in the distance, but saw no marshalling of troops. Evidently, Randor was not attacking immediately.

His flock rose from their slumbers and formed the two precise lines from which they were to repel the tribunal's attack when it did come. There was satisfaction in that. Even though it took harangue after harangue into the evening, eventually everyone understood. There would be no turning back. No option for a second exile.

Thaling looked at the portal door next to him and then the makeshift setter he had fashioned on the Earth. The logical thing to do was to set both the near and far destinations to 'Nowhere,' make the doorway vanish and then destroy his makeshift setter. It was one thing to spout 'the ship had been burned' but harder to convince everyone of that when evidence of its presence still stood boldly on the plain.

Destroy his setter, he pondered. Could he really do that? He ran one hand along its bumpy exterior. Probably the best piece of magic he had ever performed. Yes, magic, but because it was made of scrap parts, unlike most products of the craft, it was quite fragile. Destroying it would be easy. A single jolt could shatter it into pieces.

But sending the portal to Nowhere and then smashing the setter to the ground now, he could not. Despite his rage for revenge, despite his desire to see Randor beg for mercy before his throat met a dagger's blade… the outcome of every battle could never be known precisely before it played out. Suppose his flock, even after all this time in the horrible prison on Earth, still did not have the will to stand and slash when comrades on either side had already been slain or lowered their daggers in surrender.

No, if everything failed, if all of this adventure came to naught, Thaling knew he would use the portal to escape… escape back to Earth or perhaps to some other orb that could become a new home.

He thrust the thoughts aside. Enough of that. There was no profit in dwelling on a defeat that might not, *will not,* occur. He was the middle brother, after all — not endowed with an intrinsic lust for battle like Angus, nor as patient and contemplating as was Dinton. They had both staked claims on what they would be, and he, himself, was left with little else in between. The peacemaker, the one who would calm the emotions on either side when it became necessary, but one who had no other use whatsoever.

He tried to stoke the fire of his revenge for his mate, but this morning it was not as intense as the day before. Why did he not imagine the thrill of skewering Randor, feed his boldness, make himself stand taller to face his destiny?

It was because Randor had changed, he decided at last. True, the tribunal looked the same physically as he was remembered, but his manner was quite different. Except for the one bit of emotion when expounding on the righteousness of his beliefs, he was calm, almost detached. He spoke of slaughter to Thaling's face, but without emotion, no savoring of the task. Instead, his adversary seemed... annoyed or irritated. The return of the Heretics was like an itching fleabite and had to be handled before pursuing the rest of the calendar for the day.

In the distance, a flick of motion at the tower gates caught Thaling's eye. No more introspection. This was it! This was it at last! He made a series of hand signals his lieutenants passed on to those under their immediate command. The two lines spanning the flat ground rose to attention and placed their hands on the dagger hilts at their sides.

But as Thaling resumed his watch, he saw not an outpouring of many armed opponents ready to fight but a single wagon, larger than the one Randor had used the day before to transport the Earth native to and from the city.

As it drew closer, he could see the vehicle contained one shackled wizard and five imps the master controlled — five small demons plus the two larger ones who pulled the wagon forward.

The vehicle steered toward Thaling and came to a halt directly before him.

"Where is the one who is the Buddha?" the wizard asked. "The news bite yesterday evening was a hit. We have been tasked to make a documentary to be aired this evening as a follow up."

Thaling stared back at the city. "What about Randor?"

The wizard shrugged. "Rounding up warriors or some such," he said.

"I doubt he will be seen here today. But there is little time for idle chatter. Where is the Buddha? We have to record more and improve the quality of the art."

Thaling motioned toward the dessert building. "He is confined there, but only loosely. After he can stand the cold no longer, we let him emerge and take in the sun. Then when that, in turn, becomes too unbearable, he retires back inside.

"Show us," the wizard said.

Thaling did not like the hint of command in the wizard's voice, but he stowed the setter into a large pouch on his side and motioned the craftmaster to follow.

THALING TUGGED open the door and entered the freezer. Maurice had his helmet off and was sampling one of the desserts. The earthling looked up, startled.

"Cherryblossom," the wizard commanded. "Start making sketches. The one without the helmet is something we can use right after the commercial break. And this time get enough detail so the final result will pop off the page."

"I prefer to be known as 'The Crimson Avenger,'" Cherryblossom said.

"I use the name your teammates call you," the wizard said. "How many times do we have to keep going over this?"

"But it is derogatory," Cherryblossom protested.

"Do as I say," the wizard said. "Only four more months of this, and I can be free," he muttered aside to Thaling. "If I had only known how bad this would be…"

"Sweetplum," he resumed his commanding tone. "Start on the title credits. The first will be… The first will be 'The Buddha Says.' Then the shot with the helmet on, cleaned up from yesterday. Then… then, what was it he said to the tribunal?"

"There are only two mistakes, one —"

"Right," the wizard cut him off. "Flash that one next, then we will do another pose. Alternate the quotes and the poses, one after the other."

"What is all this?" Maurice asked. "Poses?"

"You're a star," the wizard said. "A hot new property. Everyone was ready for it. Not one of the reruns was working anymore. Thoughts were beginning to crop up. People were thinking rather than letting the entertainment pour in to placid minds."

"But poses?"

"I don't know. Just do something with your limbs. Arms outstretched and palms turned inward. Arms raised high. For a negative, wave your hands back and forth across your chest. That sort of thing."

"Like this?" Maurice followed the first of the wizard's instructions.

"Exactly. But hold it there. Give Cherryblossom a chance. He's good but not fast."

"How long?"

"He'll tell you when to move to the next. And while were waiting, say some more of that way out stuff."

Maurice frowned. "You mean like, Buddha says 'Do not dwell in the past, do not dream of the future; concentrate the mind on the present moment'."

"Exactly. Keep them coming. We have two thousand heartbeats of prime time to fill up."

A Star is Born

MAURICE'S FINGERS cramped. The cold was now unbearable. A true Buddhist should be able to withstand it, but he could not. He put away his phone containing the long text he was composing for Briana. Time to go outside and warm the air trapped by his swathing. The events of the previous evening had been puzzling at first, but eventually he figured out what was happening. The aliens had some primitive form of television — no motion, more like a slide show — a series of intermingled text and static images.

He pushed opened the door and was startled by what he saw. Thaling's followers stood in more or less straight lines as they had before. But beyond them and closer to the city were thousands more of the aliens milling about.

When the crowd caught sight of him, almost in unison, they roared, "The Buddha. It is the Buddha."

Maurice frowned. "I am not the Buddha," he shouted back.

"I am not the Buddha," repeated an imp standing beside the door. He was gnarled and gangly like most of his kind but was distinguished by a large and robust chest, seemingly out of place on its spindly legs. Its voice was loud, booming loud, loud enough to pierce Maurice's helmet and still hurt his ears.

"I am not the Buddha," the crowd echoed, this time in complete synchrony. Many knelt on their knees, extended their arms, and bowed in Maurice's direction.

One of the smaller demons he thought he recognized from the day before trotted up to explain. "Another smash hit," he said. "Ratings through the roof. New and exotic. Scratches an itch that has been festering for years. No more delays. This is reality, baby. We are going *live*."

A hush like that found in a lifeless desert fell over the field. Even

Thaling's minions had turned to watch, waiting for Maurice to say more.

Maurice thought for a moment and then began with the first thing popping into his mind. "Buddha says 'When the student is ready, the teacher will appear.'"

The stentorian imp — what else would you call it — repeated the words out over the crowd.

"The Buddha. It is the Buddha," the assemblage responded.

Maurice looked again at Thaling's followers and compared their number to the larger mass of others before him. He remembered the shaman on Bagana and how receptive he was to the pull of the great one's words. Yes, there was opportunity here.

"The first noble truth — life is frustrating and painful," Maurice said. "The second — suffering has a cause. The third, that the cause of suffering can be ended. The fourth is that there is a path, a way to end the cause of suffering."

"The Buddha. It is the Buddha," the crowd responded,

The tension in Thaling's troops melted away. Everyone was watching and listening, straining to hear what he would say next. Definitely, now was his chance.

He stepped away from the doorway, and no one forced him back. He took two more long strides, and no one rushed forward to stop his motion. He eyed the portal door shimmering in the near distance. Only Thaling was standing near it. Only the stentorian imp followed him, and the imp remained a respectable distance behind.

Maurice continued quoting. If he could keep this up long enough, he could reach the flock leader, push him aside and race through the portal back to the Earth.

"Buddha says 'We are what we think.'" he called out. "'No one saves us but ourselves. No one can and no one may. We ourselves must walk the path.' He felt he was getting the rhythm of it now and felt a growing confidence to improvise. "Trying to push aside fear and despair by amusements and distractions is a futile effort. One must meditate. Seek wisdom through thought, not push it away."

Maurice stumbled on a rock underfoot and brushed against one of Thaling's warriors. The alien shrieked in ecstasy and fell to the ground. "The Buddha. He encourages thought. Games and puzzles are worthwhile."

"Not necessarily that," Maurice said. "Each of us must find our own way along the path.

"Buddha says 'The whole secret of existence is to have no fear.'" he tried to continue, but more troops broke rank and converged on him, arms extended, beckoning to be touched.

He tapped all of the offered palms he could, stepping around prostrate bodies beginning to pile up in front of him, picking his way onward toward his goal.

Just as Maurice reached the flock leader's side, another stentorian boomed from the direction of the city. "I am Randor, the tribunal," the imp called out. "I have come to end this heresy once and for all."

Maurice looked in the direction of the challenge. There was Randor threading his own troops through the mass of others and forming a line in front, directly opposed to the one Thaling had built. Maurice would have expected, approximately the same number as commanded by the returning exile. The difference was that, whereas Thaling's troops were enraptured with Maurice's pronouncements, Randor's stood at attention, ready for the signal to attack.

It would be a slaughter, exactly as the tribunal had threatened, and after that would come the attack on the Earth. It was not only a matter of his own escape. He had to save the rest of his home planet as well.

Prelude to Enlightenment

"RANDOR," THALING said as Maurice drew near. "I see the reason for his delay. Look at his minions. Wizards, all of them. Criminals who probably have been offered freedom in exchange for what they have been asked to do."

Maurice looked across the parched plain and considered. The door to the portal was only a few feet away. But escape by itself would not be enough.

"What would happen if he were not the leader?" he asked.

Thaling managed a forced laugh. "You see the impact of your words. If I were not here to harangue them, my followers would fall to the ground and roll on their backs like pet dogs hoping for your touch. Randor's troops would do the same."

"Then we should get him away from the scene," Maurice said. "Make him vanish..."

He stopped speaking. The strands of an idea began to weave together. "Who were you talking to in the hole in the ground in front of the other portal door?" he asked.

"The rock bubblers," Thaling shrugged. "I have released them. Besides, it will take two to roll a stone large enough to contain them."

"I will help you," Maurice said.

Thaling laughed. "Of course you would. As soon as you set foot back on your own orb, you would vanish as rapidly as you could."

"I give you my word," Maurice said.

"Your word? What is the worth of that?"

"There is much in life one cannot control," Maurice said. "Most, in fact. But one thing over which you have complete mastery is your *honor*. It is yours to shine brightly or let be tarnished and scorned. I said I will help you — on my honor."

Thaling's brow furrowed as he pondered Maurice's words. He stared at Randor's straight line of armed wizards.

"You go first," the magician said. "I will follow as soon as you are there."

IN ONLY a few minutes, Thaling was able to summon Littlebutt and Mintbreath into a small boulder near Oscar's hut. Together he and Maurice rolled it into the portal to stand against the far door. Maurice returned to the field with the assembled aliens, and Thaling followed shortly after. The two pushed the rock through the doorway..

Thaling's minions, Randor's troops, and the undisciplined crowd — all three groups stared at Maurice as if he had them entranced. He raised his arms, palms downward in one of the poses he had performed the day before. Immediately, an anticipative hush fell over everyone.

"Pain is inevitable," he said. "But suffering is optional. Do not accept what is said by others. Look within yourself to discover truth."

As Maurice finished speaking, an astonished cry erupted from Randor's ranks. In the blink of an eye, the tribunal sank into a hole in the ground that immediately closed.

"Randor is gone!" Thaling shouted. "Look! Look! Without him to lead, his minions will not fight with verve. Yes, see, even some of them are laying down their arms. My flock will win! I will win! After a millennium, revenge is mine!"

Then the returned exile stopped, and exhaled a great sigh, one almost collapsing his stooped body to the ground. "I had wished to tear away Randor's throat myself. Even in victory, my rage will not be assuaged."

"Holding on to anger is like drinking poison and expecting the other person to die," Maurice said. "There will always be for you the pain of loss, but you can learn not to suffer because of it."

A chant started by the crowd of aliens between the two war lines drowned Thaling's answer.

"A miracle!" those nearest the disappearance cried out. "The Buddha has performed his first."

As those farther away looked and saw that Randor was no longer there, they added their voices to the chant. "A miracle! The Buddha has performed his first."

Thaling's followers threw their daggers to the ground and joined in as well.

Like a tide receding from a stormy shore, everyone who had been standing, even the stentorian, prostrated themselves to the ground. "The Buddha," they chanted. "The Buddha."

"I am not the Buddha," Maurice protested, but his words were drowned out.

"I would not have thought it possible!" Thaling as he took in the massive reverence arrayed before him. "You are the solution," he declared in wonder to Maurice. "The fresh voice from another world to heal our wounds."

Maurice looked about. Only Thaling remained standing. With a sudden thrust, he pushed the exile aside and flung open the portal door.

"You gave your word of honor," the flock leader scrambled back to his feet.

Maurice hesitated for a second. "I came back. I did not promise to stay."

Thaling dove at him and the two tumbled to the ground.

"Don't you see?" Thaling shouted. "You have united us as none before has ever been able to do. Stay and be the dispenser of wisdom for us all. Everyone will listen and obey your words. You are the one who can grant us eternal peace."

He raised his head and yelled, "Help me. Help me convince the Buddha he is to stay."

Two more exiles slammed into Maurice and flattened him to the ground. His phone bounded out of his swathing and skittered a few feet away.

Briana, Maurice thought as he struggled to get free. No matter what, she needed to know and understand what was happening. With a burst of strength, he reached out, grabbed his phone, and dialed Briana's number. There was no reception on wherever this place was of course, but, maybe, just maybe near the other portal door, the one by Oscar's hut...

He pushed 'Send' and flung the phone down the length of the passageway. It clanged as it struck the far door. Thaling shut the one closer, picked up his makeshift controller, and then began to manipulate its settings.

"To Nowhere," the flock leader said. "I should have done this when we first arrived."

Maurice looked back to the door, and in horror saw it fade and vanish. The portal was his only way home. The implication of what was happened hit him like a cannon ball shot directly into the gut. He wrenched himself free of the two exiles struggling with him and frantically grabbed at the device in Thaling's hand.

The setter slipped away from the flock leader and crashed to the ground, exploding in a shower of metal, glass, and wires.

"Remove his glove and hold him steady," Thaling commanded to one of his followers. He removed the ring of eternal youth from his hand and thrust it on the middle finger of Maurice's. "Now twist and bind it to his palm so it cannot be extended. Our Buddha will be with us forever."

Maurice staggered to his feet as the fetter was applied. It was a ring of twine with a simple enough knot, but somehow he felt a slight tingle where it touched his skin. Instinctively, he knew he would not be able to remove the ring.

A second cannon ball, as violent as the first, slammed into his being. Not only cut off from home, but also marooned for an *eternity* — the worst thing that possibly could happen. Here he had no friends, no familiar surroundings. Nothing was comforting. It was as alien as it possibly could be.

Somehow, he had to get back. Back to Briana's quest, his studies, his meditations. His walk along the eightfold path. Searching for the truth, to remove the suffering from his own life, to…

Maurice stopped struggling. He let Thaling lead him back to the sorbet parlor, and slumped onto one of the chairs. The enormity of what had happened bore down on him, sinking him into despair.

No, not that, he recoiled. He would meditate. Perhaps in that, there would be a crumb of solace. He settled into the posture and cleared his mind.

Almost immediately, with a feather touch, the realization hit him. Return to what? Would what he sought be any different from what was before him here? A simple place to stay. Food to satisfy his needs. Dispensing wisdom to others who sought it. Was not *this* the path he was to walk from the beginning? As the temple master had said. He knew the teachings of Siddhartha in his head; what he needed was to understand them in his heart.

Yes, that was the way he would endure. Accept the world around him as it was. Do not yearn for what could never be. 'Peace comes from within. Do not seek it without.' Meditate and find the answer. Yes, he could do this. He looked at the magic ring of eternal youth bound to his finger. After all, he would have an eternity to get it right.

He stood up, emerged from the parlor, and straightened out his arms toward the crowds of followers now intermingling among one another.

"I am not the Buddha," he cried out.

"I am not the Buddha," everyone called back. "You are. *You* are the one."

Part Six

Briana's Choice

1

Counter Incantation

BRIANA LOOKED at the row of cabs lined up in front of her along the street. Four at once this time. Word was getting around. She hoped so. Three days of asking the same questions repeatedly with nothing to show for it.

The sun was setting on this side street in the old part of Hilo. At least the heat and humidity would not continue to be so oppressive. Fig approached her after slipping the Benjamin to the next cabbie in the line. He shook his head again. Behind him, Ashley and Jake stood in the shade as best they could, dialing for more pickup reservations.

Fig was the most exhausted of their group. Taking the red eye back to SoCal so he could round up the micromites and then immediately bringing them back to Hilo was a good idea. But so far, they had not spotted a man wearing a hoodie anywhere on the nearby streets.

"I remember now," the driver nearest Briana said when she stuck her head into the open window on the passenger side. "Yeah, took me a while. Two of them. A man and a woman. The guy wore a hoodie and did not say much. Dropped them off on Iwalani. So, I get the two hundred bonus, right?"

"What about the woman," Briana asked. "Anything unusual about her."

"Nothing stood out. Dressed okay, but nothing high fashion. Didn't say much either."

Briana waved him away. "No thanks," she said. "Not quite the right description." She sighed in frustration. She felt the guilt more than any of the others. It had been a wrong decision. Fig had warned her, but not one of them had objected to her rapid fire tasking the night before.

When they had returned to the warehouse with the truck, the food, and the blanket, they found Jake still unconscious on the back office floor. Angus, or Dinton, or whatever he called himself was gone, and so was Ursula.

But perhaps more important was what they found near the microphone in the front office — the papers with the strange text Briana had surmised might be the incantation for producing more of the SF_6 gas.

The bottom of the last page was torn off and missing — probably the final few words that would break the spell, release the pent-up energy and cause the volcanos to erupt.

It was a conclusion that none of the group wanted to believe — that the incantation at each of the volcanoes has been started. The concentration of SF_6 was building with each passing moment.

After a full backup to a flash drive, they dismantled and destroyed the warehouse computer so it could no longer be used for transmission. Then they traveled to Oscar's hut, removed the equipment there and verified the portal door was still shimmering nearby.

When Briana went inside, she recognized the other entrance's destination was set to 'Nowhere.' She picked up Maurice's phone and read his lengthy text. Knowing the rest of the exiles were no longer anywhere on the Earth was the only satisfaction. Maurice was marooned somewhere impossibly far away.

Even though everyone was getting punchy from lack of sleep, Ashley had led them through another brainstorming exercise with no real result other than returning to Hilo and interviewing cabbies about a fare in the evening two days ago.

The lack of anything positive was tearing at all of them, Briana knew. They had so little time left now. The exile could break the incantation at any moment, and then everything would be over.

Rather than interview the next cab in line, Briana slumped against the building wall behind her. She was so tired, so depressed, so lacking in energy. She reached into her backpack and withdrew the portal setter. When it had first stopped working, she had spent hours clicking the buttons and watching the displays, but nothing worked. The next day, she tried only for an hour before giving up.

Without thinking, she pressed the 'ON' button for perhaps the thousandth time. A ready light started blinking. The transport device was indicating it was accepting commands!

"Guys!" she cried. "The remote is working. Something has happened. I don't know what. We can use the portal again."

"How does that help us find where the exile has gone," Ashley called back.

"Well, we can widen the search without walking," Briana answered. Her energy began to return. "Dismiss the remaining cabs. That doesn't seem to be working anyway."

A few more Benjamins from Jake's bottomless wallet thanked the remaining taxi drivers for their trouble. Briana thought for a while after they were gone, then punched the instructions. Soon the portal door shimmered a little ways up the street in the growing dusk.

"This changes everything," she said. "I should have thought things through more thoroughly, considered all of the possibilities." Her shoulders sagged. "I have no excuse."

"Excuse for what?" Fig asked.

Briana coiled and uncoiled a tress. She did so a second time, then a third. "I am going back," she said at last. "Back to Murdina. My personal problem is small compared to what now has to be dealt with."

"You're abandoning us?" Fig's voice rose almost a whole octave.

"No, you and Jake are coming with me. Ashley can remain behind and continue searching here in Hilo in case."

"You're talking in riddles," Fig continued complaining. "Why?"

"I will need you for your knowledge of chemistry. To talk to Fordine, the thaumaturge. He tutored me when I was quite young. Probably the reason my father put him on the council. Quite wealthy for one of his craft. Came up with the idea of... an academy he calls it. Trains apprentices and journeymen. Other thaumaturges pay a good fee to be free of the bother of instructing their own. And Jake because, well, believe it or not, Murdina is even less civilized than it is here."

"Talk to Fordine about what?" Jake asked. He was tired also, but his interest perked up.

"How to construct another incantation — a new one, a *counterspell*. One that will reverse the one the exile started in motion here and then release the pent up energy over a long, long time."

"You told us the crafts of the exiles were more advanced than yours," Fig said. "How will any thaumaturge on Murdina be able to do that?"

Briana waved the papers that had been left at the warehouse. "It will take me a few hours, but this will be the key. I can translate phonetically the symbols that were written — change them into words understood on Murdina."

"So, one of your thaumaturges can repeat the charm?" Jake asked.

"No, don't you see? What the exile left is like… like part of a Rosetta stone. We know both what the incantation does and how to speak it. If a master studies the sounds, he will learn the underlying concepts used. And once he grasps those, a reverse catalyst spell should be possible."

2

Two Brothers, Not Three

DINTON SAT on the hard floor of his alcove and brooded. He had tried so hard. Over all the years, he was the one keeping everything together — giving his brothers enough freedom so they would think rationally before they acted — reminding them of his implied authority when necessary — averting one disaster after another.

Now there was nothing to show for his efforts. He was the last of the exiles. He was alone. The heavy oppressiveness of the silence hung over him like a stone propped by rickety sticks. He grasped the ring on his left hand with his right and gave it a few tentative tugs.

It would be simple enough. Take it off. Climb to the surface and let the cold take away what remained of his life. Perhaps he would even find Angus' body nearby and could lie down beside him to await the inevitable end.

Yet, there was no satisfaction in that. It would mean Randor and the Faithful had won. Their father — suicide by duel. Thaling by abortive escape. Angus by... did he really care how?

"You look quite glum," Angus' voice suddenly broke through Dinton's reverie. "A little bit down, perhaps, because there is no one left over which to rule?"

"Angus!" Dinton cried. He rushed forward and swept the other exile into a tight embrace.

His brother shook him off. "No need for that. Since you have no means for enforcement, I even forgive you for the error in judgement about my use of the crafts."

"What do you mean? How did you escape? How — "

"There will be time enough later to explain," Angus said. "There are two other matters first." He pointed behind himself at another — one completely swathed with no way to tell who it was.

"I don't understand," Dinton said. "Who is this? Thaling told me I was the only one of our kind who remained."

"True enough, brother," Angus said. "The first item on the list is an introduction. This one calls herself Ursula. She is a native — was a native. Now she is my concubine."

"We do not know if we can — "

"Only a technicality. Surely, aided by the crafts, we will come up with a way to repopulate the surface."

"Repopulate! — "

"You should have donned the ring when I did," Angus replied. "Some said you delayed so many years so we all would see the beginning of gray in your fur. But no matter. I will speak slowly so you will understand. See what Ursula is carrying? It is what the natives call a microphone. The wires trailing it travel up to a computer in Oscar's shack.

"You are right," Dinton said. "I *do not* understand."

"When I was temporarily... detained, I learned that Thaling and the rest had left. That meant I did not need fear recapture by those loyal to you. It was safe to return to Oscar's shack and prepare."

"I discovered the natives had trashed the place," Angus continued. "All of the computer gear would no longer work." He chuckled. "But in their haste, the marauders did not also destroy Oscar's notebook. It was so complete. Apparently, a recluse has much time on his hands." He shrugged in the manner of a native. "So, it was a simple matter to reorder everything and hook it up again. Overnight delivery is a wonderful thing.

"And I have decided to send the final message not from above with only Ursula to witness," Angus rattled on. "Well, she could not do that anyway. Not from above but here, in this alcove, your alcove, so you could be the one to watch with me the beginning of the end. All that remains is speaking three more words — only three simple words more. The rumble from Kilauea's eruption will be the signal they have worked."

"Evidently the cold has worked upon you, brother," Dinton said. "You are the one who is deranged."

"I have brought this from my own humble lair." Angus reached into his pocket and pulled out the small clock that had adorned his table for so many years. "See, it has both the date and the time. In only two more passes of the sun overhead, it will be exactly five days since I spoke the incantation. Exactly five days. Not too short a time nor too long. As the native children's myth of a golden one relates, 'It will be just right.'"

"Ursula," he called back over his shoulder. "I will go with you back up to the garden this first time — to fetch a meal for Dinton and myself. Keep your senses sharp. In the future, you will have to make the journey on your own."

"What senses?" Dinton asked.

"She is blind, brother," Angus replied. "But has had a lifetime to compensate. She does that very well."

Dinton watched Angus and Ursula leave, puzzled. What was his brother talking about? It made no sense. He sighed. But whatever it was, he was sure to have it explained to him over and over again. Angus never missed a chance to brag. So non-productive. Their father had been right from the very start.

Reflexively, he reached down and patted the baton hanging from his waist. Thaling had given it to him when he refused the plea to return home. Now there was only his brother and he, but still, the rules of a thousand years should apply.

Angus would object, of course. What would the argument be when they disagreed? Over the years, when Thaling, occasionally had refused to offer an opinion to break a tie, they had resorted to asking all of the exiles, to vote. But now everyone was gone. There were no more flocks. No more…

Dinton snorted. What was the name? Ursula. Somehow, she needed to be neutralized, and it should be done now. His thoughts wandered a bit. And perhaps he should obtain a little insurance as well.

3

A Stranger in Paradise

JAKE LOOKED at the strange surroundings. He was in a practice yard enclosed by a low brick wall next to some dormitories. Nearby were practice labs, a kitchen and dining hall, two wells, and one smaller structure with a richer façade, the dwelling of Fordine, himself. Beyond were rows of crops and fields of alfalfa for beasts of burden.

He parried a thrust easily and tapped the journeyman gently on his chest. Besides learning craft, a good student of thaumaturgy was taught skill in arms so that his master did not have to bother with such things. The man facing him smiled, and Jake smiled back. He had progressed rapidly — already now far more able than what he had learned from Briana's simple instructions. An excellent balance, and the quick adjustments he had learned from surfing were serving him in good stead.

This thaumaturge's academy was quite a production, he thought — self-sustaining so that the focus was entirely on the craft. Jake had no interest in learning incantations, but when it came to arms, with a few more days, he felt he would be the equal of any one here, except for perhaps the seneschal himself.

He inhaled deeply. There was a hint of some fragrance he could not place, but it smelled wonderful, like orange blossoms but somehow more enticing. He scanned the small village that lay beyond the academy's walls. It reminded him of a rustic town in the old west, except the buildings were of stone rather than wood. Although he could neither see or hear any of it, he imagined vendors hawking fresh produce in a central square, a smithy at a stable reshoeing a horse who had lost a shoe, a tavern about to serve another round of ale.

Remarkable. Only a day ago, he was standing on a street corner in

Hilo, Hawaii, hailing cabs. Now as Briana had been, *he* was the stranger in a strange land. No, that was not quite right. He liked it here.

The door of one of the practice labs opened, and Briana and Fig rushed out. A group of apprentices ran to surround them. One of the youngest, twelve at the most, solemnly bent on one knee and offered up what he held in his palms. It looked like a miniature stone wheel with a tiny crank attached. Briana took the offering and with her thumb and forefinger turned the handle. A tiny light began to twinkle on the wheel's frame.

All of the assembled apprentices started jumping up and down and yelling. Jake only understood the barest smattering of words, but what he heard was easy to interpret.

"Briana. Briana, Daughter of the Archimage," the young men chanted repeatedly, each repetition more animated than the one before.

"I am not royalty," Briana had explained when they had arrived. "My father has no title to any land at all — not in Procolon nor any in Arcadia across the Great Ocean. But here in the western hinterlands, a lord or lordling rarely appears, and I am by default given a deference I do not deserve. But let it be. It would be too much bother now to explain."

"Master Fordine said he needed time to think, to be alone and not distracted," Briana called out to Jake as the crowd finally dispersed. "And with Fig's help with the chemistry, he did not need to bring in an alchemist to consult. A few hours more and he should have something."

Jake saw Briana suddenly sag, and he rushed to prop her up. "We have been pushing very hard," he said. "Little man, get her a chair."

Fig frowned at the words as he always did, but rounded up three. They sat and began watching the door to the practice room, each to their own thoughts. Jake started looking at his watch every five minutes or so until Briana frowned for him to stop. They all knew that even an instant too late would not be good enough. But watching the minutes tick by did nothing to help. Either they would succeed or they would not. They had to wait and hope for the best.

Jake watched Briana stare into the distance, looking at the other buildings, out into the village and up the road leading to the east. He was not sure, but perhaps he could tell in her eyes that there was also a slight relaxing of the strain. She was home, he thought. After so many months of paved streets, busses, and laptops, she was home — returning to her old childhood mentor at the academy, the one she had visited when she was as young as the youngest of apprentices here.

In this setting, Jake saw Briana in a different light. Here, she was not merely another woman like the rest. True, from what he had seen, the society here was male dominated exactly as it was on Earth, but a daughter of the Archimage did deserve a special respect. Yes, she was more than... she was *Shangri-La!*

And he had to admit his respect for her had grown also. Without her clever action on the slopes of Mount Etna, he would have suffered a fate... for him, literally a fate worse than death. A hint of a warm feeling began to flow into him about her — a strange one he had never felt before.

Jake watched Briana manage a polite laugh when one of the serving wenches approached, passed her a note, and looked for a second at Jake before retreating. A second woman out of the fields shouldering a scythe came by, and another note was presented as well. A third with a low-cut blouse approached with some sort of roasted fowl on a platter and stooped to place it on the ground in front of Jake — bending forward far lower than was necessary.

Briana would not like him staring, he decided abruptly. He pointed to the scraps of paper in her hand. "What are those? These women are acting like schoolgirls."

"Let me read them to you," Briana said with resignation. "I am sure you will be pleased." She unfolded the first. "Are you willing to share?" Then the second. "He has very long arms. Excellent for fighting and reaping the hay. Are all his other members lengthy, too?" She looked back at Jake. "You are considered to be *exotic* here — different from all the journeymen they normally see."

"I am no journeyman," Jake snorted. "And why would they ask these questions of you?"

"Because they think you are my consort," Briana answered. "And there is too much on my mind now to explain about the bizarre relationships of the Earth."

Jake smiled for a moment, but then drew his face back into what he hoped was neutral. He should have been pleased by this interest, but surprisingly he was not. He thought of what would happen after all of this was over. Saving the Earth or not, eventually Briana would want to return here... and so would he! Why not? Consort to a daughter of the Archimage. A swordsman. Her protector. Yes, that felt very nice indeed.

As Jake pondered, Fordine emerged from the practice room. He moved slowly with age but carried himself rigorously erect. His robe was made not of simple brown cloth but the fine fur of some large beast. Running an academy evidently was very profitable.

The master craftsman extended a folded parchment toward Briana, and she stuffed it into her pack.

"We can return now!" Fig burst out. He sounded happy despite the fatigue. "Set up some equipment like what we found in the warehouse and broadcast the spell. You've done it, Briana! The Earth will be saved!"

Jake sighed in relief. Just like that, the ending was coming. Soon, the struggle and tensions would be over, and then he and Briana could —

"Sound the alarm," someone shouted from the east. Everyone looked to the road running alongside the compound. "The Procolonian Guard has abandoned the Archimage. The way to Ambrosia, completely undefended. Slammert's forces can march to the capital unopposed."

Briana sprang to her feet and began speaking rapidly to Fordine. Jake could not understand anything being said.

"What is he talking about?" Briana challenged the thaumaturge. "Abandonment of my father? Master Fordine, you said none of this when we arrived."

"It is a delicate situation, milady," Fordine said. "I have much wealth at stake here. I cannot choose sides until I am sure who will win." He shrugged. "I thought it best not to distract you."

"Distract me! Didn't you think — no, never mind. Tell me what has transpired while I have been gone."

"Your father went into a deep depression when you were reported missing," Fordine said. "He began paying attention to the affairs of the council less and less. Whisperers began saying perhaps he should step down. Let some other master assume his role."

The thaumaturge stroked his beard for a moment, then continued. "But we could not be sure. Your father is so wily. A man never at a loss. Maybe he was up to something that would be revealed in the fullness of time. And then when Slammert produced the wedding contract you had signed, he said your father had merely secreted you away. 'The Archimage cannot act on his own self-interests,' the baron had thundered. 'His authority had not been won by force, but merely was loaned to him by the noble lords.'

"When the date of the ceremony passed, Slammert issued an ultimatum. Produce you as his bride, he ordered, or he would call for the west to rise up with him in rebellion, strip away your father's power, sentence him to death."

"But my father has acted wisely for over thirty years," Briana protested. "Three decades of unblemished service. Everyone on both sides of the Great Ocean have prospered. Thirty years of peace. Little need for any standing army. Border crossings unencumbered. Commerce flourishing."

Fordine shook his head. "For every decision Alodar made, there was always a winner and a loser. Over time these little resentments build up." He shrugged. "Finally, many agreed with Slammert without thinking of the consequences. Many now say, 'Why not? We are ready for a change.'"

"Most of us on the council *did* think the wedding contract was merely a ploy. Slammert knew Alodar would never agree to have it honored. One of his precious daughters bound in marriage to one such as him? Of course not. It was the excuse to launch what he really wanted to do — become the king of Procolon. Without a standing army. With no one in the position of Warmaster after Cedric passed away... And after Procolon, then who knows? Wage war against Arcadia and the Southern Kingdoms? All have grown soft after so many years of peace."

"You should have told me this when I first arrived," Briana shouted. "Would you have merely said nothing after I was again on my way?"

"And you, milady, with all due respect, you should not have signed the contract in the first place."

Another messenger came running onto the glen from the other direction. "From the west," he panted. "Slammert's army approaches. Over one hundred men. He even has a few masters of the crafts with him as well. They will be here by tomorrow morning." He looked at Fordine. "You must decide now, venerated Master," he said. "Either flee, or prepare to receive on bended knee, your new lord when the sun again rises."

Briana slumped back onto her chair. She looked from Jake to Fig and saw their puzzled expressions. Quickly, she summarized for them what was happening.

"Only about a hundred," Jake said. "Surely there are enough men-at-arms about who could be rounded up to defeat the threat."

"It doesn't work that way," Briana said. "Not in our society — not how wars are fought on Murdina. It is a matter of which side gathers momentum the soonest. If a small army has a victory, additional warriors will swarm to join in, wanting to share in the spoils, making the next victory even more certain. With each step toward Ambrosia, Slammert's forces will swell even more. If he is to be stopped, it must be now."

"Not one world in peril, but two," she bemoaned.

"There still may be sufficient time." Fig leaped up and took the incantation scroll from Briana's pack. "I can take this to Ashley now." He pulled a flash drive out of his pocket. "She can configure what is needed, and speak the words as well as any of us. Write me out a quick pronunciation guide for your speech as you did for Fordine, only for English rather than for the words of an exile. And after Ashley gets going, I will return and help out here."

"The apprentices," Jake said. "They have some practice in arms. They can stop Slammert's march."

"But they are only boys!" Briana protested.

"From what I've seen, they will fight for you, Briana," Jake said. He felt alive, even more alive. Yes, he had tagged along with the others on Briana's quest in order to win the reward she promised. But this. This was different. He was not merely an obedient minion. He was key. He was central. He was meant for this.

4

The Eve of Battle

LIKE AN overwound clock spring, Briana felt as if she was going to snap. Surveying the ragtag line of young men milling around on the road, she shook her head. Clearly, what Jake was doing was not going to be enough. With the seneschal translating his plea, he only had been able to enlist half or so of the apprentices and journeymen to abandon their studies of thaumaturgy and take up a sword. Fifty or sixty only. The rest of the underlings in the compound were toting lunch baskets up the side of the nearby hill to watch the massacre when Slammert's horde appeared from the west.

A shimmer in the air caught her eye. The portal door reappeared. Fig finally must be back. He had left the previous evening, and shortly thereafter, the magic entranceway had disappeared as well.

"What took you so long?" Briana shouted. "Were you in time?"

"Can't tell for sure," Fig said.

"What does that mean?" Briana felt the last thread of civility dissolve away.

"Ashley had moved the portal back to her place. From there, it was easy to buy what we needed online and have it delivered immediately." Fig pushed his glasses back into place. "But Ashley... something was bothering her. She was not quite right. Complained her head hurt. That she had trouble focusing."

"I tried to help with the configuring," Fig continued. "There are always a few little steps that need to be worked out. But she kept pushing me away. Insisting she could do the job by herself. Said she needed peace and quiet."

"It took you all this time?"

"I did not return alone," Fig said. "I have been a little busy. Watch."

The portal door opened again, and a familiar figure stepped through, pushing a shopping cart.

"Slow Eddie!" Briana exclaimed. She looked back at Fig. "How did you ... Never mind. Why is he here? What can he do?"

"Slow Eddie and a few others jumped at the chance. They were near Hollywood Boulevard, as you had told us."

"Chance? Chance for what?"

"A new beginning, missy," Slow Eddie said. He looked at the grounds of the compound. "Yes, it looks like this Fig fellow described things well. Listen to the birds singing. Smell the clean air. And the way your servant tells it, there are jobs here. Lodging and food."

"But what would you do?" Briana persisted.

"Don't care much what it is, so long as we are not judged by our pasts, only by what we might become. This thaumaturgy stuff sounds quite interesting." He eyed one of the apprentices nearby. "We're not as young as these sprouts, but, as I say, a new beginning none the less."

"I mean the battle," Briana pointed down the road. "Everything could change."

"We can help with that, too." Slow Eddie set on the ground a box from the shopping cart and started ripping open the cover.

"Drones," Fig explained. "Remember when Ashley was lecturing us about operations research. Said the most important thing on the battlefield is not the headcount ratio, but intelligence. Knowing where to strike. From where an enemy thrust might come. It's a multiplier. It can amplify the effect of what we do many fold."

More of the homeless began emerging from the portal, each pushing a cart carrying his own newly acquired little machine. In only a few minutes, the air filled with their annoying whines.

"No, not so close together," Slow Eddie called out. "Each of us should take responsibility for a single sector. That way we can see everything going on."

"There's more," Fig said as the portal door continued to shut and then open again. Someone who obviously was not dressed in the tatters of Slow Eddie or one of his comrades emerged. He wore a long white surcoat cinched at the waist and emblazoned with a Maltese cross over what looked like chain mail. He carried a leather shield in one hand and a pack similar to Briana's on his back.

Briana blinked at what she saw. Where did someone like this come from? She examined him from head to toe. "The weaponry looks like it's only for sham battles, not a real fight," she said at last.

"The seneschal can exchange what they have brought. There is an arsenal here."

Another warrior appeared and then another. Briana felt slightly dazed as more and more began to appear. "Where did you find them?" she asked.

"The SCA," Fig said. "Forty-two of them. If I had thought there was sufficient time, I probably could have recruited more."

"Forty-two! Fig, the counter. It must show a number smaller than that now. Even if we win, not all of them will be able to return."

"None of them are going back!" Fig said. "Like Slow Eddie and his pals, *this* is the life they want to lead. Not only on weekends and with play battles in which no one actually gets hurt. Many have dreamed about a place like Murdina for years. Now, for them, it will be real." He looked at the line Jake was trying to assemble. "These guys can be the center. The apprentices can be on the flanks. Maybe the younger ones in a row behind."

Briana counted as the warriors emerged. When the last appeared, she expected the portal door to remain closed, but instead, she then heard from behind it a deep throaty roar. The entrance flew open again, and a burly man dressed in steel-studded black leather rolled out astride a two-wheeled beast of ebony and chrome. The back of his sleeveless jacket proclaimed 'Hell's Devils. Mess with us and you die."

Behind him, a woman smoking a cigar and similarly dressed emerged. A broad bladed knife without a sheath like a short machete was strapped to her thigh. Without a word, she climbed onto the bitch seat of the chopper in front of her and appraised the new surroundings with a steely glare.

The portal closed again, but soon a second motorcycle came through, and then a third.

As the procession continued, Fig explained. "Our cavalry. Before she got too hard to communicate with, Ashley said this Slammert probably has some horsemen he will use to attack on both sides. Try to encircle us from behind."

"How many bikes?" Briana asked.

"I lost track," Fig said. "I felt I was taking too much time. But the deal is the same — one-way tickets. They like the idea of miles of open road. No cops. No speed limits — well, at least until their gas tanks empty."

"They're here!" Slow Eddie called out. "Over the next rise,"

"Okay, let's get things into order," Fig said. "Slow Eddie, you guys back up a bit. Far enough not to be caught in the fighting, but sufficiently close to call out what you are seeing. Devils, fan out on the flanks. Get ready to engage their horses when they show up. The rest of you, go talk to the tall guy in the middle of the road."

The hubbub of conversation stopped. Everyone moved to their position. Briana wondered what she should do, but only for an instant. She slid away her pack, ran up to Jake, and stood at his left side. Fig scrambled after to guard her own left.

The first of Slammert's force appeared over the crest of the hill.

Almost instinctively, Jake knew what he must do. "For Briana, Daughter of the Archimage," he shouted.

A lusty cheer came from almost every mouth. "For Briana, Daughter of the Archimage."

Briana firmly grasped the short sword she had strapped to her side in place of her dagger. She looked right to left. It was the same as she had imagined so many times as a young girl. Maybe this was not with thousands, but it was close enough. No, not close. Exactly. Exactly as she imagined it be. Exactly as it was in the sagas.

She looked over her shoulder to the younger boys, some standing proudly at attention, others looking wide-eyed at the safety beckoning on the hillside. At the ends of their line, fear shown on the faces of most of the older ones — the journeymen. Several had stepped to the side to vomit out their guts. They were the ones who knew full well that this might be their last day to be alive.

5

The Technology of Warfare

THE HILLCREST was a little ways off, and Slammert's march was like that of a snail. An hour passed before they drew near. They reacted immediately when they reached the peak. The horsemen dispersed to either side and began moving forward slowly, keeping pace with the men on foot.

Briana watched the advance, giving her time to think. The lust for glory was all very well and good for those who battled. For them, this was the chance for fame and fortune... and for death. She looked at Jake on her right, his face shining with confidence, but the repeated grasping and releasing of the hilt of his sword gave him away. On her left, Fig stood at tall as she had ever seen him, his mouth open and his tongue darted back and forth over dry lips.

She was the one responsible for all of this, she thought. If only she had not let whatever good sense she had run off and hide — because of a little flattery. If she had not taken the portal to another world and been gone for so long.

Yes, Slammert might have been able to concoct a reason for raising his army — a force of only one hundred or so men. A pitiful number. She shook her head. Had her father not been distracted by her unexplained absence — vanishing without a trace, what then would have transpired? With the full regard of the council and respect of all of those who ruled, this upstart petty baron would have been squashed like a roach under the wheel of an alchemist's wagon.

The approaching army stopped two dozen yards from where Briana and the others stood. Slammert grinned when he recognized her. "Ah, my bride," he said.

Briana made up her mind. Before anyone could stop her, she stepped forth. "Yes, I am a bit late," she said. "But that has made the..." She stumbled for the words. They were hard to say. "Made my *anticipation* a little bit greater. I am here, my husband to be. There is no need for this posturing. Disband your followers. Let us return to your estate and plan for our wedding feast."

Slammert paused for a moment, at a loss for words. "It is not quite that easy," he said at last. "There is my... my reputation. It has been damaged." His face contorted into a leering grin. "Yes, by all means, come to me, my sweet. We can consummate our joining here and now. Remove all of your clothing. It will be so wonderful for everyone to watch."

Briana steeled herself and took a first step forward.

"I commanded you to remove your clothing," Slammert yelled for everyone to hear.

"I... I want you to help me," Briana answered.

Slammert frowned. He strode to the halfway mark between the two forces and extended his hand.

It is the right thing to do. It is the right thing to do, Briana repeated to herself with each step forward. What she was about to endure would be over soon enough. Her father would be saved. Ashley would speak the counterspell. All that remained would be for her to recover from the shame.

She extended her arm to his outreached hand and managed a small smile. Slammert tilted his head slightly to the side and started to tug her gently toward him.

"Tell them," Briana said. "Tell them first."

"What! Who?"

"Your recruited minions. Tell them to disperse, to go home. They are no longer needed." Briana tugged at a strand of her hair. "And sending heralds throughout the land announcing there is no longer any threat of war — that would be a nice touch, too."

Slammert's brow furled. He did not let go of Briana's hand.

Then he kicked her legs from underneath her and pulled her to the ground. Briana tried to rise, but he slammed his foot on her back.

"Put her somewhere safe," he called back to his troops. "There is time enough for this after the roadblock to our progress has been removed."

Two of Slammert's men sprang to attention, startled by the command. But before they had taken their first step, Fig burst from the defensive line, waved his sword over his head, and rushed forward.

"Unhand the Queen," he shouted. "Unhand the Queen of the Eight Universes. She will not be sullied by such as you."

"No, Fig! No!" Briana cried.

Slammert withdrew his boot from her back. He studied Fig almost stumbling as he came forward. Then, when Fig got within range, he withdrew his own blade, bent slightly forward, and with a savage sweep slashed at an unprotected leg.

Fig cried in pain and crumpled to the ground next to Briana. Blood began pulsing from the wound. "Not again!" Briana cried out. "Not again!"

She struggled to her knees, grabbed at Fig and tried to pull him erect. As she did, she heard Jake shout, "For Briana. For the Daughter of the Archimage."

Jake rushed forward, and the centermost of the line on either side immediately followed. Slammert clamored back to his own troops and yelled. "Repulse them. Cut them down."

The charging men circled past Briana and Fig and tore into Slammert's line. A loud clash filled the air, the impact of sword on shield. From both sides, Briana could hear the clop of galloping horses and then immediately afterwards the deep rumble of the bikes.

Briana stood, pushed her hands under Fig's arms, and began dragging him away from the fighting, back to the relative safety of Slow Eddie and the other homeless. As she did, several of the apprentices saw her retreat, dropped their blades, and began to run away.

The blood kept coursing out of Fig's leg, far more this time than a trickle. The cut was too deep, she realized. Many stitches were needed, and no one had thought to stash a chest of sweetbalm nearby — if there was any stockpiled anyway.

She scanned the litter of discarded backpacks and packing boxes nearby. There, in the refuse — bungy cords! Coiled around Fig's leg and stretched as far as possible, the flow of blood slowed but did not stop. He needed help now, or shortly he would bleed to death.

Back to Earth, Briana concluded. Ashley could call an ambulance. She had done so from her home before. Or, if she had to, move the portal to a hospital entrance. There might be gawking as it appeared out of nowhere, but there was no time to ponder the impact of the sudden mixing of technologies now. Drones. Motorcycles. Murdina was already tainted. The Earth may as well be also.

She struggled to pull Fig into the portal and propped him up on the far door — the one opening on Earth — where ever Ashley had placed it. Remembering how their little cadre had found Maurice's message, she executed the same trick. She patted Fig's pockets and withdrew his phone. Leaning close to the door, she dialed Ashley's number.

"Hello," a weak voice came through the speaker.

"Ashley, is that you?" Briana asked.

"I... I don't know," Ashley responded. "I seem to be hearing something in my head, a voice. It's growing louder. I don't know."

"Have you broadcast the incantation?" Briana shouted into the mike.

"No, not yet. I haven't been able to get everything to work right. The voices. I can hardly type any more. It is too — "

"Listen!" Briana commanded. "Fig is at the portal door. He is hurt, hurt badly. Get him to help and then call me ba..." No that won't work. When you have obtained some help for him, record a massage on Fig's phone and hurl it against the door here on Murdina. I will listen to it when... when I get the time."

She ran back out of the portal and immediately was distracted by the buzz in the air. The drones were close together, hovering over the battle line. Looking at the control screen in Slow Eddie's hand, she saw one of the cycles roar into a quartet of horsemen converging from the right. The mounts spooked and reared. Two dumped their riders and the others galloped away in panic, out of control.

Briana raced down the line of the homeless, looking at all of their screens. On the left, the scene was the same. Slammert's cavalry was being routed. The cyclists pursued, drawing abreast of retreating riders and... and firing guns at their startled adversaries! Drones. Motorcycles. And now, guns. Would Murdina ever be the same?

She looked up from the consoles toward the upslope. Jake and those flanking him were winning. The center of the line bowed forward. They were forcing Slammert back. But on either side, the apprentices were starting to panic. Many were already down. The ends of the line were unraveling and falling apart.

Could Jake and the others break through and start flanking movements of their own? Or would they have to fall back and protect their own rear instead? Briana could not tell. She yanked open the portal door. Fig was not there. Ashley must have dragged him out — but there was no phone on the floor.

6

Move and Counter Move

NORDO, THE leader of the Hell's Devils, felt good. He looked over his shoulder at his buddies racing full bore over the rough ground, the drivers bent low over the handlebars, the women firing wildly over their mate's backs at anything that moved. They had succeeded. Slammert's cavalry was gone. They were returning to the central battle to find out what they should do next.

Out of the corner of his eye, Nordo saw three men robed in white spring to their feet and race to a wagon a distance behind Slammert's line and far to one side. It was weighted down by a long barrel lying prone. One sprang up on the frame and began flailing a two-handed pump back and forth. In response, a frothy spray spewed out the rearmost end of the cylinder and soaked the ground.

The two other men ran to the front of the wagon and thrust themselves into a pair of empty yokes. Straining against the load, they started the wagon moving perpendicular to the road, across the field of battle from left to right. As the caisson continued, it gathered speed while continuing to spray. Finally, it came to a halt as the hill fell sharply away and further progress would lead to a runaway down the slope.

Nordo's motorcycle roared into the wet ground but did not get far. A plume of fine sand flew into the air, and the bike toppled onto its side. A second cycle followed, and it also was halted by the barrier of grit. Whatever was in the tank broke rock down into sand. The bikes would not be able to cross.

All of the riders jumped clear as their choppers became useless. Nordo saw the trail of sand coming from the wagon, and he ran alongside its trail until he caught up with the robed men.

"Mess with Hell's Devils and you die," he spat.

The two who were yoked struggled to get free, but before they could, they were shot dead at point blank range. The third fled down the hillside as quickly as he could.

On foot, the bikers continued onward toward the rear of Slammert's line. As they approached, they fired at the backs of the men-at-arms. But only one or two fell. By now, most of the guns were empty, and Nordo's buddies hesitated.

"We're in their rear," Nordo called out. "They can't fight in two directions at once. Come on, let's get 'em." Following his lead, the gang continued forward. But as they did, a few of Slammert's men disengaged from the line and turned to meet them.

A shadow of doubt crept into Nordo's mind. Yeah, this was supposed to be easy. They were behind the enemy, but an enemy with shields and long swords. All his guys had were bare hands and knives.

PHOBOS, THE dervish, soared into the air. It seemed like eons since he had been last summoned. The wizard was second-rate, but hey, what the hell. It beat sitting around waiting for a real job. He surveyed the field before him. Two lines of humans dulling their blades against each other. Same-o. Same-o.

But wait, here was something different. Little machines of metal making noises like a hive of agitated bees. And hovering, yes, hovering, staying in one spot. Four horizontal, whirling wings keeping them aloft.

Phobos swooped back to the wizard to make sure. "'Get them back to the ground,' you said. And we are the guys to do it? "

He looked up at his six broodmates flying in formation and awaiting the final word to attack. "I told you we don't do the electrical stuff. Bolts of fire and such. You need bigger guys than us for that. Prettier to watch what they do, too."

"I have deduced the weakness," the wizard said. "Dervishness is exactly what is called for."

"OK, you got it," Phobos said. He flew up to join his mates and then picked a target for himself. As he had been instructed, he flew until he hovered a hand span above it and started to spin. He rotated faster and faster, almost to the point that he became dizzy, but not quite. The friction of his body pulled the air and the hovering machine into a tight funnel, making the two of them opaque by its rapid motion.

Shouts of amazement began ascending from the ground, and Phobos smiled. He always liked that part. The speed increased a tiny bit more, and to his surprise the flying machine rose to smack him in the butt. Ah, wrong direction, he thought. The wizard had told him that might happen.

As quickly as he could, he decelerated and then started spinning again— but in the opposite direction. When he got to full speed, the flying machine began to fall away from him, just as the wizard also had predicted. Maintaining his centrifugal speed, he lowered himself gently, depositing the machine on the ground. He had made the device lose all of its lift.

SLOW EDDIE pointed skyward excitedly. What looked like small tornados had appeared in the air and were moving toward the drones.

"Whirling dervishes," Briana called to him. "Little demons that can swirl the air. A wizard, a rogue one, is on Slammert's side."

"We lost the advantage of being able to see the entire battlefield, Slow Eddie yelled. "We are blind without the drones."

"Briana, we need you." Jake's voice came through the confusion. "The flanks are collapsing. They are insufficiently trained. Come and show yourself. They need to see you have not abandoned them, to see who they are fighting for."

There was a pause, and then Jake yelled again, this time for all to hear. "For Briana. For the Daughter of the Archimage. For my... for my love."

Briana's feeling fluttered for a moment when what Jake had yelled hit home. But no time to think about that now. She looked at the flanks of their battle line. Jake was right. They were winning in the center but losing on the edges. And if the flanks rolled back, the center would not be able to stand. They needed more help, but from where? All of the journeymen and apprentices who had agreed to fight were already engaged, wounded or dead. There was no one left in the academy except for the women.

The women! Yes, the women, Briana realized. Ashley. Irma. Insight from her sojourn on Earth. The customs there were not entirely the same as those here. At the academy: cooks: scullery maids, field workers, and all the rest. No one had thought about them when the forces were marshalled. Except for a showpiece like herself, they were never called to battle. On Murdina, such things were not done.

She slapped the short sword on her side. And why not!

She ran back to the academy grounds and grabbed the arm of the first maid she saw. "Your exotic one. The one from another world. He is in danger. You can help save him."

She pushed the thought of what would happened afterward out of her mind. That too was for later. "Round up all of the others. Arm yourself with whatever you can. Pitchforks, scythes. Anything with a long handle and a sharp edge at the end."

7

A Tale for the Sagas

"THERE! THAT is where we are needed." Briana pointed toward the left flank. "Remember to keep a firm two-hand grip on your weapon. Your opponent will try to knock it away."

She looked back at the cadre she had assembled. Twenty; maybe twenty-five. The number did not matter. They would do what had to be done. Secure the flank so that all would not be lost. She pulled her sword from its sheath.

"For Jake. For Jake, the Exotic. Save him from his fate."

"For Jake," the women yelled back. "For Jake, the Exotic."

They formed into a rectangle three rows deep. Pitchforks in the first two rows, those in the second thrusting between the carriers in the first. Scythes in the rear handled by the youngest, the most nimble, ready to loop around and swing swift death from the sides.

Briana stood in front of them all. With a swift trot she led them onto the battlefield from the rear and aimed for the crumbling line on the left.

As they approached, the encircling attackers stopped their advance. At first they shouted a war cry and turned to face the new opponents. But as the women came closer, their jaws dropped open. Almost instinctively, they lowered their swords, puzzled.

"Get back to your kitchens," one yelled. "We do not fight *wenches*. There is no glory in that. Get back to your kitchens. You will have your hands full with us after we take care of man's business here."

Briana did not respond. She continued trotting up to the man in the center of the line and stopped.

With a flourish, the man facing her, dipped his blade to the ground. "Well?" he taunted.

Briana did not hesitate. With a smooth motion, she slashed her sword across his neck.

The warrior's eyes bulged. "We do not fight — " he tried to say again before he slumped to the ground with blood coursing over his tunic.

The other women charged forward, pushing with their pitchforks against the line of men. Those in the third row whipped out to the sides swinging their blades. Slammert's men, shocked into action began parrying the thrusts, pushing the blades of some of the forks into the ground.

But they could not bring themselves to swing their own weapons in attack. Cautiously they retreated one step backwards and then two. Those on the ends of their line cried in sudden pain as the scythes sliced true.

Briana sensed that they had to seize the moment now, before all of the shock wore off and the men could fully comprehend that they had comrades on the ground. She swung her sword left and right, deflecting other blades before they could do any harm.

Two more of the men fell, and then almost in unison, four threw down their arms and collapsed to their knees in surrender. The apprentices of the line seeing what was happening gathered fresh courage. Not to be outdone by mere women, one by one, they rejoined the fight. The flank disintegrated into a disorganized mêlée.

The effect was contagious. The center bulge grew deeper and broke through. Slammert's men were divided into two smaller groups. In mere minutes more, the battle was over. Slammert thrust his sword into the ground and bowed like the rest. Most of his warriors began slinking away.

"Briana, I have done it," Jake said. He looked at Briana's blood stained tunic. "I mean we have done it. Your father is saved."

He extended his hand. "It is the *perfect* ending to your quest. Come, now is the time for me to be proclaimed consort in truth."

Without thinking, Briana extended her hand forward to grasp his. Yes, she had a promise to Jake she had to keep, but after that one time…

Her father would be so proud. The problem with Slammert taken care of. Stories of another orb with customs and wonders so different from their own. Yes, a tale for the sagas to be sure. It was going to end well after all.

End well? The thought jarred. No, that is not right. The portal. Fig. Ashley. The counter-incantation. It all was not over yet.

Briana withdrew her hand and ignored the women who filled the void her action created, all clustering around the man they had help save. She ran back to the portal, and flung open the door.

This time, there *was* a phone laying there.

Briana pressed 'Play' and placed her ear to listen.

"Briana, there is something wrong with me. I can't think straight anymore. I can't even remember the number to call. Nine, one... something. I don't know. I used the portal to go to Oscar's hut. I can't remember why I did it. I barely could fumble through recording this... The command is so loud now..."

Briana heard a garble and then what sounded like Ashley speaking again but this time as if she were deliberately trying to imitate a male voice.

"I am Dinton, the eldest brother," the recording said. "It has taken a while, and this subject has been very resistive to my sorcery. But now her will is mine. She is my... my concubine. Angus and I are the only two of our kind left in these dismal caverns, and if he has one, then so shall I.

"He boasts that in minutes he will conclude an incantation that will prove he is the one to carry the baton. But no matter how potent it is, I will not agree. Possession will be resolved by a vote of our followers, and if his can no longer be found..."

The recording stopped. Briana gasped. Fig was not on his way to the hospital! The counterspell had not been spoken! Angus will speak the words releasing the SF_6 into the air in minutes!

"Briana!" Jake shouted.

Briana tried to think. The SCA, Slow Eddie, the Hell's Devils. They had made the choice to come to Murdina and stay. Jake was the only Earthling left. He would have to be the one to return and save the planet.

"Jake," she called out. "The incantation. You have to return and speak it."

"Are you kidding?" Jake yelled back. "I love it here. I want to be with *you* here." He tried batting away the arms pulling him from side to side. "Don't mind them. It is only the excitement of the moment. We will be famous, written up in these sagas that you keep talking about. What happens on the Earth is no longer our concern."

Briana watched a moment longer, but the conclusion was inescapable. She was the one who was going to have to say the incantation herself.

Instinctively, she glanced up at the counter to see how many portal passages were left.

It felt as if an icepick pierced her heart. She was stunned.

She blinked to make sure, but there was no mistaking what the translation of the symbol meant."

"1"

One more trip and then the portal would no longer work! If she used it, she could then never return!

"Briana!"

She would have to make a choice. Jake was right. Story over. The perfect ending was here.

But if she did stay. What about Fig? What about Ashley? What about the fate of an entire world?

But. But. There were too many buts. If she stayed, all would end well. If she did go, she would not be able to return — ever!

"It is not supposed to be like this," she cried aloud.

"Briana!"

Briana sucked in what felt like the deepest breath she had ever inhaled in her life. The happiness of her own life, or the salvation of many. There was only one choice really. She looked back at Jake and shook her head.

"Sorry," she mouthed without uttering aloud the word. Before she could change her mind, she raced into the portal.

"Briana!"

8

Only by Her Wits

BRIANA OPENED the portal door, stepped out, and slammed it shut. The magic transport faded away. No time to look back now. She had made her decision.

She ran inside Oscar's hut and saw Ashley sprawled on the floor, one arm with a rope wrapped tightly around her wrist and the other end tied to a pipe under the sink. Her free arm was reaching, straining, clawing toward the door and the outside.

"I had to make sure," Ashley said softly. "Sure that I did not go. Dinton, he calls himself. He demanded that I come." Her eyes rolled back in her head and she hit the floor with a thud.

Papers, books, and trash were scattered everywhere. It was not evident where in the jumble were the words to the counterspell. The computer monitor on the card table showed the same desktop as the one in the warehouse. The exiles had been here since we left.

She ran to where Fig had been tossed aside like a rag doll and looked at him. He was still alive, but barely.

No time. No time left to waste. She already had made one heart-wrenching decision and had to continue relying on her gut to tell her what to do next.

Stop Angus and Dinton. They were the last two aliens left, Maurice's last message had said. Stop the incantation. But how? She needed a clue?

"Wait! What was that?" Briana said aloud. Something not there before. A cable leading away out of the door. She ran back outside, tightening the straps to her backpack. She began tracing the cable snaking along the ground. She recognized where they were going. Back to the cave.

The entrance. There it was. The cable led inside.

Briana stopped for a moment and ripped the miner's helmet out of her pack. She put it on, and swung her head from side to side. There, off to the left, the cable led to a little opening, one she and Fig had missed the last time there were here.

She bent down and peered through the hole. Her lamplight revealed a large cavern on the other side. Large — and deep. She would have to scale down its wall, hand over hand.

Briana rid herself of her pack, and slapped the short sword on her side, reassured. It would have to do the deed.

USING ALL her strength, Briana pushed the rock plugging the entranceway to a lower cavern aside. It was hot, oppressively hot. She felt as if she were in the Sahara. No, worse even than that. She had to find Angus and Dinton soon — before her strength gave out.

Briana shone her lamp back and forth. Nothing distinctive either way. Wait! There to the left. A buzz. No, a deep hum. How did a drone get in here? And movement near the limit of illumination. Bands of canary yellow shifting within the ebony black.

Moving as fast as she could, she advanced. A slight turn in direction. And then, on the floor, crumpled like the clothing of an abandoned doll was a pile of bleached burlap. A helmet cast aside nearby. White hair. It was Ursula, blind Ursula.

And above the woman's prone form... Briana recalled in horror. Insects! Giant insects with long segmented antenna, multifaceted eyes and thick, black, hairy limbs. Two were pinning Ursula to the ground. Another stood partially erect on two legs. Carrying... carrying what looked like an egg — a giant ovoid glistening with slime. Briana took a step backwards. Not this. Not now.

Out of an indentation in the wall to the left, another of the tiger wasps, this one more yellow than black, sprang forward and coiled its forearms around Briana's throat. Forced to the ground, her helmet clattered away.

Two more wasps appeared, smaller and with stunted wings. Wrapped their forelegs around each of her arms. She tried to use her legs to burst free. Didn't work. Illuminated in the cast aside lamp, Briana saw yet another wasp approach, this one also carrying an egg. It bent over her and with its huge mandibles ripped her tunic apart from neck to waist.

Briana strained to loosen her sword arm. Slippery and dripping, it became free. Then, almost immediately, another wasp grabbed it. Four arms, not two, pulled her hand back out of the way. She kicked with both legs. Anything. Anything to avoid what she feared would happen next.

Her left arm became unfettered. Reaching clumsily across her chest and down her side, she freed her sword. Thrusted upward. Into the eye of the one with the egg. Ichor, blue as the sky spilled forth, pulsing, pulsing a thick syrup over her chest.

A cloying, sickly smell. Briana coughed. Pheromones. If these wasps were anything like those on Murdina, they would be aroused into a stinging rage. She stabbed again. The other eye.

The wasp dropped the egg and reared. Blinded, it snapped off the arm of one of its brood. More ichor. More rage. The confining arms released her. All of the wasps were angry, ready to kill. Anything that moved was a target, even another of their kind.

Briana sprang to her feet, stabbing. Stabbing as rapidly as she could. Two more eyes gone. Then four. She stumbled over an egg and kicked it out of the way. A sudden pain flash in her leg. Hot and numbing. She had been stung.

Mostly blinded, the wasps tore into one another. Implantation of eggs was no longer of interest. So then, escape. Escape from these creatures now. Coming in this direction was a mistake. She looked down the corridor. Ursula's face shone in the lamp light. No, do not go further that way.

The blind woman stirred. With surprising strength, she regained her footing.

"Let me lead," Ursula said. "I'll use my hands along the wall."

"Where are Angus and Dinton?"

"Your voice. I recognize it. You are one of Mr. Angus' enemies."

Briana stopped. Tightened the grip on her sword.

"Dinton asked me to do it," Ursula continued.

"Wait! What are you saying?"

"Told me to fetch something at the lowest levels. He wanted me to go there. Go there alone. He *knew*. He knew what I would find."

"Angus is no better."

"I know. I know it now. Mr. Angus. His demeanor. Completely changed." Ursula broke into a sob.

Briana relaxed her grip. "Where are they?"

"I am taking you to them."

"WE SHOULD be close now," Ursula said.

"I see a dim glow up ahead," Briana said. "Go back to the rock that seals the passage to the surface. Push it aside, enter, and close it behind you."

Without waiting for a reply, Briana pressed forward. It was getting more difficult to move now. Her leg was completely numb. She had to drag it along, using one hand to press against the wall for balance. Merely standing erect was becoming a challenge. Push what happened with the wasps out of her mind. It was an interlude, a distraction. There was a world yet to be saved.

As she approached the increasing light, Briana heard what sounded like the growling of competing tigers. It must be them — Angus and Dinton speaking, although she did not understand a word.

"She is *mine*, not yours to command," Angus said. "Share in pleasure, yes, I will grant you that, but not to order about."

"An oversight," Dinton replied. "I apologize. When my own slave arrives, then I will have no need."

"Your own slave," Angus snorted. "How convenient you should happen to mention that now — on the eve of putting to the vote on who should wear the baton. But no matter. Compose yourself. See the time. Prepare now to witness what I shall cause to come to pass."

Briana limped into the alcove. She saw that one of the aliens had grey in his fur. That one must be Dinton, the other, Angus, the one they had captured but then managed to escape. There was a microphone sitting on a table. This is from where the incantation was to be cast!

She lifted her sword in challenge, trying to hold the tip straight and firm.

But she could not. Her hand was shaking too much.

"This is your concubine?" Angus looked at Briana. "The one responsible for the attack on the warehouse that nearly undid my plans?"

"I do not recognize her," Dinton said "How could I. They all look the same." He scowled at Briana. "Drop your weapon, native," he said in

English. "You have no hope against two warriors of our kind… two flock leaders, no less."

He drew his dagger, and so did his brother.

Briana's chest tightened. She tried to take a breath but could not. A heartbeat. And then another. Her sword continued to quiver. A dozen beats more.

She felt no surge of strength — now, when she needed it the most.

Her shoulders sagged.

She had courage, sure. She easily could limp across the distance between her and the two exiles. But then she would be cut down. As had Fig when he faced Slammert. A single slash or two and it would be over. And after that, over for everyone else as well.

"Come on. Let's get this over with." Angus growled at her. "My brother and I — "

"My *younger* brother and I," Dinton interrupted, "have much more important things to attend to. Force your tiny and weak body to charge at us so we can move on."

A single woman against one surprised and over-confident man, yes, a possibility. But against two trained and alert warriors? There was no way a lone female could triumph. What could she do?

In desperation, Briana flung her sword forward, point first, toward Angus, hoping he would be surprised, and it would pierce his chest.

He easily batted it away.

Instinctively, she stepped backward. Okay then, get them away from the microphone. It would give her a little more time to think. She retreated, limping back up the passageway as fast as she could. Dinton and Angus followed, one of them carrying a torch. Like hunters cornering a fox at the end of a chase, they closed the distance slowly, as if anticipating the pleasure of an inevitable kill.

Briana managed to pass the rock sealing the passage to the outside and then stumbled in the encroaching darkness. Reaching down, she felt the slimy stickiness of the egg she had kicked aside. The wasps, pheromones — an idea.

She continued down the passageway, hand on the wall in imitation of what Ursula had done. She could not see anything, but she could smell. She tripped again, this time over the outstretched, hairy arm of one of the wasps. It was not moving. Grimacing while she did it, she felt over the inert body until she touched the fragrant liquid oozing from a fatal wound. Her tunic was already soaked, but she had to be sure. Using both hands she coated herself with more of the slime and then stood, fanning her arms in the air.

A sound, and then motion. At least one of the wasps was still alive. They had not all perished in their frenzy. She stepped backwards and waited. The sound came closer, the raspy rattle of the insect's body dragging over the fallen others of its kind.

The wasp pursued her slowly with an uneven cadence. Perhaps one of its limbs was injured or gone. No matter. It was doing what she wanted, following her back up the passage.

Briana saw the flicker of the torchlight ahead, and then Angus and Dinton came into view, both with daggers still drawn. And there also was the egg, glistening on the ground. Fighting back the repulsion, she forced herself to pick it up and cradle it to her chest. It was what she had to do. The slime oozed over her torso, hands, and arms, sticky beyond belief.

Angus and Dinton approached. Briana wished that both her legs were working so she could move faster, but perhaps the two aliens would be startled enough, nevertheless.

Dinton extended the torch toward her and pointed with his dagger.

Angus nodded and stopped. "I see that she returns. Perhaps resigned to her fate."

Briana kept coming. She limped up to face Angus and, before he could react, thrust the egg upon his dagger to shield herself from its sharpness. She wrenched away her own grip and wrapped her arms around the alien, hoping that some of the pheromone liquid would transfer to his chest — so that he, too, would become a target.

Dinton turned to stab Briana in the back, but hesitated when he saw the wasp lumber into view. It ignored him and moved to attack the struggling duo at his side.

"Randor's handiwork haunts us still," Angus called out as he tried to extract himself from Briana's embrace. "We should have destroyed them long ago. Why, brother did you never listen to *any* idea that I ever had?"

Dinton did not reply. He avoided the flailing arms of the wasp and moved closer so that he could target its eyes. Briana could not tell what was happening behind her and clung to Angus as hard as she could.

But the alien she embraced was far stronger. He released the grip on his entombed dagger and then ripped Briana's arms away, flinging her to the ground. She looked back and saw that ,with two deft strokes, Dinton had dispatched the wasp.

A final feeble try, but it had not worked. So much for the valiant warrior saving the day.

A sense of gloom crashed over her, one that she knew she would never be able to throw off. A victory on Murdina that she would never be able to enjoy, and here where it mattered more, total defeat.

While Briana sat stunned and felt herself fall into what felt like a bottomless pit, Angus and Dinton roared back and forth at each other in triumph — in triumph at what they had just done — wasp slain and native captured. The only word she recognized at all was 'Randor' repeated a few times.

'Randor', she puzzled. Why would she recognize that? She frowned at the distraction, grateful that it gave her a momentary respite from dwelling on her plight.

Yes, that was it. Maurice's message. What Randor had told him about the brothers. An interesting tidbit about a strange culture, but nothing of consequence.

Her tiny and weak body, Dinton had said. It was so unfair. But she could not deny it. She could no longer stand. In the end, it *was* her body betraying her, betraying her when she needed it the most.

Her body! Another thought formed. What was it Ashely had said? 'If we are ever going to be judged the equals of men, it will because we used our wits rather than our bodies.'

Yes! Not our bodies, but our wits!

Like a rock climber looking for an elusive handhold, her mind caromed through all that had happened to her while here on Earth and Maurice on the alien's orb.

Rubbish, irrelevant, of no use… Wait! What had Randor said about the three brothers? Yes! One last hope!

"You are the one named Angus, right?" Briana pointed at him. "The one your sibling calls the youngest?"

"Yes, yes. He takes every opportunity to remind me," Angus replied.

"But why do you allow that?" Briana asked. "Randor says it is the other way around. You are the elder and Dinton the youngest of all."

"What? Randor? What do you know of Randor?" Angus asked.

"A tribunal on your home world. One of three."

Angus squinted at Briana for a moment before speaking again. "How do you know these things about Randor? Why did he speak so?"

"He said you were triplets. That you, Angus, came out of the womb the first. Then Thaling and finally Dinton, here. But as you grew, your father came not to trust how you would rule when he was to pass.

"Passion and fury were everyone's lot — flaws in the character of your species, but for you, it was more extreme than most. So he told everyone Dinton was the first — the most introspective, the most deliberate of you three, the most like himself, the one most likely to ensure your flock survived."

Angus snarled. He reverted to his native speech. "Did you know of this, brother?" he challenged. "Is it true?"

Dinton did not immediately answer.

"Angus, how does that make you feel?" Briana interjected into the silence. "How long has it been for you without your birthright? A thousand years, right?"

"It was for the best, Angus." Dinton hurried to say. "Your temper would have lead our flock into continual perils. All of us would have perished long ago."

"Did you know of this? Is it true?"

Again, Dinton did not speak.

"Is it true?"

Dinton looked at the glare in Angus' eyes for a moment. "Yes, our father told me when I was old enough to understand the reason," he finally said. "But, but, I have not been autocratic. I was the one who suggested the idea of the periodic game to decide who next was to wear the baton. You had a chance at ruling, at maturing, as did Thaling, too."

"Games! Games that you won almost every time. Stupid contests so you could demonstrate over and over your superiority. The implicit message that you were the only one worthy to command. The prohibition against using magic. To work for our release."

"It was not so easy, brother," Dinton shouted back. "Holding you in check for a thousand years took a great deal of effort. The threat of the Faithful finding out we were performing the crafts was too great a risk."

"Yes, a thousand years! A thousand years of trying to keep my urges under control, for enduring the humiliation of your petty little victories. For... for enduring the shame of being sentenced to the pit of the wasps."

"If you ruled, it would have been disaster! "

"Worse than that. Dinton. It *is* a disaster! Ill-prepared, poor Thaling has returned home, to a doom you were unable to prevent. You are pathetic, Dinton. A failure. A disgrace."

"I still wear the baton," Dinton snarled back. He waved his dagger in Angus' face. "Do not speak to me that way ever again."

Angus threatened with his blade as well. "Worse than a failure," he spat. "Too paralyzed by doubt to act. You are a coward!"

"Immature youngster," Dinton shot back.

"Weakling!"

"Child!"

"Mouse!"

"Infant!"

The two circled each other for a moment, and then Angus struck out at his brother. Dinton blocked with his free arm and tried to slice into Angus' gut. Angus twirled to the side.

Dinton attacked again, this time with a fake to the face and then a thrust downwards towards the chest. Angus took a half step back, then suddenly reversed himself and thrust at his brother again.

For several minutes they dueled, the flash of their blades almost too fast for Briana to follow. A stab towards the gut. A slash at a wrist before it fully withdrew. A spin to the side.

Then Dinton sucked in his breath and hesitated rather than trying to pursue a momentary opening. He was beginning to tire. The younger in chronological age, but the one who donned the ring of eternal youth the later of the two.

Angus seized the advantage. He flung his free arm across and under Dinton's lunge, sending the blade upward and out of the way. Then, in the blink of an eye, he plunged his own dagger into his brother's chest, a fountain of blood exploding when he withdrew.

Dinton sagged to his knees, disbelief etched into his face. Rings of eternal youth halted the natural aging process but did nothing to stop a violent attack. Angus bent forward, thrusting a gloating face into that of his brother.

"Now, who is the most worthy to wear the baton?" he crowed as he reached to Dinton's belt to start untying its constraints.

Dinton tried to speak, but could not. With a dying effort he plunged his own dagger into Angus' gut, and then collapsed, dropping his blade to the ground.

Angus swiped he hand across his stomach and then looked at his palm coated in red. His eyes widened as he saw Briana at his feet. He staggered a step or two towards her, and then grinned in apparent triumph.

"Imsoarion," he yelled at the top of his lungs.

Briana recognized the word as it echoed against the cavern walls — the first of the last three that would break the incantation and cause Etna and Kilauea to erupt. She struggled to pull herself up off of the floor as much as she could.

"Transminator," Angus yelled, although this time not quite as loud as before. He fell to his knees in front of her, one hand pressing against the blood oozing between his fingers.

Briana looked about desperately and saw Dinton's dagger lying in front of her.

Angus paused for a moment to savor what he was doing and then started to speak the final word. As he opened his mouth, Briana lunged for the dagger and grabbed it. She hurled herself at the alien. With both hands, she thrust it into his mouth and up into his brain.

9

Three Scoops

BRIANA HAD been wandering the streets of old Hilo for hours. The sun was hot. She needed to stop. There was still much to do, but at least the most important things had been taken care of.

She had spoken aloud the counterspell soon after Angus and Dinton had hit the ground, and after taking care of Fig and Ashley, had checked with the gas monitor at Kilauea. The counter-incantation had worked. The accumulated energy was gradually ebbing. SF_6 levels were going down.

Fig was recovering. When she had glanced at him in Oscar's hut, she had seen the dance of the thousands of little lights clustering around his wound. The micromites were forming a clot by bridging together their tiny bodies. Most drowned in Fig's blood as it pulsed around them, but they had slowed the flow enough that, when she returned, he was still alive and able to be rushed to a hospital.

He was still there but would be released sooner than Ashley. Even though she no longer complained about a voice in her head, she was unable to shake the horror of her mental trauma. Drugs, shock treatments, and talking sessions, the psychiatrists had said, and she would recover. Although, Briana could tell, they were not sure when.

Maurice was lost forever, somewhere on another planet, who knew how far away. But then, the world he sought was an internal one. His struggle was to make the external no longer relevant. Perhaps he would achieve Nirvana no matter where he was.

And then there was Jake. In the end, he proved himself. Maybe he really did care for her. What would have been different had she chosen to stay with him rather than flee? She would never know. But judging from the way the women were fighting for his attention after the battle, he would be satisfied with his fate.

Jake would not know what became of her either. Nor would her father. Yes, the Archimage might be proud of what she had striven for, but the closure would be unknown forever.

Tears began to well up in her eyes. When she and her father had parted, it had not been on the best of terms. If she were to do this over again, she would have given him a hug and whispered in his ear that she would always love him.

A bus screeched to a stop at the curb beside her and then almost instantly roared off again, the foul smell of diesel poisoning the air. So unlike Murdina, she shook her head. Most of this orb had no soul. All noise and flashing lights. All hurry from one event to the next.

On Murdina, there was time to lounge in the green hills of spring, smell the newly sprouted flowers and the cool, pure air. Time to be the doting auntie to newborn nieces and nephews. To fend off her sisters' playful teasing when they were tired of waiting, about which of them would be her matron of honor.

Of course, eventually, she would want a life-companion and children of her own. Most ideal would be a mix of the few men she did know. Some of Jake's roaring lustiness mixed with Fig's unconditional love. And a dash of Maurice's calm demeanor and wisdom thrown in as well.

The tears swelled. The cool green hills of Murdina. She never would see them again. She surrendered to the surge of sadness that crashed over her like a tidal wave. Her home, those she loved, almost all of her entire life — gone and lost forever.

Passersby stared at her while she stood sobbing, but did not stop to offer aid. For how long she continued this way, Briana could not tell. Finally, savagely, she tore her thoughts away from the sadness. The hero's sacrifice was complete. It was over and done. There were other things to ponder now.

The sudden appearance of electronic drones and motorcycles would not be of much consequence on Murdina after all, she decided. Batteries eventually would no longer work. The gasoline all consumed. Yes, the thaumaturges and alchemists would study these things, but it would take years, decades, maybe even centuries before they would have any practical impact on the way of life.

The culture of Murdina was resilient to such sudden changes. So unlike the brittleness here on Earth, the fragility of this civilization.

One might think the instant communication, knowledge of the

working of atoms, and the harnessing of energy meant its technology was superior. Yes, a good idea could be implemented worldwide in seconds, but then so could one that was bad. A sole visitor from another planet, single handedly, had almost brought an end to everything.

Millennia ago, when the seekers of knowledge on this orb came to the crossroads for which paths to take — thaumaturgy or physics, alchemy or chemistry, magic or mathematics, irrevocable choices were made. Now, it would not be easy to mix the discoveries along the road not taken without shattering consequences.

This planet needed protection, a guardian to ensure the use of the arcane did not destroy what was already here. The tiger wasps must be disposed of. The entrance to the caverns of the Heretics sealed. Emmertyn persuaded to stop using his trances to take unfair advantage in the stock market, Iggy to give up dispensing alchemical potions of great power. The little sprites, the ones who survived, to restore the data at CERN to its original condition.

Ah, the imps. This place was absolutely infested with them! Micromites, hoseherders, hairjumblers, rockbubblers... They could not be eliminated, but maybe controlled to do no major harm.

Prevention and control. Perhaps, ultimately, that is what *she* was meant to do. She had the familiarity with all five of the crafts. She could spot their use before anyone else. Her thoughts rumbled about, but eventually came to a solid conclusion. It felt right. Yes, the guardian. After everything that had happened, that was to be her own destiny.

Fig would help, of course. Ashley, too, once she was better. And Ursula would be an excellent administrator at a home base somewhere.

Her face began to dry. She tried an energizing breath and then coughed. Some of the diesel fuel still floated in the air. So unlike spring at home, the cool green hills of Murdina. She never would see them again. The tears threatened to return, to gush into the flood that comes with deep racking sobs.

She looked at the shop door at which she had stopped and read the sign over the jamb. She blinked. Almost despite herself, the self-pity dissolved away. The corners of her mouth turned upward in the beginning of a small smile.

This is what she had to do whenever her thoughts took her in the wrong direction, she decided. Rejoice in the comfort of simple pleasures.

She pulled open the door and entered. "A French Vanilla cone," she called out. "And make it a triple decker. Three scoops. Three scoops, not just one."

Author's Afterward

IN THE *What's Next?* section of *Riddle of the Seven Realms* I did not have another book to tout. I merely had caught up with republishing three books from almost 30 years ago. I wanted to write more but concluded the section with "I will just have to see if there is enough gas left in the tank."

Well, obviously there was and *The Archimage's Fourth Daughter* is the result.

The basic idea that I wanted to explore was the dichotomy between our modern civilized life here on earth with that of the traditional fantasy — a roughly medieval setting with castles and such. This has been done many times before, of course, but usually with someone from here making the journey to a magical land — *The Wizard of Oz*, *Peter Pan* and so on.

But what would happen if the direction of travel were reversed? The protagonist was plopped down in our world and scrambling to make sense of it.

So with that in mind, I started writing. Now, thirty years ago I plotted everything out in detail before starting — an outline for each and every chapter — what engineers call *top down* design. But this time, I thought it would be fun to merely start and see where the story took me.

I started with a chapter involving a small demon imprisoned in a glass cage — with the idea that the hero after a brief sojourn on the earth would return to her home world and face the *real* challenge of the story. I even put the first seven chapters up on a blog with this in mind.

But after my hero had managed to survive the culture shock of being here and was ready to go back home, I found that I really did not have a very good idea about what to do when she got there. What was the purpose of the caged demon anyway? So, I put him aside for use some time later in the future.

Having the tale centered on earth gave me the opportunity to explore the question of what if magic *were* in use here. It could not be very noticeable because if it were, it would be quite disruptive. But stock market manipulations, falsifying high energy physics data and small storefront love potion vending seem quite possible.

Not only that, by operating on earth, I could interject elements into the story that were not fantastic at all, but things that I find interesting. Yes, one can get a door to open by manipulating the latch guided by a dentist's mirror. Surrounding an automobile by hundreds of prone bodies to prevent it moving does indeed work. Skilled engineers who are presumed to operate with cold hard logic for a greater good sometimes succumb to baser emotions. In our pursuit to understand the universe around us, we have come a long way from visual observations to looking for bumps on histograms. Will we ever decide to stop climbing deeper and deeper into what may be a bottomless pit?

Along the way, I also discovered the joy of sometimes being surprised myself by the words I put onto the screen. There was not merely one type of imp involved in the story (the token minority) but several. I enjoyed writing about them the best of all.

What's next?

ALTHOUGH I wrote three related novels in the 1980's, they were deliberately intended *not* to be sequential parts of one long story. The underlying rules of the universe I constructed were the same, but different problems and different characters were in each book.

A few decades before that, of course, *The Lord of the Rings* started the long story trend and many of our most successful authors today are directing their efforts that way as well. For me, I enjoy a one volume story that starts, has a middle, and then ends.

"Wait a minute!" you might say. What about Maurice? Does he ever get to come back home? What about Jake? Did he win the battle on Murdina? And Briana. Is the only thing she has to look forward to is weight watching support meetings?

My short answer is a cop out. I don't know.

My feelings right now is that the story for the characters in *The Archimage's Fourth Daughter* is complete. It is the ideas behind the stories that are important to me. The characters are there to get them expressed. On the other hand, this time around I did try harder to make Briana and the others more interesting, more believable, and easier to care about.

We will just have to wait and see which way I go next.

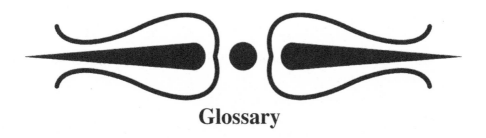

Glossary

Aerogel

Insulating material composed almost entirely of trapped air. Originally developed by NASA for use with cryogenically cooled propellants. Subsequently spun out and became commercially available for other applications.

Wikipedia: https://en.wikipedia.org/wiki/Aerogel#Applications

Alchemy

On earth, the root of the word comes from the Greek for transmutation. In the Middle Ages, alchemy focused on changing baser metals into gold, finding an elixir of life and a universal solvent. Some alchemical practices ultimately became the basis for modern chemistry.

In *Master of the Five Magics* and its sequels, alchemical procedures were described by formulas of arcane symbols kept in grimoires. Formula success was governed by probability; the more potent the result the less likely it was to succeed.

On earth, the most similar craft is that of a chemist.

Wikipedia: http://en.wikipedia.org/wiki/Alchemy

Angkor Wat

A Cambodian temple complex built around the 12th century

Wikipedia: https://en.wikipedia.org/wiki/Angkor_Wat

Arcadia

Land across the Great Ocean to the east from Procolon. Setting for *Secret of the Sixth Magic*

Archimage

A master of all five of the crafts of thaumaturgy, alchemy, magic, sorcery, and wizardry.

Aeriel

Wife of Alodar, the Archimage, and mother of Briana. Their romance is described in *Master of the Five Magics*.

ATLAS

An acronym containing another acronym! It stands for A Toroidal LHC ApparatuS. LHC stands for the Large Hadron Collider at the European Center for Nuclear Research (CERN) Whew!

Atlas is a suite of particle detectors, designed to be general purpose and able to detect a variety of particle types over a wide range of energies. In the second decade of the twenty first century, primarily it was employed in the hunt for experimental evidence of the existence of the Higgs boson.

Wikipedia: https://en.wikipedia.org/wiki/ATLAS_experiment

Bette Davis Eyes

Bette Davis was a movie star of the 1930 noted for her large expressive eyes -- made popular by the song in 1981.

Wikipedia: https://en.wikipedia.org/wiki/Bette_Davis

Wikipedia: https://en.wikipedia.org/wiki/Bette_Davis_Eyes

Buckaroo Banzai

A cult film released in 1984, noted for its many inane quotes

Wikipedia: http://www.imdb.com/title/tt0086856/quotes

Hernando Cortez

Cortez did not burn his ships before attacking the Aztecs at Tenochtitlan. He scuttled them.

Wikipedia
https://en.wikipedia.org/wiki/Spanish_conquest_of_the_Aztec_Empire

CERN

The European Organization of Nuclear Research

A particle physics research laboratory located on the border between France and Switzerland. It houses, what in 2017, is the world's most powerful accelerator for protons and even heavier ions, able to hurl them at one another at energies available nowhere else in the world.

Wikipedia: https://en.wikipedia.org/wiki/CERN

Charm

On earth, a synonym for spells in general. In *Master of the Five Magics* and its sequels, a sorcerer's spell in particular.

Wikipedia: http://en.wikipedia.org/wiki/Charm

Circles of Life

A common motif used in many designs. Constructed from a set of circles of the same size placed in a hexagonal repeating pattern. Also called the Flowers of Life.

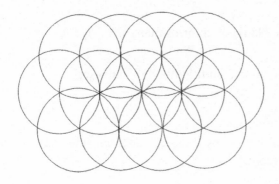

Clue

This popular board game, manufactured by Parker Brothers in the US, has been around for many years. All of us probably have played it when we were younger.

The simplest strategy is to mark off on your score sheet all of the cards you have in your hand. After all, there is no way they can be in the black envelope on the staircase marked x at the center of the board. Then when your turn comes and someone passes you a card, mark that one off, too. Eventually, you will be able to deduce which three cards must be the solution.

There are things you can do to speed up your deduction process. The following is the one I used as a youth and is similar to others found on the internet. The basic idea is to eliminate possibilities not only on your own turn but also on that of others. If you are successful at doing this, you might the first to get the answer.

The example here is truncated. It would take too long and too much space to walk through an actual game. As shown below, we are going to be dealing with four players — you and three others, three weapons, and three rooms only. Rather than just using a single column to keep track of things, assign one for each of the other players and one more for the answer in the envelope.

	Me	Alice	Bob	Carl	Answer
	• •	• •	• •	• •	• •
Rope					
Gun					
Knife					
Lead Pipe					
	• • •	• • •	• • •	• • •	• • •
Lounge					
Kitchen					
Study					

The first thing you do is cross off the cards you have. For this example, you have two cards dealt to you — the rope and the lounge. The Xs on the scoresheet eliminate these possibilities for the other players and the answer.

	Me	Alice	Bob	Carl	Answer
	• •	• •	• •	• •	• •
Rope		X	X	X	
Gun	X				
Knife	X				
Lead Pipe	X				
	• • •	• • •	• • •	• • •	• • •
Lounge		X	X	X	
Kitchen	X				
Study	X				
Hall	X				

Doing this might seem counter-intuitive. Don't we want to be finding out what *is* in the answer, rather than what is not? You are doing that, but just coming at it from a slightly different view point.

Okay, now suppose you are going first and you suggest it was done in the study with the rope. Alice, the first person on your left shows you that she has the study. From this, you mark off that Bob, Carl and the Answer do not.

	Me	Alice	Bob	Carl	Answer
	⋮	⋮	⋮	⋮	⋮
Rope		✕	✕	✕	✕
Gun	✕				
Knife	✕				
Lead Pipe	✕				
	⋮	⋮	⋮	⋮	⋮
Lounge		✕	✕	✕	✕
Kitchen	✕				
Study	✕	✕	✕	✕	
Hall	✕				

Next, it is Alice's turn. She suggests it was done with the knife in the kitchen. Bob shows Alice a card. It is either the knife or the kitchen but we do not know which one, but the possibilities are linked. If we later find out that Bob does not have the knife, you can use the link to conclude that he must have the kitchen — or vice versa. Keep track of links by numbering them on the scoresheet as shown on the next page..

	Me	Alice	Bob	Carl	Answer
	:	:	:	:	:
Rope		✕	✕	✕	✕
Gun	✕				
Knife	✕		1		
Lead Pipe	✕				
	:	:	:	:	:
Lounge		✕	✕	✕	✕
Kitchen	✕		1		
Study	✕		✕	✕	✕
Hall	✕				

Next, it is Bob's turn. He suggests the rope and the lounge. Of course Bob has neither of those cards because you do. You show him one. Put a small B for Bob in the square for the rope to indicate the card you have shown him. Then if he makes a suggestion involving the rope a second time and things rotate to you, you can make sure to show him the same card again and not increase his information.

	Me	Alice	Bob	Carl	Answer
	:	:	:	:	:
Rope	B	✕	✕	✕	✕
Gun	✕				
Knife	✕		1		
Lead Pipe	✕				
	:	:	:	:	:
Lounge		✕	✕	✕	✕
Kitchen	✕		1		
Study	✕		✕	✕	✕
Hall	✕				

Next, it is Carl's turn. He suggests the gun and the kitchen, and Alice shows him a card. On our score sheet, indicate this linking with the number 2.

	Me	Alice	Bob	Carl	Answer
	⋮	⋮	⋮	⋮	⋮
Rope	B	✕	✕	✕	✕
Gun	✕	2			
Knife	✕		1		
Lead Pipe	✕				
	⋮	⋮	⋮	⋮	⋮
Lounge		✕	✕	✕	
Kitchen	✕	2	1		
Study	✕		✕	✕	✕
Hall	✕				

Your turn again. You suggest the rope in the kitchen and Alice shows you the kitchen. You can cross off the kitchen for Bob, Carl, and the Answer. Ahah! We know that it was done in the hall.

	Me	Alice	Bob	Carl	Answer
	⋮	⋮	⋮	⋮	⋮
Rope	B	✕	✕	✕	✕
Gun	✕	2			
Knife	✕		1		
Lead Pipe	✕				
	⋮	⋮	⋮	⋮	⋮
Lounge		✕	✕	✕	
Kitchen	✕		✕	✕	✕
Study	✕		✕	✕	✕
Hall	✕				

But wait there's more. If Bob does not have the kitchen, then the linked number 1s tells us he must have the knife. And if he has the knife,

400

Alice, Carl, and the Answer cannot.

	Me	Alice	Bob	Carl	Answer
	⋮	⋮	⋮	⋮	⋮
Rope	∎	✕	✕	✕	✕
Gun	✕				
Knife	✕	✕		✕	✕
Lead Pipe	✕				
	⋮	⋮	⋮	⋮	⋮
Lounge		✕	✕	✕	✕
Kitchen	✕		✕	✕	✕
Study	✕		✕		✕
Hall	✕				

Finally, Alice suggests the gun in the study. Bob passes and Carl shows her a card. We know that Alice has the study, so Carl must have the gun. So the lead pipe must be the weapon. Make an accusation. You have won the game!

	Me	Alice	Bob	Carl	Answer
	⋮	⋮	⋮	⋮	⋮
Rope		✕	✕	✕	✕
Gun	✕	✕	✕		✕
Knife		✕		✕	
Lead Pipe					
	⋮	⋮	⋮	⋮	⋮
Lounge		✕	✕	✕	✕
Kitchen	✕		✕	✕	
Study	✕		✕	✕	✕
Hall	✕				

Of course, this example was contrived, but it shows how with X's, numbers, and letters, you can go a long way towards keeping everything straight.

Maybe, this is why Dinton was so successful. On the other hand, he was not all that crafty with other games such as Rock, Paper, Scissors and the Magic Eightball — maybe because he did not consider them to be games of pure deduction.

The Company

Jargon term used by defense contractors to refer to the Central Intelligence Agency, headquarted in Langley, VA. It is reputed that workers there refer to the National Security Agency, headquarted at Fort Meade, MD as TBARS — the bastards across the river.

Wikipedia:
https://en.wikipedia.org/wiki/Central_Intelligence_Agency

Demon

Resident of another realm different from that of the universe containing the earth and the world of *Master of the Five Magics*. With the exception of djinns, of limited physical power in our realm. Synonymous with devil.

Wikipedia: http://en.wikipedia.org/wiki/Demon

Wikipedia: http://en.wikipedia.org/wiki/Devil

Wikipedia: http://en.wikipedia.org/wiki/List_of_fictional_demons

Devil

A synonym for demon in *Master of the Five Magics* and its sequels.

Wikipedia: http://en.wikipedia.org/wiki/Devil

Wikipedia: http://en.wikipedia.org/wiki/Demon

Fluorine gas

See 'Source of Fluorine Gas' in Nature heading at

The Fort

Jargon used by defense contractors to refer to the National Security Agency (NSA) headquartered at Fort Meade, MD. It is reputed that workers there refer to the Central Intelligence Agency (CIA), headquartered at Langley, VA as TBARS — the bastards across the river.

Gluons

One of two types of new 'elementary' particles proposed by Murray Gell-Mann and George Zweig in the 1960s. Protons and neutrons, what we had thought were elementary, were composed of quarks. In analog to how charged particles interacted with one another, quarks exchanged gluons instead.

Gluons also have charge, but one different from the plus and minus of electromagnetism that we are familiar with. Gluon charge 'cancels out' for certain combinations of three gluons. In analogy with light for which red, blue, and green combined produce what appears to be white to our eyes, gluon charge was called 'color charge'.

Histograms and Bump Hunting

A data presentation technique.

We see them used all the time. For example, suppose we wanted to display the ages of all the people in a particular neighborhood. The graph could look like the following.

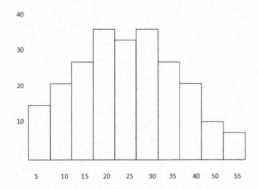

The x-axis of the graph is divided into horizontal 'bins'. Each bin represents a particular age group — 0 to 5, 6 to 10, and so on. The y axis is a count of how many people fell into each age range. We see that there are fewer inhabitants with an age of 0 to 5 than a more adult group such as 20 to 25.

Histograms are used in physics too. Suppose we are studying the reaction in which a charged pi meson collides with a stationary proton and produces a neutron and two pi mesons as a result.

$$\pi^- + p \rightarrow \pi^+ + \pi^- + n$$

(Even with this simple example, one can see how weird things are on the atomic level. Can you image a cue ball hitting a three ball on a pool table and three, not two, balls result -- with the three ball vanishing as well!)

Plowing on ahead -- There are three particles in the final state, and lets suppose we are interested in what the energy of the resulting π^- is. So, we collect a bunch of events of the type we are looking for, measure the energy of the output π^- for each event and make a histogram of the results.

If the energy of the incoming π^- is low enough, the histogram might look something like this:

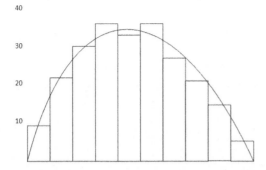

Superimposed over the histogram is a theoretical prediction —one that says that, subject to the constraint that energy has to be conserved, every possible output momentum of the π^- is equally likely. It can be anything. There are no hidden gears involved in the reaction that would favor any direction or magnitude over another.

The experiment data in the histogram agrees pretty well with the theory. Both low and high energies are unlikely, and sure enough, we find that few of our events have such energy extremes.

Of course, the match is not exact. We are dealing with a finite number of events here. It the theoretical curve says that for, say, 100 events, we expect five at the lower energy limit, we easily might get 7 or 3, because of statistical variations.

Now suppose we collect some more data, but this time the incoming π^- has more energy. The final histogram might look like the illustration on the next page.

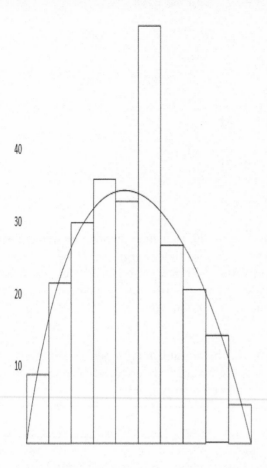

Wow! Something is going on here. A spike or bump, at one particular value indicates that sometimes we do not have three particles coming out of the reaction, but only two. Where there are only two, the energy of both is fixed.

At least part of the time, physcists finally decided, the reaction was:

$$\pi^- + p \rightarrow \pi^- + N^{*+}$$ and then subsequently $N^{*+} \rightarrow \pi^- + n$

This type of example occured a lot in the 1960's. Using the accelerators and detectors of the time, the cozy little family of proton, neutron, and electron were joined by hundreds of other particles, such as the N^{*+}. Toto was not in Kansas anymore.

But because of the statistics, when do you decide that the data deviates from what is expected? Suppose the creation of N^{*+}'s was not as prevalent as that shown in the first histogram, and instead we get:

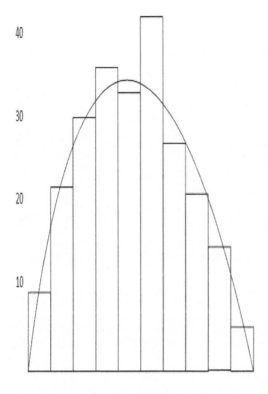

Okay, perhaps still convincing enough. Then how about:

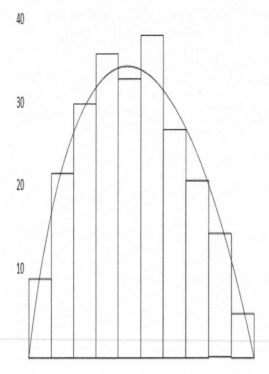

(Sigmund Freud was misquoted. What he really said was "Sometimes π^+ and n is just π^+ and n.")

As more and more physics data were being collected, scientists were moving onto shakier and shakier ground. At the end of the 1800's we saw small bits of debris jiggling in a liquid. The existing of atoms explained that better than anything else.

Then when we saw the tracks in photographic plates, the existence of particles was also the best explanation.

When we got to reactions like:

$$\pi^- + p \rightarrow \pi^+ + \pi^- + n$$

we saw the output π mesons because they were charged. A neutral neutron leaves no track. But we inferred it was there because assuming it was made the output energy equal that of the input. Energy was conserved.

As accelerators and detectors improved and more and more data were collected, many more histograms were examined. This meant that, by chance, some bumps did not indicate the existence of a new particle at all. They were merely statistical fluctuations instead.

There is no way to be *absolutely* sure if this is the case or not, but as a general rule, physicists do not publish a result if the chance of a statistical fluke causing an observation is more than 1 chance in about 3.5 million.

I have not visited CERN in over fifty years, so I am sure that with the advent of more powerful computers and the increased deluge of data, the search has become more sophisticated with techniques such as maximum likelihood comparison of 'bump' and 'no bump' hypotheses. Looking at histograms has been delegated to the realm of 'quick first looks."

Even so, part of the craft of experimental particle physics is still one of 'bump hunting' -- looking for those deviations in the data that represented something that reflects reality.

Fig's bump hunting to prove the existence of the micromites has nothing to do with particle physics, but the fundamental underpinnings are the same.

1. Make a hypothesis for both a 'real' and the 'null' result.

2. Do an experiment and examine the results

3. Decide if any 'bumps' were found -- anything that could not be explained by the null hypothesis.

Imago

The last stage of four stages of insect development. A synonym for 'adult'

Wikipedia: https://en.wikipedia.org/wiki/Imago

Imp

In *Master of the Five Magics* and its sequels, smaller demons than djinns and mostly just pranksters.

Wikipedia: http://en.wikipedia.org/wiki/Imp

Lanchester Square Law

A formula for estimating the number of victors surviving if two unequal forces combat until the smaller is annihilated. It is given by nfinal = sqrt(nsquared - msquared) where n is the initial number of the larger combatant, m is that of the smaller, and sqrt indicates taking the square root.

For example if n = 5 and m =3, the number surviving of the original 5 is 4.

Some military historians claim that Admiral Horatio Nelson's intuitive understanding of the law guided his tactics to defeat the French and Spanish at Trafalgar in 1805.

Wikipedia: https://en.wikipedia.org/wiki/Lanchester%27s_laws

Another reference:

https://www.futilitycloset.com/2016/03/20/lanchesters-laws

Lateral arabesque

Term coined in the early 1960s by Lawrence Peter, author of the Peter Principle, to refer to a change in management position that is not upwards but only to another one at the same level.

Lawrence Bragg

Bragg, at the age of 25, was the co-recipitant for the Nobel Prize in physics with his father, William Bragg in 1915 -- a well-deserved recognition, but I can't help but thinking, however, that it might have helped just a tiny bit to have been born to equally brilliant parents.

Wikipedia: https://en.wikipedia.org/wiki/William_Lawrence_Bragg

Level Three Trigger

The number of proton-proton collisions (called events) produced by the Large Hadron Collider (LHC) at the European Center for Nuclear Research (CERN) is staggering. Most of it is of little interest. A winnowing process is used to pick out those events of interest for more detailed examination.

Lower level triggers are used to select only a subset of events and perform preliminary computations upon them. Level Three triggers can be tailored to select an even smaller subset -- those for a particular researcher's needs.

See also the section titled Data Systems and Analysis at:

Wikipedia: https://en.wikipedia.org/wiki/ATLAS_experiment

Lost Horizon

A novel (1933) by James Hilton about a lamasery hidden somewhere "west of Himalaya Mountains" in Asia.

Wikipedia: https://en.wikipedia.org/wiki/Lost_Horizon

Magic

The use of means outside of normal availability to affect change. On earth, the terms magic, sorcery, thaumaturgy, and wizardry are roughly synonymous.

In *Master of the Five Magics* and its sequels, each, along with alchemy, have distinct meanings. Magic is performed by the exercise of rituals, the steps of which are derived from extensions of rituals deduced previously.

The goal of these exercises is the production of magical objects, things that are perfect in what they do, such as mirrors, daggers, swords, and shields. Once created, with few exceptions, they last forever.

The power of magic is limited by the time and expense involved in performing magic rituals. Some take several generations and the involvement of many participants. Because of the time and effort involved, magical objects are quite expensive.

On earth, the most similar craft is that of a mathematician.

Wikipedia: http://en.wikipedia.org/wiki/Magic

Magic Eightball

A toy of the 1950's. One asked a question and then shook up the eightball. After a few moments the answer would rise to show in a window at the top of the ball.

Wikipedia: https://en.wikipedia.org/wiki/Magic_8-Ball

Mark 50 Torpedo

A high speed US Navy torpedo for use against deep-diving submarines. It uses sulfur hexafluoride as its propellant.

Wikipedia:
https://en.wikipedia.org/wiki/Mark_50_torpedo

Money

Until there were banks, the amount of money in a country did not change much. Precious metals were mined to add to the supply of coins, but that led to only slow increases. With the advent of banking, however, everything changed.

Imagine if you were a merchant in ancient times. You were doing well and your gold kept piling up. Everyone could see this, including thieves, so you built a strong vault to keep it in — all 100 ducats of it.

Your friend, Nebuchadnezzar, came by one day and asked for a loan of 100 ducats to buy supplies for his building company. He would pay it all back within a year and give you 10 more ducats for your trouble. Nebi was a straight up guy, and even though building ziggurats was sometimes iffy, he had a reputation of doing what he said he would, so you agreed to the loan.

But as you started to open the vault, he asked you to stop. He didn't really want to carry the hundred ducats away with him. They were quite heavy, and thieves were about. Instead just leave the cash where it was and give him a cuneiform tablet certifying that he had the hundred ducats. So you did.

A few days passed and another friend, Daniel, came by. He had heard about the loan to Nebuchadnezzar and wanted one for himself. You were about to say that you no longer had any ducats to lend out, when an idea struck you.

"You are going to leave the 100 ducats in the vault, just like Nebuchadnzzsar, right? Not take possession of any of the gold?"

"You bet. Haven't you heard? There are thieves about."

And just like that. The role of a bank from merely being a secure place to store money, it started serving another purpose. 100 ducats of money were generated out of absolutely thin air. Merchants would use cuneiform tablets to keep track of transfers from one to another and did not have to lug around the gold. You were able to lend the same 100 ducats out several more times. With so many people (seemingly) flush with cash, business boomed. Everyone was happy. (Of course when the Hittites were threatening to attack, everyone wanted his money back, but that was a different story.)

This phenomena of money generation from nothing is related to but distinct from the idea of using substitutes such as clay tablets or conch shells or paper to represent money. In modern times, all banks, in the US, anyway, have the requirement to only keep a fraction of what is deposited available for withdrawal at all times — a reserve of approximately 20 percent. That reserve serves as the basis for the generation of an additional four times more additional money out of whole cloth.

This little tale has nothing to do with Briana's quest to find the exiles, but ever since I learned of the true significance of banks, it has always amazed me that it was true.

Murdina

In Briana's native language, Murdina means the Earth. Untranslated to English for this edition in order to avoid confusion at several points in the story.

The Prisoner of Zenda

A turn of the 20th century adventure novel (1894) by Anthony Hope.

Wikipedia: https://en.wikipedia.org/wiki/The_Prisoner_of_Zenda

Procolon

Largest country in the continent west of the great ocean.

Procolon is a feudal society with a structure similar to what was at one time here on earth. With the exception of magician guilds, in exchange for swearing allegiance to the sovereign, lesser lords held sway over their own smaller land holdings. In general, kingdoms were relatively small, like those to the south. Perhaps in part, Procolon achieved its size because of a greater reliance on sorcery to keep apprised of the happenings within its boundaries.

This structure was basically unstable. A king or queen had to walk a narrow line between wanting too much or allowing too much autonomy. A lord dissatisfied with the demands for service by his liege could assert his independence and rebel.

PYTHIA and GEANT

Names of two software simulation packages of Atlas data. With PYTHIA, one could hypothesize a particular reaction, say,

$$\pi^- + p \to \pi^+ + \pi^- + n$$

414

and produce an 'event' that gives specifies the momentum and energies of each of the particles involved.

Then with GEANT, one can produce the output that the ATLAS suite of detectors would produce for such an event.

Armed with this, Chalice could substitute actual ATLAS output with the hypothetical one he had constructed.

See also the section titled Data Systems and Analysis at:

Wikipedia: https://en.wikipedia.org/wiki/ATLAS_experiment

Robe

Practitioners of each of the five magics are distinguished by the capes and robes they wear.

Thaumaturges wear brown covered with what is on earth the mathematical symbol of similarity.

Alchemists wear white covered with triangles with a single vertex bottom-most symbolizing the delicate balance between success and failure when performing a formula.

Magicians wear blue with the palest for a neophyte and the darkest for the master and covered by circular rings symbolizing the perfect mathematical object.

Sorcerers wear gray covered with the logo of the staring eye symbolizing the ability to see far in time and place and into another's inner being.

Wizards wear black covered with wisps of flame symbolizing the portal by which the realm of demons and the realm of men are connected.

Rock Paper Scissors Strategy

Surprisingly, at least for me, there are over 700,000 google hits on this search term. Here are two that I liked best.

http://www.telegraph.co.uk/men/thinking-man/11051704/How-to-always-win-at-rock-paper-scissors.html

http://www.wikihow.com/Win-at-Rock,-Paper,-Scissors

Rule of 72

A shortcut to estimate how long it would take an investment to double in value at a fixed rate of interest. It is given by 72/n, where n is the interest rate of the investment is held. For example if the rate is 6%, then the investment will double in 12 years.

Wikipedia: https://en.wikipedia.org/wiki/Rule_of_72

The Scarlet Pimpernel

An adventure novel by Baroness Orczy published in 1905. The hero was the secret identity of a wealthy English fop, foreshadowing the advent of Superman by 29 years.

Wikipedia: https://en.wikipedia.org/wiki/The_Scarlet_Pimpernel

Sorcery

The use of means outside of normal availability to affect change. On earth, the terms magic, sorcery, thaumaturgy, and wizardry are roughly synonymous.

In *Master of the Five Magics* and its sequels, each, along with alchemy, have distinct meanings. Sorcery is performed by the recitation of charms, the steps of which are revealed from self-enchantment.

The power of a sorcerer is limited by the fact that each casting takes some of his life force, and eventually he succumbs when he has no more to give.

On earth, the most similar craft is that of a psychologist.

Southern Kingdoms

Small kingdoms on the isthmus and connecting continent below the kingdom of Procolon. The initial setting for *Riddle of the Seven Realms*

Spell

On earth the terms cantrip, charm, enchantment, glamour, incantation, and spell are synonymous — the performance of an act of magic.

In *Master of the Five Magics* and its sequels, except for the word spell itself, each of the others have particular meanings, and the word spell is a generic umbrella for any of them.

Thaumaturgy — incantation
Alchemist — formula performance
Magician — ritual exercise
Sorcerer — charm recitation
Wizard — invocation

Stock Market 128 Swindle

The method Angus used to select Emmertyn as his stock broker is a twist on a classic scam.

An initial list of 128 prospects are sent a letter touting a new stock tip service. To prove how strong it is, a prediction is made for how a particular stock will fare in the coming week. 64 of the prospects are told it will go up; the other 64 that it will go down — or in strongly moving markets, some other tip is given. The basic idea is to use events that have a 50/50 chance of going either way.

After a week passes, half of the predictions will be wrong. These prospects are never contacted again. Another letter is sent to those remaining. 32 are told that another stock will go up and the other 32 that it will go down. Again, the prediction will be correct for one half. Now, interest might pick up a bit. Two correct tips in a row!

The process continues until only a single pigeon is left. By now he is convinced that the new tip service is indeed amazing. Seven weeks and not wrong once! The final letter is the solicitation. No more free tips. The next one will cost.

The pigeon pays and so long as the predictions do come true by chance, he continues to pay for the information. When it no longer works, the swindlers start with a new list of 128.

There is nothing magic about 128 of course, other than if the starting number is too low, the results might not be regarded as amazing enough. If it is too high, it takes too long to earn a living.

Subordinate

The first four crafts have named subordinates in *Master of the Five Magics* and its sequels.

Thaumaturgy — Journeyman, Apprentice

Alchemist — Novice

Magician — Neophyte, Initiate, Acolyte

Sorcerer — Tyro

Sulfur hexafluoride

The elements sulfur and fluoride combine into a variety of compounds. One of them has six fluoride atoms bound to one of sulfur. This result, SF_6, is a dense gas that some 3000 times as potent as carbon dioxide in causing global warming.

Wikipedia: https://en.wikipedia.org/wiki/Sulfur_hexafluoride

Commercial Sulfur Transport

Sulfur is transported in a liquid form using special temperature controlled gas cylinders.

Reference: http://www.sulphuric-acid.com/techmanual/storage/trans_sulphur.htm

Supersymmetry

Speculative theories of particle physics that suggests there is a relationship between two classes of elementary particles. The hope is that it might form a basis for unifying gravity, electromagnetism, and the strong and weak forces of nature into one coherent whole.

As of 2017, no experimental evidence has been obtained verifying predictions of any of the theory variations.

Wikipedia: https://en.wikipedia.org/wiki/Supersymmetry

Test and Set

At first thought, it seems an easy thing to make sure that only one of two users have access to some resource at the same time.

It is not easy; it is hard. Reliable solutions did not come for many years — until it was realized that in a single machine cycle time, the instruction that tests to see if the bit is set also sets it if it is not.

Wikipedia: https://en.wikipedia.org/wiki/Test-and-set

Thaumaturgy

The use of means outside of normal availability to affect change. On earth, the terms magic, sorcery, thaumaturgy, and wizardry are roughly synonymous.

In *Master of the Five Magics* and its sequels, each, along with alchemy, have distinct meanings. Thaumaturgy is performed by the reciting incantations that bind together objects at a distance that once had physically been together and with a source of energy that can perform work.

The power of thaumaturgy is limited by the fact that all incantations must conserve energy or, as sometimes stated, the first law of thermodynamics.

On earth, the term derives from the Greek for miracle and the most similar craft is that of a physicist.

Wikipedia: http://en.wikipedia.org/wiki/Thaumaturgy

VIN

Vehicle Identification Number. Commonly used in the phrase 'VIN number'. Both this and 'PIN' number must have been coined by the Department of Redundancy Department

Wikipedia:
https://en.wikipedia.org/wiki/Vehicle_identification_number

Wizardry

The use of means outside of normal availability to affect change. On earth, the terms magic, sorcery, thaumaturgy, and wizardry are roughly synonymous.

In *Master of the Five Magics* and its sequels, each, have distinct meanings. Wizardry is performed by the invocation of demons from another realm from that of the earth.

The potency of a wizard is limited by the power of the demons that he can dominate.

On earth, there is no such craft as such, although one could argue that the practices of witches and warlocks is similar.

Wikipedia: http://en.wikipedia.org/wiki/Witchcraft

Zorba the Greek

A 1964 film based on the novel of the same name by Nikos Kazantzakis. In it, Zorba heats the air in small rounded glasses (like brandy snifters) and then seals them against Madame Hortense's bare back. The air cools and a partial vacuum is formed, ostensibly sucking the poisons created by pneumonia out of her body.

Wikipedia: https://en.wikipedia.org/wiki/Zorba_the_Greek_(film)

Made in the USA
Coppell, TX
22 December 2021

69877522R00256